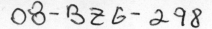
Praise for *The Heiress's Deception*

"Exceptional . . . This series launch is an intoxicating romp sure to delight fans of historical romance."
—*Publishers Weekly* (starred review)

"Sizzling, witty, passionate . . . perfect!"
—Eloisa James, *New York Times* bestselling author

Praise for Christi Caldwell

"Christi Caldwell writes a gorgeous book!"
—Sarah MacLean, *New York Times* and
USA Today bestselling author

"In addition to a strong plot, this story boasts actualized characters whose personal demons are clear and credible. The chemistry between the protagonists is seductive and palpable, with their family history of hatred played against their personal similarities and growing attraction to create an atmospheric and captivating romance."
—*Publishers Weekly* on *The Hellion*

"Christi Caldwell is a master of words and *The Hellion* is so descriptive and vibrant that she redefines high definition. Readers will be left panting, craving, and rooting for their favorite characters as unexpected lovers find their happy ending."
—*RT Book Reviews* on *The Hellion*

"Christi Caldwell's *The Vixen* shows readers a darker, grittier version of Regency London than most romance novels . . . Caldwell's more realistic version of London is a particularly gripping backdrop for this enemies-to-lovers romance, and it's heartening to read a story where love triumphs even in the darkest places."

—NPR on *The Vixen*

In BED with the EARL

OTHER TITLES BY CHRISTI CALDWELL

Heart of a Duke

The Heart of a Scandal

His Duchess for a Day
Five Days With a Duke

Lords of Honor

Seduced by a Lady's Heart
Captivated by a Lady's Charm
Rescued by a Lady's Love
Tempted by a Lady's Smile
Courting Poppy Tidemore

Scandalous Seasons

Forever Betrothed, Never the Bride
Never Courted, Suddenly Wed
Always Proper, Suddenly Scandalous
Always a Rogue, Forever Her Love
A Marquess for Christmas
Once a Wallflower, At Last His Love

Sinful Brides

The Rogue's Wager
The Scoundrel's Honor
The Lady's Guard
The Heiress's Deception

The Wicked Wallflowers

The Hellion
The Vixen

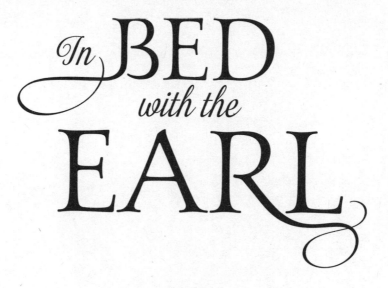

In BED
with the
EARL

CHRISTI
CALDWELL

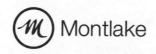 Montlake

Text copyright © 2020 by Christi Caldwell Incorporated
All rights reserved.

Published by Montlake, Seattle

www.apub.com

Amazon, the Amazon logo, and Montlake are trademarks of Amazon.com, Inc., or its affiliates.

ISBN-13: 9781542042574
ISBN-10: 1542042577

Cover design by Juliana Kolesova

Printed in the United States of America

Around the time I was to begin work on my first Lost Lords of London book, I found myself a victim of plagiarism. From the moment I discovered my words had been stolen, I was gutted. I was outraged. I was filled with so many different emotions, all of them consuming and powerful. During that time, I turned to the incomparable Nora Roberts, who encouraged me to put all that emotion onto my pages. Those pages came to be Verity and Malcom's story. Ms. Roberts, I am so very grateful to you for guiding me back into my books. In Bed with the Earl *is for you.*

Prologue

Some twenty years earlier
London, England

"Keep up, ya little shite, or ya're going back in the bag."

Noooo. Not the bag.

Percival couldn't go in there again. He couldn't breathe in there. And it was so dark. So very dark. And he hated the dark.

That alone was enough to jar Percival Northrop into quickening his pace.

Or he tried to. He really did.

But he was just so tired, and every part of his body ached.

"Oi said faster." A rough fist caught him hard between his shoulder blades, and he stumbled, pitched forward, and would have landed flat on his face.

The only thing to prevent it was when the tall, toothless man who'd been herding him along caught Percival by his hair. "Stay on yar feet," he growled, yanking those strands so hard he whipped Percival's head back.

His head hurt.

And not even like the sickness that had made him and his parents and all their household ill.

The stranger released him, and Percy bit his lip to keep it from trembling.

The man scoffed. "Ya're a slow shite, aren't ya?"

Tears filled Percy's eyes. But he didn't want to cry. He didn't want them to see him do it. Even though his papa and mama had always said there was no shame in weakness, the men who'd snatched him didn't seem to be of the same opinion. Neither the man who was hurting him nor the other ugly man, hairy like the bear his papa had shown him in an illustrated book, didn't like tears at all. It made them angry and impatient.

Unlike Percival's mama and papa.

Mama . . . Papa . . .

And this time, the tears fell freely. They coursed down Percy's cheeks until they were warm and itched his face.

He missed his mama and papa. He missed them so much. He didn't care what the mean men who'd taken him from that horrible place said about his crying.

Trembling, he stumbled, trying to keep up. Not because he wanted to go with them. He didn't. He was trying to move as quickly as he could because when he slowed, they prodded him in the back, forcing him forward.

Only it was so hard to keep walking.

He still hurt from the fire in his chest, as his mama had called it. It burnt inside even now, and Percy hadn't been out of his bed—any bed—since his sickness.

Until these men had come to his bed. Stood over it. Then, one of the men had given the mean nurse some coins, and the other stranger had tossed Percy into a sack and over his shoulder. Percy had been struggling to breathe since.

Now, Percy's heartbeat came loud in his ears. Like the times he'd race his papa so fast and so hard that it had climbed into his ears and pounded hard there. So loud he could barely hear his and Papa's laughter.

It was too much. He couldn't do it.

Percy fell down.

He yelped, and put his hands out, but they scraped the rough stones, ripping up his skin.

"Oi said not a word, ya shite."

The man hit Percy on the back of his head so hard it slammed him forward into the stone. He couldn't even cry out. Blood filled his mouth. There was a rock on his tongue. Only it wasn't a rock . . .

He spit a tooth out.

They broke my tooth. "You broke my tooth," he whispered.

And then he cried.

Because he'd never lost one before. His tutor had said they'd one day fall out, and Percy hadn't slept for nights and nights because he'd been so very afraid of when that day would come: his teeth falling out of his mouth. But now, these men had done it. These mean, ugly, angry strangers. Percy cried all the harder and curled his hand around his tooth.

"Let's just cut 'im," the bearish man whispered. "Oi told ya he was too weak. We'll find another one."

"We already paid the coin for this one," the other stranger spat. And then he turned to Percy. "Forget yar damned tooth. Or Oi'll break yar bloody head," he growled as he yanked Percy up on his feet. "Get movin'."

And Percy *knew* he was supposed to be afraid. He *knew* they were going to hurt him and then kill him. But he didn't *want* to die. Even though when they killed him, he'd get to go see Mama and Papa. But he was an earl's son and had responsibilities that now fell to him.

Papa was now in heaven, and Percy was all that remained of the Northrop line.

"Let me go," Percy whispered. And when the ugly stranger tightened his hold, Percy used all the energy he had to fight. "I said *let me go.*"

Except they weren't impressed. They merely laughed.

Anger shot through Percy. "Stop laughing at me," he yelled, and they only roared all the more. "Do you know who I am?"

At last they stopped laughing, and then Percy wished they hadn't, because they'd gone all quiet. And the quiet was scarier than when they'd yelled. "Oh, yeah, Oi know."

He did? Percy's heart jumped. They knew him. Which meant they'd free him. Because they couldn't hurt an earl's son. No one did.

"Ya're the fuckin' king of England."

Both men exchanged a look, and then—

"Bwahahaha!" The bear of a man bent over and clutched his side.

They were . . . laughing at him. None had ever dared laugh at Percy's father. But these men, these ugly, stupid, dirty strangers, would make fun of Percy . . .

All the rage and pain and heartache he'd felt snapped him. "I said stop laughing at me," he cried, and with all the energy he could manage, he rushed at the pair of brutes.

One of the men easily caught Percy by the thin shirt he'd been given, lifting him by its front and raising him so that they were at eye level. He stared at Percy for a long time. Close as they were, the smell of the other man burnt Percy's nose and stung his eyes—putrid, like the sick that he'd thrown up.

"Put me down. I demand it." Percy had never heard his papa be mean to anyone, but he had heard him use big words and make demands, and people always listened.

"Ya hear that, Sparky? The bloody king demands it."

Sparky . . . What a silly name for a man who looked like a bear.

Sparky's buglike eyes went wide. "Oi 'eard 'im, Penge."

And then the pair of strangers burst out laughing.

Percy cried out as Penge set him down so hard his knees buckled and he hit the ground again.

The tooth slipped free of his hand, and, his cheek pressed to the wet stones, Percy stretched his fingers, reaching for it.

"Boy's mad," the bear—Sparky—was saying. "Ain't of any use to anyone. And certainly ain't going to be of any use to 'im."

Him? Who is "him"?

And Percy quite decided then that he didn't want to be of use to anyone who knew these men.

"We already paid coin for the little shite. Another mad king we 'ave here in England. Let's go, Yar Majesty. Ya've subjects to meet."

And as the two men dragged him off, all his bravery faded. Tears fell once more, staining his cheeks. "I want to go home," he begged. "Please." Even if Mama and Papa weren't there . . . he wanted to go where it was safe and warm, and where people were kind.

Penge cuffed him on the back of his head so hard that stars danced behind Percy's eyes. "Didn't ya know, King?"

"Kn-know what?" he whispered, his voice trembling from both pain and fear.

Sparky flashed a toothless grin, cold, empty, and missing all warmth. "This is yar home now, Yar Majesty. King of the sewers. Get used to it."

Another surge of energy burst through Percy, and he didn't care that he'd been sick. Or that his stomach turned like he was going to throw up. "This isn't my home. Do you hear me? This will never be my home!" He kicked and twisted and fought the mean men. "Someone will save me." *Only* . . . Percy sobbed. Who would save him? There was no Mama or Papa anymore.

Penge slapped him across the face, rattling his teeth. "Get the bag," he ordered Sparky.

And this time, as the scratchy fabric was brought over his head and Percy was shoved inside and flung over one of the strangers' shoulders, he closed his eyes, grateful when the darkness crept in.

"No one is comin' for ya. Ya 'ear me? Ain't no one lookin' for an orphan."

That cruel threat echoed, coming as if from a distance, far, far away.

Someone was coming. They had to be . . .

He tried to speak the words aloud but couldn't make his mouth move. Or make a sound.

Someone was . . .

Percy closed his eyes and remembered no more.

Chapter 1

THE LONDONER
MYSTERY!

All of London is in search of the gentleman who's been
robbed of his title by treacherous relatives. The new
Earl of Maxwell remains a mystery to all . . . There is only
one certainty: the Lost Lord has no wish to be found!

V. Lovelace

The Seven Dials, London, England

Shite.

Having dwelled in the sewers longer than he'd moved amongst men
on the equally fetid streets of St. Giles, Malcom North held slogging
through that muck as the most familiar memory of his existence. It was
also the oldest.

Malcom picked his way through the dank grime that eventually
tunneled out and emptied into the Thames.

He timed each rise and fall of his foot to the flow of water. He
used the sounds of London's true underbelly to mask his steps. Using

the seven-foot pole that he'd carried for almost fifteen years now, he navigated the underground system.

He stilled, the water sloshing around his ankles, as the distant whine of an approaching herd echoed around the tunnel. Shoving the pole into the clever loop in his shirt, Malcom caught a metal chain in both hands. He climbed his feet up the walls, and hefted himself higher. Then, grabbing for the metal hooks left by the scaffolding that had built this underground world, he held himself aloft as the army of rats splashed ahead, racing through the filth and waste. The creatures squealed and chirped as they ran, climbing over one another in search of a poor blighter to feast upon.

Malcom's arms strained from the exertion, but he channeled the stinging discomfort. Over the years, he'd learned one discomfort transmuted into another. A man wasn't capable of feeling two hurts at once, and as long as he mastered one, he could defeat anything. His biceps and shoulders strained; sweat dripped from his brow.

He grimaced through the pain and remained hanging there until the last of the rodent pack, a lone white creature, went scurrying past.

Malcom lowered himself. Waiting. Waiting. The rapid splash of water breaking grew more distant, and he let himself fall. His previously strained muscles exalted from that release, the prickling that shot through his limbs a peculiar blend of pleasure and pain.

As his feet hit the stone floor, the water splashed noisily, splattering his trousers with the residual waste. He'd long ago ceased to smell the stench of this place, the tepid air more rotted than the coal-infused scents which those who dwelled in East London were forced to breathe daily.

As a boy, this had represented a choice . . . a luxury Malcom and all those born of his rank were without. Which sewer would he search? How would he find the means to survive? He'd not relied on the support of any gang leader. Every decision had been made by Malcom without any influence from the derelicts above. The life of a tosher represented all he knew.

And all he wished to know.

Gathering up his pole, Malcom resumed his march through the tunnel, scanning the brick walls as he cut a path through the water. Walls which had been a home, a place to hide from bastards bent on buggering a terrified street lad alone in the world. A haven from the constables who'd rid Polite Society of the guttersnipes sullying the air with their mere presence. And a place to hide from the gang leaders who'd built their empires on the backs of boys and girls.

Malcom stopped; his gaze zeroed in on a brick that jutted out, the difference between it and the others so slight it might have been an optical illusion. And yet there were no illusions in these parts. Just harsh realities.

Unsheathing the crude dagger he'd found in another tunnel when he'd first begun as a tosher, he did a sweep of the darkened space and then started forward, lifting his legs and lengthening his strides to minimize the echo left by his splash.

Sticking the weapon between his teeth, Malcom pressed his back against the wall so he could search for the foes who lurked everywhere.

Because for all the uncertainty that met a man in East London daily, there was only one fact which held true: there was always someone waiting in the hopes of usurping from a person his power.

Malcom always remained one step ahead of those trying to take his territory. It was why he was here even now.

Reaching behind him, his fingers immediately found the brick jutting out no more than a quarter of an inch. When he was a boy, digging in these spots had proven a simple, effortless task.

The brick immediately slipped into his hand. Setting it aside, Malcom probed the surrounding stones. He immediately loosed four bricks until a two-foot-wide opening gaped in the sewer wall. Angling sideways so he could both maintain a watch on the tunnels and assess that opening, Malcom stretched a hand inside . . . and immediately found it.

His fingers collided with a familiar, heavily patched burlap sack. Malcom yanked it out and fished around.

Empty.

The bloody bastard.

Swallowing a curse, Malcom pushed the bricks back in, and shoving his hat back into place, he rested a shoulder against the wall.

And waited. Waited with anticipation singing in his veins until he heard sloppy footfalls draw closer.

The figure, several inches smaller and two stones heavier, came crashing through the opening of the tunnel and then stopped. His gaze landed on Malcom North, and a burlap sack slipped from the other man's fingers. It fell with a noisy splash and then disappeared under the grimy water. "North?" the man croaked.

"Alders," Malcom called out, almost pleasantly. Cheerful, even. So jaunty that one who didn't know him might have taken it for a pleasant greeting.

"W-wasn't expecting you."

No, he hadn't been. Fury whipped through Malcom, but he'd become a master of reining in his emotions.

"N-not what it l-looks loike, N-North," the man stammered.

Malcom took a perverse glee in the way the trembling bastard's eyes bulged as they landed on the weapon he held. "Oh." He stretched that syllable out slowly, layering it with a silken steel warning. "And how is that?" He dusted the tip of the blade back and forth over his callused palm.

Even with the dark set to the tunnels, Malcom caught—and relished—the paling of the other man's skin. "W-wasn't . . . w-wasn't . . ." Alders's voice emerged garbled as he choked on that guttural Cockney, unable to bring forth the lie he no doubt sought. "These tunnels, th-they've been empty. Fair game, they w—"

Malcom stopped that deliberate glide of his dagger upon his palm. He took a slow step forward.

Whimpering, the other man hunched, covering his head protectively.

"Oh, come, Alders," Malcom murmured, continuing his path toward the quaking man. "I'm not going to hurt you."

Alders peeked out from between his arms. Fear spilled from his bloodshot eyes. "Y-ya ain't?"

"It is not as though you are stealing from someone you shouldn't be . . . You know the rules of this place." Every tosher grew up with them ingrained in his soul.

"Don't t-touch another man's t-tunnels," Alders stammered.

Aye, they all knew the rules. Except all rules were forgotten when toshers grew desperate and started to poach the lesser-used areas—territories belonging to older, less adroit toshers.

"Does the name Fowler mean anything to you?" Malcom murmured.

If it was possible, the bastard's skin paled all the more at the mention of one of the ancient toshers who searched these sewers.

"Ah, I see that it does. You don't happen to know anything about the latest men who've come after him, do you?" Malcom dangled the question as a threat and a lure.

The man trembled with a force that had the water slapping around his sizable legs.

Deliberately drawing on the moment, and stretching the man's terror along with it, Malcom scoffed. "You wouldn't ever do anything of the sort . . . unless perhaps you wanted to face me?"

The blubbering, pathetic mess of a man looked at Malcom and frantically shook his head, knocking loose his wool cap and exposing his shiny, bald pate. "I wouldn't—"

"Because," Malcom interrupted, "the only stupider, more dangerous thing a man could do than lie to me would be to come after that which isn't theirs."

Alders immediately clamped his fleshy lips tight. A damp splotch marred the front of his wool trousers.

Malcom glanced pointedly at the stain. "Ah, well, *that* is telling."

"I—I was s-sure these tunnels were free. Fowler is old—"

"Tsk. Tsk." Malcom lifted his dagger blade up. "Wrong answer."

Alders blubbered; tears spilled down his cheeks.

Where they lived, there was every danger in showing weakness. Exposing oneself in any way saw a person with their neck sliced, and a blade in their belly for emphasis. "Another wrong answer." He closed the remaining distance, and Alders scrambled to escape. Angling his stick, Malcom caught the other man's left foot and sent him toppling into the running water.

"Please," Alders cried, shielding his head once more. "P-please."

Blade in hand, Malcom leaned down, relishing in the way the attempted usurper shrank from him. "The rest of it, Alders."

Alders slowly let his arms down and glanced at Malcom with befuddlement stamped in his fleshy features.

"Surely," Malcom exclaimed, dropping his palms on his waist as he placed himself so that he was deliberately towering over Alders, who had to strain his neck back to meet Malcom's gaze. "Surely you don't think I'm going to turn the other cheek while you steal things that aren't yours?"

"I . . . I . . ." Tears filled Alders's eyes, and he hugged his arms around his knees and rocked. "Please. Please, don't."

Using the tip of his dagger, Malcom flipped open the front of the man's jacket. As one, his and Alders's eyes went to the pair of watches dangling from two clever linings sewn into the article. Malcom slipped his blade into the thread, instantly severing it. With his spare hand, he caught the gleaming gold piece and stuffed it inside his jacket. Keeping his blade aloft, he motioned to the silver piece. "Now the other."

The directive hadn't even left him before Alders was scrambling to relieve himself of the damning item.

The findings, however, didn't belong to this man, but another. "Now the bag." Malcom turned those three words into an order. When Alders remained shaking in his spot, he leaned down and whispered, "Now."

Squeaking, the burly man scrambled around Malcom, crawling on his knees through the water. "I've got i-it. Somewhere," he cried, talking to himself as he searched. A moment later, he surged upright, whipping the bag from the water, sending drops flying. "'ere it is."

Malcom peered quickly inside the sack. Even in the dark tunnels, the familiar spoils one could always expect to find gleamed back: watch fobs, miscellaneous gemstones that had come loose from whatever settings they'd once adorned. Grime-covered sovereigns. A veritable treasure existed underground, fair game for the taking, and one was able to sell them without a penalty of thievery.

"Now . . . What. Are. The. Rules?" Malcom asked, flinging the bag over his shoulder.

"Don'ttakewhat'snotmine," the man said in a rush, his words rolling together and barely intelligible.

"From what?" Pointing his knife to his ear, Malcom shook his head. "I didn't hear you."

"These tunnels—"

"Sewers," Malcom corrected. "Let us not make them more than they are," he taunted.

After contemplating Alders for a long moment, with his dagger he motioned the man forward. "Come, come."

Alders hesitated; tears sprang to his eyes once more, and with all the joy of a man having been summoned for his walk to the gallows, he joined Malcom.

"What else, Alders?" he asked coolly.

"I'm so sorry," the older man said through tears.

"And you won't do it again, now, will you?"

"No!" Alders cried. "N-never. My girl. She be the one who thought . . . said—"

Malcom lifted a single finger, instantly silencing the man. "In these sewers, my word is law. Are we clear?" When the other man hesitated, he stuck his face close and whispered, "Are we clear?"

The old tosher gave another shaky nod.

Malcom grinned. "Off with you, then," he said with his earlier false cheer.

Alders hesitated, as if he recognized a trap and had to pick his way out of it. Then he took off racing, splashing noisily through the water, the echo of his footfalls growing increasingly distant and then fading entirely.

The old tosher forgotten, Malcom flung his things over his shoulder, grabbed his pole, and followed a different tunnel away, this one narrower.

Darker.

The dark.

And there it was . . . Despite his infallibility over the years, that child's weakness mocked him. Attempted to drive back logic and replace it with only fear.

Malcom kept his gaze forward and forced himself not to look sideways and note the cramped walls, walls that were closing in around him.

Refusing to give in to that irrational fear, he hummed a song in near silence.

Roome for a lusty lively Lad,

dery dery downe, That will shew himselfe blyth be he ne're so sad,

dery dery downe . . .

The corridor widened, and some of the tension eased from his frame. Malcom strode quickly forward and didn't stop until he reached the familiar grate. Setting his belongings down, he pulled himself up and scoured the space through the slat in the grate. Waiting. Waiting. His ears attuned to every slightest sound—the distant drunken revelry, the rattle of a lone carriage.

He pushed the covering off and shoved it aside. Dropping once more to the ground, he tossed his stick out first. Clamping his knife between his teeth once more, he grabbed the brown bag, shoved it through the opening, and then climbed out fast behind it.

The moment his feet found purchase on the East London cobblestones, a faint *click* sounded just behind him. "Ya've gotten careless in your old age," the low, rough voice containing a trace of Cockney taunted. His palms up, Malcom inched slowly around and then, with a swift move, swept his leg out, capturing the other, broader figure, taking his feet out from under him.

Cursing, the man went down hard. His pistol clattered just once before Malcom had it in hand and turned on the man knocked clean on his arse. "And you've gotten sloppy in yours, Giles."

Dark eyes glared up at him, and then a reluctant grin curved those scarred lips. "Bloody hell, Malcom," he cursed, and yet, there was a thread of admiration as Malcom stretched a palm out.

With his only hand, the other man, Malcom's associate, took the offering and made to wrench him forward.

Anticipating that movement, Malcom compensated, angling his weight back, and then drove Giles back onto the ground.

"Oh, fuck yourself," Giles muttered, and this time, a scowl replaced his earlier smile as he ignored Malcom's hand and jumped up with an impressive agility for a man of his powerful size. "Damned smug, you've always—" The other man's words cut off as his gaze went to the bag Malcom hefted over his shoulder. Giles whistled slowly. "You caught him."

"Aye."

"He's had his sights set on these tunnels since Fowler began to slow," Giles said, speaking of the old tosher who'd trained Malcom years earlier.

Ever since, Malcom had been defending his own territories—and his livelihood—from potential usurpers such as Alders . . . people who'd try to take from him. If a tosher didn't keep those people out, if he didn't take back what had been stolen, one lost one's operation and people starved because of it.

"Did you take care of him?" Giles asked as they fell into step, as casual asking that question as if he'd asked whether Malcom had invited his nemesis for an ale at a tavern.

"I handled him."

"Someone's looking for you."

So that's why Giles had searched him out.

It wasn't uncommon for a man to be hunted in St. Giles. This, however, had been eerily different. A persistence that didn't fit with constables looking to cart a guttersnipe to Newgate to ease the worries of some fancy toff. Someone had begun asking the other toshers and street waifs who hung 'round these parts about Malcom. As such, Malcom had stayed low, keeping to the shadows even when he embarked on his work.

"Fowler sent me to bring you back immediately." That briefly gave Malcom pause. "He said there's a fancy-talking blighter who's come 'round."

Malcom's place was a lair, built amongst the rot, an unsuspecting kingdom hidden by a shattered facade and dirtied windows. The key, not only to survival but also to thriving in these places, was remaining hidden. And now, someone had found him. Through his frustrated fury he managed a single word: *"Who?"*

"The man's a detective." Giles gave him a look. "Connor Steele."

"Connor Steele." Malcom flashed a contemptuous sneer. That illustrious detective known by all. One of the few who'd escaped, Steele had been an impoverished street bastard who'd climbed out and built a *respected* name for himself—by betraying the men he'd run amongst. Respect in the streets, however, and respect on the side of the law and Polite Society were black to white. Malcom had less time for rats like Steele than he did for the sloppy toshers like Alders. "Where is he?"

"Fowler's with him. Bram is on guard outside."

Bram. More brute than human, the nearly seven-foot-tall mountain of a man had taken apart—literally and figuratively—opponents who'd crossed him . . . until he'd found himself making a trek to the gallows. Malcom had saved him from a certain hanging on more than one occasion, and because of it, the old man had set himself up as a de facto right hand, whether Malcom wished it or not.

And the truth would always be . . . the latter. There was no place for friends or family in these parts. Eventually, the streets claimed them all. As such, there was no point in creating dependents if one wasn't going to be around to take care of them.

Malcom crossed the street to where a young urchin with a tosher staff in hand was watching his mount and handed over a coin.

The small child looked up at him with wide, adoring eyes Malcom had never been, nor would ever be, deserving of. "Mr. North, sir."

"Billy," he greeted the girl, and offered a word of thanks. Not more than eight, she didn't have many options awaiting her. It was a miracle she'd survived as long as she had in her disguise. "Billy's going to need training," Malcom said.

"Girls don't have any place in the sewers."

It was not every day that Malcom met someone more diabolical than himself. "I wasn't asking. Find her a drain, go over the rules of the sewers, and then train her."

"*Train her?*" the other man protested.

"She'll need a tosher pole. Get her one. And then teach her how to use it to get herself underground, and how to navigate the tunnels." He paused. "And teach her how to use it to defend herself," he ordered, the matter done.

A short while later, Malcom rode up to the front of the unassuming structure between Tottenham Court Road and Willow Street. Sandwiched between two businesses, it was cleverly insulated, protected on both sides.

As he dismounted, Malcom patted his horse on the neck and did a sweep of the area, homing in on the street urchin who held the reins of an enormous black mare—horseflesh too expensive to belong to any of the people who dwelled here. Steele was doing well for himself.

One of Malcom's men came loping over, his gait slightly uneven, yet nearly indiscernible. "North."

Handing his reins off to Dore, one of many toshers who worked for him, Malcom found his way down the narrow alley until he reached the back of his residence. He leapt up the steps and, after inserting the small key, let himself in through the back entrance. His boots slopped water and grime over the rotten wood flooring. Not bothering to discard his jacket, Malcom moved through the narrow hall and quickly found his way to one of the three small rooms on the main floor.

The door sat open, with Fowler seated in a too-small-for-his-frame wooden chair.

The moment the old tosher caught sight of Malcom, he struggled to his feet, but Malcom waved the bruised bloke back. His right cheek was still swollen from the beating he'd taken a fortnight back. Fowler peered at the satchel Malcom held.

"Here." Malcom tossed the findings over to their rightful owner.

Fowler caught them against his concave chest. "Ya found it," the old man whispered, glancing up.

"Aye." The moment Fowler had come home bloodied, with a foot broken from a ruthless assault in the sewers, Malcom had resolved to flush out the ones responsible.

"Never made a mistake like that before," Fowler said, his throat working. The old man briefly looked into his bag at the contents and then hugged it once more. A glassy sheen misted those pale eyes. "Won't happen again—"

Discomfited, Malcom waved off those assurances.

Fowler coughed into his hand. "It's me damned eyes, is all," he defended, wiping at those drops.

Even a visit from one of London's most capable detectives was preferable to the old tosher's tears. To any tears, really. Like his heels were on fire, Malcom entered the makeshift office . . . and immediately found him.

In fairness, one would have to be blind to miss a tall, ugly brute like Steele. The detective's face and form bore the marks of his years on the street. And he stood there, his arms clasped behind him, his expression a mask of impassivity as he watched Malcom's approach. "You're North," he said without preamble.

It wasn't a question, but rather a statement spoken by one who'd been searching and at last had found his quarry. It deepened the warning ringing in Malcom's head that had pealed since Giles had tracked him down.

"I don't like company," Malcom said by way of greeting, pushing the door closed behind him. "And I like even less people asking questions about me." He layered a warning within that. Coming forward, Malcom shrugged out of his damp jacket. He deliberately tossed it close enough to Steele to soak him with the remnants of the sewer water.

He'd hand it to the other man: he made no outward reaction to the state of Malcom's dress . . . or to the stench clinging to his garments or the dusty, sad conditions of this East London office. Of course, Steele, even having climbed out of East London and having established a new life for himself, couldn't truly divest himself of this place.

"Steele," Malcom said, with mock joviality. "I would offer you a brandy, but alas, I'm afraid in these parts we don't have such luxuries to hand out." To underscore that very point, Malcom fished a small flask from his pocket, another token of his time in the sewers. Taking a swig of the harsh whiskey, he wiped a hand over the back of his mouth, and held out the flask in a taunting dare.

Steele lifted a palm in a polite declination.

Malcom's lips curved in a jeering grin, and he took another deliberate drink, and then tucked his flask into one of the many pockets lining his wool jacket.

The steely-eyed detective took in Malcom's every movement, lingering briefly on the clever pocketed garment donned by every tosher in London. Garments all different in their texture but similar for the purpose they served.

"There are matters of some import I would speak to you about." Steele at last let his arms fall to his sides and revealed a thick folder he held in his fingers.

Malcom forced himself to not linger his focus on the folder. To do so would reveal a weakness. Instead, he smiled coolly. "Ah, I'd offer you a seat, but alas, I fear I don't have one that would suit a fancy swell such as yourself."

Expressionless, Steele assessed the stack of wood crates lining the floor before collecting a solid egg-transport box. "This will do," he said, despite Malcom's disdain. The man didn't shrink from the discomforts of Malcom's office the way any other man of the law would and did.

Either way, the detective had overstayed his welcome. Nothing good could come from his being here. "Ah, but you see, I'm not offering you a seat," Malcom drawled, folding his arms at his chest. "That would suggest you intend to stay some time, and yet, I've no interest in entertaining you . . . or anyone."

"I understand my presence here is no doubt uncomfortable."

Malcom snorted. "Getting chewed up by sewer rats is uncomfortable. Having you here as unwanted company? An easy annoyance to be dispensed of." With that, Malcom started for the door.

"Does the Hope Foundling Hospital mean anything to you?" the other man asked, refusing to budge from his spot on the bloodstained floorboards.

"Nothing," Malcom said automatically. And it didn't. There were any number of those hellish institutions, those holding places for children who would eventually be turned loose as pickpockets and whores. "Now, if you'll excuse me?" He clasped the door handle.

"What of the names Sparky and Penge?"

Malcom paused; those names whispered forward. Vaguely familiar . . . and yet . . . not. Feeling the other man's eyes burning into his nape, Malcom took a path over to the desk he'd made out of an inverted phaeton wheel.

"I don't know them. I've never heard of them or of your hospital."

"How did you come to be here, Mr. North?"

"The same way as the rest of London's orphans." Rotted luck and even more ill fortune. "Alas," Malcom said icily, "if you've come for philosophical discussions, you're better served returning to the nobs you rub shoulders with now."

Steele, however, was unrelenting. "Ah, but you are not quite like the rest of London's orphans, are you?" Malcom didn't move. "You don't have the rough Cockney of one from these parts."

The other man wasn't going anywhere. It was not, however, the first time Malcom had been mocked or called out for the quality of his speech. He faced Steele once more. "Neither do you," he pointed out.

"I was rescued and raised as the adopted son of an earl."

The question came through clearer than if he'd spoken it aloud: How could they account for Malcom's proper English?

"Is that why you've come?" Malcom goaded. "To trade stories with a fellow street urchin similar to yourself?" He didn't wait for an answer. "Allow me to disabuse you of that notion. If you're looking to find someone like yourself? You're going to want to try Mayfair."

Steele pounced. "And are you familiar with Mayfair?"

Malcom silently cursed himself for revealing too much. The detective was searching for a street thief, then. "The only places I rob, Steele, are the sewers, where anything is free for the taking." As long as a man was brave enough—or stupid enough—to go claim it.

"I wasn't suggesting that you were committing theft."

"Am I familiar with Mayfair? No. Do I take cream in my tea? Don't drink the stuff. Should we move on to another polite topic? Weather, perhaps? Rain. Enjoying more of it than usual in our sunny old England."

Giving no outward reaction to that baiting, Steele snapped open the previously ignored folder in his hands. He sifted through several pages and then extended one sheet of parchment across the phaeton wheel. "Is this familiar to you?"

Making no attempt to take the page, Malcom dipped his gaze slightly enough so he could scan the information written there while keeping an eye on the detective.

126 MAYFAIR

LONDON PROPERTIES OF THE EARL OF MAXWELL

"Nothing. Now—"

"And yet, you can read it," Steele interrupted.

That gave Malcom pause.

The detective returned the sheet to his folder. "You not only speak proper King's English but also are able to read. Who instructed you?"

"I . . ." And for the first time since Steele had shown up and he'd sought to divest himself of the detective, Malcom faltered. For . . . he didn't know. Just as he'd never had an explanation of why his speech had come clipped when all the other boys and girls he'd foraged with had those guttural Cockneys.

"You don't have an answer, do you?" Steele asked quietly, without inflection. "Or an explanation?"

He didn't. He never had. When the other people he'd dealt with had all been illiterate and near impossible to understand with the thickness of their speech, Malcom had always been different. So different that when he'd been younger, smaller, he'd been beaten and mocked for it: the shite who thought himself royalty. That name, "King," once had been used to taunt him, but with the passage of time and Malcom's growth into a formidable street opponent, it had evolved into an acknowledgment of his strength in these parts.

"How about this?" Steele murmured, withdrawing another page, this one a sketched rendering of a fancy townhouse. The artist had captured the white stucco, the gleaming windows, and the gold knockers on the front of the double doors.

Malcom opened his mouth to deny any knowledge of the residence, but froze. Then, almost reflexively, he took the sheet.

His gaze locked on the minutest detail—the door knocker that didn't know if it wished to be man or lion, and had somehow perfectly melded the two into a bewhiskered half beast.

. . . the doors scare me, Papa . . . it looks like a man-lion . . .

The page slipped from Malcom's fingers.

The blood rushed to his ears, and he whipped his head up, the moment shattered. "I don't recognize that door."

"I didn't ask if you recognized the door, Mr. North." Steele gave him a long, slightly sad smile. "But rather . . . the residence."

A fancy Mayfair townhouse? He and his sort didn't venture out to those parts of London. Not if they sought to preserve their necks as long as possible. Malcom scoffed. "And why would I know anything about a townhouse in West London?"

"I was hired to investigate the possible whereabouts of a series of children who were taken."

"If you think I can help, you're wasting your time," he said tightly, clasping his hands behind his head. "I don't deal with anyone." As a rule, he kept people—all people—at arm's length.

"Yes, well." Steele cleared his throat. "The child who lived in this residence," he went on as if Malcom's insistence meant nothing, "fell ill alongside his parents. The parents perished. The child was turned over to a foundling hospital."

"I haven't been in a foundling hospital." *Not since . . .* He shoved back thoughts of that night. Those memories were, at best, murky. "Why don't you say what it is that you've come to say?" He had a sewer to rob.

Absolute silence filled the room, quiet so heavy that Malcom could hear only the periodic drip of water clinging to his trousers.

The detective held his gaze with an uncomfortable directness. "Because, Mr. North, I have reason to believe, and proof along with it, that you lived there . . . only"—Steele glanced around—"under different circumstances," he murmured when he returned his focus to Malcom. "Back when you were a boy, and the son of the late Earl of Maxwell."

Chapter 2

THE LONDONER
SCANDAL!

The Rightful Heir, the Earl of Maxwell, kidnapped as a boy by his grasping relatives and turned over to a foundling hospital. One can only wonder at the strife endured by that then young member of the peerage...

M. Fairpoint

Over the years much had been taken from Verity Lovelace: the comfortable cottage she'd grown up in. Her collection of ribbons. All her frocks and satin slippers.

But this loss . . . this was the keenest, unlike any Verity had suffered before. This was the first time she'd been robbed of her written words.

Motionless, unbreathing, incapable of moving, she stood in the middle of her room, the paper her sister held facing her.

How am I not shaking?

Or was she? It was all jumbled in that moment. Confused by the words hovering before her. Time stretched on. Verity tried to breathe. She tried to tell herself to get a proper breath. Inhale. Exhale. The simplest of a body's functions. And she could not do it. The air remained lodged, painful in her chest.

"They're not . . . all of your words," Livvie murmured with a startling optimism that life had not yet managed to quash in the seventeen-year-old. "I've read it."

Some of the words or all of them . . . it wasn't the amount that mattered. They'd been taken from her, and along with them the coin earned from the articles she wrote. The monies Verity relied upon to feed herself, her younger sister, and Bertha, their nursemaid turned all-purpose servant. As such, Verity's security—their collective security—was threatened.

But it was about more than money . . .

"The title is different," Livvie murmured.

Verity briefly closed her eyes.

"Too trusting, you've always been."

"Hush, Bertha," Livvie chided, just then sounding more like a woman ten years her senior. "Ignore her," she said softly. "You're not. She's not, you know."

And yet, the former nursemaid's opinion meant next to nothing, compared with what this moment represented.

Bertha snorted. "Don't know any such thing," she countered, blunt as the London day was dreary. "As fanciful and hopeful as your mother."

Their mother had been the daughter of a Scottish tavern keeper, and because of that, she'd the misfortune of crossing paths—and falling in love—with a roguish nobleman who never did right by her.

And yet, the irony of their nursemaid's words was that Verity had prided herself on being *nothing* like the woman who'd given her life. Not because she hadn't loved her mother. She had. But neither was she desiring to repeat the same mistakes that hopeless romantic had made.

In this, however, Verity had been hopeful.

About her future.

Nay, not just about her future . . . but being in full control of it. For her and Bertha, and more importantly, for Livvie.

Her sister cleared her throat. "Would you like me to read the article to you?" she murmured.

I'll read it. She wanted to get that assurance out. And failed. Verity yanked the pages from her sister's fingers. She forced herself to read the whole of the words printed there, paragraphs assembled under a story that belonged to her, but with credit given to another.

THE RIGHTFUL HEIR RESTORED

At last, the world has a name. Questions have swirled, cloaking society in the same fog that rolls over the darkened streets inhabited by the man whose identity everyone longs to know.

She couldn't make it any farther in the article. Her stomach churned, a pit forming in her belly. Livvie hadn't been completely incorrect; they weren't all Verity's words inked on the pages of *The Londoner*. Only the important ones belonged to her. There were a handful of empty descriptions, extraneous ones that advanced nothing in the article, ones that cheapened her original draft, ones belonging to another.

Not her.

I'm going to be ill . . . "Bloody rotter." That exclamation tore from a place deep inside, where rage dwelled. Verity tossed the pages, and they fluttered through the air, caught by her quick-handed sister.

"You gave him access?" Bertha pressed.

"I didn't." Her fists clenched and unclenched. "He stole it."

None other than Mitchell Fairpoint.

Verity began to pace. She should have been properly suspicious the moment he'd ceded the assignment over to her. With the paper struggling, as many were, only the most successful reporters found themselves maintaining their assignments. As such, the competition to retain one's post had been fought out amongst the articles written and the readership drawn in.

Her stride grew more frantic; her dark skirts whipped about her ankles, that *whoosh* of fabric grating.

For years she'd been fighting for her place at *The Londoner*, taking on the most menial roles. Finally rising to the ranks of a reporter. Reporting on tedious affairs that only the world of Polite Society could or would ever care about . . . until this. Until this story . . . still about a nobleman. But the first story of substance. The story the world craved. The story that was to have saved her . . . and her family. Gotten them out of their small apartments in the most dangerous part of London.

She had broken the story, only to have it ripped from her.

All the energy went out of her, and Verity abruptly stopped midstride, and then slid onto the edge of her usual kitchen chair.

Gone. It was gone. Except—

"It can't be gone," she whispered.

"It is," Bertha muttered, earning a frown from Livvie. "They've been looking for a reason to sack you, and now they have it."

Aye, Bertha spoke the truth. Verity's throat moved spasmodically. She'd been hired on as a mere girl of twelve, that post one her father had helped coordinate for her before he passed. And in her time there, Verity had worked within every capacity possible at *The Londoner*: she'd swept the floors and seen to the overall tidying of the establishment. Before being promoted to the role of note-taker, and then eventually . . . reporter.

All while the owner's son, that miserable bastard she'd despised since they'd first met, had expressed nothing more than boredom and disdain for his family's work.

Now that same clueless-to-the-workings-of-a-newspaper blighter had taken over ownership from his aging father, and she'd been fighting for her livelihood since.

For no other reason than her gender.

He didn't care about the fact that she'd spent nearly half her life working in this damned office. Or about the quality of her work.

Her passion.

He would simply turn her out and allow a thief of words in Verity's place instead.

"Over my dead body," she gritted out. Exploding to her feet, Verity sprinted over to the coatrack and yanked off her cloak.

"This isn't the time to speak to him," Livvie said, correctly anticipating Verity's intention and exuding far more restraint than her older sister.

"The hell it isn't." Verity snatched her bonnet and jammed it atop her head.

As if to make a mockery of that very idea, a bolt of lightning streaked across the afternoon sky.

"I have to agree with the girl," Bertha warned as Verity yanked the strings of her bonnet into a sloppy bow.

"I'll return shortly," she said, grabbing up the morning edition of *The Londoner* and her small satchel.

She flew from their apartments. The scents of the bakery below, the smells of baked goods and fresh bread that penetrated the thin walls and had always been soothing, now proved sickeningly sweet.

Verity stormed down the narrow stairway so quickly she stumbled at the bottom step. She caught the railing to keep herself upright. When her feet found the floor, she took off running for the doorway that led out to the crowded streets of East London.

The streets were bustling and noisy, with shopkeepers hurriedly hawking the remainder of whatever goods they had for that day before the rain broke.

Bypassing an old Rom woman trying to sell her jewels, Verity raced onward. She kept her gaze forward and wove amongst the passersby, her skirts whipping in angry time to her furious footfalls. As she found her way along the familiar path she'd traveled these past eighteen years, her chest rose and fell from her exertions. From the burn of her fury.

The offices of *The Londoner* drew into focus. She staggered to a stop, her gaze leveled on the neat little building, the one spot of white amongst a row of grey and brown stucco establishments.

I've found you employment, poppet. I hate that this is the future that awaits you. I wish it was more. I want it to be more . . .

And what her father had secured had been the most she ever could have hoped for as a bastard-born girl.

He'd secured her employment. And he'd cared for her as much as any bankrupt nobleman might care for his by-blow daughter.

And now she was on the cusp of losing it.

Verity briefly closed her eyes and focused on taking a slow, steadying breath. And then another.

When she opened them, she brought her shoulders back and marched into battle. She climbed the handful of steps, and her trembling fingers fumbled with the handle.

Damning that shake, a sign of weakness, Verity yanked the door open and stormed inside.

The din of the room continued; writers and editors clamoring to meet the day's deadline didn't so much as lift their heads from the tasks focusing them.

Drawing the door closed behind her, Verity scanned the room, searching the neat rows of desks. With all the men at work and Miss Wright, the only other woman on staff, filling the inkwells, it may as well have been any other day. Only it wasn't.

"Excuse me, ma'am," Miss Wright murmured, hurrying in front of Verity to reach her next inkwell at *his* desk.

Rage narrowed Verity's gaze into thin slits.

Pen poised over his page, Mitchell Fairpoint glanced up from his papers. His midnight hair slicked back, his nose faintly too sharp, and his eyes too cunning, he'd the look of the Devil to him.

"You bastard," she hissed, flying across the room.

That managed to penetrate the activity around the room. Shouts went up in echo to her cursing.

Ignoring the pathetically offended sensibilities, she reserved all her fury and channeled it onto one person. Verity slammed her bag down hard on Fairpoint's desk. "You stole from me."

His thin lips drew into a tight line as he smoothed his palms along his jacket. "How dare you!"

It didn't escape her notice that he remained seated, deliberately insolent, mocking. Her rage skyrocketed as she rested her hands on his immaculate desk and leaned forward. "I dare because it's true," she sneered. "You stole from me."

"I won't have my honor impugned by one of your ilk, Miss Lovelace."

She wavered. For a moment, she thought he might be referring to her birthright. Which was impossible. Only Mr. Lowery Sr. knew. And he'd pledged that secret to her father.

Fairpoint cried out, "Have a care!" Yanking a kerchief from his pocket, he wiped at the smattering of ink Miss Wright had spilled upon his fingers.

"My apologies, sir," the young woman murmured. Turning, she held Verity's gaze for a moment. She gave an almost imperceptible nod of approval, then rushed off to see to the supplies of another desk.

"Now, if you would go, Miss Lovelace. I don't have the time for this." He gave a flick of his fingers, like one brushing off a bothersome child. "I've my next story to see to."

My next story.

His.

As though the Lost Earl had *ever* been his.

From across the desk Miss Wright gave Verity another look; that taciturn show of support bolstered her. For this injustice, Verity's fight for respect and a place in this office, was about even more than just her and her security. It was also about the other woman who'd been working here for five years now and who also was denied a meaningful role. And though she'd never appreciated it before now, as long as she held her post here, Verity served as a reminder that women could do and be more in these professions men were so very determined to keep them out of.

Rage darkened her vision, and, snarling, she swept his papers from his desk. "Bastard."

Cries went up, the indignant shouts muffled by the whir of blood rushing in her ears.

"Miss Lovelace, that is *enough*."

That voice managed to penetrate her rage, and all at once, Verity became aware of several things: the pall of silence amongst the all-male staff now staring on in horror. And the annoyed figure standing in the middle of the offices. A figure who rarely visited. A man who left the daily affairs to his staff and swept in to grace them with his presence only when he wished to play at being the proprietor.

And this would be the day he'd be here.

Her stomach turned over. "Mr. Lowery," she said in belated greeting, her voice hoarse.

Out of the corner of her eye, she caught the smug stamp of Fairpoint's features and curled her fingers into balls at her sides to stop from scraping her nails down the bastard's face.

"I'd speak with you in my office." Not bothering to see if she followed, he started across the rooms.

Verity scooped up her copy of *The Londoner* and her bag. She stomped around the desk and leaned close to Fairpoint. "We are not done here," she whispered.

"No," he agreed with a snide grin. "I'd venture only one of us is."

Verity flared her eyes and made to lunge at the thief of her words and future.

"Miss Lovelace," Lowery snapped, his voice carrying from his offices, "I don't like to be kept waiting."

"I suggest you be going, Miss Lovelace," Mr. Fairpoint advised, setting the contents of his desk to rights. "I trust you've displeased Lowery enough this day."

She fisted her hands so tightly her jagged nails dug sharply into her callused palms, the rough skin dulling any pain. Verity reached the offices and lingered outside. *Always be composed. Always be in control. Never show emotion.* These were the expectations for any woman who wished to be considered seriously in this—or any—profession. Women were not permitted furies, even when the greatest of injustices had been committed. Even as men could slap one another across the faces with gloves and fingers and then meet on a dueling field to fight for their honor, women were expected to pour tea and be meek.

Verity intended to fight for her job. Smoothing her features into a calm she didn't feel, she clasped her hands before her so that her satchel swung as she moved. "Mr. Lowery," she murmured, stepping inside.

He opened his mouth.

"I'd speak with you, please," she continued before he could speak. Before he could sack her or call her out for her improper behavior on the floor. "Regarding my recent research and story on the Lost Earl."

"'Lost Heir.' That is how it was recorded by Fairpoint."

Verity set her jaw so hard her teeth ground audibly in the office and her temples throbbed. She forced her lips up into something that felt more grimace than smile. "Ah, yes." She swept forward. "However, when I broke and wrote the story, I'd originally titled it as the Lost Earl because, well, the gentleman who'd been lost"—who still eluded the world—"was, in fact, an earl."

"'Lost Heir' sounds better," Lowery said impatiently. "It's the titles of the articles that sell."

Was it, though? She'd rather say it was the content . . . however, given the precariousness of her position and her future here, she'd not belabor the point. "May I?" she asked, gesturing to the chair across from him and claiming it before he could toss her out on her buttocks. "That story, as you know," she began calmly, "was one you assigned to me."

Removing a cheroot from his jacket, Mr. Lowery touched the tip to the candle at the corner of his desk. Ignoring the way her nose twitched at that pungent odor, Verity fixed on the head editor of *The Londoner* as he puffed away on the noxious scrap. "And?"

And? he asked.

Verity placed her bag on the floor. "And Mr. Fairpoint stole my story. He put his name on it and presented it to you." She set the damnable pages on his desk.

Lowery didn't so much as glance down. Taking another draw from his cheroot, he tipped the ashes into the silver tray on his desk. "Don't care about some rivalry between you and Fairpoint." A rivalry. That was how he saw it. And of course, Verity would be taken for some emotional female as opposed to the wronged party she, in fact, was. "What I cared about, Miss Lovelace," he went on, dropping his elbows on his desk, "was the story."

Her livelihood was crafted of words. As such, as Lowery raised his cheroot to his lips and took a slow, deliberate draw, her writer's mind clung to two words: "cared" . . . and "was." Both spoken in past tense. Panic sent her heart thudding in her chest. There'd be no righting the wrong done to her. Lowery, as he'd indicated, didn't care. Only profit mattered.

And therefore, as Lowery exhaled that plume of smoke in an uneven circle, she shifted her focus to fighting not about her stolen story but rather her future here. "I've an idea for a story on the Lost Earl . . . Heir." She forced that hideous title out.

That gave Lowery pause. "Oh?"

Now that the world had the name of the missing nobleman, everyone craved details about his life and his whereabouts with the same ferocity with which English people craved their tea.

She had his attention; now there was the matter of retaining it. "Everyone wants to know about him—"

"Stop wasting my time with theatrics, Miss Lovelace," he snapped, exhaling another puff of smoke from the side of his mouth. "Do you have information on the gentleman or not?"

No. Not yet anyway. She sidestepped his question. "Each publication, we might put forward possibilities about where the gentleman has been—"

"Possibilities?" His brow puckered, those five creases conveying his disapproval.

Verity nodded enthusiastically. "Oh, yes." There'd not been much Verity Lovelace hadn't done in order to survive. "The possibilities. Can't you just imagine them?"

"No," he said flatly. "It's your job to tell me precisely what they are."

"Well." Her mind raced as she searched around for the proper pitch. Bastard born, with a mum dead too soon, and left to navigate the world alone as a child, she'd learned right quick precisely what the world had in store for a young woman on her own. Though in fairness, with the passage of time, she'd come to witness firsthand that where women were concerned, the world didn't discriminate by age. It was harsh, more often than not unfair, and ruthless to all women. As such, there was not much Verity wouldn't do to hold on to her current post as a reporter with *The Londoner*. And that explained why, at that moment, she was making a desperate pitch of a nonstory.

"Miss Lovelace," he snapped impatiently.

"We whet the world's appetite with a thirst for more. Feed their craving until he is at last found."

Lowery paused. And then . . .

"Ain't a story."

Bloody hell.

"Egregious offense, you coming in here, trying to have me publish something that ain't a story. In fact, not sure which is more egregious . . . that, or your making a show of yourself. It is unbecoming of my staff."

Verity bit her tongue to keep from pointing out there'd been any number of egregious offenses that day: Fairpoint's plagiarism. Lowery's own use of the word "ain't." "Ah, but I disagree."

His high brow creased, his thin lips pulled tight at the corners.

Oh, bloody hell. Verity spoke on a rush, in a bid to defuse his anger. "That is, I most respectfully disagree, sir."

"As long as you do it respectfully."

She brightened. Mayhap she'd unfairly misjudged the gentleman, after all. "Truly?"

Mr. Lowery snorted. "Of course not 'truly,'" he snapped. Stubbing his cheroot out on a silver tray, he grabbed the pages Verity had tossed down a handful of minutes ago. "This is a story."

"It was my story," she could not keep from pointing out. The fury of having her work stolen redoubled in her breast.

He hurled them across his cluttered desk.

Verity hurriedly caught them to her chest, wrinkling those recently completed pages, the ink, still slightly damp, marring her fingertips.

"Papers are costly to run, Miss Lovelace. With the taxes—"

"I'm familiar with the state of taxation on newspapers," she clipped out. In addition to having her work ripped asunder by a buffoon with poor grammar, she'd not be lectured on political events she was well versed in. "Quite so," she added for good measure. It's what accounted for the ruthlessness that had developed amongst reporters who were desperate to keep their assignments.

Mr. Lowery peered down his lengthy nose with such condescension she ground her teeth together again. "If you know that, then you know I can't keep you around if this is the manner of nonstory you've given me." With that, he came out of his chair. "I told you your assignment here was contingent upon your delivering the Lost Heir story."

"And I did." She could not keep the thread of desperation from her voice. Panic knocked around Verity's chest as she followed her employer as he stalked off, but he began rummaging around the stacks of papers throughout the room. Muttering to himself while he searched for whatever it was he'd lost this time. Verity stopped on the other side of the table he currently searched. "It is a teaser, Mr. Lowery." It was a desperate bid on her part. "Something to *entice*."

He snorted. "Do you expect me to buy into that idea?"

Actually, since he'd newly taken over control of daily decisions from his father, she rather had. Either way, she knew men, and she knew their egos and, more specifically, how easily those egos were bruised. As such, she kept her lips wisely shut.

"You knew your post was on the line."

"Yes, and I—"

"And it's been four months," he snapped. "Four months of you writing some other nonsense while you bring me nothing on the story that I really want."

In fairness, it wasn't solely the story Mr. Lowery wanted.

It was the story the whole *world* craved: the tale of the Earl of Maxwell, who'd been kidnapped as a boy and thrust onto the streets of St. Giles while usurpers had availed themselves of a lavish lifestyle at the child's expense.

People had followed the downfall of those who'd robbed from the late earl, his wife, and his son. The only thing the world was missing now was the restored earl and an accounting of just how he'd survived these past years. What he'd done. And where he was . . .

She tried to reason with Lowery. "The gentleman has proven elusive. He does not wish to be found." It was undoubtedly why Lowery had given her the blasted assignment. He'd been attempting to sack her for months.

"I don't care what he wishes, Miss Lovelace. I expected you to find him. I expected you to interview him. Find out where he's been. What he's done. And publish that story in our damned paper."

Expected . . . which signified the past tense and a telltale mark of her future here. And when she lost her employment here . . . what then?

What of Livvie's future?

Bertha's?

Our futures, together.

As if watching the life of another play out before her, she followed Mr. Lowery as he gathered up an armful of papers and beat a path to the door.

And when he stepped through it, then all hope would be lost. She'd no longer be Verity Lovelace, a woman with a respectable position and secure employment. She'd become an unemployed, unmarried, on-her-own female, prey to the whims and cruelties of heartless men, and with a younger sister to care for. And a rent she could not pay.

Verity came whirring back to the moment.

"Mr. Lowery," she cried out, rushing after him. Ignoring the triumphant smile worn by Fairpoint, Verity gripped her employer by the arm. She ignored the outraged glint in his eyes as he took in her bold fingers. Panic lapped at the corner of her senses. "Please." There were many too proud to beg. Verity, however, did not do this for herself alone but rather another, and it was that which made her able to swallow her pride and plead for her future. "I *need* this post."

Shrugging off her touch, he proceeded over to his cloak and shrugged into it. "And I needed this story." Mr. Lowery gathered several files and stuffed them inside a leather bag. And with that, he disappeared through the door.

Yes, a struggling paper needed every advantage, and Lowery had pinned the hopes for his paper's rise to its former greatness upon that story.

Verity sprinted after him, and again inserted herself into his path. "Another week," she appealed, all but shouting through the din of the room.

He wound his way around her, making for the entrance. "And what do you think a week will do, given that it's been months?"

Hope. It was what had fueled her and enabled her to survive the whole of her existence.

Mr. Lowery opened the door, and a sharp blast of wind whipped through.

"We're done, Miss Lovelace," he said, drawing his gloves on.

Verity followed him outside. The previously bustling streets were now eerily quiet because of the impending storm reflected in the thick black clouds rolling overhead. That symbol of darkness and gloom . . . *It is an omen* . . . She thrust aside the tingling of unease working along her spine. "I've made progress," she called after him. *Lies.*

And as he seemingly knew it, he continued on to the waiting carriage.

Verity bit the inside of her cheek, and then called, "I've determined his whereabouts." Another blast of wind carried those words, stretching their echo.

That managed the otherwise impossible until now: Mr. Lowery stopped, one foot poised inside the carriage.

For one agonizing moment, she believed he'd climb inside that black barouche, ride off, and leave her hopeless once more.

Mr. Lowery stepped down and faced her. "You have three minutes, Miss Lovelace."

Gathering up her skirts, Verity sprinted down the handful of steps and joined him.

"I've uncovered some of the details you've sought."

"You?"

She nodded.

"You know where he lives?" And by the suspicion coating that inquiry, he was rich in doubt.

She'd not a damned clue. Alas, the lies came easily when one was desperate enough. "I do."

Rubbing his gloved palms together, Mr. Lowery contemplated her. All the while, she made herself remain still through that scrutiny.

Suddenly, her employer stopped. "Where is he?"

Verity lifted her chin in mutinous defiance. "Why would I freely give you that?" she scoffed. "My last story was already stolen from me. You've been wanting to sack me since you took over the operations of *The Londoner*. As such, if I give you that information, you'll hand it to one of the men in your employ and allow him to complete the story."

For a long moment, she believed he would call her lie out for the falsehood it clearly was.

But then, desperation made a person do funny things, like trust where one oughtn't. Verity herself was proof of that. "You have until the end of the week, madam. I want that story not only researched but also written and on my desk by Friday's time."

Elation, swift and palpable, surged through her. "Yes, sir," she said on a rush, her relief real even if her assurances for Lowery were not.

Mr. Lowery pulled himself inside the carriage. A moment later, his driver closed the door behind him, and the conveyance leapt forward.

Verity stood there, her face carved into an expressionless mask, her frame immobile, as the carriage pulled away. Fearing the owner of *The Londoner* would have his eyes on her even now, searching for the truth of her deception.

When it disappeared over the horizon of the eerily empty London streets, she let her shoulders sag. "Oh, bloody hell," she whispered. Giddy with relief, she set her shaking palms atop her knees and leaned over them.

A week. She'd bought herself one week more of security.

The reminder of the promise she'd made, the one her future now hung contingent upon, managed to penetrate her relief.

One more week to find a man who'd no wish to be found. And reveal a story that her employer—and all the world—wanted told.

A bolt of lightning zigzagged across the afternoon sky, nearly black from the ominous storm threatening. With that, reality came streaming back in as it invariably did.

Cursing, she ran back inside, fetched her worn brown cloak, bonnet, and leather satchel, and stepped back outside.

The moment her feet touched the pavement, the skies opened up. A deluge of unrelenting rain poured from the heavens, and in mere moments it had flattened her bonnet and sent water running in rivulets down her face.

Sputtering around a mouthful of water, Verity raced the short distance back to her apartments. Her boots sank into a large puddle, the grime and cold penetrating the thin, breaking soles. So that when she climbed the stairs of her apartments, every part of her and her garments was sopping.

Her sister immediately opened the door.

"I got caught in the rain," Verity muttered the obvious.

Her sister took her by the arm and pulled her in. "I see that. You look terrible," she said.

"I—I c-can always c-count on you to b-be truthful," Verity said gently through teeth that chattered. She dropped her bag, and it hit the floor, immediately leaving a small puddle on the hardwood.

Her sister returned her smile. "Of course you can." Smiling. Always smiling. Would she still be so if tossed out of their apartments and forced to live on the streets?

Dread slithered around Verity's belly. If anything were to happen to her, what would become of her sister? It was something she'd not given thought to—until now. Until she hung on the cusp of being unemployed. In her quest to care for Livvie, she'd left her vulnerable: a woman of seventeen, unable to properly care for herself.

Livvie's brow dropped. "What is it?"

Her sister missed nothing. Verity made a show of wringing out her skirts. "I'm cold," she lied, because soggy skirts were far easier to speak to a girl about than the possibility that they'd find themselves homeless.

"Here," her sister murmured, falling to a knee beside her. She proceeded to help Verity from the too-tight boots that were all but falling apart. "These won't do you much longer, Verity." Livvie struggled with the ancient footwear.

"I kn-know." There weren't funds. Certainly not now. Not when their future remained up in the air.

"Oh, bloody hell," her sister whispered.

"Livvie," Verity gently chided. "You should not . . ." She looked down . . . and her stomach sank. Livvie held the threadbare boot aloft, a small, circular scrap of leather that had once been attached to the sole in her other hand. Closing her eyes, Verity leaned against the door. "Bloody hell."

"We'll fix it," her sister hurried to reassure her.

Only they wouldn't.

"It's fine," Verity said tiredly. There were far greater concerns—at the moment anyway—than her stockinged feet being exposed to the London elements.

Livvie scoffed and set to work helping Verity out of her other boot. "You can borrow my pair when you go to work."

When you go to work . . .

Verity bit the inside of her cheek. "I'm not worried about my boots."

That snagged her astute sister's notice. She sharpened her gaze on Verity's face, and then slowly stood. "What is it?"

She hesitated. "It is nothing."

Fire immediately flared to life in Livvie's eyes. "Don't you dare do that."

"Wh—"

"Consider withholding truths. We don't do that. Not in our family."

No, they didn't. Just Verity did. To protect Livvie as best she could.

"He sacked ya, didn't he?" Bertha emerged from the kitchens. "Foolish ya were, thinking ya could ever make a serious go at that work. Men's work it be," she said with a faint pitying in her eyes and words.

Verity glared at the older, gap-toothed woman. "Hush, Bertha. That's not true."

The heavyset woman sailed over. "And filling this one's head with hopes that women aren't afforded the luxury of."

Yes, because the options that the world had for all women existed of two fates: a respectable path of marriage . . . or the path of shame and finding oneself in some man's bed, as had been the case for Verity's mother.

As Bertha set out to school Livvie on the ways of the world, Verity walked in her drenched stockings over to the door and pushed it closed. Then, drawing in a slow breath, she glanced between them. "When we left Epsom, we knew that it would not be easy, and yet we survived."

"Because your da set you up with work," Bertha said with her usual bluntness.

When Livvie went to speak, Verity put a hand on her sister's arm, staying her words and ending her inevitable defense. "I've not been sacked." That statement chased away the worry from her sister's eyes. "I've been given another opportunity—"

Bertha snorted. "To find that bloody duke."

"He's an earl," Verity muttered, struggling with the clasp at her throat. "But yes. He is the reason."

Livvie moved aside Verity's fingers, and swiftly saw to the task herself. Taking the garment, she draped it over one of the two chairs in their apartments. "You've searched for him. You can't find him. Why can't you simply make it up?"

"I cannot make it up, Livvie," she said gently. She'd dealt before in fabricated truths. Her entire existence on the outskirts of London had been one.

Bertha thumped the table twice. "The girl is right. You make it up."

Verity hugged her arms around her middle. Of course they'd be of a like opinion. But then, desperation compelled people to make any manner of decisions they'd not otherwise make. For them—for herself—she wished to do it. "I cannot," she said tiredly. Not if she wanted to live with herself in good conscience.

"'Course you can," Bertha cried out.

Livvie tugged Verity by the hand and led her to the small kitchen table, forcing her into a seat. "I don't see why not," she said softly. "The gent doesn't wish to be found. He's not coming out."

"And better off for not finding him, I say. Any man who prefers living in the sewers to being a fancy duke is madder than the late King George," Bertha mumbled before quitting the kitchen and heading for her rooms.

After she'd gone, Livvie waited several moments, then sank to a knee beside Verity. "The people want a story," she said. "They don't care about what was real and what is false . . . A story is what sells."

"The girl is right." Bertha's voice came muffled from the other side of the panel.

They looked toward the older woman's room and then back at one another, sharing a smile. It appeared Verity had found the one topic that had managed to unite the pair that so often failed to see eye to eye.

Verity's smile was quick to fade. "I'm not fabricating a story."

"But—"

"Please, don't ask me to do that. For when the lie came to light"— which it invariably would—"we'd be precisely where we are now." Only with no chance of keeping her post, and a reputation ruined. "I'll not lie to sell a story." And certainly not a lie about a person's past.

"Lying's a good deal safer than starving," her sister said.

Verity flinched. "I'm going to find him."

"And how do you intend to do that?"

Seated at the table, staring into the lone flame dancing, Verity found she rather didn't know. But she would find him. There was no other choice. Someone in East London must know of—

Her lips parted.

"What is it?" Livvie asked, concern in her voice.

Ignoring that question, Verity fixed on not what her sister was saying but earlier words uttered by another. Verity froze. After all, known as Garrulous Bertha by all those in their corner of East London, the older woman tended to easily spew words, as she was wont to do. Still . . . Verity jumped up, and with Livvie calling after her, she bolted to Bertha's rooms. She didn't bother with a knock.

When the door exploded open, the woman didn't even look up from her knitting needles.

"How did you know that?" Verity demanded.

Bertha's gnarled fingers continued darning away. "Huh?"

Verity sprinted across the room and plucked the needles from her hands. "You said something to the effect of a man who prefers to live in the sewers." Words that had been too specific.

Bertha lifted her rounded shoulders in a lazy shrug. "That be the word on the streets." She reached for her darning needles, but Verity held them out of reach.

"By whom?" she asked slowly, as if speaking to a child.

The older woman's lips formed a wide, slightly gap-toothed smile. "My sweetheart."

Her . . .

Livvie's giggle sounded from beyond Verity's shoulder.

Bertha scowled. "Hush. You think it so shocking that I might have found myself a suitor?"

The girl's laughter only deepened.

Verity gave her sister a look and, when she'd finally silenced her, returned all her focus to Bertha. She fell to a knee beside her fraying upholstered chair, one of the remaining pieces left from the lifetime of comfort they'd enjoyed while the earl had lived. "And . . . who is this gent?"

"He's a tosher."

What . . . ? Puzzling her brow, Verity glanced over at Livvie, but the younger girl merely stared back with wide eyes.

"What is a tosher?" Verity pressed Bertha.

"*Pfft.* One would think you were two fancy gels." Instead of the by-blows they were. The implication hung there . . . without inflection, and yet, still stinging as it always had . . . being bastard born—even if it was to an earl. "*Tosshher,*" she repeated, as if adding an extra syllable and slight emphasis to the word might somehow make it mean something to Verity. "He's a sewer hunter. Scavenges. Pans and retrieves tosh. Well, more than *tosh* because 'tosh' is copper," she explained. "This fellow finds himself a whole lot of riches down in that waste-filled water."

Livvie's face pulled. "That is disgusting."

"Be that as it may, the fellows doing it are better off than your sister here, trying to write a story for a gossip column."

Her mind racing, Verity fell back on her heels. It made sense. All these months she'd been scouring London for anyone with a hint of the gentleman's identity, she'd been searching the wrong places. Asking the wrong people. In short, the Earl of Maxwell didn't walk amongst them. Rather, he'd been under her all the while.

There was a tug at Verity's sleeve, and she glanced over.

"What are you thinking?" her sister asked.

And for the first time since she'd been handed the impossible assignment, Verity smiled. "I'm going toshing."

"That isn't a word," Bertha corrected, much as she had when instructing Verity as a child.

Verity's smile deepened. "It is now."

Chapter 3

THE LONDONER
THE HUNT!

All of London is in search of the gentleman whose fortunes have been reversed. He remains a mystery to all . . . There is only one certainty: the Lost Heir has no wish to be found!

M. Fairpoint

Verity had done next to everything in order to survive.

Or so she'd believed.

The following evening, attired in one of her only three dresses and a pair of too-tight slippers belonging to her sister, Verity realized just how wrong she'd been.

"Are you having second doubts, gel?" Bertha asked loud enough that her voice carried damningly down Brook's Mews.

Nay, more like third and fourth and fifth doubts. *"Shh,"* Verity said gently.

"Now you're so worried about getting yourself caught? We've been standing here for the better part of five minutes."

"I'm going, I'm going," she muttered, and then forced herself to kneel. Ignoring the cold of the pavement penetrating her thin skirts. Wishing all the while she'd had Livvie accompany her instead. Knowing this was no place for her sister. Furthermore, Bertha was the one with connections to the toshers, and having two women and a sheltered young woman hovering around the sewer opening would only risk notice. As it was, Bertha, with her failure to appreciate the importance of silence, posed danger enough. Verity wrestled with the grate, her muscles straining under the unexpected weight of the protective covering. At last, the unrelenting cover gave, and she used all her strength heaving it up.

The stench of rot filled her nostrils, and she gagged, covering her nose in a futile bid to block the smell of it.

Bertha leaned forward, and then swiftly drew back. "Good God." She pressed her forearm over her face.

Nay, there was no God down there.

"I suspect it is going to get a good deal harder when you're in there," the older woman pointed out with her usual blunt honesty.

And damn if she wasn't right. Forcing her arm to her side, Verity eyed the opening.

She could do this.

How difficult could it be? Climb down—

And search for a man who didn't wish to be found? So much so that he'd forsake a title in place of . . . this?

Verity scrabbled with her lip. Mayhap Bertha was right, after all. Verity was a-hunting a madman. For no sane person could prefer this life to the one awaiting him if he simply claimed his fortune. And for the first time since she'd been handed her assignment from Lowery, unease wound its way through her for altogether different reasons. Not from the sheer desperation to locate and tell the story, but from what would happen if—when?—she did locate the man in question.

An image slipped in: a beastlike figure, with the stench of filth clinging to him. Wild eyes. A feral mouth.

I cannot do this . . .

"Mayhap you don't go in," Bertha murmured with her first vocal doubts raised. "Mayhap there is another way to find him."

There wasn't.

"I'm going, I'm going," she muttered again. Only, as she remained standing there, she couldn't determine whether she was trying to convince the other woman she was going to climb down—or herself.

Either way, before her courage deserted her, Verity shimmied onto her belly until she dangled with half her body in and the other half out of the opening. Then, slowly, she lowered herself down into the sewers.

She choked on the acrid scent that slapped at her.

Her arms ached. Her muscles screamed. But for the life of her, she could not let herself make the final descent.

There has to be another way.

"There isn't," Bertha whispered, confirming she'd spoken aloud. "Only way down into the sewers is through one of them grates," she murmured, misunderstanding Verity's wonderings. "Now you should hurry on with yourself. Before someone comes and we don't have either our lives or your story to show for it."

And in the end, it was that ominous warning about either of the fates awaiting her that compelled her. Verity closed her eyes and let go; her stomach dropped along with her in a fall that seemed eternal.

She landed hard, sinking into a small puddle, the freezing-cold water instantly penetrating the thin soles of the pair of slippers she'd received just that morning. "Bloody hell," she whispered, her voice pinging off the stone walls.

Verity climbed her gaze up the six feet between her and that lone exit, and her stomach flipped over once more. How in blazes was she to get back out now? "Bertha," she whispered. "Bertha," she repeated, this time more insistently. And for one horrifying moment, she believed she'd been duped, lured, and left to die in this dark pit where none would ever know.

But then . . .

Bertha ducked her greying head into the opening. "What?" she cried, her voice ricocheting around the brick walls.

"Shh," Verity implored. "It's fine. It is just . . . I . . . I'll need help climbing out."

Even in the dark, she caught the pull of Bertha's high forehead. "Help? You only just climbed in."

And despite herself, Verity found herself laughing. "Not now. Later."

"I'll wait here—"

"I've told you. You cannot." Too many would be watching and questions would be asked, and Verity wouldn't have her story stolen once more. "Go with your fellow . . . Return in thirty minutes."

Bertha hesitated, then caught the sides of the grate. Panic swelled as the older woman slid the covering back into place.

Oh, God.

There was a sharp clatter that echoed with an eerie finality, as with its closure the fragile glow cast by the moon was stolen, and Verity was plunged into complete darkness.

Her breathing increased, growing more ragged, the sharp sound of it echoing around the tunnel.

Verity briefly closed her eyes.

You've done far worse . . . You've . . .

Only, had she? Had she truly?

She'd had rocks tossed at her by village children who didn't want to keep company with a whore's daughter. Been hungry from an empty belly. Cold in the harshest of winters. But had she truly known the full extent of life's ugliness and depravity? An ugliness and depravity she continued to learn the endless bounds of. Plunging herself underground, locked away from the world, trapped.

Her breath rasped loud in her ears.

"Enough," she whispered, needing to hear her voice. Verity forced her legs to move, and focusing on the simple command of placing one foot in front of the other, she wandered deeper into the tunnel.

Tunnel.

There, that was a better way of thinking of it . . . tunnel, and not sewer. Sewers were dark. Dank. Dangerous. Tunnels, were . . . well, similar, but—

Verity shivered and huddled deeper into her wool cloak.

Drip. Drip. Drip-drip. Drip. Drip. Drip-drip.

As she walked, she scoured the narrow pathway, lined with increasingly deepening water. "Bloody hell." She sighed at her slippers, the silliest of shoes to ever go traipsing through London—let alone the sewers of London—in. And now hopelessly ruined. They'd take days to dry, and even when they did, the leather would be threadbare.

Verity reached the end of the tunnel and stopped abruptly, the grimy, stone-slicked path sending her foot sliding forward. Gasping, she shot her palms out and braced herself against the uneven bricks. Catching herself.

Verity looked beyond . . . at a network of tunnels. That led off in both directions. She squinted in an attempt to better see how far down the current path led.

It was an infernal maze that a person could simply get themselves turned around in and wade through waste until he—or, in her case, she—drew their last noxious breath.

And all the questions raised about the Earl of Maxwell's sanity whispered forward, for no sane man should choose . . . this . . . over a life of untold comforts. Verity held her sleeve against her nose in a bid to mute the stinging odor permeating the air. "You had better be here," she muttered, conflicted even with that utterance as to whether she wanted to run face-first into a man who preferred to call this place home over his Grosvenor Square residence.

Verity hefted her skirts around her waist and continued forward.

She waded through the deepening water. Her submerged skin quickly went numb from the frigid cold.

"Where are you?" she whispered.

And when you find him . . . then what?

"Then you convince him," she assured herself in the eerie silence, her own echo oddly terrifying. And she'd certainly convinced any number of men—more than she could count or remember, men of all stations—to share their secrets.

It had been the blessing and curse of her thirty years of existence.

This earl would be no different. This earl, who'd identified as a commoner for more years than he'd ever lived his comfortable existence as a peer.

A faint rumble went up, ominous, cutting across her musings.

It froze Verity in her tracks.

Squeak. Squeak.

She cried out as a flurry of rats bolted toward her, and she raced out of their path, hugging the brick wall.

Just as several loose stones overhead gave way, toppling into a heap, the clatter of those rocks crushing the rats who'd found themselves in the place where she'd just been.

Breathless from relief and terror, those competing emotions twining in her chest, Verity struggled to get air into her lungs. Leaning against the wall, she took support from the dank bricks.

"Everything about this damned place is dank," she whispered, needing to hear herself talk in this underground crypt. Fearing the *drip-drip, drip-drip* pattern of sewer water plinking would drive her mad. "The air, the walls, the ground . . ." She froze. "The ground," she echoed. *No.* With dread slipping through her, Verity lifted her left foot from the water.

She groaned. *"Noooo."* Her heart plummeted to the sole of her now naked foot.

She'd lost one, which may as well have been a pair of shoes. And what was worse . . . it wasn't Verity's, but Livvie's.

Closing her eyes once more, she knocked her head lightly against the brick.

Damn *all* men.

The one who'd loved her mother, but not enough, and for it, had left Verity a bastard with few supports in place when he'd died.

Lowery and his damned son with his ill opinion of women and their capabilities.

And Fairpoint. Hatred sizzled through her veins, crackling and lifelike.

She forced her eyes open.

And damn the gentleman busy playing at street rat for the perverse devil he was. Her fury compelled her away from the wall, and she found solace . . . nay, strength in it. It enlivened her and gave her a focus that would keep her from surrendering to the panic of her circumstances.

Gathering up her wet skirts, she trudged through the water, scraping her toes along bricks slicked with grime.

She flinched. "What in God's name is that?" she whispered. As soon as she gave the question life, she shook her head hard. *No. Don't think about it.* "Think about the fact that you're scurrying around the gutters like a rodent." And all because a man who had a fortune and future awaiting him was more content to dwell here? "Lunacy." She exhaled a hiss of anger. Sheer lunacy was all that accounted for it.

Verity toed the floor.

How far could the damned scrap have gone?

And then her foot caught a patch of grime, and she cried out as her leg came out from under her and she tumbled onto her buttocks, landing with a sharp splash.

Freezing water immediately soaked her skirts, the sting of cold as biting as the pain that throbbed up her spine from where she'd fallen. There, braced on her elbows, up to them in grime, she didn't want to consider, until she was out of this hell, bathed, and the gowns she now wore properly laundered, just what she was drenched in. Every part of her, from the roots of her hair to the tips of her toes, was soaked.

Her toes.

My toes.

She froze, and with a sickening dread winding through her once more, Verity slowly lifted first one bare foot from the water—and then the other.

Two slippers, gone.

Something built in her chest; a half groan, half sob rumbled up and then exploded from her lips. Verity hugged her arms around her middle and laughed.

It could not possibly get worse than this.

With that empty assurance rolling around her mind, she struggled to her feet and set to searching for *two* missing slippers.

Chapter 4

THE LONDONER

At last, the world has the name they've been searching for. Questions have swirled, cloaking society in the
same fog that rolls over the darkened streets inhabited
by the man whose identity everyone longs to know.

V. Lovelace

Every muscle in Malcom's arms ached. His biceps and triceps bulged
and screamed in protest.

Sweat dripping from his brow, he shoved himself up another fraction, using the wood bars to lever himself higher. And then he held
himself there, suspended.

And even that torturous exertion was preferable to the man droning
on behind him. Or attempting to. Since he'd let the fancily clad old
man in nearly thirty minutes ago, the servant had done more stammer-
ing than speaking.

"My lord." Sanders, the aging man-of-affairs Malcom had inherited
some several months back, sifted through yet another stack of papers.
"I—"

"I told you not to call me that," he said coolly as a bead of sweat slipped down his forehead and hit his eye.

"But you *are* the Earl—"

Malcom silenced the rest of that protestation with a look.

Even if Steele had laid a paper trail that could stretch the length of London with proof of Malcom's claim to the Maxwell title, Malcom wanted nothing to do with the earldom. With any of it. It might be his past, but that was precisely what it was . . . his past. At that, one he didn't have a single recollection of. "It's enough that I've accepted my rightful *claim* to the damned title."

He blinked back another bead of sweat from his eye, the sting of discomfort transmuted by the strain he put his body through. God, how he despised the blighter. The reason—and the only reason—Malcom forced himself through the old man's company was to spare himself from having to oversee the mess he'd inherited. "I also advised at our last meeting—of which there had already been too many—that we were done," he gritted out through the strain of his efforts, fixing his gaze over the top of the older man's head. Everything Malcom had gleaned about his new circumstances changed nothing. Or he'd been determined that would be the case.

"That is also true," Sanders said with more aplomb than he'd shown since he'd entered. "However, my . . . Mr. North," he amended, and then grimaced as though the reduction in title, even in speech, were physically painful to concede. "I also informed you that there would be matters that came up."

"Matters came up when Steele came to me," he muttered, inching his frame along the parallel bars.

"Yes."

"And the following week after that."

"Yes, but given the extreme nature of the circumstances, it was to be expected that—"

"And then when you came to me, each week thereafter." Malcom may have dwelled outside the world of Polite Society, but he knew enough what the servant had done—he had set himself up weekly appointments with the intention of tricking Malcom into taking a role in his newly inherited *business*.

Footsteps sounded from the hall. A moment later, the door opened, and Giles let himself in. The only person in London who'd dare that insolence, and yet, here they were.

Sanders paused midsentence, his gaze lingering on the empty place the larger man's left hand should be.

Catching that horrified focus, Giles raised the empty nub to his forehead in mock salute.

Sanders's skin was leached of color, his throat moving frantically before he shifted his focus back over to Malcom.

"You were saying?" Malcom asked coolly.

His man-of-affairs swallowed loudly. "I—I understand your concerns—"

"If you understood them, then you'd not be wasting my time now."

"However," the older man went on with a tenacity that even Malcom was hard-pressed not to admire, "there are certain responsibilities that come with your new station that cannot simply be left undecided, my lord."

Shoving himself up with one arm, Malcom looped himself around, facing the opposite direction, giving both men his back. "And why not?"

That question was met with a shock of silence. And he could all but see the gears of the old servant's mind as they came to a grinding halt. "Because . . . well . . . because you are the—"

Malcom swung himself around and leveled Sanders with a single dark look that brought him to silence once more.

Sanders set his folder down and stood. "Because you are the earl, Lord Maxwell. Whether you wish it or not . . ."

Not. He wished *not*, because in short . . . he wasn't. He didn't give a fucking damn what some detective with the same rotten birthright as himself had to say. He didn't give a shite what the world wanted to believe—a story they craved as a diversion from their own miserable lives. The *ton*, bored with their tedious fucking lives. And the people here, dreaming of a way out. And then there was Malcom, who didn't give a rot either way, because his life was his and he was content with it.

Malcom let himself drop; his feet hit the floor, and every muscle in his arms rejoiced at the cessation of his earlier efforts. "You indicated that you would see to everything." When Sanders remained tight-lipped, only a guilty flush suffusing his cheeks, Malcom arched a brow. "Did you not?"

"Yes, and I'm quite capable of seeing after your affairs," Sanders said stiffly. "All the ones that I am able. And yet, I've not the ability to make decisions for you. Now . . ." The stubborn servant picked up that stack of belongings he'd come in with and held them aloft. His arm wavered, and he let it drop to his side. "Unless you . . . cannot? In which case I'd be—"

Cursing, Malcom stomped over. He yanked the leather folio from his fingers.

Sanders hurriedly backed away.

Flipping open the file, he raked his gaze over the words there. A name jumped out, familiar. "Who the hell is Bolingbroke?" he snapped. Good God, what had become of his existence? His hours and days now spent sifting through details and information about some fancy lords.

"Bolingbroke . . . was in possession of your title before you were . . . found."

"Found," he muttered.

"Per your advice, I enacted the paperwork to begin securing all debts accrued while he'd been in possession, along with interest on items he purchased in your absence."

He read through the neatly written notes about the gent. "And?" he prodded, increasingly impatient.

"And he's recently married. As such, I expect we might collect sooner than anticipated. In which case, I require guidance on what you'd have me do with the collected funds."

He caught the glint in the servant's eyes and could almost pity Maxwell or Bolingbroke, or whatever the hell his name was, for having failed to see the ruthlessness that had been greater than any loyalty possessed by his servant. Trust was something Malcom would never give this man . . . or anyone. But the plan Sanders had hatched for collecting interest on top of everything else Bolingbroke had been required to turn over was a plan that made sense. If another tosher had come onto his territory and stolen from him, he'd do the same—take the stolen goods and then some for good measure. Taking in order to build a fortune and security was something he understood . . . and respected. And in short, it was why Malcom suffered through the servant's company. He'd resumed reading when his gaze snagged on the lines in the middle of the page.

Country manor . . . Kent estate . . .

A throbbing pulsed at his temples.

Another echo.

Laughter. Whispering in his mind. Haunting.

"My . . . lord?" Sanders ventured, jarring Malcom to the present.

He snapped the file shut and tossed it to the servant, who caught the packet with a surprising alacrity. "Do you have the funds?"

"Do . . . I?"

Malcom swiped his hands down his face. Good God, the man was a damned parrot. Returning to the wood parallel bars, Malcom drew himself up and swung his legs forward. "Do. You. Have. The Funds. From Bolingbroke?" he added.

Understanding dawned in the older man's eyes. "No. Not yet."

"Then see me when you do, and I'll determine what to do with them then. In the meantime, get the hell out."

Scrambling, Sanders hastily gathered up his things and beat a retreat from the room.

As soon as he'd gone, Giles chuckled. Laughter. It was foreign in the Dials, and yet somehow the other man had retained the ability to do so. Unlike Malcom. The sound of mirth grated and marked a weakness in a person. "You're fucking mad," the other man called as Malcom brought his body in line with the parallel bars. Every muscle in his body quivered and screamed at the strain. "Do you know that?"

Given Malcom's partner well knew the rules on interrupting his sessions, the charge could have been easily flipped. As it was, after ten years of working alongside one another, Giles had granted himself far greater familiarity and freedoms than any person unfortunate enough to have dealings with Malcom.

Maintaining his posture, Malcom kept his gaze fixated on the circular window that overlooked the streets of the Dials. Alas, he didn't want that fortune Steele had come in here and dangled. He was content enough and didn't need a single bit of what Connor Steele had said awaited him: not the land, not the fancy Mayfair townhouse.

His life was his own.

Resting a shoulder against the wall, the bastard watched on with entirely too much amusement in his eyes. "You're the only bloody person in the whole of England to be sitting on a damned fortune and content to let it languish."

"You know the rules on interrupting me."

"Aye." Giles flashed a wide grin. "And you know I don't care."

No, he didn't.

It was an insolence Malcom didn't tolerate in anyone else. Likely because there was an obstinacy to the other man he could relate to, and had since he'd come upon him nearly dead in the sewers of London.

"Answer me this . . . ," the other man said, dropping into a chair and kicking his legs out.

"No." He didn't answer questions about himself. And not simply because there was no need for a person to know anything about him, which did hold true as well . . . Rather, it was because much of Malcom's life was a mystery . . . even to him, and he preferred it that way.

"If you've no interest in that title or that life, why've you gone and hired yourself that bootlicker to see to those riches? To take more from the blighter who's now out a title?"

Riches.

It was the correct word to describe the several hundred thousand pounds he'd inherited. And the countless pounds more sitting there in properties . . . properties all over England. Places he'd never been . . . and more . . . places he had no desire to be . . . *Please, don't. God, don't* . . . His own cries of long ago ricocheted in his mind until vomit churned in his belly. "What do you want?" he asked impatiently. "Don't you have a sewer to see to?"

"I found information, information you should be aware of . . . Someone is coming for you . . ." Giles's words droned on as a memory trickled in.

Long ago. A faint echo that hummed and buzzed in his mind. A child's voice . . .

Someone is coming for me . . . Someone is coming . . .

Then, all at once, the present rushed up to meet him. Blinking, Malcom shoved aside the foreign memory. Or imagining. Those weren't his memories.

"What?" At last, he let go. His feet hit the floor, and Malcom flipped his hair, shaking the excess sweat from those strands.

Giles grabbed a towel from the hook on the wall and tossed it over, and Malcom wiped his face. "Someone has been asking questions about the sewers. Tonight, I saw a pair entering."

He slowly lowered the damp cloth. "When?" he whispered.

The other man lifted a shoulder in a loose shrug. "Twenty minutes—"

Malcom's black expletive drowned out the remainder of those words. "And you waited to tell me?" He shoved the tails of his shirt inside his trousers, stalked over to a hook, and yanked free a dark wool jacket.

"Seemed like you had important business to see to," Giles said dryly.

Sitting on a wood stool, Malcom proceeded to tug on a boot, all the while tamping down another curse. "Is there nothing you don't find amusement in?" he snapped.

"Is there anything you *do*?" the other man drawled.

"No," he said flatly as he pulled on his other boot. There wasn't time for laughter or amusement in the rookeries. Not as long as one wished to stay living.

"Corner of Charing Cross. Here." Giles grabbed the seven-foot pole and tossed it to Malcom.

He easily caught it and started out. After Sanders's visit, he was spoiling for a damned fight. And he intended to have it.

A short while later, Malcom slid the grate off. Using his right arm, he lowered himself through the opening, and then reached up with his free hand to drag the grate into place.

He let himself fall.

The sound of his feet striking the ground was muted by the distant mutterings echoing down the tunnel.

Narrowing his eyes, Malcom did a meticulous sweep, and then started forward. As he walked, he scoured his gaze over tunnels and crevices more familiar than the place he now slept. The commotion that had greeted him had since faded and ushered in a silence broken only by the occasional *drip-drip* of the sewer water and the desperate squeak of a hungry rat.

Up ahead, the forward path he'd traversed so many times before stood blocked. Malcom slowed his steps, taking in that small heap of stones that had fallen.

Those loose bricks had seen countless men and children dead in these places, discovered long after they'd been pinned or knocked out, their bodies feasted on by the rats so that only bones were left to greet the toshers there to replace them.

And then he heard it . . .

A soft mumbling . . .

And then he saw it . . . No. Not *it*. The person responsible for the earlier noise, the person who'd been scouring Malcom's territory.

"Where. Are. You?"

He froze, his entire body stiffening as he unsheathed his dagger.

With Giles's warning, Malcom had anticipated any manner of people to greet him: a ruthless street tough. A desperate member of some gang, seeking something to assuage his liege.

What he'd not expected in any of his musings on the way here was to find a diminutive girl in skirts, crawling around the sewer floor. Fishing her hand through the murky water. And talking to herself.

"Whereareyou? Whereareyou? Whereareyou?"

Mad.

That explained it. Her words all rolled together, falling over one another.

Even so, those besieged by insanity proved the most precarious, the ones to most closely watch for their unpredictability.

Malcom pointed the tip of the blade at the girl. "Rise," he commanded in quiet tones that immediately froze her on her hands and knees. "Now," he ordered when she made no move to comply.

For a moment, he suspected in addition to mad, the girl might be hard of hearing. But then she removed her hands from the water and slowly straightened.

"Palms in the air." He infused steel into that directive. "Turn."

The girl hesitated; it was, however, the slight stiffening of her shoulders that indicated two truths about the interloper to his world: one, her hearing was fully intact, and two, she'd a pride that bespoke her stubbornness.

"Now," he repeated, and as she faced him, Malcom ticked a third item onto his list of discoveries. The girl was, in fact, no girl at all. But rather . . . a woman. Five feet nothing, and generously rounded, she possessed a set of wide hips and a generous bosom that pressed against the dampened fabric of her cloak. With that, he had his fourth piece of discovery. "You're a whore, then," he said flatly. Of course. It hadn't been the first or even the fiftieth time he'd come upon women plying their trade away from the eyes of society—polite or impolite. Here in the tunnels underground, anything went, and it was enough to lure even the finest-born deviants down.

"Wh-what?" she croaked.

Except the only whores who descended to these pits were ones in hiding . . . or ones searching out something . . . or someone. "Who are you meeting?" he demanded, keeping his dagger trained on her.

"Who am I *meeting*? What manner of question is that?" His head spun as the minx prattled on, asking a slew of questions he couldn't keep up with. "A meeting? What type of formal meeting do you think occurs down here?"

With that last query and the clipped tonality more similar to his own speech pattern than the usual gritty ones reserved for the coal-roughened Cockneys of the souls who dwelled here, she proved herself different from nearly all in the streets of East London. If she was a whore, she'd have to be a fine one at that.

"I don't—" Her words ended on a squeak as he stalked over and, tucking the blade between his teeth, swept his hands over her frame, searching her for a weapon. "Wh-what in hell do you think you're doing?" she stammered, slapping at his fingers.

And Malcom noted a whole sea of new details, ones vastly more interesting and dangerously distracting: the lush curve of her hips. The flare of her waist. Despite himself, despite the fact that she was a stranger and undoubtedly dangerous for it, his fingers reflexively slowed their search, lingering, exploring. Still methodical despite the wave of lust that wound through him, he pressed his hands along the front of her coarse wool.

"You blackguard!" The lady's sharp gasp split the quiet, followed by the crack of flesh striking flesh as the minx dealt him a shockingly impressive backhand that barely missed knocking his knife loose and whipped Malcom's head back.

A heavy silence fell, punctuated by the uneven patter of the water's drip.

Sheathing his weapon, Malcom rubbed at his wounded flesh.

Hell. "You struck me," he said, disbelief pulling the obvious from his lips. No one had dared put a hand on him in fifteen years. It was a date committed to memory—the near-death beating Malcom had doled out that day to the older, bigger, and stupider fellow.

With the exception of the bright-crimson circles that splotched her cheeks, a common mark of the sewer's cold, the woman went a sickly shade of white. "I—I did hit you." He braced for blubbering tears as she begged forgiveness. "In fairness, you c-certainly had it coming."

God, she was brave. Malcom curved his lips up in a slow, cold smile. Either way, no one struck him. Certainly not a strange slip of a woman invading tunnels that belonged only to him.

"You should not have done that."

Chapter 5

THE LONDONER
WHO HAS HE BEEN?

What did the Lost Heir turn to in his absence? Thievery?
Begging? Worse? Society can only wonder . . . for
now . . .

M. Fairpoint

You should not have done that . . .

No truer, more *accurate* words could have been applied to Verity
and her decisions this night.

All of them.

Since Verity had discovered her story had been ripped off, there
were any number of things she should not have done: climbed into the
bowels of London's underbelly. Unarmed, at that. Waded through filth
in search of her sister's slippers.

"I—I disagree," she said on a rush; terror brought her voice creeping up an octave, and yet, neither would she be silent in the face of the
ominous threat glinting in his golden stare.

Golden, like a feral cat's.

The thought had no sooner slipped in than he took a slow, predatory step closer.

Her heart thudded, and she backed up. This had been a mistake.

"You . . . what?" he murmured, his voice a shade deeper than a
baritone.

Verity's bare foot caught an uneven cobble. She stumbled and managed to right herself. "I disagree. You deserved a good s-slap."

Thankfully, those words managed the seemingly impossible.

The stranger stopped his menacing approach. "Did I?" He dusted
the tip of his dagger, a blade that glimmered even in these tunnels, along
an enormous palm.

She took in that menacing drag of his blade. By God, she'd not
let him unsettle her any more than she had been. Verity gave a shaky
nod. "Indeed." Of its own volition, her gaze slid longingly behind the
stranger; with wide shoulders and enormous thighs, he stood, a mountain of a man, blocking her path to freedom. She'd never make it past
him.

"Indeed," he echoed, a taunting edge to his voice. A cool, emotionless grin tipped the right corner of his mouth, leading hard lips into a
dangerous half smile. As if he'd followed her thoughts and celebrated
her fear. "Fancy lady, are you?"

Verity scoffed. "Hardly." She might have the blood of an earl in
her veins, but that blood was tainted by birthright. Either way, this
hulking figure hardly cared; he merely mocked, and as such, she met
that disdain with the stony expression she'd perfected with the villagers'
children. "My birthright, however, shouldn't matter. You've no right to
put your hands on any woman," she said crisply. And yet, how many
times had she witnessed her mother in the village, subjected to that fate
because the world had known she was nothing more than the mistress
of a nobleman? And how many times had Verity herself encountered a
less-than-subtle touch? The only difference was . . . there'd been nothing sexual about this man's hands on her. There'd been a perfunctory,

all-businesslike purpose to it. Even so . . . there'd also been a thrill of danger, a whispered warning echoing through her that said *Run.*

He touched his middle and index finger to an imagined hat's brim. "I'll remember your lesson on propriety when I'm not stalking through a sewer."

She'd have to be deaf and dumb to fail to hear the jeering edge there. Only through her terror, Verity noted the details that had previously escaped her: the quality of his dark wool trousers and matching cutaway jacket. His cultured tones better suited for an English gentleman. She ran her eyes over the gleaming strands of blond hair drawn back from a clean-shaven face. And there could be only one certainty: this man who taunted her even now was no sewer dweller. "Who are you?" she asked quietly, the question born of a curiosity that came from the work she'd done and loved.

"The Devil."

That whisper scraped chills down her spine.

He was on her before she could form a proper, useless scream. Covering her mouth, he muted that cry, drowning out a futile plea for help. She'd been a fool to challenge him. Verity bucked and writhed and thrashed. *Oh, God. I'm going to die here . . .*

Bearlike in size and strength, the man caught her wrists in one hand and brought them above her head. In one fluid move, he spun her around and pinned her palms to the brick wall, anchoring her in place. "Be still," he commanded like a king.

Terror lapped at her senses, stealing any logical thought beyond the evil he intended with her. Verity increased her struggles. She bit at his callused palm but couldn't part her lips enough to catch the coarse skin. Blackness tugged at the corners of her vision. And even as unconsciousness was preferable, she could not give in. Because she'd never awaken. She'd die here.

He placed his lips against her ear, and her eyes rolled toward the dank stones overhead.

"I said, be still," he whispered. Spearmint wafted in the air, conjuring memories of the treats her father had tucked into her palm as a girl when he'd come to visit, that child's treat contradictory with this brute now at her back.

Ever so slightly, he eased some of the pressure in his hand, allowing her to draw some breath.

"Are you going to be quiet?" The question hadn't even fully left his mouth before Verity was nodding her head in a jerky shake.

He edged his enormous palm away, and her entire body sagged, but her captor kept her upright as easily as if he played with a child's doll. Verity gasped, struggling to bring air into her lungs.

"Now," he said coolly, "you're not the one asking questions. Are we clear?"

Fighting still for a proper breath, Verity managed nothing more than a nod.

"Now." He lowered her arms but still kept them wrapped in a manacle-like grip, one with a shocking amount of strength, and yet there was also a gentleness to it that belied any criminal intent. Or was that merely hope and wishful thought on her part? He turned her back so that Verity faced him. "Who are you?"

"V-Verity Lovelace." Her voice emerged hoarse from fear and the useless fight she'd put up against him. She pressed her eyes briefly closed. All the while trying to put disorderly thoughts to rights. To plan her escape. To answer his questions.

The stranger released her. "Miss Verity Lovelace," he murmured, bringing her eyes open.

Another gasp burst from her; he had his dagger in hand, casually angled at her chest. *Flee.* She arched forward, poised for flight.

"Uh-uh." Her captor had perfected the cheerfully delivered threat. "I'd advise against that."

He'd end her. She saw the promise of her death reflected in those gold eyes.

"Now, what were you searching for, *Miss* Verity Lovelace?" Verity had been jeered and mocked the better part of her life for her birthright alone. This stranger before her, however, was the first who'd managed to gibe so perfectly with a single syllable. "Or . . ." He did a sweep of the tunnels. "Is there a husband whom you are here on behalf of?"

"N-no. There's no husband."

"A client?"

A client? And then the meaning of his question hit her. "No." The denial burst from her, that indignation preposterous to her own ears, given that he was a thug of the streets with a clear intent to kill, or at the very least harm, her. Even so . . . "I'm here of my own volition."

He slid closer; his stealthy steps barely stirred the water around them. "And what were you searching for?"

Not a "what," but rather a "who." And yet, less was more. She knew better than to reveal too much about her purpose here. Shivering, she huddled in her soaked cloak. "Sli-slippers," she whispered.

He angled his head, setting the long knot of hair drawn at his nape to fall over his shoulder.

At the piercing, unasked question, Verity lifted first one foot and then the other. "I've lost them. They are my s-sister's." Her voice broke. For it was easier in this moment to focus on the idea of returning home with Livvie's footwear missing than the fact of her current interrogation at the hands of a stranger who oozed lethality.

He was coldly implacable. "And yet, something drove you into the sewers to risk your sister's slippers."

It wasn't a question but rather an observation doled out by a man who was as clever as he was well built. As such, Verity set her mouth. To hell with him. To hell with his questioning. And her patience—with him, and with every man who made it their mission to suck control from her—snapped. "Are you going to kill me?"

His mouth moved, but no words slipped forward, and knowing that she'd knocked him off guard strengthened her. "Cut me with your knife?" Lifting her heavy hem above the water, she marched forward. "Rape me and leave my body to rot?"

The stranger scraped a disdainful stare up and down her frame, clear in his gaze what he thought of her body. "I don't rape women," he said frostily, not disputing the former charges she'd leveled.

And every last bit of gooseflesh upon her body that hadn't already been on end from the frigid water soaking her through stood.

Her courage flagged, and when she again spoke, she forced a strength she didn't feel. "What is it to you if I'm in these tunnels?"

"Sewers," he said flatly.

Yes, she knew where they were.

The stranger touched the tip of his knife to the clasp at her throat; she sucked in a breath, braced for the thrust of that dagger—that didn't come.

"And it matters. The reason you are here matters very much, Miss Loveless."

"Lovelace." It was an inane correction to make, given that she was one wrong utterance away from being stabbed through the heart.

His gaze sharpened on her face, one that searched for insolence? Or was it her secrets he sought? Or mayhap both. And with an intuitiveness born of the need to survive, Verity knew she'd never leave these sewers unless he had the information he sought. "You were correct. I was . . . I am searching. I'm desperate."

"Your sister," he ridiculed, as though Verity's caring about anyone were foolhardy and a folly.

But if Verity drew her last breath alone in this pit of hell, she'd own that her every action, her every decision in life—including this very one now—had been with Livvie in mind. "My sister," she said quietly, and for the first time since she'd let herself fall the six feet into these tunnels, a calm settled over her. "I've lost employment. My apartments will follow. And our survival depends on my being here amongst the toshers."

His brows lifted slightly in a near imperceptible elevation that could have been a trick of the shadows playing off the darkened walls. "And what do you know of toshers, Miss Lovelace?"

"Next to nothing," she confided, and her heart thumped erratically as she looked upon her captor in an altogether new light—a necessary one. Verity drifted closer. He was well over a foot taller than her, and she had to crane to look at him. As she did, she searched a face shockingly symmetrical in its beauty: carved features, hawklike nose, slightly bent from having been broken. Nicked and scarred as it was from his high forehead to sharp cheeks, the marks still did little to diminish an astonishing handsomeness. It momentarily distracted, made him . . . human. And therefore, safer for it. The man was preferable to the Devil he'd professed to be. "Are you familiar with the toshers who work these tunnels?"

"Toshers don't work the tunnels," he said flatly. "They live here."

Before Verity could pose the question hovering on her lips, a portentous rumble sounded in the distance.

She froze; her gaze locked on her captor, and where his features had been carved of stone before, now there was a disquiet reflected in his eyes that riddled her with more terror than the previous weight of his blade against her. "Wh-what . . . ?"

With a curse, he sheathed his dagger. "Come on," he barked, and raced off, not bothering to see if she complied.

At that unexpected freedom, Verity backed herself in the opposite direction.

He suddenly stopped and spun back. "Are you mad?" he thundered.

The only madness would be remaining here and facing his wrath head-on. Except . . . the pandemonium at her back reached a fever-pitched crescendo that gave way to chirping and shrieks. Her stomach twisted. "What is that?"

Muttering a black curse that carried through the tunnels, the man raced back and snagged her wrist.

"What? I don't—" Her words ended on a squeak as he yanked her through the tunnels.

Verity tripped and stumbled, her heavy skirts slowing her. The wool dragged in the water, and frustration welled within her. "What is that?" she cried for a second time, this time her question nearly drowned out by a deafening uproar; it licked at their heels.

And her captor became the unlikeliest savior, pushing her ahead, propelling her in front of him. Her feet numb, her body trembling with a combined fear and cold, she allowed him to shove her on.

Her breath rasped, noisy in her ears.

Or was that his?

She paused to glance back and found his focus singularly forward. "Move," he thundered.

Verity stumbled, and righting herself, she pressed on.

They reached the end of the tunnel passage, and he yanked her by the back of her dress, wrenching her close. Except . . .

"My slippers," she cried out. Only they weren't hers. They were Livvie's. Livvie's favorite pair. Livvie's only pair.

"You're off your head," he shouted down at her. "If you go back, you'll find your feet a feast for a thousand rats and no need for any damned slippers."

Before she could formulate so much as a thought, he hefted her up and tossed her atop a two-foot-wide ledge; the path led onward through a narrower, darker tunnel.

Her sudden savior drew himself up as easily as one drawing one-self upon a swing. "Get moving," he clipped out, nudging her lightly between the shoulder blades.

Bile stung the back of her throat.

At his order.

At being caught alone with this lethal figure.

At herself for having made so many mistakes this night.

Going off with this brute, however, would mark the height of the greatest folly.

Verity considered the five-foot drop down.

"That would be a mistake." He sounded almost bored as he correctly predicted her intentions.

A moment later, a sea of black came rushing forward.

Verity swallowed a cry and told her legs to move. To no avail. She stood frozen, her bare feet locked to the brick floor, and she closed her eyes, prepared for the rising flood of water and rats to gust over her.

And then she was lifted off her feet. Propelled up. Verity tried to scream. Tried to breathe through the wave.

Only . . .

Her eyes flew open as she was jarred by the quick footfalls of the stranger. She reflexively twined her arms about his neck and clung tight as he raced onward; with the added weight of her sodden skirts and frame, he may as well have moved with the same ease as when Verity had once carried Livvie as a babe.

They—he—continued on, and after an endless path of twists and turns, he crashed through a wide opening. And the coal-tinged air had never smelled safer. A faint glow bathed the bricks, heralding their return to Earth.

"Loosen your damned grip," her captor muttered.

Only, was it truly fair to think of him in that light? Given that he'd saved her life no fewer than three times in that short span? Those efforts had made a lie of his threat of death. And—

"Are you going to faint?" he snapped.

Verity bristled. "I don't faint."

"Aside from you removing your talons from my skin, I don't care what you do or don't do."

She glanced down at her fingers, curled like claws into the fabric of his wool coat.

"I'm not interested in your services," he said tautly.

"My . . . ?" Verity followed his pointed stare to where she gripped his chest. She gasped and released him. "I assure you, I am *not* selling services." Quite the opposite, really. She was searching for her story, the source of her security, and soon to be the reason for her unemployment. Verity burrowed into her cloak, her efforts to find warmth futile. Even so, she rubbed her gloveless palms together frantically in a bid to bring warmth back into the digits. As she glanced around, dread, an increasingly familiar feeling, pitted her belly. "Wh-where are we?"

"Ludgate Street."

"Wh-what?" she whispered; her shivering intensified, racking her frame until her teeth rattled painfully in her mouth. Bertha would be waiting. Wouldn't she? Surely, with all that had happened since she'd descended into the sewers, the thirty minutes had passed. And with nothing to show for it.

Nothing but bare feet, feet which had at some point gone numb from the cold. "I suggest you be on your way, lass." With that, her savior turned on his heels, and she'd no more than blinked before she found him vanished into the shadows.

A sob climbed her throat, and she forced it back, strangling on those useless tears. Could this night be any worse? As if in answer to that very question, the London skies opened up and poured down a deluge.

Squinting through the heavy curtain of rain, she began the long trek home.

Verity made it to the end of the pavement.

A stranger stepped into her path; with a fine French umbrella shielding him and his elegant garments from the elements, there could be no doubting he wasn't one of the coarser sets that roamed St. Giles. And that truth made him and his presence here all the more dangerous.

"Well, you look a sight."

That pronouncement was shouted into the noise of the rainstorm, and even through the din, Verity detected the clipped quality of his speech, confirming that which she'd already gathered about the man's rank.

Hugging her arms around her middle, Verity lifted her chin and made to step around the gentleman. "Step out of my way, sir."

Undeterred, he angled his umbrella and blocked her retreat once more. "It is raining." He motioned to where a carriage waited at the end of the street. "Why don't you let me help you, miss?"

"I've nothing to discuss with y-you." The chattering of her teeth, along with her bare feet, made a liar of her.

"Actually, you do." He flashed a hard grin.

The storm eased, but the rain persisted. Even as she stood up to her ankles in a puddle, barefoot, with the wind and rain battering at her, she refused to be the mouse to his cat. "What do you want?"

That already flimsy display of a casual grin faded, replaced by a frosty ice. "I want to know what you're doing around these parts." He looped a surprisingly strong hand about her forearm.

Verity gasped.

"What are you looking for?"

"Release me." She wrenched at her arm. To no avail. She cried out when he tightened his hand in a blindingly painful grip.

"You'd be wise to have a care. Nothing good can come from a woman visiting these—"

With a sharp jerk of her knee, Verity brought it betwixt the stranger's legs.

A hiss exploded from his lips as he crumpled to the ground. His umbrella fell to the pavement, and then the wind whipped it along. The fine article caught a lamppost and ceased its tumbling down the street. "You bitch," he barked, and then he grabbed for her.

Verity already had her knee up, catching him square in the chest.

He tilted, and then lost his already precarious balance, toppling onto his side. His temple struck an uneven cobblestone.

The stranger's mouth formed a small, surprised circle, and then his eyes slid shut as he fell facedown.

Verity didn't move, hovering there, standing over the gentleman. Unable to breathe past the horror.

As she'd been wrong on every score earlier . . . the night indeed had gotten worse.

Good God, she'd killed a man.

Chapter 6

THE LONDONER
QUESTIONS!

Of all the questions about the Earl of Maxwell, there
is one pressing question for now . . . Where does he
live? And more . . . where has he lived these past two
decades . . . ?

V. Lovelace

Two things were confirmed in short order: one, Verity Lovelace, the
suspicious woman in the sewers, had found herself in another spot
of trouble; and two, she certainly hadn't required any rescuing from
Malcom.

She leaned over the unconscious form of a well-dressed man at her
feet.

"You're incapable of finding anything but trouble."

With a loud gasp, Verity retrieved her umbrella and wielded it like
a rapier she was prepared to spear him with. She stared at him through
blank, unblinking eyes for several moments, and then her lashes drifted
slowly down and up. "You," she muttered, lowering her makeshift
weapon.

And then she followed his gaze to the prone form behind her. "Are you gonna finish him off?" he asked curiously.

The young woman blinked those enormous eyes. "Finish him . . ." She slapped a hand over her mouth. "No. Of course not. I'd *never* . . ."

Aye, and her shock at that supposition was just another clue that marked her an outsider to the rookeries.

And yet even with that, the small slip of a woman had managed to fell a man more than a foot taller than her and a good stone heavier. Despite himself, admiration for the peculiar creature stirred. Nay, she hadn't needed rescuing. Not this time.

As such, he should go . . .

The young woman hugged her arms around her middle. "I think I've killed him."

Alas, she was determined to keep him at her side. "Would it be so awful if you did?"

"Yes." Her voice emerged threadbare. She'd faced down an army of rats and flooded sewers, and yet this is what should affect her. And shivering in a soaking gown as she was, with her hair hanging in a tangle of equally sopping curls, and barefoot, against all better judgment, Malcom found he couldn't leave her. Just as he'd been unable to turn out Giles, who'd had his hand severed. Or Fowler, with his damned leg. Or . . .

Bloody hell.

Malcom joined her at the nob's side. Falling to a knee, he felt around the man's neck.

Verity gasped, and squatted beside him. "Are you *robbing* him?" she squawked, stealing frantic glances about, proving once again that she wasn't from these parts. All knew that, like the real rodents that roamed these cobblestones, street rats, too, scurried to their respective corners whenever the London skies opened.

"And tell me, is thievery worse than murder, Miss Lovelace?" he drawled.

That managed the seemingly impossible: it silenced the lady.

Malcom resumed his search and then found it: a pulse. Strong and hammering away. "He lives."

Verity exhaled a small prayer.

She couldn't remain here.

He couldn't remain here. The foolish minx was free to do whatever she wanted. Only . . . it was because Miss Verity Lovelace hadn't given Malcom the answers he'd sought as to why she'd been in the sewers. That was the only reason he even considered taking her with him.

It was absolutely the sole reason.

And not because she was barefoot and brave and spitting mad like a feisty cat. Only . . . Malcom squinted. With her cheeks crimson red, he'd taken that color to be her body's response to the cold. He'd failed to note her swollen eyes—bloodshot ones. "Were you crying?" he demanded, horror creeping into his question. Tears . . . the ultimate sign of weakness in the roughened streets of East London; there was no place for them, and he'd not a single memory of shedding those drops—ever. Not even the rain falling upon her could mitigate the clear drops of her misery.

She bristled. "Absolutely not. I do not c-cry." Her voice trembled from the force of her shivering.

"You're a lousy liar," he said flatly.

All at once, the downpour eased, and his shout was left echoing on the remnants of the previously gusting wind. *Oh, bloody hell.* He did a sweep of the still-quiet streets. Now that the rain had abated, the filth would creep from the cobbles, and along with them, the constables.

"I'm not crying, but even if I was, I'd certainly be entitled to whatever it is I'm feeling without making apologies to you."

"Shh," he warned.

"I will not."

Of course she wouldn't. The chit wouldn't do anything she was supposed to do. As such, he should leave her to her own devices. And yet, with logic screaming at him, he jumped up and took her by the hand. "Come on," he muttered, tugging her to her feet.

She emitted a squeak better suited to a bird. "What are you doing?" she cried, digging her heels in and forcing him to a stop.

"Would you be quiet?" He gritted his teeth. God, she was more stubborn than the English sun. "Unless you care to wait for a constable to come by and inquire as to what you're doing with an unconscious, bleeding gent at your feet, I suggest you start walking, mada—" She'd already kicked her stride into a double time.

Fool. "You're a damned fool," he said under his breath as the rain picked up, drowning out most of that sound.

Alas, not enough of it. The minx, with her catlike hearing, sputtered, "I beg your pardon. Did you call me a damned fool?"

"I wouldn't be off the mark. Climbing into sewers you have no place in, wandering St. Giles alone," he muttered as they continued their flight. "You may as well hang a sign around your neck and invite trouble to join you for tea and biscuits."

That effectively silenced the chit.

For a moment.

"Well, I didn't originally begin here," she needlessly reminded him as they turned the corner, at last putting some safer distance between her and the man she'd felled. "You were the one who brought me here. And left me."

Oh, hell, he'd had enough of her ramblings. Malcom stopped abruptly, and with a gasp, Verity Lovelace crashed against his side. He swept his soaking cap off and bowed his head. "I'm sorry; did you expect an escort home?"

"Well, not an escort, per se," she said, giving her skirts a shake. "But . . ."

And for the first time in more years than he could remember . . . nay, mayhap for the first time in forever, he laughed, the sound rusty and hoarse, and more growl-like than amusement filled.

Verity pursed those temptingly full lips. "Are you laughing at me?"

"Yes," he confirmed, not missing a beat. "Now, come on." Malcom hurried on.

Several moments passed before he registered his solitary flight. Cursing, he spun back.

Verity remained where he'd left her, wringing out the front of her dress, her gently rounded features pale. Good God . . . he really should leave her to her fate. So why couldn't he? Why was he determined to make this woman's problems his own? It went against all he was and believed in. Cursing blackly, Malcom marched over to her. "What now?" he snapped.

The young woman sank even white teeth into a plump lower lip. "I left him for dead."

"*We* left him for dead. Now, let's go."

Wholly uncaring about that distinction, Verity remained rooted to the pavement.

"What *now?*"

"Should we send someone for—"

"He was going to rape you," he said bluntly. Color rushed to her cheeks, even as the matter-of-fact reminder of the fate that had awaited her sent a primal rage pumping through him. "Do you really care what happens to him?"

"I . . . shouldn't," she agreed.

"Precisel—"

"And yet, I'd still not have someone's death on my hands." She glanced down at the cobblestones.

He opened his mouth to chide her for that nonsensical logic, but then something made him call those words back. "You've never done this?"

She bit her lip and shook her head. "No." Hers was a whisper.

Swiping at the rain that ran down his face and into his eyes, Malcom took in the soggy creature before him: her soaking skirts were matted to her frame. Her hair hung in a tangle of thick, albeit limp strands around her shoulders.

And then there were her bare feet peeking out from under the frayed hem of her skirts. Blood-soaked toes that she'd not complained about.

Bloody hell . . .

Malcom swept the slip of a woman up; even soaked through to the bone as she was, her frame was light against his.

"Wh-what are you doing?" Verity Lovelace's voice pitched.

Ignoring her, Malcom loped over the barren cobblestones. At this hour, this end of London generally brimmed with seedy life and danger. But then, even in the sewers, water sent the rats scurrying off to hide.

The woman struggled against him. "Where are y-you taking me?" she demanded in an impressive display of strength and fury.

Malcom tightened his hold, quelling her attempts at freedom. He'd have his answers as to why a woman who spoke like a lady, and wore her indignation like one, too, had been in his tunnels. "Somewhere that isn't here," he muttered. The woman went limp in his arms, effectively silenced. Was it silence that checked her questions? Fear?

Fear was safer. When he had her in his residence, her fear would give him answers to the questions he—

Verity Lovelace slammed her fists into his chest with a startling force for one her size; the unexpectedness, along with several uneven cobbles, brought Malcom crashing to his knees, loosening his hold on the termagant.

He cursed, ignoring the pain that shot along his legs.

The woman punched him in the temple, bringing his head whipping sideways. Malcom relinquished his hold, and Verity Lovelace took off running.

Her skirts, along with her bare feet, hampered her flight, slowing her progress.

As Malcom set out in quick pursuit, she shot a glance over her shoulder. A streak of lightning lit the night sky, illuminating her face and deepening the terror that spilled from her gaze.

Another man, a weaker one, might have been affected by the paroxysm of dread that contorted her features. She hefted her skirts higher, and—

All his muscles coiled. "Watch out," he bellowed.

The young woman ran face-first into a lamppost. Her entire body jolted as the force of her collision sent her flying backward into a puddle.

His heart hammering in his chest, Malcom cursed and quickened his stride.

The damned fool. What was she thinking?

He skidded to a halt and leaned over her prone form.

Verity Lovelace lay motionless on her back, her thick, dark lashes closed with moisture clinging to them. Blood poured from her nose, blending with the rain slapping down at her, turning the crimson pink.

"You are a damned fool, do you know that?" he snapped, going to a knee beside her. And stubbornly resistant. And damned if his admiration didn't grow tenfold. Grown men, even taller than his six foot four inches, had backed down before challenging him.

Leaning over her, Malcom lightly tapped her cheek. "Wake up, now," he murmured, unable to explain the panic knocking around inside his chest.

She groaned. "I'm awake."

And a wave of relief swept over him.

His response merely stemmed from the fact that the woman was a spirited adversary. One who, despite the fear that had cloaked her slender person, had challenged him at every turn, and as such, it was nigh impossible to be anything but vexed by such a woman.

"Verity Lovelace," he repeated more insistently, giving her opposite cheek another little tap. Mud stained her skin but did nothing to conceal the satiny-smooth texture. Like the finest fabrics he'd unearthed in the unlikeliest of places.

At last, the young woman's lashes fluttered. She struggled to open her eyes, and then she did . . . and out of the sewers, with the lamppost illuminating her face, Malcom found himself leveled by those eyes. A shade not quite blue and not quite purple, but a melding of both, held him spellbound.

"Wh-who?" She closed her eyes once more, and that dangerous spell was thankfully shattered. When she opened them again, pain glinted in their depths, along with a return of her earlier fear. "You."

He forced his lips up into the requisite sinister smile he'd donned over the years—the one he'd made himself wear in the name of survival. "Aye, me."

A lone wind gusted down Great Russell Street, carrying away with it the softest sigh that had slipped from her lips, one of resignation. Except, with a show of strength he was hard-pressed not to appreciate, the minx struggled to her feet. "Do you intend to kill me?"

"I don't kill women."

Her eyes worked over his face. "Do you hurt them?"

"Only the ones in need of hurting."

Verity's cheeks went several shades whiter. She shivered in a likely blend of fear and cold. And then with that same impressive boldness, her nose still bleeding, she went up on tiptoe and studied his face.

Making some indistinct murmur, Verity fell back on her heels. "I don't believe you."

And she'd be right. He'd dealt with any manner of men and women and children in East London, some women who'd been as ruthless and cold as Malcom himself. Malcom damned the nearby lamppost that cast a light about him and his mottled cheeks. He didn't know whether to be outraged at the minx for calling him out as a liar, or himself for having been unable to deceive this chit before him. "I don't care what you believe."

Did she seek to reassure herself? Or him? Either way, his appreciation grew all the more. "Of course you don't. I'm not going with you," she said tightly when he reached for her a second time. She stiffened. Like one of those London blackbirds ready to take flight.

"You there!"

The shout went up, and as one they looked to the swift approach of the burly stranger who'd been determined to drag her off—the very-much-alive stranger. A flash of silver sparked in the inky-black London night. In his lifetime living in these streets, Malcom had found himself cornered and approached by any number of adversaries. As such, with the man's swift approach came the rush of blood in preparation of fighting his foes.

The previously recalcitrant virago slid closer to Malcom.

"I trust he's not a friend of yours?" he drawled, even as he drew a pistol.

"This isn't funny," she whispered, her cheeks pale. "Help me."

Malcom caught the young woman and propelled her ahead of him. "Go," he bit out.

She took off flying with an impressive speed for one of her shorter height and bare feet.

The steady footfalls echoed behind them, increasing, and gaining.

Malcom directed a glance over his shoulder and cursed at the pistol pointed at his back. "Bloody hell," he clipped out. Pausing, he stopped, turned, and, drawing back his hammer, he let a shot fly.

A cry went up as his shot found its mark in one of the assailant's hands, effectively knocking the gun from his fingers and bringing their pursuer to a halt.

Verity skidded to a stop and spun back. "Did you *shoot* him?" she cried.

"I grazed him." He'd always been an expert shot.

"It's all the same," she rasped. "A shot is a—"

The wounded stranger was already moving toward them—albeit slower, but still with the same dogged determination.

"Would you care to remain here, debating the point and waiting for your company to return, or continue as we were?" This time, he didn't allow her a say. Malcom scooped her into his arms and took off running. And miracle of miracles, the minx made herself silent. She clung to him, and with her face pressed against his shoulder, her still-bleeding nose soaked the fabric of his shirt.

"You are losing him," she whispered.

Of course he was. Malcom knew these streets better than the gangs that roamed them.

She peeked her head up. "I think it is safe for you to set me down. I don't see—"

"*Shh,*" he warned. "He's there."

"How do you . . . ?" And blessedly, self-preservation won out over the chit's infernal curiosity.

Adjusting her in his arms, Malcom lengthened his stride and took an abrupt shortcut along a narrow alley between two abandoned structures. The remainder of the way, Miss Verity Lovelace, a proverbial magnet of trouble, remained quiet in his arms.

Even with the mud of London's sewers clinging to her garments, a whispery hint of lavender filled his senses. Fragrant blooms, crisp, sweet, and . . . clean, unlike the women who dwelled in these parts. Or the whores whom he'd taken to his bed over the years.

And unbidden, like a moth to that damned flame, he leaned closer and breathed deep of that scent of purity.

Why did his heart thump funnily at the feel of her against him? Aside from the worry about his place in East London, she wasn't his concern.

They went the remainder of the way to his residence in silence. Winding them through the alleys that led to the back of his lodgings,

Malcom reached the kitchen doors. He kicked the panel with the heel of his boot.

"You can set me down," she said, struggling against his chest.

He snorted. "And have you run off? I don't think so, minx." He'd not make the mistake of underestimating her again. And he'd certainly not risk losing her before he had answers to his questions. Failure to properly size up one's opponents and their capabilities marked the difference between a slit throat and another night's sleep. And God help the weakness, admiration for the spitfire swept through him.

When nothing more than the gusting winds greeted him, he kicked again, this time harder.

There was another moment of silence.

And then Bram drew the panel open a fraction and stuck his shaggy white head through. His eyes bloodshot, the man peered out. He squinted. "Why ain't ya use the front door?" he asked, his voice heavy with sleep.

Malcom adjusted his hold on Verity Lovelace, bringing her closer to his chest. "Next time, I'll have a care to bring any guest I return with through the front door for all the world to see," he drawled.

The door at the opposite end of the kitchen burst in, and Fowler limped through. "Why didn't you say the lad was home?"

The lad.

Good God.

He felt Verity Lovelace's wide-eyed stare taking in everything.

Bram's gaze landed on the stranger Malcom cradled, and all vestiges of sleep lifted. The older man instantly yanked the panel open. Pushing past the old tosher who'd trained him, Malcom did not break stride. "Have a bath prepared and brought up," he called out.

"Where?"

"My rooms."

"But . . . ," Fowler sputtered. "But . . ."

Aye, the old codger was entitled to his shock. As a rule, Malcom allowed no one in those suites. "And towels."

"Aye," Bram said.

Malcom paused and, thinking better of it, looked back. "See that Giles is on the lookout for any suspicious figures in the street."

As he walked, his boots trudged water over the scarred hardwood floor, leaving a murky trail of mud and grime that he made a habit of never trekking abovestairs. And yet, now that the immediate danger of their pursuer had abated, he noted the violent trembling that shook the woman in his arms, spasms that racked her body, and climbing the dark stairwell, Malcom held her closer.

"I n-need to leave," she managed to get out between her chattering teeth.

"Is that what you want? For me to turn you out so you can risk meeting your would-be assailant? One who's no doubt angry at being taken down by you?"

"He didn't f-follow us here."

"Are you sure about that?" Shifting Verity Lovelace so he could access the key hanging around his neck, Malcom shoved the key into the lock and entered his private suites.

Private suites only three had dared enter, and now he'd let another person in. A woman . . . one who'd been lurking in the sewers, searching for someone. And yet, gender mattered not in these streets. Man, woman, or child, each was capable of ruthless intent. Malcom shoved his hip into the door, closing the panel behind them.

He carried her over to his bed. "Can you stand?"

Her head moved against his shoulder in something that might have been either an uneven nod or a shake of denial. Malcom angled her away from him.

"I—I told you," she whispered, her voice threadbare, her teeth rattling. "I—I'm fine." She reached between them and struggled with the clasp at her throat.

He snorted. Aye, just fine. "I have it," he said quietly and, pushing aside her hand, saw to the task himself. Malcom set the young woman down, and she immediately swayed. The forever-ruined cloak, bearing the stains of the sewers, fell with a heavy thud at their feet.

He caught her around the waist, holding her upright, and then reaching inside his jacket, he withdrew his dagger.

Her breath caught noisily. "Don't—" she rasped out.

Malcom slid the tip of his dagger along the top button of her serviceable dress. Or her once serviceable dress. "I said stop," she hissed like an angry cat, and, unfurling her claws, she lashed out at him.

Catching her by the arms, he lightly held her. "I know, given that I discovered you in a sewer, you don't have a brain in your head. You're in my rooms, slopping filth over my floor. Your garments are soaked and not doing you any good." He caught the blade in the top button and it popped free.

"It's one of my only garments," she whispered; her chin came up a mutinous inch as her pride once more proved greater than her fear . . . or the vulnerability that admission seemed to cost her.

And despite everything he knew about trusting strangers, once again awareness stirred within . . . for the bedraggled creature who'd challenge him at any turn. "Fine."

Some of the tension dissipated from her narrow shoulders.

Malcom raised his hands to see to the next button.

She gasped and struggled against him. "What are you doing? I—I thought—"

"You're not wearing this garment." He'd already lifted an elbow, shielding his face from another of the hellcat's attacks. Her blow bounced off his arm. God, she did not quit. With her struggling like the cornered cat he'd accused her of being, Malcom made slow work of her buttons. When they were at last free, she clutched that sorry garment close and glared at him. Her face smeared from the blood of her injured nose. Her hair tangled and hanging about her shoulders. Hers was an impressive display of fury.

A knock sounded at the door.

"Enter," he boomed, not taking his gaze from her.

Fowler entered and, with two buckets in hand, made for the porcelain tub in the corner. He dumped first one bucket and then the next, and then took his leave. From the corner of his eye, Malcom caught the young woman's intent study of the tub. As if feeling his stare and resenting him for that impudence, she yanked her gaze forward.

After Fowler left, Malcom unfastened the buttons at his jacket.

"Oh, God," Verity Lovelace whispered, darting her eyes about the room, a cornered creature seeking escape and knowing there was none.

"No need for theatrics," he said dryly. "As I've assured you, rape is not amongst the crimes to my name." *Theft. Assault. Murder.* There were any number of sins blackening his long-deadened soul. Harming a woman, however, remained the one not to taint him. Shrugging out of his jacket, Malcom tossed it across the room; the garment caught one of the hooks alongside the door. The young woman's eyes bulged in her face, enormous saucers that she directed up toward the ceiling as he tugged free his shirt—

And for the first time since he'd set to undressing the both of them, he froze, stopped by the continued evidence of her innocence.

Surely it was an act. It was always an act.

Even knowing that, even silently chastising himself for being ten times the fool, he released the soaked article and left it dripping. He turned his attention to his boots, and was in the midst of divesting himself of them when Fowler reappeared with another two buckets. While he poured them, Malcom started for the armoire at the corner of the room. Yanking the doors open, he fished around and then tugged out a black garment. "Here," he said, returning to the woman. He tossed the muslin article at Verity Lovelace, and she reflexively released her hold on her wet gown and caught the clean article to her chest.

She eyed it like she'd never before seen a dress . . . but said nothing. Her clear, wary stare continued to take in everything, alternating between Malcom and Fowler, until the older man left and all her energies were trained once again on Malcom. "What is this?" Her nose began to again bleed, trickling down her nostril.

"I think it should be obvious." He stalked over to the steaming bath and grabbed one of the white cloths Fowler had set out. Malcom soaked the article and then twisted it. Droplets plinked upon the smooth surface, rippling the water. He twisted the cloth several times, until he'd squeezed out the residual moisture. Wordlessly, he returned to his *guest* and handed the garment over.

The young woman hesitated, and not taking her gaze from Malcom, she ripped the cloth from his unresisting fingers and backed away until she had placed his bed between them. She stopped abruptly, glancing down at the mattress.

Her brows shot to her hairline as she tripped over herself in her haste to be away from him.

As he came around the bed, she continued backing away, until the backs of her legs collided with his wall. The sharp thump jarred the painting above her head, and the young woman shot her gaze up to that pastoral landscape of pale-blue skies and emerald-green earth, and then she whipped her focus over to Malcom once more.

The gown she clutched slipped and revealed a far more bounteous display of flesh.

Unbidden, his gaze lingered on that tantalizing cream-white flesh.

Verity Lovelace gasped. "Do *not* come any closer." She held her fists up, positioning herself in an awkward pugilist's stance.

Malcom slowed his steps. And for the first time since he'd come upon her in his sewers, he found himself smiling—a *real* smile. The muscles of his mouth protested that foreign movement. It was an expression he'd never managed but only ever manufactured—to intimidate. To mock. To threaten. This was . . . different, and unnerving for it.

"Do you find this amusing?" she spat, and all her impressive bravado ended on a squeak as he closed the remaining space between them.

Abandoning her dress for a right hook, Miss Lovelace brought her arm back.

Alas, the hellcat had revealed her penchant for a well-timed blow too many times before this to ever land another.

Catching her wrist in a firm grip, he brought her arm back to her side.

"Please," she whispered, her eyes sliding closed.

"Please" had long been the word he had heard and preferred to hear from the mouths of the women he'd bedded over the years. Never, however, had it been uttered in fear.

Still, he had less experience in assuaging the fears of any person, let alone those born outside the rougher set he'd kept company with through the years. "Here," he said gruffly. Relieving her of the damp cloth, he swiped at her face.

She flinched, and he gentled his touch.

The woman's earlier bravery appeared restored as her lashes swept up; still, she regarded him with weariness spilling from the spellbinding, purple-blue depths of her eyes.

Resting the damp rag, now stained crimson, over his shoulder, he stretched a hand between them.

She shot her hands up protectively once more.

"Stay calm. Nervousness makes it worse."

"And you know because you've h-had so many?"

"You ask a lot of questions." Even in the sewer, when he'd had a knife at her person and demanded answers, she'd met them with queries. It was another foreign experience for him; people in the rookeries didn't ask questions . . . unless retribution or revenge waited at the end of that query. "Don't lean your head on the wall. Tilt it forward." He reached and angled her head slightly. "Otherwise you're going to choke on your blood."

She blanched.

Malcom caught her pert little nose between his thumb and fore-finger and pressed.

The young woman resumed thrashing.

"I'm not trying to suffocate you," he said curtly. It was foolish to be offended by her continued fear—bloody hell, he should relish her unease, for it would make it easier to have answers to the questions he sought. "If I wanted to, I'd squeeze your neck."

"Is that meant to reassure me?" she countered, with some of the strength restored to her voice.

"Breathe through your mouth."

Those perfect rosebud lips formed a little moue, a bow like a cherub in a painting he'd plucked from the sewers and should have sold, and yet had retained for some reason. Malcom released the appendage, and the suspicious hellcat touched her nostrils. "It stopped."

"I put pressure on the part of your nose that was bleeding and stopped the flow."

"Thank you." Those words came almost grudgingly, as if it cost her a pound of flesh to deliver them.

Another smile tugged.

"What do you want with me?" she asked quietly.

Not bothering with assurances about his previous promise, which meant nothing to her, he folded his arms at his chest. "You were going to land both of us in trouble."

Those thin, arched brows slid back into their proper place, and then a smidgeon lower. "And I'm supposed to trust that you're some chivalrous figure rescuing a woman who'd become lost in the sewers?" Suspicion swirled in her eyes. "That you've brought me here to clean me up and care for my nose?"

Actually, he had. The sight of her, bedraggled and dazed and her eyes brimming with terror, had reached into a place inside where a soft-ness dwelled, a weakness that he'd believed himself incapable of.

"I never proclaimed to be chivalrous. Only practical." And ruthless in his determination to protect that which was his, and to bring down those who'd infringe upon it. But then, something she'd said penetrated those uneasy thoughts. *Lost in the sewers . . .* Malcom mentally tucked away that unwitting admission. Malcom crossed his arms at his chest. "Have your bath, change your dress, and then we will speak."

She darted her tongue out, the pink flesh trailing a nervous path along a rosebud seam he'd failed to note . . . or properly appreciate . . . until this moment. Until that action. "Speak about what?"

He'd be the one asking questions. Not this minx. Not allowing her the opportunity to pepper him, Malcom started for the door.

Of course, the impudent spitfire stole another query before he could exit the rooms. "What is your name?"

"North."

With that he left, and found his way to the kitchens.

Seated at the table, with his broken foot resting on one of the small kitchen chairs, Fowler frowned. "Giles is doing a sweep outside. Water's ready for you." He nodded his balding head toward the wood bathtub. "Wot in 'ell are ya doing, bringing a fancy piece back?"

"She's not a fancy piece," Malcom muttered. With the polished speech of a lady and a blustery pride and spirit, she was nothing like the hardened women he'd kept company with through the years.

The other ancient tosher limped over to the table, his lame left leg dragging as he walked. "Oi went ahead and assumed ya wanted the porcelain one for yar number."

"She's not—" He caught the glimmer in those ancient eyes. "Oh, go to hell," he muttered. "Both of you," he said for the pair of them. "I should turn you both out."

"Aye," Fowler agreed, a dimple marring his sunken, wrinkled cheeks. "But you won't."

Nay, he wouldn't. And they knew it. Malcom removed his shirt and tossed it aside. Shucking out of his damp garments, he submerged his frame in the steaming water, slid under, and hurriedly scraped his hands through his hair.

He was greeted with a flask under his nose. Malcom took a long swallow, then handed it over.

"Ya 'ave to admit. This 'as been a bit of a surprise," Bram noted, tenacious as a starved St. Giles pup with a bone tossed to the cobblestones.

"What?" Malcom asked between tight lips.

Fowler shrugged. "Well, it's just it ain't every day that ya bring back a foine one loike her and her foine talk . . . and let her into your rooms."

A fine one like her . . . and her fine talk . . .

Malcom scrubbed the water from his eyes.

"I've questions to put to her," he said, unable to keep a defensive edge from creeping in.

The other man snorted. "Ya've put questions to lots of women . . . lots of people before. Never done it in yar private suites."

Malcom washed the filth from his body. "This one is . . ." He clamped his lips closed. Different. She was—

"Different?" Fowler drawled, taking another sip.

Malcom rinsed off the soap. "Go to hell," he muttered, earning a round of laughter from the old codgers.

The mouthy former tosher tossed a towel to him, and Malcom caught it and wiped the water from his eyes. "*And* she's got ya repeatin' yarself? That ain't loike ya. Over yar heels for a pretty piece."

She wasn't a pretty piece. "This has nothing to do with . . ." The fact that she'd enormous siren's eyes, eyes that had been filled with an innocence he'd believed to be mere fiction splashed upon the pages of literature. Or the way her wet gown had clung to her every curve.

Fowler lifted a bushy brow.

"We were set upon. And I'd have answers as to who was after her and what she was doing in my sewers."

Bram's thick brows crept up a fraction, creasing that already heavily wrinkled forehead. "She was in the sewers? *That one?*"

Unease trickled in. Were the toshers truly incorrect in their skepticism? As a rule, Malcom didn't trust anyone.

"Aye." Precisely. "Fowler, get the hell out so I can enjoy a moment's peace." And so the old man could get some proper rest. No good could come from him being on his still-unsteady feet.

The battered tosher levered himself to a standing position.

Malcom frowned. He wasn't careless. It was a charge that had never been leveled at him . . . in large part because he'd no people that he called friends or family. In larger part because he was nothing if not cautious at every turn. Or he had been. "Bram—"

"Oi'm already headed up there now," he assured him, not bothering to look back. "Oi'll stand guard until ya're ready for her."

Malcom hurried through the remainder of his bath so that he might seek out the enigmatic Miss Verity Lovelace and determine what in hell a woman like her was doing in a place like the rookeries.

Chapter 7

THE LONDONER
FROM BEGGAR TO EARL . . . !

There have been reports that since he was kidnapped, the Earl of Maxwell survived on the streets by begging . . . It is hard to expect any such person might fit in within the world of Polite Society . . .

M. Fairpoint

Verity remained motionless long after the man—*North*—had brought the panel shut behind him.

Heart hammering, she pressed her cold, bloodstained palms against the door, and borrowed support from the frame. And concentrated on drawing in slow, steadying breaths.

Since her parents' deaths, she'd prided herself on the life she'd made as a reporter. She'd conducted research and crafted stories that society had craved more of. But those? The men and women whom she'd written of in her articles . . . they had all been people of the peerage. Their lives largely comfortable with the exception of scandals that, though interesting on-dits, had not been dangerous. In short, her work, and that which had gone into it, all had been safe.

Turning, Verity rested her back against the panel and hugged her arms around her middle, bunching the muslin fabric of a quality she'd enjoyed only long, long ago when her father had been alive and there had been funds to attire his by-blow daughter in fine garments. She took in the rooms belonging to Mr. North—her prison?

She'd nearly been drowned, eaten by sewer rats, and then set upon by a stranger. And by the weapons he'd pointed at her and Mr. North, there could be no doubting how that exchange would have gone—had it not *been* for Mr. North. He'd delivered her from certain peril. A panicky laugh bubbled past her lips. He'd delivered her from peril . . . this same man who'd placed a blade to her throat, demanding answers.

Who was he? Hero or beast?

Or was it possible for a man to be both a redeemer and monster, all rolled into one?

Her gaze found the painting hanging near Mr. North's bed, that gilded frame better suited to the articles her late father, the earl, had brought to Verity's mother and personally hung about the modest cottage. The rendering upon that canvas, done in oils, captured a blissfully peaceful, bucolic country scene. It was an image so vivid and still so real.

And yet, this . . . ruthless Mr. North hung that work here. In fact, now that her terror had receded to a disquiet she could control, Verity took in the other details of her surroundings. Of Mr. North's rooms. His mahogany bed frame. His porcelain bath. The muslin he'd pulled from an extravagant walnut armoire with its beveled mirror and painted floral scene upon the heavily carved wood panels.

Verity's mind raced with questions. He wasn't a tosher; so what was he? Who was he? He wasn't her business. Any interest in him was irrelevant to the information she truly sought—nay, needed. So why was she unable to shake the countless questions tumbling around her mind?

Verity wandered over to an exotic green-and-pink embroidered chessboard. Intrigued, she gripped her towel in one hand, and with the other picked up the pink queen. She ran her thumb along the contoured ribbing of that most powerful piece before setting it down.

Verity did another sweep of the place she'd been brought to.

How did such a man come to be in possession of such wealth? Furthermore . . . who was he, this man who prowled the streets in fine garments and spoke flawless King's English, but carried himself with the ruthless ease of any London street tough?

He'd gibed her at every turn, then tended to her injury. Granted, there'd been nothing warm about his ministrations; he'd been perfunctory, as methodical as a doctor tending a patient . . . And yet, he'd cared for her. And he'd not left her to fend for herself in the streets. Therefore, that surely said something about the stranger?

Or mayhap you're merely telling yourself that. Mayhap that was far easier than considering the possibility that she'd, in fact, traded one threat for another.

Unable to shake those misgivings, Verity loosened her death grip on the dress North had given her and made her way to the bath.

"A bath." She exhaled those two words for the reverent prayer they were.

Nay, not just any bath . . . not the tepid water at best, cold water at most, dunkings she suffered through in the name of cleanliness and hygiene. But rather, a bath that beckoned with steam that rose from the water like little puffs of white clouds.

Verity warred with herself in a shamefully short battle before shucking the borrowed dress aside, and her soaking undergarments. Before logic screamed at the folly of climbing into a stranger's—a strange man's—bath, she stepped in.

A blissful sigh spilled from her lips, and her eyes slid closed; the temperature of the water was so hot it nearly hurt. It *did* hurt. Her toes tingled, and those needlelike pricks radiated up the expanse of her legs. And she reveled in them. But it was the most glorious form of pain. The heat penetrated the chill left by the sewers.

Verity sank into the water until it covered her shoulders.

Then she closed her eyes and simply welcomed the warmth driving away the cold. The aches in her arms from descending into the tunnels eased.

And for a moment, she allowed herself to forget that she was, in fact, in the home of a stranger who wielded a weapon with dangerous ease.

Forget . . .

Cursing, Verity sat up so quickly water sloshed over the edge of the tub.

Bertha would be waiting.

If she'd even remained when Verity failed to return.

And Livvie would be beside herself.

But neither could Verity return to them as she'd been, her face bloodied and the stench of the sewers clinging to her garments and person.

And the man who'd sought to drag her off . . . and who undoubtedly would have if Mr. North had not intervened . . .

Taking a deep breath, Verity slipped under the surface of the tub and soaked the dirty strands of her hair. She ran her fingers through the mud caked upon the tresses, and emerged, gasping for air. Wiping the water from her eyes, Verity searched for a bar of soap amongst the items that the hulking figure who'd come carrying the water must have set down at some point.

Except . . .

Going up on her knees, Verity peered at the peculiar item atop the towel, and then grabbed—

"A bar of soap," she whispered, sparing another glance at the door Mr. North had departed from, and then back once more to that finest of luxuries. She weighed the smooth item in her hand, turning it over. For not only was it a bar of soap, it was a clear one at that. Almost too glorious to use.

Almost.

Alas, the desire to scrub her body free of that filth overcame her reticence, and she dunked the soap and proceeded to lather herself from head to toe. The slightly bitter orange scent of the bergamot was crisply masculine, and yet so very preferable to London's grime that streaked her skin and turned the white soap bubbles black. Returning the sudsy bar to the tray, Verity hurriedly rinsed. She inhaled deeply, then sank under the water; her ears immediately filled, the previous quiet becoming a muted, muffled ringing in her ears. She cleaned the soap from her hair, and emerged from the water.

Even as the pull of regret was strong, Verity forced herself from the bath. Limping over to the neatly folded towel, she dried herself off, and then mindful Mr. North would return, she reached for the undergarments—and a blush instantly scorched her red as she took note of the details that had escaped her while Mr. North had been here and she'd clung to her gown to keep herself shielded from that piercing stare.

Midnight-black lace—she turned the article over in her hands—*delicate* lace of the finest quality. A quality befitting one of means, and yet—her cheeks warmed—scandalous for the color . . . and the cut of the neckline. When presented with the option of donning the outrageous article or stepping into the filthy garments resting at the foot of the bath, she chose the former. Hurriedly, Verity tugged the chemise on. She smoothed it into place, taking in the ornamental crimson tie that wrapped about the middle, and ended in a bow at the juncture of her legs.

Her stomach muscles tightened, bunching the fabric of the piece North had given her to wear. And just like that . . . all the reservations flooded to the surface. The reminder that he was a stranger. That she'd entered not only his household but also his bedrooms, and now, now wore shameful numbers only ever worn by a mistress.

It was an understanding Verity had from being the daughter of a woman who'd filled that very role for a man of power and influence.

Once again, questions whirred and swirled about the identity of this man—she could not determine whether he was friend or foe.

No man who put a blade to your chest would ever be considered friend.

She shivered, the dread tripping along her spine having nothing to do with the cold. The same fear to grip her in the sewers found its way to the surface. For fine baths and soap and garments aside, there could be no doubting the man who went by the name North was dangerous. And along with that revelation, something else grounded her . . . those questions she carried about her unlikely savior.

With hands that shook, Verity hurried into the dress and drew it overhead. It clung slightly to her bosom, but as she slid the garment into place, it proved an otherwise remarkable fit that one might have believed had been designed specifically for her.

If gowns were designed for her.

Which they had been . . . once upon a lifetime ago, when she'd been the cherished daughter of a lord, who'd lavished her with fancy ribbons and fineries. And slippers. Her eyes went to that luxury. She lunged for them, ignoring the pain that shot along her scraped feet, and scrambled into the delicate scraps. Her eyes slid closed at the bliss of the satin cushioning within.

A quiet knock sounded at the door, and Verity jumped. "J-just a moment." She made her legs move to the oak panel, and against all better judgment, she turned the lock to let the stranger . . . North . . . into his rooms.

Framed in the doorway, he made no immediate move to enter. Rather, he eyed her through thick, dark lashes that obscured his gaze, and yet somehow she still managed to be seared by the directness of it. "May I?" It was a slightly mocking request, one that sought to illustrate the ridiculousness in him asking permission to enter his own chambers.

And yet, they were his chambers, the place he slept. With an enormous bed situated in the center of the room. Verity's fingers clenched and unclenched on the panel.

Reluctantly, she stepped aside.

Mr. North swept in. His keen eyes missed nothing. He touched that assessing gaze on every part of the room. As though he searched for a hint that his kingdom had been somehow set askew. And then he focused on her.

Verity felt the blush stealing up her chest and neck, and then setting her face awash in color. "Thank you for the garments," she said lamely. "I'm ready to take my leave."

"Close the door, Miss Lovelace," he said flatly.

All the moisture evaporated from her mouth, leaving her tongue heavy, and as she spoke, her words came out slightly garbled. "Am I a prisoner?"

"Trust me, had I wished to hurt you, it would have happened in the sewers, where I'd have left you, and none would have been any the wiser that we'd met."

Verity didn't know whether to be terrified or reassured by that blunt admission. Pushing the door shut, she leaned against the panel and eyed him warily. After all, it hadn't escaped her notice that he'd not answered her earlier question. Therefore, there was only one conclusion: she was his prisoner.

As he wandered to the opposite end of the room, Verity silently gave thanks for that space between her and her captor. The immediate threat that had her pleading for his help had since eased.

Since they'd arrived and he had deposited her in his room, he'd also gone and washed the filth from his person. And without the murky darkness that had served as the setting for their first meeting, Verity studied the broad back of the man who went by no other name than North.

He reached the windows and drew the curtains back a fraction to peer out.

Nervously twisting the fabric of her borrowed skirts, Verity made herself stop. "I didn't thank you for your . . . assistance earlier," she said into the quiet.

North continued perusing the streets, only pausing to briefly look back at her. "Is that what you think? That my efforts tonight have all been to help you?"

She dampened her lips. "W-were they not?" He was a glorious specimen, and yet his features were slightly *too* pronounced to ever be lauded as handsome by society's standards. He had slashing, bronzed cheekbones. A hard set to a square jaw, slightly too heavy. Prominent scars that stood out starkly. And perhaps she'd the same ill judgment her late mother had shown toward the wholly unsuitable, for her belly danced with her awareness of him as a man.

"Don't make more of my actions than they were," he said bluntly, and resumed his inspection of the outside scenery. He released his hold on the gold velvet curtain, letting it slide back into place before he turned around once more. "The only thing I seek is answers."

"I don't have any to give you."

His lips quirked up in a detached half grin. "I didn't even ask you a question." *Yet.* It hung there clearer than had he spoken.

"Fair point," she allowed. Verity found herself gripping her black skirts once more. That smile, however, softened him. It marked him more man than the beast she'd first taken him as and worse . . . *feared* him to be.

And yet, he'd also brought her here, saving her from that fiend in the street.

"Who was the man on the street? Is he why you were hiding in the sewers?"

Why she'd been hiding? Her brow furrowed, and then she realized the conclusion he'd drawn. He expected she'd been in the sewers not in search of something, but because she'd been in hiding. Over the years, such similar assumptions had been made. People of all genders made determinations about her presence and her role in life for no other reason than because she was a woman. Those erroneous conclusions had proven a valuable tool that had allowed her to collect information from the unsuspecting. As such, Verity weighed her next words carefully. "I don't know who he was. Only that he wished me ill."

"And what was your first clue? The fact that he had a gun pointed at your chest?"

"Actually, yes. That and . . ." She felt herself blushing. "You were being sarcastic."

"I was," he said drolly.

"Oh." Verity sighed. "As I said, the man was . . . *is* a stranger to me." Which was, in fact, the complete truth. She could venture and speculate any number of potential enemies, but the list would be long, and the ranks of those foes great.

He quit his place at the window, and took slow, sleek steps toward her. Verity found herself contemplating the doorway and the path to freedom.

"Would you like to leave, Verity?" he asked in that smooth, slightly-too-deep-to-be-considered-a-baritone voice.

"Would you allow it?" She answered his question with one of her own, more than half-afraid of the answer, because she suspected she already well knew the truth.

"I would," he said surprisingly.

Verity started for the doorway.

"Although I should mention that the bloke who cornered you earlier is circling outside."

That ominous warning jolted her midstep, and she made herself face him. She felt the color drain from her face; it left her dizzy and off-kilter. "You're lying."

Sweeping one arm toward the window, he wordlessly invited her to verify for herself. Verity was across the room in four long strides. Curtain in hand, she peeled it back a fraction to peer out.

Sure enough, that same stranger did a sweep of the streets. To what end would he be searching for her? Because she'd knocked him cold, no doubt.

"Do you still wish to leave?" North taunted.

Reluctantly, she let the curtain fall back into place. Nay. Not when there was a ruthless stranger bent on revenge for her bringing him down. "I don't know him," she repeated, carefully selecting her words, sharing that which she knew.

North snorted.

"I don't." She lifted her palms. "I'm not lying when I told you I don't know." Based on the work she'd done, earning the ire of the *ton* through the years, there could have been any number of people who'd sent the stranger to speak to her.

North hooded his eyes.

He stalked past her, and unlocking the door, he turned the handle and let the panel hang open. "That's not sufficient enough for you to stay, Miss Lovelace."

"Please, don't send me out there. I can't leave. Not yet. Not until . . ." *He's gone.*

Chapter 8

THE LONDONER
THE SEVEN DIALS

We've received reliable evidence confirming just where
in London the Earl of Maxwell has called home . . . the
Seven Dials.

V. Lovelace

Everything about Verity Lovelace, from her presence in the sewers to
the man circling for her now, screamed danger.

As such, he'd be wise to turn her out on her generously rounded
buttocks.

In fact, he'd be a damned fool to let her stay.

And yet, he couldn't very well send her outside and on her way. Not
without assigning her to a death sentence.

Bloody hell. Malcom shoved the panel closed. "Fine."

Verity's eyes lit, transforming her from someone quite ordinary to
someone . . . who enthralled. "I can stay?"

Unnerved by his appreciation of Miss Lovelace, Malcom crossed to
the mahogany drink trolley and poured two glasses of brandy. "Don't
get any ideas that you're moving in."

"Oh, I wouldn't. I've a place, a family," she prattled, garrulous in ways that gave him a damned megrim, and yet also intrigued. "So you needn't—" The young woman caught the look he leveled on her. "You were being facetious."

"Aye."

She wrinkled her pert nose. "Oh."

Who was this woman with her absolute lack of artifice?

He held a brandy out. "Here."

Verity hesitated, and then tiptoed over. Eyeing him with that same wariness she had in the sewers, she accepted that offering, and took a sip. She grimaced. "Good God, that's vile!"

"Aye." He'd always detested the stuff himself, and yet, there'd been a familiarity to the sight and smell of brandy that had proved oddly comforting. Those peculiar details he'd never before shared with anyone, and he didn't intend to begin with a minx who cloaked herself in more secrets than Malcom himself.

Cradling her glass, she wandered about the chambers uninvited.

He stiffened.

This feeling of being exposed was an unfamiliar one. Largely because he'd never let anyone inside his rooms, and now because of whatever damned spell this spitfire possessed, he couldn't bring himself to bully her into stopping.

Though something told him that Verity Lovelace, who took down grown men in the street and didn't so much as flinch at a bloodied nose, wasn't ever one to be bullied.

Cradling her still-full snifter in her palms, she paused periodically to examine various pieces he'd fished from the tunnels. Ones he'd not brought himself to sell for reasons he didn't understand and had never cared enough to examine.

Verity stopped, and with almost mechanical movements, she set her drink down.

And Malcom knew the very moment she'd forgotten his presence and become wholly engrossed in the crude painting in an ornate, gilded frame that juxtaposed with the unsophisticated rendering on the canvas.

Angling her head, Verity stepped closer, contemplating the small beggar girl crouched on a corner stoop. In that small child, the artist had perfectly captured the wariness, exhaustion, and absolute lack of hope that came from living here.

Verity raised her fingertips close to the basket of ribbons the tiny peddler hawked.

"You like it?" he asked gruffly, not knowing where the question came from. Only knowing he himself hadn't ever been able to sort out why he'd kept this particular piece.

"I . . . There is a realness to it," she said softly. "I was her."

That admission came so faint he barely heard it. Or mayhap it was the first straightforward admission, voluntarily given, that took Malcom aback.

He moved closer, stopping just beyond her shoulder, and examined that piece with new eyes.

"I had a ribbon collection, until I didn't. I placed each one in a basket and sold them at a corner until they were gone."

That clue into her roots and background should be nothing more than a detail he locked away. Yet the image she'd painted of herself as she'd been—a struggling girl—was more vivid than the portrait before them. The desperation she spoke of was one he could understand. One that, despite all he'd amassed, the fortune he'd attained, stayed with him still. But then that was what set people in East London apart from the elevated members of the peerage, the strife that could never truly be forgotten. Not even when one rose up and freed oneself from the struggles of surviving.

Verity continued on to the next frame. He stood so close that her shoulder brushed his chest as she walked.

"Are you familiar with that, Verity?" he murmured. The young woman gave no indication of affront at his laying claim to her name. "Have you been that child?" *Too.*

Malcom had.

Bone weary with exhaustion as he'd regaled passersby with Scottish jigs for any coins they might toss his way.

Verity shook her head slowly. "No," she murmured. "I was spared that."

Aye, but wasn't that the way of East London? One was spared one injustice but was the victim of ten more.

"Were . . . *you*?" she ventured, casting that always assessing glance over her dainty shoulder, and leveling him with it. "That child?"

Malcom set his mouth, and ended the exchange that had become entirely too intimate. Abandoning Verity to her examination of his things, he returned to the window to search out the man who'd been looking for them.

"Is he still out there?"

He peered out at the darkened streets. The lone figure out there, a small lad, darted along the cobblestones. No doubt on his way to streets that were filled with potential pockets to pick. "I don't see him." That should be sufficient enough to send her on her way. So why didn't he?

Verity gave her head a slight, almost clearing, shake. "Do you believe he's gone?"

It didn't matter. She needed to leave. *That* was the only answer that made sense. So why couldn't he bring himself to get those words out?

For some inexplicable reason, he settled for vagueness. "I'm not certain."

She sighed, and with a restless energy resumed her circle about his private rooms.

Making a show of watching the streets, he alternated his study of the outside view and the woman reflected back in the slightly smudged lead panels. Her steps were gliding ones. More in line with the men and women he'd spied at a frost fair years ago, skating on silver blades over the frozen Thames, than with a woman walking on her own two feet. Her hair hung loose down her back; the dark curls glistened in the candle's glow. There was something compelling about her.

"It's a stunning set."

He started. His neck went hot at being caught woolgathering. "Beg pardon?" he asked gruffly.

Verity motioned before her, and he followed her vague gesturing to the burled-wood chess table and the embroidered chess set that rested atop it.

Malcom grunted. "Never played it."

"Oh, you should learn," she said almost cheerfully. One might forget what had brought them together this night and that she even now hid from those wishing her harm. "It's been years since I've played." There was a wistful quality to that admission. "We could always . . ."

"What?" he asked tightly.

She lifted one shoulder. "It's just, while we wait to be sure he's gone, we might . . ." She nodded at him as if he were supposed to understand what she was suggesting. Which would be bloody nigh impossible with this one. Every last word out of her mouth left him spun around, and upside down.

"What are you saying?" His question emerged sharper than he intended.

Either way, she gave no indication that she'd detected the crisp edge.

"That we might play chess, of course. I could teach you."

"You, teach me?"

"Chess," she reiterated. Pulling out a chair, she sat, and urged him over.

Good God, the minx was mad. Of course, he'd had confirmation of as much when he'd stumbled upon her. This was just a needless reminder. "I didn't invite you for tea and biscuits," he said flatly.

Dismissing her outright, he tugged the curtains back for another sweep of the streets.

"No," she murmured. "I know that. It just seemed a way for us to keep busy."

Keep busy. He scoffed. What a rubbish phrase. The whole of his existence was devoted to his work and scouring the sewers. There was no need to "keep busy." He *was* busy.

Or perhaps he was the mad one, for Malcom found himself abandoning his place at the window, and joining her at the other end of that table. He yanked out the chair and seated himself.

Verity beamed, her full cheeks dimpling and her soft violet eyes aglow.

He'd never known a person could smile like that. All honest and real and luminous.

And then, as if she feared revealing her joy might make him quit the table, her smile slipped, and he lamented the loss of that earlier lightness. "Now," she began, all matter-of-fact business that strangely proved as endearing as her earlier joy. "The chessboard is always arranged the same way. The second row"—she pointed to the area in question—"is filled with pawns. The rooks"—she gestured to those pieces—"they go in the corners, and the knights are next to them." She held one of her two knights aloft. "Then there're the bishops, and lastly the queen, who always goes on her own matching color, and the king on the remaining square." Verity briefly paused in her telling to look up. "Have you gathered all that?"

"I think I'm following along sufficiently," he drawled.

"Now, each of the six pieces are capable of different moves. You cannot go through another." As if to illustrate that point, she knocked the rook in her hand against the pawn on her end of the board. "The knight, however, can jump"—she demonstrated, leaping one of her two knights over one of her pawns—"but you can't ever move onto an area with one of his own pieces. You can use him to take the place of your opponent's piece, which is then captured. This is the king," she went on, lifting hers up. "He's the most important but the weakest."

As she prattled on with her instructions on that piece and all the remaining ones, he found his gaze drawn to her mouth as she spoke. That full lower lip and slightly narrower upper one that set her mouth into a perpetual pout. Hers was a mouth that conjured all manner of wicked imaginings of even more wicked delights to be known. "The other special rule is called 'castling,'" she was saying, completely oblivious to his lust-filled musings over her mouth.

He tamped down a wave of disgust.

Get control of yourself.

Malcom forced himself to focus on his unlikely tutor's words.

"Do you have all that?" she asked, glancing up from the board.

"Aye."

"Pink is paler than green, and the rules are white first. Therefore, it is your move . . . Mr. North."

Barely sparing a glance at the table, he moved one of his pawns to the center of the board, and then waited for her to make her first move.

She frowned. "You didn't even look."

"I looked." He nudged his chin at her, urging her to get on with her turn.

"Chess is about strategy and taking one's time," she intoned, her gaze firmly trained on the board. Verity chewed at a fingernail, the distracted worrying endearing. Fifteen loud ticks of the wall clock marked the passing time before she moved a pawn.

He moved his queen.

Verity eyed him quizzically. "Do you remember what I'd mentioned about the queen?"

Nay. It had been somewhere between that lesson and the one of the rooks that he'd become lost in improper thoughts about her mouth. "I know what she does."

The young woman dropped her elbows on the edge of the table. "You're just moving the pieces."

Malcom matched her pose. "Would it matter if the only purpose is to pass the time until it is safe for you to leave?"

They locked gazes in a tense battle—and yet, this battle was altogether different from any he'd ever fought before. This had nothing to do with life or death or a fortune to be made and then grown. This was simply about . . . playing a damned game. And damned if he wasn't enjoying himself . . . and her company.

Verity was the first to relent. "I suppose not," she conceded, going back to her study of the board. Another fifteen beats of the clock passed as she hovered her hand over her pieces before settling on a pawn.

They didn't speak for the remainder of the game. And this companionable silence was just as comfortable as their earlier discourse.

Malcom slid his piece and knocked her queen. "Checkmate."

Verity didn't move for several moments. Her eyes widened as she frantically scoured the board. "But . . . that's . . . not possible." She scrambled forward in her chair, and then moved her hand around the chessboard as if she re-created each of her previous steps.

His lips twitched. "You were done at the beginning. Not only did it take away your control of the center, it blocked the center square for the knight. It didn't allow development of any pieces, and also it seriously weakens safety of your king. Hence . . ." He waved the captured piece. "Chess pieces are like people. They should all be working for you." It was how he'd built his empire. "Even your queen, at the onset."

Sputtering, Verity sat back in her seat. "Why . . . why . . . you've *swindled* me."

"Nay. One has to be playing for something in order to be swindled out of it."

"I don't know if that's true," she groused.

"It is," he said bluntly.

"But you said—"

"I didn't say I couldn't play, Verity. I said I hadn't played this chessboard. You incorrectly assumed I hadn't played with another."

She peered at him. "Are you a barrister?"

"A . . . ?" And then that question fully registered. A laugh exploded from his chest, shaking his frame. Good God. Hers would be the first and last time that Malcom would ever find himself confused for a man on the right side of the law. "No."

"You argue like one," she mumbled.

A sharp knock at the door shattered their exchange, and with it ushered in reality.

Climbing to his feet, Malcom stalked over to the door and yanked it open. "What?" he snapped.

Bram peered boldly beyond his shoulder, over to where Verity remained seated, toying with a chess piece.

"I asked 'what,'" Malcom repeated.

"Giles arrived. Wants to speak with you."

"I'm not taking company." He made to shut the panel, but Bram shoved an elbow in the doorway.

"Said it's important."

Giles wasn't one to ask for help. Not even when Malcom had first come upon him, buried under bricks from a cave-in, and his hand severed. Instead, he'd lifted up the middle finger on his sole remaining hand to convey just how much "help" he wanted from the then-stranger. In short, it was the one reason he'd taken him on as one of his associates.

He let the old tosher in. "Keep Miss Lovelace . . . company, if you will?"

He'd hand it to the woman. Anyone else would have wilted or plain fainted dead away at the sight of the towering, burly Bram. She dropped her head in greeting and, with the exception of a slight tremble to her hands, revealed no outward display of her nervousness. "Hullo."

More wary of strangers than even Malcom himself, which was saying much, the old man narrowed his eyes.

Before Malcom turned to go, Verity called out. "Has he located our whereabouts?" she asked quietly.

Our whereabouts.

It was a singularly odd pairing of words from one in the rookeries. Here, people knew better than to put the collective welfare before one's own well-being. Unnerved, he ignored her question. "I'll be back shortly."

With that, he quit the rooms and found his way to the kitchens. Unable to make sense as he made the march through his household of the pull Verity Lovelace had that made him want to stay in his damned rooms, playing chess and baiting the spirited young woman.

He reached the kitchens.

Still attired in his heavily pocketed tosher trousers and jacket, Giles stood at the center of the kitchen, slopping water onto the floor. The moment he spied Malcom, he straightened. "There's someone searching for you."

Again.

Malcom tensed, as with that revelation, he at last managed to set aside thoughts of Verity Lovelace. Prior to that damned title being thrust upon him, Malcom had always faced threats from other men seeking to usurp him from his position of power in the sewers of London. Now, since Steele and the discovery of Malcom's title, there'd been any number of others in pursuit of him, which had made it all the harder to discern who was the threat to be dealt with. "Who is he?"

Giles glanced over to Fowler and back to Malcom. "There've been several strangers looking for a 'lost earl.'"

Oh, bloody hell. His stomach knotted.

"Who?" he asked impatiently.

"This time, they are reporters with newspapers." Giles held his gaze. "And according to the people talking, they've begun searching the sewers for you."

Damn it all to hell.

Chapter 9

THE LONDONER
ALONE!

Though there is no confirmation from sources, the safe conclusion has been drawn, he's been a man alone. Otherwise, surely there would have been someone to share his whereabouts . . .

V. Lovelace

This evening, Verity had nearly been killed.

First by rats. Then by water. And then by a ruthless stranger on the street.

And now the latest threat: the old man who may as well have been carved of stone for as much as he'd moved since Mr. North had left Verity.

He was her guard.

It hadn't been stated, either explicitly or implicitly.

But neither could there be a doubt as to what Mr. North had intended with the older man's presence.

With his back against the wall and his arms folded at a barrel-size chest, her guard remained motionless with his rheumy gaze firmly locked on Verity and her every movement. She repressed the nervous shudder that ran the length of her spine. *He is just a man. He is just a man. Albeit a large man. But a man.* Harmless, surely. With long white hair lazily drawn back and equally white brows, the nameless man put her in mind of the wizard Merlin from the book her father had brought her as a girl and read passages from each time he visited.

That memory of her father proved strengthening.

Verity forced a smile. "My name is Verity Lovelace."

He grunted. "Don't. Care."

Well, then.

Verity tried again. "Do you have a name?"

Another grunt. "*Of course* I have a name."

And mayhap it was the madness of this entire night, but a smile pulled at her lips. "Do you wish to share it?"

"No."

Hmph.

They were a tight-lipped bunch, the peculiar men who lived here . . . wherever "here" was.

With a sigh, Verity stole another restless glance around at the chambers which had become a prison of sorts. That was, a *comfortable* prison with porcelain baths and delicious soap and warm garments, but a cell, nonetheless. Verity tried again. "Given that we are keeping one another company, mayhap it would be important for us to exchange n—"

"No."

She tapped her foot on the gleaming hardwood floor . . . Mahogany floors that gleamed. It was another peculiarity in this place. "You don't like me, do you?"

"I don't like anyone," he said instantly.

"Do you like Mr. North?" she asked, rabidly curious about the older man's relationship to her savior that night.

"Do ya ever shut up?"

"Actually, no. Very rarely," she allowed. Such had been the way since she'd been a girl, which, in the work she'd eventually come to do, had proven only a skill and a benefit to her.

Alas, Mr. No-Name went even more tight-lipped. Who would have imagined *that* was possible?

That deliberate silence only intensified her intrigue. Was the bear of a man Mr. North's father? They certainly were both of a similar impressive height and size. Except their tonality was altogether . . . different. She nibbled at her lower lip, her mind growing with questions as it was wont to do. Or perhaps the older man was a servant?

Except if he was one . . . what manner of man was Mr. North that he had them in this place?

A small crystalline drop leaked out of the inside corner of Mr. No-Name's left eye. In the candle's glow, she caught the trail it wound, and also the discreet attempt made by her guard to hide it.

"Do your eyes always leak in that manner?"

And with that question, she managed to unsettle the older fellow into uttering something other than "no" or some other condescending response.

He angled his head, sending a shock of white hair toppling over one of those leaking eyes in question. "Wot?"

Encouraged, Verity took a step toward him. "Your eyes." She motioned to the slight crystalline leakages, tear-like in color and consistency, which had left his eyes red. "They're rheumy."

"So wot about it?" he snapped like a cornered pup.

"It is just I've some experience with them."

He remained unbending in his silence.

Abandoning any attempts at discourse, Verity resumed her study of Mr. North's rooms when the surly stranger at last spoke.

"*You* have experience with it?"

"My former nursemaid," she murmured. Verity crooked four fingers, urging him over. "I've several ways to help with that."

Reluctantly, he quit his place at the wall and ventured over. And for a moment, with him unfurled to his full height, she questioned the wisdom of engaging the giant of a man in any way. He had to be nearly two feet taller than her. Broad, like the ancient oak she'd climbed in Surrey. And as scarred as that old tree, too.

When he stopped before her, Verity craned her head all the way back until her neck muscles arched and ached. "This isn't going to work," she muttered. "You're entirely too tall. If you will."

He followed her gaze over to one of the chairs in Mr. North's rooms. "If Oi will, wot?"

Drawing out the scrolled green armchair at Mr. North's desk, she patted the watersilk squab cushion. "I can't very well help you from all the way down here." She flashed a smile.

And then, miracle of miracles that day, Mr. No-Name sat.

Verity reached for his face, and the older stranger jerked away, giving her his cheek.

She sighed and let her arms fall to her side. "I cannot help you unless I have a look."

"Didn't ask for help."

No, he was correct on that score, but he *had* claimed a seat.

Just then another tear slipped from his eye, and wound a path down his cheek. "It's just me eyes," he barked. "Oi ain't crying."

"Of course you aren't." She spoke in the gentling voice she'd used when Livvie had suffered a fall and scraped knee over the years. "That's the rheumy. It's quite common, I'll have you know," she explained, probing at the swollen corner of his right eye, and his like-swollen left eye.

"Is it?"

It was a grudging concession from a man who seemed more likely to toss her out the pair of windows than answer any query.

"Oh, yes," she said conversationally. "The older a person gets, the more their eyes tend to tear, and then this coal and soot in London certainly doesn't help anyone."

"Aye, ya're correct there."

"Though mine are also quite bloodshot from the quality of the air." To demonstrate as much, Verity lowered her head a fraction so she faced the old man squarely.

There was another one of those familiar grunts from him. "Yar eyes are foine enough."

Knowing the stranger even just a handful of minutes, she'd wager everything that it was as close to a compliment as the old codger had ever allowed.

Silently mouthing a list of items, Verity did a sweep of Mr. North's quarters until she found a stack of still-untouched white linens. Gathering one, and thinking better of it, she grabbed another, and then made a beeline for the bath. "Well, this won't do," she murmured, studying the grimy film coating the top. Her gaze landed on the untouched brown bucket of water that had gone unused. Falling to a knee, she rinsed her two cloths, wrung them out, and returned to Mr. No-Name's side.

"Wot's that?" he asked, eyeing her suspiciously.

It did not escape her notice, however, that the harsh, clipped edge when he spoke had gone.

"They're compresses." She held one of the soaked linens aloft. "May I, sir?"

"Ain't a 'sir.' Moi name's Bram." He hesitated, then gave a small nod.

Verity applied the warm cloth. "This will soothe them some." She proceeded to explain. "I believe the air dries out the eyes, and they require moisture. That, and who knows what becomes trapped within them." She applied the second damp linen to his other eye. "How does that feel?"

A little groan escaped him.

She smiled. "My nursemaid said that her eyes often feel gritty, and this will help with that sensation. But you should take care to do it often to ease that discomfort." When the cloths had gone from warm to lukewarm to cool to the touch, she removed the compresses, soaked them, and reapplied those damp cloths. "This is not all you can do to help them."

"Oh?"

That response was muffled by the fabric covering his mouth.

"There's any number of easy treatments. Why, Bertha hardly suffers any bouts of rheumy."

"Ya don't shut up, do ya?" he murmured from behind the towels, this time without the previous malice.

"I told you I didn't. But I prefer to think of it as 'speaking a lot' and not so much as 'not shutting up.'"

His shoulders shook slightly in a silent laugh.

"Now, pay attention. The remedies, I'll write them down for you." Verity scanned the gleaming surface of Malcom's immaculate desk. There wasn't so much as an inkwell or pen contained within the neat tray along the top. "A pencil. A pencil," she muttered, bringing the lid up; the well-oiled hinges didn't so much as squeak a warning.

Bending over the desk, she peered inside, and her gaze collided with a small, official scrap of paper.

> Mr. North,
>
> I well understand the most recent of your instructions; however, as your man-of-affairs, it is my duty to inform you that I will require an additional meeting so we might discuss the transfer of ownership of properties.

"Wot are they?"

"What, indeed," she murmured. It took a moment to register that it had been Mr. Bram who'd spoken. *"Hmm."* She blinked slowly, still riveted by the intriguing words dashed in a flawless scrawl. And then she jolted. "Oh, uh—yes! The remedies. The first is rose water. You'll need to mix it with a dash of diluted honey, and it will make a fine paste that you can apply to both eyes."

Even as she prattled on those directives, her mind spun and raced. It wasn't her business. Mr. North's affairs were his own . . . and yet, as a woman whose entire existence had become shaped by asking questions and exploring peculiarities, she could no sooner halt her questions from coming than she could will herself to stop breathing.

Mr. North had a man-of-affairs? It was as though Mr. North had carried her to some upside-down world where nothing made sense and everything was murky. How else to explain why a ruthless stranger running through the sewers should have . . . a man-of-affairs.

"And then, there's chamomile," she murmured distractedly. "You'll need a dash of dried flowers, and add it to a cup of hot water." By rote, she recited the remainder of the instructions to Mr. Bram, and resumed reading.

Baron Bolingbroke's been divested of all his properties.

"Bolingbroke," she whispered, that name blaring in her mind, familiar for the number of times she'd seen it and written of it herself. Her heart kicked up a beat, this frantic rhythm having nothing to do with the earlier fear. She quickly worked her gaze over the handful of sentences written there in that meticulous scrawl.

"Wot?" Mr. Bram asked, reaching for the linen.

"Nothing," she said quickly, and that stayed his hands. She read the remainder of the words written there.

In the meantime, per your request, I've issued severance to the staff at your property located at:
4 Grosvenor Square.
Each will be suitably vacant, per your request.
Respectfully,
Sanders
Your Man-of-Affairs

Verity remained absolutely motionless; unable to so much as draw a single breath into her lungs, her mind whirred and careened. Impossible. Only . . . Verity did a sweep of the lavish furnishings. Considered the man who lived amongst this palace in the pits of hell. Devilishly handsome, wicked, and yet possessed of a smooth, clipped English suited for any fine parlor.

She rocked back on her heels as the truth slammed into her. He was . . . Maxwell. The man whose story her future—Bertha's and Livvie's futures—hinged upon.

She'd found him. Giddy in ways that she'd not been in more years than she could recall, Verity found a giggle climbing up her throat as she worked her eyes once more over the words written to the Earl of Maxwell. Afraid they'd change. Afraid that, in her hope for a future and security, she'd even now merely imagined the words written there.

"May I help you, Miss Lovelace?"

That lethal purr sounded from the front of the room, a silky taunt.

With a gasp, the page slipped from her fingers and fluttered to a damning place at her feet.

Mr. Bram yanked the cloths from his eyes, and he took in Verity beside Mr. North's open desk. And all the color left his face. "Oh, bloody hell."

Oh, bloody hell, indeed. And all thoughts of having been rescued by a savior, and even the importance of this story, fled in the face of the danger staring back at her in his ruthless gaze.

He is going to kill me . . .

Verity swallowed hard.

"If you'll excuse us?" Mr. North . . . Lord Maxwell murmured.

Verity took a step toward the door.

"Not you, Miss Lovelace."

Mr. Bram climbed awkwardly to his feet. "Oi'm so sorry," he said hoarsely, an apology that went ignored by Mr. North.

Her heart lurched. Every muscle in her body lurched. This was bad. Which would have been the understatement of the century. She curled her toes into the soles of her borrowed slippers and followed the stranger's—nay, he was no longer a stranger in name—the Earl of Maxwell's gaze. As dread slowly wound its way through her, Verity curled those digits all the tighter.

And as it was all the easier to focus on matters within her control, she looked to her older patient as he limped across the room. "Be sure and try out those remedies, Mr. Bram." She felt Mr. North sharpen his gaze on her person. "And I've something that might help with that limp, too," she promised.

The older man stopped. "Do ya, now?"

She may as well have promised him the sun, moon, and stars for the way he looked at her. "Oh, yes. You'll require—"

"Bram," Mr. North snapped, and the older man instantly scuttled off, but not before flashing her an apologetic look.

"It is really not Mr. Bram's fault. He's not done anything wrong. You really shouldn't take your . . ."

Not taking his eyes from her person, he reached behind him with an agonizing slowness and drew the door shut. *Click.* That soft but decisive snap that served as a seal of her fate.

Just like that, Verity's bravado flagged. She clutched at the fabric of her skirts. Wanting to be the composed reporter gathering her research, and undaunted in the face of peril.

And she came up . . . pathetically empty.

That cold smile affixed to hard lips remained in place, a grin that no person would dare mistake for anything but the feral threat it was. He pushed away from the door and started a languid stroll toward her.

Had she truly been relieved about determining the identity of her savior and captor?

It was now all muddled.

"Now, Miss Lovelace? If that is your name?"

"M-my name?" Wasn't it? Even her name eluded her in that moment. "Of course it is." Her voice ended on a croak as he drew ever closer; the ice that frosted his gaze sprang her to the reality now facing her, the menace that spilled from his broad frame. Mayhap she'd been wrong. Because she'd experience with earls—was, in fact, the daughter of one. They were nothing like the predatory devil who stalked her now. "I *am* Miss Verity Lovelace. What grounds would I have to lie?" She hurried to place the chair of his desk between them as another barrier.

He stopped his pursuit. "And how may I help you?"

Ironically, the stranger—the gentleman—could have uttered no truer words than those.

They fortified her, and sent resolve creeping into her spine as she brought her shoulders back. Verity met his gaze squarely. "Are you the Earl of Maxwell?"

Except she already knew as much . . . she simply sought the confirmation from the gentleman's mouth.

His eyes grew shuttered, but not before she caught the flash of horror in their depths.

He was a man unaccustomed to being challenged. And his unsettledness eased away further frissons of fear. Verity slid out from behind his desk chair and glided slowly across the room. She stopped when only a handful of steps separated her from the very stranger who'd put a knife to her earlier that night.

"Do I look like an earl?" he countered, belated with that reply—that deliberately evasive one.

Taking that as an invitation to study him, Verity peered at Mr. North.

That slightly hooked nose, which had been broken one or more times, did little to conceal the aquiline appendage that served as a signal of his birthright. The small white nicks and scars merely marred a canvas of otherwise flawless high, chiseled cheeks and a hard, square jawline.

Glorious. Her pulse throbbed a beat harder. His features, melded with those *flaws*, only served to mark him beautiful in his masculinity.

His mouth crept up in a tight, one-sided smile that didn't meet pitiless eyes. "Did you have a good look, Miss Lovelace?"

He'd noted her appreciation. Verity's cheeks burnt, and she curled her toes into the soles of her borrowed slippers. He merely sought to disconcert her. It was a familiar state she'd found herself in many times before, with many men before him. Feigning nonchalance, Verity gave her head a little toss. "You have the look and the tones of an earl," she pointed out. "And more . . ." She gestured to those private missives she'd availed herself of. "You have letters written regarding Baron Bolingbroke." Verity stretched up on her tiptoes so she could at least hold his gaze and not be peered down at. "Therefore, Mr. North, I would say you are, in fact, the Earl of Maxwell, after all."

Chapter 10

THE LONDONER
INVISIBLE

The Earl of Maxwell remains a specter . . . lurking. Hiding. Waiting to show himself to the world. When will he decide it is time? All society—polite and otherwise—holds its collective breath . . . for now.

M. Fairpoint

What a goddamned fool he was.

He, who kept all out, had fallen prey to Verity Lovelace's indomitable spirit and strength.

And those same damned traits that had made him lower his guard remained on full display even now. The moment he'd caught the hellion snooping in his desk, he'd anticipated a rightful fear from the young woman. Certainly, he'd expected tears. At the very least, pleas for forgiveness as she'd blubbered on useless excuses.

He'd hand it to her. She'd offered none of the likely responses, and unsettled him by going on the offensive, boldly unapologetic.

And damnably accurate in the conclusions she'd reached.

Damn Bram.

Except as soon as that thought was given life, Malcom killed the blame.

Malcom was the one who was responsible for this. He had brought the chit here. He had let her into his rooms. He had only himself to blame.

For all the good that self-acknowledgment did.

Unnerved, Malcom called on every shred of control he'd mastered through the years to keep those sentiments concealed. To give himself something to do, he stepped around her, brushing her shoulder as he passed. Coming close enough to detect the steel that infused her spine.

She stood proudly erect, that imperceptible stiffening a mark of the expected terror. She did not, however, back away.

Malcom made a show of folding the damning page she'd availed herself of. Her eyes followed his every movement as he ran his thumb and forefinger along the crease.

All the while he silently cursed himself for falling lax. Good God, he'd sat down and played chess with her.

He'd been careless, an all-too-unfamiliar misstep on his part. One he hadn't before made.

Until her.

Malcom made a bid to reclaim his footing. "*Tsk, tsk.* That was a mistake, Verity." He didn't want to notice the long graceful glide of her throat as she swallowed. The lone bead of water from her bath that clung to her still, lingering persistently there, a crystalline drop as stubborn as the woman herself. Malcom placed the note inside his desk, and then brought the lid closed with a quiet snap. "I do not take to having anyone go through my belongings, Miss Lovelace," he whispered, starting a path around her.

Once again, she didn't make apologies or excuses. She just lifted her chin another fraction. "You are the Earl of Maxwell."

His neck went hot. God, she was tenacious, her spirit a confusing mix of breathtaking and infuriating, and blast if he didn't know what in hell to do with her . . . or more, with his response to her. "I've already told you; I'm not the man you think I am."

Which wasn't a lie, but rather a deliberate stretch of the truth.

"Actually," she said with a gentle smile, "you've not already told me that. Rather, you've called me out for—" Those rosebud lips immediately compressed into a silencing line.

"For?" he purred, stalking a circle around the minx. "*Hmm?* Going through my possessions?" She remained silent, her gaze suitably wary, following the path he walked about her.

"I wasn't going through anything." She scrunched her face up. "Not intentionally anyway. I was searching for a pencil."

"A pencil," he repeated flatly.

"Exactly," she said with an enthusiastic nod that sent drops of water flinging from her wet hair. Dark tresses with a thousand shades of brown to them. "How else was I to write down the remedies for Mr. Bram?"

The remedies? . . . Mr. Bram?

As a boy avoiding street lords determined to make him part of their gang, and escaping the cold, he'd taken to hiding inside various Covent Garden theatres. A number of kindly actresses and actors had taken mercy on him and let him hide above the rafters, high above the stage and the audience, watching from afar. This moment, with Verity Lovelace, felt a good deal like one of the many farces that had played out before him.

Malcom jammed his fingertips hard against his temple. What in God's name was happening here?

"I understand why you're angry," the young woman murmured in soothing tones better fit for a child. "You're upset I was snooping, and I'd have you not take it out on Mr. Bram."

Malcom's self-control broke. "His name is not 'Mr. Bram,'" he bellowed. The lady jumped several inches off the floor. "His name is Bram. Just 'Bram.'"

She paled. Her body trembled. She did not, however, back down. "You needn't be so angry about it, my lord," she shot back, her breathless timbre ruining whatever courage she otherwise displayed.

My lord.

There it was again.

Malcom sneered. "You've made the mistake of confusing me with someone who is safe. And why is that, *hmm*?" He caught the ends of several dark strands that hung, twisted and tangled, down her back. Twining the curls about his fingers, he held her effectively trapped. "Because you take me for an earl?"

The blood slipped from her cheeks, leaving them an ashen hue. "Release me," she whispered, resistant through and through.

He didn't relent. "Because you, like all the world, believe those men are fine and good and no harm can befall you as long as you're with one of those vaunted lords?" Malcom twisted the lock once more. "You believe the title 'earl' affixed to a man's name somehow erases who he is." *Who I am.* Malcom lowered his head until their brows touched and their eyes were aligned. "What he is." He placed his mouth close to hers; their breath mingled and danced. "Well, if that is the case, you're about to be disappointed, Verity."

They remained locked in silence, warring with one another.

Malcom's gaze dipped to her mouth. To those provocative lips that existed in a perpetual pout and, because of it, flayed his logic. Desire took on a lifelike energy, crackling and hissing like ten thousand embers that burnt in a hearth.

Then she darted the pink tip of her tongue out, hers a siren's temptation. "Are you the Earl of Maxwell?" she repeated.

"And if I am?" he countered, unable to look away.

"Then I've been searching for you." There was a lilting quality to her words as she spoke, a lyrical singsong, pure and unsullied by the dirt-clogged streets, and it heightened the reminder of all the ways in which this woman, this *stranger*, was different. And it was because of that maddening pull she had over him that it took a moment for him to hear that admission.

"*You've* been searching for me?" All his defenses went up, swiftly dousing the maddening haze of lust that had clogged his damned senses.

She gave a hesitant nod.

Oh, the bloody fucking irony! He tossed his head back and erupted into a harsh, guttural laugh. He'd stumbled upon one of those bastards seeking him and his story. At numerous points, he could have been on his way and free of her. But not once but twice, he'd gone back to the blasted termagant's side, and then brought her into his residence.

And at last, the minx edged away from him, displaying a belated but justified fear.

"What do you want?" he asked flatly, unfurling so that he towered over her more diminutive frame.

She backed up another several steps.

Did fear send her retreating? Or the need to look him directly in the eyes? He'd known the minx for barely four hours, and he'd wager the life he'd built as a tosher that it was, in fact, the latter.

"My name is Verity Lovelace," she began.

"You said as much," he said icily. "What were you in search of? Handouts?"

She sputtered, "Of course I didn't come looking for charity. I work for *The Londoner*."

"*The Londoner*," he echoed, dumbly. Oh, God in the heaven he didn't believe in.

This time, they are reporters with newspapers . . . And according to the people talking, they've begun searching the sewers for you . . .

Impossible. She couldn't—

"It is a newspaper."

"I know what *The Londoner* is, Miss Lovelace," he snapped. "And I'd hardly call it a newspaper. It's nothing more than a gossip column."

By the slight pout of her lips, she took umbrage with his opinion, and yet this time, the damned virago managed to retain control of her usual obstinacy. She cleared her throat. "Although I disagree—"

"You have two minutes." And then he was tossing her out on her deliciously rounded buttocks.

Verity cleared her throat again. "Yes. As I was saying, I work for *The Londoner.*"

"What manner of work do you do there?"

The woman bristled. "Do you find it so hard to believe that a woman would have honest employment?"

"A fine one like you?" He flicked a finger at the puffed sleeve of the gown he'd given her. "With your fine speech and lily-white, unblemished skin, I've you marked as a lady."

She swatted at his hand. "First, my garments should not factor into any assessment of me. I'm merely wearing them because you destroyed mine and provided these. Secondly . . ." A pretty blush blossomed on her cheeks. "I'm not a lady."

"Some fancy lord's by-blow, then?"

The color flamed several shades of red brighter. "We're not talking about my past, my lord," she said between her teeth.

Ah, he'd struck a nerve. Invariably, he discovered his opponent's vulnerabilities. Verity Lovelace was no different. Not in the ways that mattered. "So that is it, then? *Hmm?*" And the gaze she leveled this time upon his chest was so direct it ran through Malcom. Sightless, unseeing.

She held her mouth with such tension, white lines formed at the corners of her lips.

"Tell me this, Miss Verity Lovelace," he whispered. "What makes you think you've the right to probe into my life, and yet insist on privacy and secrets for yourself?"

"My life is of no interest," she said, her voice so hushed he had to lean close to make out what she said. "But yours? Yours is a tale of injustice and wrong and—"

"Do not presume to make your efforts out to be any sort of social crusade," he hissed, and Miss Lovelace tripped over herself in her haste to move away from him. "What you are in search of is gossip, is it not?"

"No. Yes." She wetted her lips again.

"Which is it?"

"Both," she elaborated. "There is, of course, a desire for society to learn about your identity, and additionally, it would do well for the world to see that Polite Society is not so very—"

"Polite?" he taunted.

She gave another one of those nods. "Precisely."

"I was being sarcastic," he said coolly. "I take, by your choice of rather predictable words, you aren't writing for the papers, Verity Lovelace."

The young woman folded her arms at her chest; her eyes flashed with indignation. "How dare you?" The affront in her tone and body's response merely confirmed . . .

Malcom tossed his head back and bellowed a mirthless laugh. "That is it." And then her name and why it was familiar hit him. "V. Lovelace of *The Londoner*." The bloody huckster, peddling in the curious details of Malcom's life, was no "he" but rather a "she."

The lady brightened. "You've read my work?"

Her work. "Your rubbish column where you speculate about the Lost Earl? Aye."

She beamed like he'd plucked a damned star from the sky. "*The Lost Earl.* I, too, felt that had a lovely sound to it."

He whistled. "Daft." The lady was daft. "I just called your writing shite."

Miss Lovelace wagged a finger at him. "Ah, yes, but you *have* heard of me."

He'd entered some manner of upside-down universe. There was no other way of accounting for the facts: one, that he'd left a woman alone in his rooms; and two, that when presented with evidence of his fury and outrage, the chit before him responded with nothing more than a too-pleased smile and an insolent lift of those remarkably long digits.

As if to confirm that very truth, the young woman stalked with purposeful steps over to his desk and—

His brows shot up. "What in blazes are you doing?"

Verity froze, with the lid lifted in her fingers. "Uh . . . I require a pen. And you don't use the designated tray for what it was intended." Only a man who was deaf would have failed to note the subtle chastisement there . . . and even had the man been deaf, he would have seen with his very eyes the censure in her smile that wasn't quite a smile. As it was, Verity Lovelace proceeded to fish around the inside of his desk, muttering to herself.

Nay. Not daft.

Mad. The chit was madder than the late King George himself.

"Ah, here." Sounding entirely too pleased, the termagant withdrew a pencil and then set to work searching for something else. "This will do."

More than half-dazed, Malcom shook his head. "What in hell are you doing?"

"Looking for paper." She directed that reply at the contents of his desk. She rustled through it a moment, and then paused briefly to glance up. "So that I might record your responses." With that, she resumed her search.

Record his responses . . .

She'd sought him out, and then invaded his belongings, all with the intention of sharing his story with the world. That was the price to be paid for his misstep . . . and a reminder served to never again falter.

"The world knows you as Percival Northrop," she was saying. "And yet you refer to yourself as North. How did you come by your new name, my lord? And do you have any intentions of adopting your rightful name?"

A growl started low in his belly. It made it no farther than his chest, trapped there. A rumble that managed to penetrate the harebrained minx's efforts. Slowly, she picked her head up.

Her already impossibly round eyes formed a perfect circle as he stalked over.

Snatching the pencil from her long fingers, he snapped it in half, and let the scraps fall to the floor.

She scowled. God, he should have anticipated that insolence. "You've gone and ruined a perfectly good pen—" Her words withered.

"I don't believe you've any idea of the peril you're in, Miss Lovelace. No idea at all."

Chapter 11

THE LONDONER
QUESTIONS . . .

Questions remain surrounding the Earl of Maxwell's
past . . . and present. But only one is begging to be
asked: Where *is* he?

V. Lovelace

Verity had a million and one questions for the man known as the Earl of Maxwell, but only one word surfaced through them all:

Flee.

That urging snaked around her mind.

She should leave.

In fact, the moment he'd stepped inside and caught her reading through his artifacts, she should have made a beeline for the door.

Even if she couldn't have made it past his powerful frame.

Even if he would have ultimately stayed her and played the game of cat and mouse that he did in that moment.

Mr. North . . . or the Earl of Maxwell or whatever name he went by . . . was a man in possession of secrets, with no desire to share.

And worse, ruthlessly determined to hold them tight.

She had experience with surly subjects, those who'd caught her about their properties, seeking out servants and invariably finding ones willing to share the family's darkest secrets. This, however, was different. This was Verity, trapped away with a feral monster of a man, with no one aware of her whereabouts.

His silence proved stark, more terrifying than any bellow or previous sharp retort. That quiet sent her unease ratcheting up, twisting in her chest. And suddenly, the desperation to uncover the story of the Lost Earl and secure her post at *The Londoner* seemed a good deal less important than preserving her own life.

Forcing a smile that stretched the muscles of her cheeks painfully, she dipped a curtsy. "I see that I've offended you. That was not my intention. If you'll excuse me . . ." She made it no farther than two steps—one and three-quarters of a step if one wished to be truly accurate—to the doorway.

The earl placed himself before her, blocking her path to freedom.

North—nay, she'd think of him as Northrop. It was a good deal easier facing an adversary if one thought of them by their given name. It humanized them. "Now you'd rush to leave?" he jeered.

He moved with stealth. From the moment he'd come upon her unannounced in the sewers, to his bedroom doorway. That was a detail she'd gathered in her time with the man.

The earl.

You've made the mistake of confusing me with someone who is safe . . . Because you take me for an earl?

Only survival mattered.

Mr. North moved a hand close to her face, and she drew a breath in sharply. But he merely stroked his knuckles along the length of her cheek, a touch that was unexpectedly gentle for the roughness of his skin. It was madness. He was a stranger. And yet, his touch mesmerized. Her eyelashes fluttered.

"I'm not opposed to staying."

Interest flared in his eyes. "Oh?" he purred.

Verity's face flamed, and she resisted the urge to press her palms to her burning cheeks. "Now you're being crude, and I'd have you know, it's uncalled for. All of *this*."

"All of this?" he repeated.

"The whispers, the rasping breath, the growling. You're making all this very uncomfortable when it needn't be."

He eyed her like she'd sprung a second head, which, though annoying, was vastly safer than the previous he-wanted-to-remove-her-head look.

"Now," she went on. "I . . . see that I've upset you. That was not my intention."

"And what was your intention?" He didn't allow her a chance to answer. "To gather up my secrets as your own? To share them with the world?"

Verity frowned. When he put it that way, she could certainly appreciate how he—or anyone—might take offense with her work. "I'm only willing to share that which you are willing to share with me."

Pure, unadulterated masculine interest glinted in his eyes. "Oh?"

The air crackled; the suggestive utterance robbed her of a suitable response. Needing space between her and this man whom she could not figure out, Verity made to draw away from him and his tantalizing caress.

His eyes mocked. "Never tell me you're afraid?" he murmured, resuming his gentle stroking. Refusing to allow her that distance. "I'm disappointed. I'd expect more from a woman on her own, darting around the sewers of London, Verity."

He laid ownership to her name with an ease better suited to one who'd been speaking it for years. That theft undoubtedly as much a part of the fabric of his person as the hard set to his scarred features. "Sh-should I be afraid?" she whispered, latching on to the mocking question he'd put to her. Fear, of course, was the suitable response. And there was something inherently wrong in her lack of that proper, justified reaction to this man.

"Oh, yes," he murmured. "Very much so."

The fact that he sought to rouse that sentiment in her was in and of itself reason enough to fear him, and yet, everything tunneled on that back-and-forth glide of his fingertips. "I'm not afraid of you," she said quietly, and then his fingers ceased their distracted caressing.

North rotated his palm and cupped her cheek. He lowered his head close to hers. Closer still. His dark eyes pierced her, running her through with the intensity in them. And more.

Desire.

"You should be." Their breath mingled as he spoke. The faintest hint of brandy wafted over her senses, more dangerously intoxicating than the actual spirits themselves.

"I—I should be what?" she managed, her voice thick even to her own ears. What had he been saying? What had they been talking about?

A slow, faintly mocking grin curled his hard lips up in that all-too-pleased, feral masculine grin. He was a man who knew the effect he was having on her. "Afraid."

With that, his mouth covered hers.

And she was very much her mother's daughter, for as he devoured her with his kiss, it was not fear or indignant outrage at this stranger who dared to embrace her that she felt, but a searing, gripping need.

There was an almost violence to the bold slash of his lips. He slanted his mouth over hers. Again and again. It was her first kiss. And as heat sang through her veins, she at last had an answer to why women threw away reputations and honor for fleeting moments of passion.

Verity gripped his shirtfront and drew herself closer. Heat poured from him, and she moaned against his mouth like the wanton she'd become. Or mayhap had always been.

He slipped his tongue past her parted lips, and Verity met each bold lash. He mated his mouth to hers, this man a stranger. This embrace forbidden. And mayhap it was the thrill of that wickedness. Or mayhap it was the fact that she was thirty and had never experienced, nor understood, the temptation of carnality. But she wanted this moment to stretch on. She wanted the desire battering at her senses to continue to drag her under.

He cupped her buttocks in his impossibly large hands, and drew her close. The feel of him—steel and heat burnt through her skirts, and moisture pooled between her legs, the desire to be closer still. Of their own volition, her hips rolled against him.

With a primitive growl, he plunged his tongue more violently, and she whimpered; her body bowed to that melding of fear and desire his embrace stoked.

And then he released her.

Her body sagged, even as she silently cried out at the sudden loss. Verity forced her eyes open, and struggled to push back the desire blanketing her senses. And ignore the agonizing ache at her center.

Oh, God.

What had he done? What had *she* done?

Verity took a lurching step forward, making a beeline for the door, but he caught her in a lazy grip. Looping an arm around her middle and anchoring her to him.

"Found your fear at last," he breathed against her ear.

Little shivers raced along the small shell, trickling down the sensitive skin of her neck, and she resisted the reflexive breathless giggle. "You've prevented me from leaving and continue to do so." Except he didn't truly hold her captive with anything more than the loosest of holds.

"Is that what I did before, love? And here my chest bears the marks of your nails from where you gripped me."

She gasped. Mortification chased away whatever maddening spell he'd woven. Verity spun out of his arms. "You are no gentleman, my lord."

He smiled again. "Ah, given our recent familiarity, Malcom should suffice."

Recent familiarity, indeed.

"You'd run off without gathering the information you sought about me . . . unless"—he gave her a suggestive look—"*this* was the information you—"

Her outraged gasp drowned out the rest of that shameful charge. "You're incorrigible." Her weak insult merely earned another of those mocking smiles. "And here all I sought was information about you, my lord."

"Malcom," he dared.

"Malcom," she ground out between clenched teeth.

His gaze worked over her. "All you sought was information?" he asked quietly.

The absolute lack of mockery and ice in those golden eyes gave her pause. Mayhap she'd reached him. She nodded slowly. "That is all." For her. For her sister. For Bertha. For her employment at *The Londoner*.

"You've your pencil ready?"

A pencil? It took a moment for that question to register, and when it did, along with what he offered, Verity sprang into action. He'd help her. She scrambled to retrieve a remnant of pencil she could still write with. "I do," she said quickly, cursing the fact that she was without her journal. Glancing hurriedly about, she slid into a seat at his desk, and stared expectantly at Malcom North, the Earl of Maxwell.

"Society, Polite and otherwise, with their interest in me and my life, can go hang, Miss Lovelace." He dropped his hands on his desk and leaned across the stretch of surface. His lip peeled back in a black snarl. "Write that on your paper. Now, lest you wish to see what I'm truly capable of, I suggest you leave," he whispered. There was a beat of silence while she sat there, frozen, numbed by all the original terror she'd faced in this man's presence. "Now," he thundered.

Verity jumped to her feet with such speed her chair flew backward, landing with a heavy crash. Her heart pounding, she raced across the room and scrabbled with the door handle.

Locked.

Verity's neck prickled with the heat of his approach. Her clumsy fingers struggled with the lock, and as it gave with a satisfying twist, she tossed the door open and raced out.

The hulking figure who'd greeted them at the back of the earl's residence waited in the hall. Gathering her skirts, Verity darted around him. Waiting for him to shoot a hand out and catch the back of her skirts. Braced for it.

But it did not come.

Hurrying down the narrow stairwell, she followed the same path Malcom North had carried her down. An hour ago? A lifetime ago. As soon as she reached the outside, she lengthened her strides. And she didn't stop running. She ran until her breath came in great, heaving spurts. Painful ones. And a stitch formed in her side.

Verity's steps slowed, and she forced herself to continue on. Knowing he was close.

She felt him and his presence.

Mayhap he'd been correct and she was mad, after all. For no sane woman would have ventured into the lair of Lord Maxwell.

But she'd not known what had awaited her there . . . who had awaited her.

At last, the bakery that had come to be home pulled into focus, and a relief so great swept through her she was nearly dizzy from the power of it. Verity forced her screaming muscles to move the remaining way to the bakery and the small stairwell that led to her apartments. The moment she reached the landing, the door exploded open.

"Verity," her younger sister cried out. She burst through the doorway and tossed herself into Verity's arms.

With a grunt, Verity staggered under that slight weight, and managed to keep them both from tumbling back down the stairs.

She folded her arms around her younger sister.

"Bertha came back and you didn't, and she didn't know where you were." Her sister's words rolled together, muffled against the fabric of her dress.

Nay, this wasn't her dress. This belonged to another.

She glanced over her shoulder, more than half-fearing that Malcom would even now be there, waiting. Watching.

"Come," she said, setting her sister aside. "We should go inside."

Bertha stood wringing her hands. "Oh, saints preserve, gel." The old woman's eyes closed. "You made it."

The moment Verity closed and locked the door, the questions came flying.

"Where were you?" Livvie demanded.

"You said you'd return in thirty minutes, gel," Bertha chided, slapping a palm on the table. "Thirty minutes. It's been hours, and—"

"What are you wearing?" Livvie blurted, silencing the room of all further questions.

Verity smoothed the fine muslin skirts. "A dress . . ."

Her sister frowned. "Don't be obtuse. Of course it's a dress. It's not, however, *your* dress."

Bertha came forward and stroked her fingers along the puffed sleeve. She whistled softly. "Fine garment. Finest you've ever worn."

The pair stepped back, and lining up, they directed accusatory stares at Verity.

"I can explain . . ." And then she proceeded to do just that; in her telling, she took care to avoid the details that would most alarm her sister: The perils in the tunnels. The stranger who'd carried her to safety and then to his lair. And who'd then kissed her. "I lost your slippers, Livvie," she said, her voice breaking. Those finest of articles her young sister had cherished.

There were several beats of silence.

"You found him," Livvie whispered. She cupped her hands around her mouth. "You did it."

"Yes, I found him." Avoiding their eyes, Verity made her way to the kitchens. She picked up the copper kettle and proceeded to make a cup of tea.

"That's it?" Bertha asked flatly.

Verity gave thanks that her back was to the older woman. With her sharp gaze and nearly six decades of life on this earth, she was savvy enough to detect the details Verity sought to conceal.

"This fine gent brought you back to his household, bathed you, and gave you a fancy garment, and that's all there is to the story?"

Verity made herself face her former nursemaid, damning the blush that scorched her cheeks. "He didn't"—she glanced pointedly at her ingenuous sister—"bathe me."

Confusion lit Livvie's eyes. Of course, she was clever enough to know that she was missing out on the undercurrents of a conversation, but still innocent enough to not be able to identify what those undercurrents, in fact, were.

"Men don't simply give fancy articles from the goodness of their hearts," Bertha persisted. "And certainly not a filthy tosher."

"He's not—" Verity made herself go silent.

"Oh?" Bertha prodded.

"Dirty," she settled for, the simplest and easiest truth about Malcom North, the Earl of Maxwell. Regal and chiseled, with a hint of sandalwood clinging to his frame, he was nothing like what Bertha expected him to be . . . Nor, for that matter, what Verity had expected.

"*Hmph,*" Bertha muttered as Verity, in a show of calm, settled into one of the kitchen chairs and proceeded to sip her tea.

Livvie climbed into the opposite seat. Scrambling onto her knees the way she had as a young girl, eager for the mints Verity would sometimes bring home after work, she leaned across the oak slab. "Your work is saved, then?"

Guilt assailed her, an all-too-familiar emotion.

At the fact that Livvie carried the worries she did.

At herself for having fled instead of demanding answers from Malcom.

Though she'd wager her soul to Satan on a Sunday that Malcom North wasn't one who'd have given over those answers to Verity . . . or anyone.

"Verity?" her sister prodded, impatiently.

"I . . ." She studied the tea leaves at the bottom of her glass. Which left Verity and her sister and Bertha where? The muscles of her stomach knotted.

Livvie fell back on her haunches. "You don't have the information."

God, how intuitive she was.

"I have enough. Some," she allowed the lie. An address. An address was all she had.

And the taste of his mouth on yours still. Unbidden, she touched her fingertips to her lips.

"Why are you touching your mouth like that?" Livvie blurted. "Have you hurt it?" Then her golden eyebrows went shooting up. "Did *he* hurt you?"

"No!" Verity hurriedly dropped her hand to the table, and took another sip of her drink to avoid Bertha's knowing eyes. "He didn't hurt me."

"And if he didn't give you the story, then neither did he help you."

Aye, there was truth there. And yet it was vastly more complicated than Bertha's blunt assessment. For Malcom had helped her. Saved her, even. The moment danger had crept up, he'd swept her into his arms and then brought her into his home.

A little tug at her sleeve startled Verity from her reverie. She found her sister staring at her with wide, worried eyes. "What now?"

Verity mustered a smile for Livvie's benefit. "Why, I offer Mr. Lowery the story I have, silly."

And then she prayed that the information she gave him was enough to spare her work and assuage society's fascination with the man known as the Lost Heir.

Chapter 12

THE LONDONER
SAVED!
RESCUED BY A HERO IN THE ~~SEWERS~~
TUNNELS OF THE SEVEN DIALS!

The world has long wondered about the Earl of
Maxwell. At last, he has been found. By me . . . I am a
woman who was rescued by him. I learned firsthand
that despite what he's endured in his time outside of
the peerage, Lord Maxwell is first and foremost . . . a
gentleman.

V. Lovelace

A fortnight later

Verity had managed that which no one else in London, of any station,
had accomplished—she'd not only located the Earl of Maxwell but also
brought forth the story that the world craved.

The story that had all London abuzz, talking about it.

The one people had pored over as they read their papers on the
streets of the city, devouring each word.

She'd given them the tale of the Lost Earl. She'd done it, when no one else had managed anything more than his birth name. She'd uncovered his whereabouts, a general description of the man himself . . . and a glimmer of how he'd spent his years exiled from the nobility.

And never had she felt more horrible for it. Betraying the stranger who'd saved her.

Perhaps that was why she was being so richly punished, just then.

Mayhap she'd not heard her employer correctly. That was all that made sense. The only way to explain . . .

"I am sorry, Mr. Lowery," she began slowly. "I'm afraid I did not hear you correctly."

"You heard me," he said flatly. Holding a quizzing glass to his eye, he scanned the inked pages in Fairpoint's sloppy hand. "I was clear in what was expected of you. You had an assignment, and you failed, Miss Lovelace." He briefly deigned to look at her. "Now, if you'll excuse me. I need to see to these edits so they might go to the presses."

If you'll excuse me. It wasn't a question but a command, as men were wont to do.

And it also served to confirm that there was no misunderstanding. Even so, it bore repeating. "You are sacking me?"

There, she'd said it. She'd said it, and hadn't shattered under the weight of her dread.

"If you prefer to think of it as parting ways, that is fine, Miss Lovelace," he said impatiently as he set aside one page for another. "Either way, you're done here."

Verity stared blankly down at the top of his head bent over those papers. "You cannot do this . . ." She could not squeeze out another word behind those. All this had become too real, in ways that didn't allow for coherent thought or well-articulated arguments.

"I can." He flipped to another page. "And I did."

This could not be it. Verity slid onto the edge of the lone seat opposite Lowery.

He briefly lifted his gaze, and catching sight of her sitting, he frowned. "I don't have time, Miss—"

"You don't have time?" she asked, and the frenzied quality to that query silenced the remainder of that coldhearted pronouncement. "You don't have time?" For the love of God, she'd climbed into the sewers and nearly been mauled by rats for her efforts. "I have given almost twenty years of my life to *The Londoner*, Mr. Lowery." All while he'd been traveling the damned Continent, living high off the earnings of his family's business, taking no role in the overall upkeep of the operations, Verity had been here and devoted. Tempering her voice, she attempted reasoning with him. "I've worked harder than every man who has ever sat at any desk. I've stayed longer, well past when they go home for the day. All the while earning less." For no other reason than because of her gender, and with all her dedication to her role, she'd simply be turned out?

Color splotched his cheeks. "Please, Miss Lovelace." He tugged at his collar. "It's crass for a young woman to speak about money."

"But it's not too crass for you to pocket the small fortune you made off my story," she shot back, and then thumped a fist to her breast. "*My story.* I brought you the tale of Lord Maxwell," she said, hating the shrill quality to her tone. Lowery expected her to be emotional. Verity exhaled slowly through tight lips. "I brought you exactly what you sought," she said again, this time more measured in that deliverance.

"You brought me *a* story," he clarified, at last setting down those damned pages. "A story. Not what I requested, but rather an exaggerated romantic tale."

"It was not . . . romantic," she sputtered; her indignation flared, far more comfortable than the earlier panic lashing at her. He'd paint her column as something romantic for no other reason than that she was a woman. There'd been no mention of the toe-tingling kiss that still haunted her memories and robbed her of sleep. More than half-fearing Lowery could see those scandalous thoughts parading through her mind, she brought her shoulders back. "It was—"

"A romantic story about the earl," he said flatly. "And it was fine for the purpose it served. It briefly assuaged the desire for any information, but this . . ." He fished around his cluttered desk, and then lifted the first-ever front-page story she'd managed. "This was never the story I or the world sought, and you know it. You merely gave them something they didn't know they wanted."

"Isn't that the whole point of writing?" she cried.

"No." Lowery slapped the copy of *The Londoner* down. "The purpose is to do your job."

And he was a damned fool.

Verity stormed to her feet. "You bastard," she hissed, curling her fingers into the edge of his oak desk to keep grounded. "I've given everything to my work here. And do you know something, Lowery? I am going to destroy you. I'm going to one day have my own damned paper, and I'm going to write the stories that the world doesn't know they want or need, and watch gleefully while your business is shuttered for your absolute inability to locate a damned good story if it were to slap you in your smug face."

Silence met her tirade, punctuated by the rapid breaths Verity sucked in.

He tightened his mouth. "Get out, Miss Lovelace."

"Get out," she breathed.

That was what awaited a woman after a lifetime of loyal service.

"To hell with you," she clipped out. To hell with all men.

Lifting her skirts, Verity spun and marched from the room. Taking immense satisfaction as she slammed the door hard in her wake and all the male employees around the office jumped and fell quiet.

Except Fairpoint.

Arms tucked behind his head, reclined in his seat as he was, his legs stretched out onto the corner of his desk, and a smug, self-satisfied grin on his thin lips.

She curled her hands tight to keep from smacking him in his smug smile.

Except, by the horrified expressions painted on the seven occupants of *The Londoner*'s offices, this was the response that they expected of her.

How was she still standing? How, when with a handful of casually tossed words, he'd thrown her entire future—her sister's entire future—into peril? Just like Lowery, just like any and every man, they all expected Verity's outburst because that was how the world saw women. Incapable of controlling their feelings, even as men moved through life, the hotheads they were, easy to anger, and even easier to take up a spot across from another on a dueling field, all in the name of honor.

Verity gave a toss of her head, and with very deliberate steps, she made her way over to Fairpoint. There was a wave of satisfaction as his previously pompous smile fell, and he hastily dropped his legs to the floor.

Good, she'd unsettled him. It was a small consolation on this bloody miserable day.

When she reached his desk, Verity stopped.

Fairpoint eyed her warily.

"You've had it in for my post since the moment you came here three years ago. You attempted to displace me when Mr. Lowery's father served as editor, and you've made it your mission since he ceded his responsibilities over to his son."

"Yes." He fiddled with an immaculate cravat.

"Why?" she demanded. Why should his life's goal have been to see her sacked?

He eyed her like she'd begun speaking gibberish. "Because there's no place for your sort here, Miss Lovelace. This isn't women's work," he said bluntly. "No matter how much you wish it to be."

Women's work? *What* was truly women's work? Marriage to a man? Mistress to a gentleman? Whore to a sailor? Servant in a fine lord's house? The options were few, and each no less vile than the other.

Pushing back the black rage creeping over her eyes, she took a step toward him.

Fairpoint hunched over.

The damned hypocrite. He'd mock a woman, and yet, feared one still. But then, perhaps that was what it was ultimately all about: men of every station truly feared women and what they might do to their ordered world. "Go to hell, Fairpoint."

And before she lost control as they all anticipated, Verity stormed out of *The Londoner*'s office . . . and the only employment she'd known almost all her life.

The moment she closed the door behind her, she stood there on the stoop.

All around, East London carried on as East London did: every side of the pavement overflowed with passersby and vendors hawking their wares. Their shouts and enticements deafening, a dissonance that wreaked havoc on her already jumbled mind.

The sting of London's stink slapped at her face; the fragrant odors of horse urine and dust burnt her nose.

Street sweepers hurried to clear manure from the uneven cobblestones, and she walked along those just-cleaned paths, her legs moving through the rote motions of a walk she'd made so many times before.

And as she reached the front of the bakery, only one thought sharpened into clarity: *I've no work.*

Gone. The security she needed to care for her family. The funds that paid for the rent of their modest apartments above the bakery.

Oh, God.

Her legs went weak under her, and she shot a hand out, catching the rail to keep herself upright. Unable to muster the strength to move, she sank onto the bottom stoop. Had she failed, had she not done her assignment to the utmost, there would have been frustration at being dismissed. But to have written the piece requested of her and garnered the sales she had for *The Londoner*, only to find herself with this ignoble fate?

The wind rustled her skirts, a soft breeze that wafted the rotted scents of St. Giles and could never be a true balm.

And yet, it was warm. But spring and summer faded, and would give way to autumn and winter . . . and as rotted as London was in the summer months, there wasn't the gripping cold.

Just as there was no cloak. Her cloak had been cut from her, and she'd left it behind at Malcom's. And it wouldn't be replaced because there'd be no funds for garments for herself—or her sister or Bertha. A sob caught in her throat, and she buried her head in her hands in a bid to hide that weakness from the folks about her.

Only they didn't care.

She straightened, and sure enough, the world continued to spin with fancily dressed strangers walking briskly, hurrying about whatever business brought them to these parts of London so they could ulti-mately escape and make for Mayfair or Grosvenor Square as they were wont to do. Everyone went about their way, and their day, without worry for the plight of others.

They were the fortunate, free of those worries.

Men and women like her late father's legitimate family.

And Lord Maxwell.

Her chest heaved, and little flecks danced behind her eyes from the sudden, sharp intakes of her breathing.

Lord Maxwell, who had a future and a fortune but was content to live a life of pretend in the most lethal corner of England. Concealing his secrets at the cost of her and Livvie's security.

But he's also the man who saved you . . . when he could have easily left you for dead in those tunnels. He'd cared for her injury and seen her bathed and clothed, and yes, he'd sent her running in terror, but he'd not proven himself so wholly without compassion.

Verity bit the inside of her cheek and forced herself to enter and face Livvie and Bertha.

At her arrival the women, darning a pair of stockings each, looked over.

Verity attempted to force a smile . . . that would not come. Instead, she pushed the door softly closed behind her.

"What is it?" Livvie whispered.

Only, Verity saw in her sister's eyes that she already knew. Despite the ways in which she'd maintained her innocence, Livvie wasn't wholly immune to the precariousness that was life for those outside the comfortable ranks their father had been born to.

"He sacked me," she said quietly, and hung her satchel from the same hook it had resided on these past years.

There was silence, and then—

"Miserable bastard," Bertha hissed.

Another time Verity would have chided her for speaking so crassly. In this moment, she couldn't muster sufficient concern for proper talk.

"He cannot do that," Livvie cried. "Surely he cannot do that?" She turned to Bertha when Verity failed to provide the reassurance that her sister desperately craved.

"He can do anything. Men can do anything they want," Bertha spat.

And through the cacophony of that back-and-forth, Verity remained motionless. Her gaze went to the stack of luggage used as makeshift furniture about their equally makeshift parlor. Soon, they'd have to put that small collection of mismatched articles—two embroidered valises, the once vibrant flowers long since faded by time—to use. To use once more, that was. For the first time in eighteen years. The lone trunk with its rusted latches.

Only . . . Verity tipped her head, eyeing the luggage. What did one do with trunks and valises when there was no place for them? An image danced behind her eyes: of her and Livvie and Bertha balancing the pieces between them as they wandered the streets, homeless. It conjured thoughts of the wandering Roma her romantic mother had once told her of. Except East London could hardly ever be considered the lush lands the Rom traversed. A nervous little giggle bubbled in her throat.

Out of the corner of her eye, she caught the concerned look that passed between Livvie and Bertha. And Verity, who'd served in the role of older sister, de facto mother, and caregiver for their trio, couldn't bring herself to find a suitable word of assurance.

Because she had none.

There was nothing.

And what was worse . . . there was *nowhere*. Nowhere for them.

A humming filled Verity's ears. The rush of blood pumping from the panic threatening to pull her under.

Her life had been upended before. After her mother's passing, Verity had been forced to leave behind her small cottage. She'd moved to London and settled into a new *home*—those sorry apartments.

There'd always been a roof. There'd always been walls. There'd been a loss of the comforts once enjoyed, but still, security.

This? This was—

There was a light tug on her sleeve, and Verity jumped.

Livvie drew her hand away. "Perhaps you might . . . speak to the Lost Earl again?" her eternal optimist of a sister ventured.

"The Lost Earl," she echoed dumbly.

I'm not the gentleman you take me for . . .

The ragged retort still echoed in her mind, his voice husked by desire, his callused hands upon her, searching her body in a touch that had bordered tender and rough. And . . . no. There was no gentleness in him. He'd been clear with his words and every action that he'd cede nothing over to her. "No," Verity said, making herself look back at Livvie and Bertha. "I'm not speaking to him." Never again.

"But he *might* be able to help?" Livvie pushed with a persistence that could come only from innocence. "After all, he saved you. Or you can speak to Mr. Lowery—"

"Mr. Lowery's not going to change his mind," she cried, frustration bringing her words rolling forth. "He's not some kindhearted gentleman." And neither was Malcom. She opened her mouth to say as much, but the words would not come. For Malcom wished to keep his secrets, and he should be entitled to that privacy.

A rebellious glimmer sparked to life in her sister's eyes. "Well, if Mr. Lowery won't, I'm certain the earl and—"

"And you blindly trust that someone is good because they are born to the nobility?" She gripped her sister by the shoulders. "For the love of God, Livvie, our father was an earl." That reminder whitewashed her sister's cheeks, and still, Verity couldn't bring herself to stop. "Our father was an earl, and what did he do? He married another woman because she was a lady, while all the while—"

"Stop," Livvie whispered.

"Making our mother his mistress. And have you ever known any comfort in life because of him?" She didn't allow for an answer. "I'll tell you, we did not." They'd not because the extent of the security he'd offered had come in the form of securing work for the twelve-year-old girl Verity had been. Releasing Livvie, Verity slammed a hand against her chest. "I'm the one who has kept you safe and secure and provided for. Me. *Me*. Not him. Not some damned gentleman." Not their father. Not Malcom, the Earl of Maxwell. "Not some bloody earl." Her shrill cry echoed in the rooms empty of furnishings.

No one spoke.

No one so much as moved.

In the end, it was not Verity who slid into the role of comforter, but rather the unlikeliest of their trio. "Here, now," Bertha murmured, showing traces of the once warm nursemaid she'd been. She rested a hand on Livvie's arm.

Her lower lip atremble, Livvie ripped away and stalked off to the lone room that had served as the sisters' shared bedchambers as long as they'd lived here. And then she closed the door behind her with a soft click more powerful than had she slammed the oak slab.

Verity briefly closed her eyes. Good God, what had she become?

Bertha frowned. "It's not the gel's fault."

"I know."

"And she certainly shouldn't have you yelling at her for it. She's scared, too."

"I know. I know." Restless, Verity pressed her palms over her face, when Bertha caught her hands and brought them back to her sides.

"It is all right to be scared yourself, but it's not all right for you to be taking that out on Livvie."

The older woman was correct. Fear over their future or not, Verity had no place lashing out at her sister. When she'd been the same age that Livvie was now, Verity had been caring for her baby sister. From that moment on, Verity had committed herself to taking care of her sister, and ensuring she didn't know the strife Verity herself had. It was no state she'd ever want her sister to find herself in. No position that any child had to be in: grown up too soon. Employed. Supporting one's family. And yet, that was the way of the world. Nay, not the world. The peerage knew nothing of children becoming caregivers. "You're right," she said quietly, absently; she wandered through the barren room, over to the window that looked down on the streets below.

Her sister truly believed Malcom North was the man to help them.

It was utter foolishness, built off the hopes of a young girl and her naivete.

Only . . .

"What are you thinking, gel?" Bertha asked gruffly.

Do not even think about it . . .

It was a quest born of foolishness . . . fueled by desperation . . .

"See after Livvie," she said breathlessly. Racing over to the hook, she gathered her satchel once more. Perhaps if she explained her circumstances, and explained the importance of this story, he might relent, and she in turn might secure her post with Lowery—nay, better—some other respectable column.

Bertha groaned. "Don't ever tell me you're going to see him."

Verity set her jaw. "That is precisely what I'm doing."

And before the older woman could try and talk her out of her decision, Verity hurried from their apartments and set out for the most ruthless end of St. Giles.

Chapter 13

THE LONDONER
FORGIVEN!

The Lost Earl has found himself again fortunate . . . this
time by the magnanimity of Polite Society. The peerage
has proven gracious in their willingness to overlook his
mysterious—and certainly dark—past. They are eager to
welcome him to Polite Society. If he wished it, that is . . .

M. Fairpoint

Malcom was being hunted.

It wasn't the first time in the course of his almost thirty years he'd
found himself prey that a foe sought to capture.

It was, however, the first time he'd faced this particular type of
adversary.

"As you can see, based on all the arguments I've enumerated here,
my lord, I would make . . . *we* would make one another a most conve-
nient match."

Silence met that pronouncement. A pronouncement delivered in
clear, soft English tones befitting a perfect English lady. Which there

could be no doubt the elegantly attired, golden-haired woman opposite him in fact was.

That was, all except for the part of the lady asking a damned stranger to marry her.

A fact that was clearly not lost on the pained-looking maid hovering close to the lady's shoulder.

"Ahem," the young lady said. "If you would like me to continue with additional reasons you should consider an arrangement between us?"

"Even with that whole impressive list, there's *more*, sweetheart?" Giles drawled.

The lady—Lady Denny . . . Lady Denton . . . or whatever the hell her name was—glared at Giles in the first real display of emotion she'd shown since her arrival. She immediately had her mask back in place. She turned to Malcom with a smile. "As I was saying, I can—"

"That won't be necessary," he quickly interrupted. He'd rather be the feast of hungry rats in the sewers of London than marry an English lady—this one, or any one.

The young woman scrambled to the edge of her seat. "But you've not considered all—"

Malcom leveled her with a look that immediately quelled the remainder of her protestations. Her cheeks went white, and she, not for the first time since her arrival, avoided his gaze. As every woman who'd walked through his doors had been wont to do.

Nay, there'd been one who'd been fearless and unapologetically bold in their every dealing.

Pushing back unwanted thoughts of Verity Lovelace, Malcom stood. "We're done here," he said coolly.

The lady hesitated and then, with the regal bearing of a princess, shoved to her feet. "As you wish, my lord." Gathering up her bonnet, she set it atop her head, unhurriedly tied it at her chin, and stalked off.

Giles was across the room in three long strides, and had the door opened for the woman and her maid. "Your Highness," he said dryly.

The lady's lips pursed like she'd sucked a lemon. With a grand *swish* of her skirts, she swept from the room, her maid following close at her heels.

A moment later, Bram ducked his head in.

"Oi'm sorry." The old man twisted his hat in his hands. "'ad a hard time saying no to that one."

As had been the case with any number of the desperate lords and their blushing, pale daughters Bram had shown in. Malcom had been tolerant, but now his patience snapped. "Not. One. More. Visitor."

"She'll be the last," the tosher vowed before ducking from the room.

As soon as he'd gone, Giles shoved the door shut behind him and took up his place at the window. "You must admit, she was a lovely one."

Giles merely sought to get a rise out of him. It had been the way of their relationship over the years. As such, with the latest fortune hunter now gone, and seated at his desk once more, compiling a list of his plans for the week, Malcom didn't even deign to pick up his head. "If you're interested in the lady, I suggest you summon her back and marry her yourself."

The other man drew the curtain back and glanced down. "Ah, yes," he drawled. "But I'm not the earl, am I? As such, I trust she wouldn't be interested in one of my kind."

One of his kind. It was a statement that set Malcom's teeth on edge, that mistaken belief held by all that because of a sudden trick of fate Malcom should be elevated to a different level than the one he'd lived these past years.

"Nor do I believe the lady's father, whomever the gent might be, would take to me approaching the pretty miss, let alone speaking with her," Giles was saying. "I know you're out of sorts with that, but it could be a great deal worse."

He drew his brows together. "I hardly see how."

"The newspaper columnist. You know . . . the one responsible for your never-ending parade of ladies . . . might resume writing about you," Giles said, turning his attention to the window once more.

Malcom gave an angry flip of the page in his journal, and studied the map he'd constructed of the tunnels.

She'd duped him, and Malcom had been paying the price ever since.

His gaze landed on his rendering of the tunnels at Canal Place. With the pencil in his hand, he ran the tip of it over the spot he'd come upon her. And mayhap there'd been some otherworldly quality to her, after all. For how else to explain the lapse in his very judgment?

I'm only willing to share that which you are willing to share with me . . .

Share only what he was willing to allow, his arse.

She'd printed a delusional, fantastical story about him that the world had lapped up. Polite and impolite Society alike. The unsavory sort he shared these streets with salivated at the chink in his armor he'd revealed after all these years. The fancy lords had frothed at the mouth for altogether different reasons—a *heroic* earl with gobs of wealth could be forgiven nearly anything, including the stench of the sewers on his person.

Then there was the matter of her printing his bloody address. The minx had described the understated buildings he'd purchased, rented, and hidden within, outing his location to all.

She'd dragged him out into the open, there for the world to see. And the world had seen—his foes as well as the members of the peerage who'd become his foes.

The pencil snapped in his hand under the weight of the pressure. "Bloody fucking liar," he muttered under his breath.

"What was that?"

"Nothing," he ground out. Malcom tossed aside the scraps and reached for another pencil. "Nothing at all." He attempted—and failed—to redirect his attention where it should be: on mapping out the schedule of the tunnels to be scoured that night.

For despite his earlier insistence, *it* was not nothing.

Not truly.

Malcom had allowed himself to be weak. He'd let his guard down, even as the incongruity of Verity Lovelace's presence in the sewers—with all her fancy speech and damned innocence—had screamed "trap." And he had stepped his foolish toes into it and had been paying the price for it ever since. Day after day, he was besieged by visitors: young women and their desperate, fortune-seeking fathers who'd believed the drivel Verity Lovelace had written upon the pages about him.

Painting him as some kind of hero.

A gentleman stalking the sewers and rescuing ladies.

And in sum, lying to the masses to sell her story.

And Malcom was the only one to pay the price.

"Though, I will say of all the women paraded before you, the golden-haired beauty is by far my top contender for the role of countess."

"Fuck off." Malcom stuck up his spare middle finger for emphasis, earning nothing more than a round of boisterous laughter for it. Abandoning his attempts at work, he tossed down his pencil and rubbed the stiff muscles along the back of his neck. "If you are unable to focus on our business together, you know I can simply replace you. There are a hundred other toshers who'd happily take your place."

"I do know as much." Giles widened his grin. "I also know that you won't. For all your annoyance and talk of sole focus upon the business, you rather like me."

"I don't like anyone," he muttered. "I tolerate you." His associate, through the years, had preferred his secrets like most in the rookeries. He'd kept his life a mystery . . . a luxury Malcom had enjoyed until the bloody minx had stolen that coveted gift in these streets. A hot wave of fury whipped through him, as potent as the day Fowler had approached, gaze averted, head down, and dropped that damnable paper on his desk.

The one that had unhinged Malcom's world.

Giles gave a tug at his lapels. "It certainly helps that the only one as capable in these sewers is me."

Malcom grunted. "As close to capable."

"I'll take that as praise."

"It wasn't praise, either. I'm merely stating fact," he said bluntly. "We're associates because of what you contribute." In fact, he tolerated more than he should where Giles was concerned. Theirs, however, was a mutually beneficial relationship, and it would be foolish for anyone to mistake the work they did with Malcom as kindness in any form.

"Ah, as we are speaking with blunt honesty, shall we discuss the tall, blonde-haired beaut—"

"No," he said before the other man could even finish. Malcom set to work, dividing his paper into columns and assigning those underlings who served their work for that week. At last Giles fell silent so Malcom could finish divvying up the operations for the upcoming week.

The silence was short-lived.

Giles plucked the curtain back, and peered out. "Another's arrived."

Oh, bloody hell.

"Not your usual taste, either. Dark. Small."

There'd been one young woman who'd been both dark and small, and who'd bewitched him. Malcom had learned his lesson, however. "She could be Athena, and I wouldn't give a damn," he muttered.

"Well, she's not. Athena, that is," Giles clarified, as though it mattered which hopeful lady or woman in search of a fortune sauntered up to his doorway. "Short. Almost childlike in size but not . . ."

Again, Verity Lovelace slipped into his thoughts. And he forcibly thrust back the unwanted memories of the shrew, just as he'd fought them each time: as she'd been that day, alternating between breathtaking courage and fear. With more displays of the former. And then there'd been her kiss.

He swallowed a sound of disgust. *Get ahold of yourself* . . . "*Childlike* . . . you say?"

"But clearly not a child." Giles pressed his forehead against the glass and peered out. "She's still rounded in the right places."

Lusting after the woman who'd ruined his existence was a new and entirely unfamiliar low. That reminder was sufficient enough to kill all thoughts of Verity Lovelace.

"I will say this one is a bit severe. More so than any of the other wide-eyed innocents to come your way."

"I don't need a damned cataloging," he said tersely.

"Come, you catalog everything. Even those things you've had taken from the Maxwell earl before you." Giles prattled on anyway. "With the way the lady's drawn her hair back, she must be giving herself a deuced headache."

Malcom continued writing. His pencil flew over the page.

"That is . . . odd, though."

Unlike prior attempts at riling him, the genuine stupefaction stilled Malcom's hand. "What is it?" After all, the only thing more perilous than incongruities were incongruities that went ignored.

"There's no doting papa. No protective maid. This one has come alone."

Alone . . .

"Completely alone," Giles clarified. "She must be a different sort of desperate than the others."

Plump and short? Severe hairstyle? A different sort of desperate . . . Nay. It was impossible. After all, there were any number of women to fit that physical description.

"And she's a determined look to her."

Malcom went absolutely still.

And that was when he knew . . .

Surging to his feet, he stormed over, pushing Giles out of the way so he could have unobstructed access to the window. He peered out the grimy pane, and damned the dirt.

And sure enough, there, attired in an all-too-familiar black muslin dress, she stood.

Nay, his mind merely played tricks on him. Malcom jammed the backs of his hands into his eyes and rubbed, and when he looked out once more, the sight remained. She remained.

"Impossible," he whispered.

"I take it you know this one?"

He ignored Giles's question, his gaze riveted on the minx thumping a fist away at his front door.

A door that Bram had been instructed not to open in greeting of anyone else that day . . . or any day until Malcom gave word—which he had no intention of giving.

KnockKnockKnock.

She paused midhammering, and let her arm fall. Verity backed away from the door.

Malcom narrowed his eyes. She'd gathered, then, that he'd no intention of allowing her entry. Good, the miserable harp—

Just then, she lifted a hand to her eyes, shielding them from the early-summer sun. And then slowly, ever so slowly, she crept her gaze higher and higher—until their eyes met.

And with two hundred feet between them, tension sizzled like the earth just before a lightning strike.

Verity's full mouth formed a perfect pout as she motioned—

At his shoulder, Giles broke out into a laugh. "Good God, is she ordering you to open your door?"

"Indeed," he muttered.

With a regal toss of her head, Verity returned to her post at the door and set to pounding it again. This time harder, the heavy boom carrying the stretch of distance between there and Malcom's window. It was an impressive, continual beating sure to drive a man mad—

And apparently had already driven Bram to the point of lunacy. The rapping stopped as the older man appeared below.

Giles peered down. "What in God's name is she saying to him?"

"I've not a damned idea." After Bram's last misstep with the shrew, he'd learned his lesson well. "I only know Bram is aware that if he values his post, he'll not allow—"

The old tosher smiled and beckoned her forward.

Verity Lovelace entered, and then the door closed.

Several beats of silence passed. "He appears to have allowed it," Giles said with more of that infernal amusement.

⬥

There was something a good deal safer feeling in walking through Malcom's *front doors*.

At least, safer than being secreted away through the alleys with none the wiser, and whisked inside back entrances.

Or at least, as she was permitted entry to the cramped foyer, that was what she told herself. That was what she attempted to convince herself of.

Nor was it her current company she was worried after. "Your eyes look better, Mr. Bram," she lauded as she tugged off her gloves.

He flashed a crooked grin. "And they doesn't sting anymore, either."

"That is splendid news, indeed," she said, giving him a cheerful pat on the back. "There's still the matter of your limp."

The brutish-looking man who'd met Verity and Malcom in the kitchens a fortnight ago marched forward, his left leg dragging slightly behind him as if the muscles had ceased to work. He blocked them at the bottom of the stairwell. "North ain't wanting visitors."

"Yes." She flashed him her most winning smile, the same one she'd donned when she'd asked to be admitted. "But surely His Lordship will accept one." Verity directed that at the only hope she had.

Bram grinned back, but a sharp glare from the other fellow killed that smile and her hopes.

A mask descended over the sentry's scarred face. "He don't go by ''is Lordship.'"

Not for the first time, a question reared itself: Who were these old, scarred men who dwelled here? Nor did that question come from the story she sought to write, but rather from a genuine need to know about the enigmatic figure that was the Earl of Maxwell.

"No," she murmured, beating her gloves together lightly. "He doesn't prefer to go by his title. That is true, is it not?"

"Just said as much," he said with an absolute absence of the rhetorical. "Now, Oi think ya need to leave."

I think, not *You must*. And it was that which confirmed he'd never be able to comfortably toss her out. Verity stuffed her tattered gloves inside the pocket sewn along the front of her gown. "I'm afraid I can't leave."

He paused. Narrowing his eyes, he looked her over. "You can't?"

And she wouldn't. Not until she spoke with Malcom.

"There are matters I need to discuss with Malcom." Once again, she did a sweep of the darkened halls. She knew he was here, and she wasn't leaving until she had an audience. Verity opened her mouth to say as much.

Just then, the resolute guard shifted his weight. His face pulled in a grimace.

His leg pained him. "I've something that can help with that."

"I told ya she did," Bram piped in on a loud whisper.

Encouraged by the angry fellow's silence, she went on to explain. "I grew up in Epsom Common. Have you ever heard of it?"

There was a beat of silence. "No," the older man said grudgingly.

"Some years back there was a cow herder who stopped to allow his cattle a drink from a nearby pool. The animals could not drink it—"

"Why?" Bram cut in.

"It was bitter tasting," she explained before looking back to the more stoic guard. "That same day Mr. Wicker allowed his livestock to wander into the water, and the ones who were injured? They saw their wounds healed." Both men stared on with wide eyes as she shared the telling. "Tales of the healing properties spread, and from then on, visitors would come to the pool. People suffering from gout and stomach upsets all were cured."

There was silence. And then—

"Impossible."

"Moi eyes are clear," Bram reminded the other white-haired fellow.

"You can find Epsom salt for purchase. Add a liberal dose to a hot bath, and soak your hurt limbs. I trust that should help greatly."

Some of the tension left his frame, and he took a step away from the stairwell, abandoning his spot.

"You've also been with Mr. North for some time."

He grunted. "Aye," he allowed, unwittingly confirming that bit of information she'd sought. Just as she'd intended when she'd tacked that statement onto the idea that he should somehow know her.

It was a knack she'd perfected in the work she'd done over the years. Subtle questions that people didn't know they'd been asked, which resulted in them revealing information they had never intended to share.

"How was it again that you came to know Mr. North, Mr. . . . ?" She cloaked the more probing question behind another.

"Fowler," he blurted, and Verity tucked that detail away. It was another skill she'd learned over the years. One proffered two questions, with one safer that lowered defenses and made a person more susceptible to revealing an answer to the first.

"And how—"

"Good God, you do not quit."

Her stomach dropped out from under her, and with a slow dread, she faced the one she'd come here requesting an audience with. He stepped from the shadows, more broadly powerful than even she recalled of the man who'd occupied her thoughts, both sleeping and awake.

For reasons not solely about the story she'd hoped to have from him, and shamefully having to do with the brief but explosive moment he'd taken her in his arms.

And previously unsettled by the darkness cloaking the halls, she gave thanks for the cover it provided her flaming cheeks. "Lord Maxwell," she greeted, and automatically dropped a curtsy as he stepped closer.

Both old toshers chuckled, earning a sharp glare from Malcom.

The pair immediately went silent.

And the desperation that had sent her fleeing to Malcom North gave way to a belated unease. After all, what did she truly know about the man who'd saved her, and who'd then sent her fleeing at their first—and last—meeting?

"I'll deal with you later, Bram."

At that cryptic threat, Verity took a commiserative step closer to the old man. "Now," she chided. "There isn't a need for that. Mr. Bram has done nothing to merit your displeasure." She patted the old man's coarse, coal-stained fingers and earned a besotted-looking, crooked smile. "He simply let me—"

"If you know what is good for you, Miss Lovelace, you won't go ordering my people about."

His people. Not servants. Not staff. Not family.

Malcom gave a jerk of his head, and Fowler and Bram went rushing off. Both of their gaits were slightly uneven as they walked, but still quick. Aye, that she could understand. Malcom North had that effect on people. Verity followed their retreat, more than half-envying the men their escape.

"You needn't be so surly," she said after they'd gone. "Unless you're always in such a state?" She pressed him with her gaze, and when no confirmation or denial was forthcoming, she sighed. "I took your surliness a couple of weeks ago as a product of our tense circumstances that night. Either way, you should be a good deal kinder to them."

"Would you rather I let you continue on, grilling those in my world with questions about me?"

By the hard smile on his face, he expected—and relished—her unease. As such, she'd be damned if she let him see her fear. Verity brought her shoulders back when another figure started down the stairs.

Verity gasped. Whereas Malcom wore his experience on the streets in the scars on his rugged face, the even taller stranger bearing down on them had the face of Gabriel, and the ice-hardened eyes and smile of Satan. And . . . he was missing a hand.

That realization gave her pause. All the men who resided here were scarred in some way.

And you should be a good deal more worried about how they've come by those injuries than the marks they possess . . .

Despite herself, Verity shivered.

The stranger stopped at the bottom of the stairwell.

"Shall I handle this one for you?" he asked, almost cheerfully beating the empty nub where a hand should be against his open, callused palm. It was not, however, that menacing gesture that snagged her focus but rather the stretch of his vowels as he spoke, ones that glided from a high pitch to a low pitch, and whispered at a Welshness to his tonality.

"I do *not* need to be handled."

"I have her," Malcom advised, as though Verity hadn't spoken, as though the two men were more than content to carry on their conversation about her as if she weren't present.

She gnashed her teeth. "I'll say it once more—"

They turned simultaneous stares upon her, withering the rest of that brave retort.

That black-haired Lucifer touched that nub to the brim of his cap and then, with one last look for Verity, let himself out. The London street sounds spilled inside before he closed the panel, swallowing the noise once more so that only an agonizingly thick silence fell upon the cramped foyer.

Verity wanted to be the one to break the quiet. She wanted to be brave in the face of bullying—even if it was veiled intimidation, and yet, fear sapped the moisture from her throat and mouth, making words impossible.

Malcom dropped a shoulder against the wall, and she jumped. "You next."

Confusion settled in her already-muddled mind. "Me next?" she asked slowly, seeking clarification.

"The door, Miss Lovelace," he said tightly. "See yourself out."

He wanted her gone. *Did you expect he'd want you to stay?* "You're displeased with me," she murmured, getting to the heart of the matter.

He stilled, and then tossed his head back, bellowing a sharp, short bark of laughter that echoed from the ceiling. It ended as quickly as it burst from his hard lips. "Good God, mad or stupid—I can't determine which you are."

It was faintly similar to an insult he'd leveled at her a fortnight ago, and it stirred indignation. His ill opinion, on the heel of her firing and society's disregard of all women, was too much. She snapped. "Does it make you feel good to bully a woman about?" She stalked over until the tips of their shoes brushed. "To go about shouting names and insulting me?"

"My charges have nothing to do with your gender," he said coolly. "I know very many women who are plenty smart and capable."

And oddly, that rankled even more, that insult that found her wanting, compared to the women he kept company with.

"And do you know, Miss Lovelace?" he whispered, dropping his face near hers, so near his breath fanned her lips.

All the earlier confidence that had sent her forward to confront him to his face flagged. "Wh-what?"

"Every one of those women would have the sense God gave a London sewer rat to not seek me out as you've done—again."

She trembled, a never-ending shiver that rolled through her. One that should be ripples of fear. And yet her body's awareness made a lie of sense and good reason. Verity wetted her lips. "Because of my column," she ventured, her voice husky and breathless.

His brows came arching down, and his eyes went to her mouth.

Oh, God. He was going to kiss her again. And what was more . . . *I want him to . . .*

"Because of your column," he seethed, banking the embers of that foolish haze of her desire. "Because you stole that which you'd no right to take. Because of no other reason than because I decreed it. *Get out.*"

"I am sorry for that," she said softly. A memory slipped in of she and Malcom playing chess when they'd simply been strangers together in hiding and not adversaries at one another's throats. A pang struck in her chest. "I am sorry for so much." Where he was concerned. She'd had no other choice, however. Not when it had been his privacy versus Livvie and Bertha's security.

Malcom peeled his lip in a hate-filled snarl. "As if your apology means shite to me."

Verity winced. "I deserve that." Her fingers shook, and to hide their quaking, she clasped them behind her back. "But I'm afraid I cannot leave." Which was the absolute truth. "Not until we've spoken, and I've explained . . . my circumstances."

Malcom cocked his head. "You're refusing to leave?" Frost chiseled off that question into a curt, syllabic response.

Aye, no doubt he was one wholly unaccustomed to having his wishes gainsaid. Was that arrogance a product of his roots in the peerage? Or of the reputation he'd earned outside of it?

And this time, as questions whispered around her mind, they stemmed not from the need for information for any article, but from a genuine desire to know about the guarded man before her.

"I . . ." She dampened her lips. *Go. This is futile. He'll give you nothing. You already took that which he didn't wish to share.* Livvie's face flashed to mind. But Livvie's face red from the cold, frost clinging to her hair in an imagined world of them living on the streets this winter. Verity dug in her heels. "I do believe I am. You see, *I* knew it was fool-hardy in coming to you again."

"And yet, here you are."

"Livvie, however, my sister," she clarified, hating the fact that her words rolled into a rambling manner when she'd always prided herself on being a master of her words. "She—" Verity cleared her throat. "Livvie, that is, believed it would be wise for me to speak with you, and I was at first resistant, and yet ultimately decided to come here." Malcom just stared at her; his expression carved of immobile granite. "To speak to you," she finished lamely when he didn't respond. All through the continuing silence, Verity realized the absolute madness in her being here. The futility in having come to Malcom North for this request. Or *anything.*

He slashed a hand forward, and with a gasp, Verity brought up her arms protectively.

A cool smile frosted his lips. "In my offices."

It took a moment for that offer to register through the pounding of her heart. Verity let her limbs fall to her sides. "You'll . . . meet with me?" she blurted, exhilaration humming to life.

"I suggest you start walking before I change—"

Verity was already striding forward, and for the first time since she'd begun the quest to find the Earl of Maxwell, she felt the stirrings of hope. Mayhap Livvie had proven correct in her supposition.

Mayhap there was more to the ruthless tosher, after all.

Chapter 14

THE LONDONER
SQUALOR!

Upon his kidnapping, the Earl of Maxwell traded
wealth and luxury for strife and sorrow. Of that, the
world is certain. The world holds its breath, awaiting
answers to the questions: What were his struggles, and
why should he not gladly embrace his lost life amongst
the peerage?

V. Lovelace

This was nothing short of a mistake.

Of course, it was not the first Malcom had made where this damned
woman was concerned.

The last had proven costly.

So why did he even now lead her through the halls of his residence,
and allow her any more of his time?

*Because she possesses some mystifying pull you cannot explain, nor
resist . . .*

He pushed back at the taunting gibe pinging in his head.

It would be far greater folly to send her on her way because of her past wrongs without finding out what the little deceiver sought from him this time.

They reached his offices, and he urged her on ahead of him.

The young woman hesitated; she peered tentatively inside, but made no move to enter. "These are not your offices," she said with a canny smile, a product of her *last* visit.

"If you think I intend to show you any more of my private suites, then you're even more cracked in the head than I'd originally taken you for in the sewers. Now move."

With a snap of her muslin skirts, she swept inside with all the regal bearing of a queen, muttering something under her breath that sounded a good deal like "Well!"

The muscles of his mouth strained from what felt damningly like a grin drawing at the corners.

Entering behind her, Malcom drew the door shut.

Verity's keen gaze touched on each corner of the room, those shrewd eyes taking in every detail. So that she could no doubt use it against him—again. Her stare briefly lingered on the chess table they'd played upon what felt a lifetime ago. He'd moved the damned thing out of his private suites and into his offices because he'd not wanted to be confronted with the memory of her in his rooms that night. The young woman ripped her gaze from the board and shifted it over to the unique metal piece hanging on the wall. She drifted over, presenting her back to him, highlighting yet another time that she didn't belong to his world. Men, women, and children who'd lived in these streets knew one never turned their back—on anyone. "I've never seen anything like it," she murmured.

"What the hell do you want?" he asked, leaning against the panel.

The young woman continued her examination. "What is it?" Her voice was hushed.

"An amputation saw," he said, taking delight in the way she stiffened. It was best she knew whom—what—she was dealing with. Malcom pushed away from the door, and wound his way over. He stopped at her shoulder. Lowering his mouth close to her ear, he whispered, "Have you ever seen one, Verity?"

She gave an unsteady shake of her head. "N-no."

He stretched a hand past her, and she drew into herself; the defensive response of her body inadvertently brought her back resting against his chest. Malcom motioned to the rusted steel. "See those locking nuts?" He didn't wait for an answer. "That holds the blade in place. And here," he went on in silken tones. "This ornate handle"—the mahogany had been carved into the shape of an eagle—"is what the surgeon would use to saw through muscle, skin, and bone."

"Would?" She angled her head back slightly, revealing cheeks that sometime in his telling had gone pale.

Not taking his eyes from her, he retrieved the object in question.

Fear spilled from her gaze, and as he brought the saw lower, she recoiled.

Smirking, Malcom pressed the handle into her palm, and curled his hand around hers, forcing her to grip the saw. "The world oftentimes has a preference for the pretty"—he touched his gaze on her face—"things," he finished. "So much so that they'd allow them where there's no place for them." He guided her hand in an up-and-down sawing motion. "See how awkward it is to grip," he breathed against her ear. "Now imagine cutting through skin and muscle." She quietly gagged but did not pull away.

"And do you have experience . . . with using a surgeon's saw?" she whispered, her voice faint.

Always working. The woman was always working. With his own devotion to the work he did, he'd be otherwise impressed—if the subject of her assignment weren't, in fact, him. Either way, he'd hand it to her, that as horrified as she was—as he'd intended her to be—she asked those uncomfortable questions anyway.

He placed his lips near her ear. "In search of more details for your story, love?"

"Actually"—she faced him; then, drawing in a breath, she notched her chin up an inch—"that is why I've come."

Malcom opened his mouth but couldn't get out a reply. None that was suitable. He tried again.

In the end, only a strangled, hoarse laugh burst free. "The insolence of you."

"It's not insolent to try and do my job."

"It is if you go about it the way you do, Verity." To keep from taking her by the shoulders and giving her a solid shake, he freed the saw from her grip and returned it to the wall. "I told you before I didn't have anything to share. And yet what did you do?" An irritating muscle twitched along his eyelid. "You fed your fabricated story—"

"My story wasn't fabricated." She spoke with an earnestness etched in every delicate plain of the upturned diamond shape of her face. "Everything I wrote was true, Malcom . . ."

He scoffed. What rot. Either she sought to butter him up for information or she was a damned romantic without the sense the Lord gave a creeper. "My actions that day were—"

"Heroic." Verity turned her palms up. "You saved me. That was the only story I had that day, and that was the story I wrote."

His eyes went to the rough skin of her palms, the chipped nails, the ink staining the intersecting creases of her hands. It was the ink. The black mark of her treachery, reminding him that anything spilt from this one's lips was only about the story she was intent on snagging to sell. "I didn't give you anything. You took it, Verity." And he'd give her nothing else. "Now, if you know what is wise, don't darken my door or path again."

The young woman sank her teeth into her full lower lip. "I can't leave. I've no choice. I need this s-story."

Malcom remained unmoved by the faint crack in those last two syllables.

"My sister—"

"Ah, yes, the sister with the slippers. The same one who convinced you to come to me."

Fire flashed in her eyes. "Are you making light of me?"

"I would have to care enough to make light of you. I don't."

She flinched, and something completely foreign, so foreign it was almost indistinguishable but felt a good deal like . . . guilt . . . slapped at a conscience that proved not as dead as he'd expected—or hoped.

Verity hugged her arms to her middle, and wandered out from behind him. Making for the front of his offices and the doorway, and more importantly, her long-overdue exit.

She stopped on the threadbare circular wool rug in the middle of the room, making herself an unwitting bull's-eye in a target. "I'm employed by *The Londoner*."

Of course he shouldn't have anticipated she'd leave. "You said as much at our last meeting."

"My employment rested on my providing my editor with this story."

"*My* story." One that he'd few details on himself. Distant whisperings of moments that dwelled in murkiness, that he couldn't pull from the shadows and had no intention of wading through for this woman—or anyone. His past didn't matter. All that did was his future. "And I'm supposed to care about your circumstances more than my own?" he snapped.

She ran saddened eyes over him. "No," she said quietly. "I suppose not. But I thought it might matter to you that my family's well-being hinges upon my successfully attaining this . . . your story, Malcom."

"It doesn't," he said with his usual bluntness. Only . . . why did it feel as though he lied to himself?

Verity sucked in a juddering breath. Moving her gaze just over his shoulder, as though she couldn't bring herself to look at him, she then spoke again. "Do you not have people you care about? People whose well-being matter to you?"

"No," he said with an ease born out of truth. There'd never been anybody. And there never would be. No good came from one's dependence on another.

She briefly shifted her focus to him. "Your Mr. Fowler and Mr. Bram. The black-haired man who was here earlier?"

He flicked a glance over her. "No one matters to me outside of the business dealings I have with them."

"Treating those close to you as though they are somehow less." A pitying glimmer reflected back in her expressive eyes. "That is a sad way to go through life, Mr. North."

"Ah, yes, but then, I'm not the pitiable one humbling myself before a stranger, abandoning honor and good sense because of a sibling, am I?"

Instead of the rise he'd intended to get out of her, she flashed a sad smile. "I'd still take a life . . . how did you phrase it? Humbled and pitiable? With people I love in it to this cold, empty, emotionless existence you've set up for yourself."

He'd not set anything up for himself.

He'd simply lived the life he'd been dealt. It was on the tip of his tongue to tell her as much. It was a physical effort to keep back that admission she'd no right to.

As if she sensed that weakness, she drifted over to him. "What is it that makes you so determined to hold on to your secrets, Malcom? Is it guilt? Fear of acknowledging to the world what you lost?"

He was upon her in two long strides, catching her lightly by the arms. "I've not lost anything, Miss Lovelace," he hissed. One would have to have memories of something in order for it to be truly gone. "There is nothing more, nothing less. This is my life."

"But it's not," she cried, pounding a small fist against his chest. "You are an earl."

A sound of impatience escaped him. "I don't want it." His fingers curled reflexively into the satiny-smooth skin of her arms, and he forced himself to relinquish her. His hands flexed, much like when he'd burnt his hand as a lad, making a fire in a home he'd found for himself one winter. "I don't want any of it."

"You don't know how lucky you are," she cried. He made to step around her, but she darted into his path. "You're content in this miserable end of London any one of us would sell our souls to climb out of. And all the while you sulk."

He sputtered, "I do not—"

"Because of what?" she continued over his indignant interruption. "Because you had the misfortune of being born an earl? Well, forgive me if I don't feel badly for you, Mal—"

He covered her mouth with his. It was nothing more than an attempt at quieting the seemingly never-ending tirade prattling past her lips. And yet the same explosive hunger when she was near, in his arms, blazed to life.

She moaned and caught herself against him, clinging like tenacious ivy.

Malcom swept his tongue inside, and she met that invasion with a bold lash of her own flesh against his. He groaned as lust pumped through him.

Working his hands over her generous hips, the equally generous swells of her buttocks, he explored all of her again as he'd longed to in ways that had kept him awake these past weeks. He devoured her mouth, its hint of honey shockingly seductive in its sweetness.

"I'm not the gentleman you take me for." He panted against her mouth, and then catching the hem of her gown, he tugged her skirts up and exposed her legs, then sank his fingertips into her hips.

A keening cry spilled from her lips, and her head fell back.

Malcom swept down and suckled and bit at the long column of her neck. Working his lips over her, dragging more and more breathless sounds of desire from Verity.

He caught one of her legs and looped it around his waist; that deliberate angling brought his throbbing shaft against her core. Even through her modest undergarments, the heat of her burnt him. And an embrace that had begun of one purpose took on more powerful, all-consuming overtones that reduced Malcom to the feeling of this woman in his arms. He rocked himself against her.

Her lips formed a small circle. "Oh!" She breathed a ragged, hungry whisper of discovery, and it enflamed him all the more.

"Who are you, Verity Lovelace?" he whispered between each slant of his mouth over hers. Her reply was nonexistent beyond the little puffs of her every exhale.

His hunger for her was mindless, his body's need for her all-consuming.

And was the reason he didn't hear the door open—until it was too late.

Cursing, he wrenched away from Verity and shoved her behind him. "Bloody hell, Fowler."

The old tosher stood in the doorway, making no attempt to hide the amused grin on his lips. "Merely came to see if you wanted me to toss 'er out." His smile widened. "Oi see that ya don't."

"Get the hell out," Malcom shouted.

Fowler was already drawing the panel closed.

The sound of his laughter carried in the hall, muffled, and then distant, before fading altogether.

Malcom scraped a hand through his hair. *Bloody hell.* It was one thing to have been weak not once, but twice where Verity Lovelace was concerned. It was an altogether different matter to have that weakness on full display before Fowler—or anyone.

He faced the young woman and found her busily smoothing her skirts. "You've quite unconventional servants."

Had it not been for the faintest shake to her palms, he'd have believed she was as unaffected as her composed tones suggested.

"I don't have servants," he clipped out.

Her clever and revealing gaze revealed the interest there. "Then who are they?"

More information he'd given her. Too much already. And he'd wager that was the very game she'd played when she brought up those names again. With a sneer, he stuck his face in hers. "I haven't given you enough today to print in your column?" Heat splashed his cheeks. "It is unfortunate for you Fowler entered," he taunted, determined to at last silence her. "You had me a moment's away from having my trousers down. Imagine the story you could have written then. Hardly as romantic. A fancy woman rutted against the wall by the Lost H—"

She slapped him.

Hard. The ferocity of that blow, combined with the unexpectedness of it, brought his head whipping back and his ears ringing. Malcom flexed his jaw. Well, he'd certainly managed to end her questioning. A new appreciation swelled for the fearless minx.

"You d-didn't have to be crude," she shot back, bold even in her fear. He started over to her. Verity backed away until she ran into the curtains that shielded the streets below, and out of space. "And I'm not a fancy woman," she went on, holding her palms up when he stopped in front of her. "I'm simply a woman attempting to do her work and care for her family. And you?" She gave him a pitying look. "You are so self-absorbed that you don't care at all about the plight of anyone. You have properties. Ones that you keep empty. Not caring that you sacked servants who needed work."

Malcom scraped his eyes over her, this woman who'd unsettled his world. "No, I don't. And I've told you: I'm not a man who cares." Or knows. He dropped a hand beside her head, half framing her in his arms. No good could come from speaking with her any more than he already had. No good had come from it, and only problems had faced him since he'd found her in the sewers. "And do you know, Verity? Those fine properties can stay empty until they crumble with time. Now get out."

Instead of the last hasty flight she'd made in the dead of night two weeks earlier, Verity slowly straightened. "Very well. I won't bother you again."

"Good—see that you don't," he called after her retreating frame. "Oh, and Miss Lovelace?" She paused. "If you cross me again, I'll ruin you."

A faint shudder shook her frame, and despite that fear, she sent her chin tipping defiantly up. "You needn't worry. I'll not." A moment later, Verity Lovelace was gone.

"The miserable minx." How dare she enter his world and tell him how he ought to live. Or question the decisions he made. He owed her nothing. He owed no one anything, which was by design.

Stalking over to the window, Malcom edged his curtains open. He scoured the pavement, and then found her.

The young woman descended the four steps with all the regal grace of a queen. She drew her shoulders up, and for a moment, he expected her to look back. To challenge him with her gaze, just as she'd defied him at every turn. But she didn't.

"Good," he muttered into the quiet, the sough of his breath fanning the smudged glass panel and blurring the figure below. It'd be a good day when he never saw Verity Lovelace again.

You'd be lying to yourself if you don't admit the exhilaration you feel run through you whenever she's near.

As if she'd followed those damning silent thoughts, the ones indicating that she knew the unwitting fascination he had with her, the young woman stole that final look back.

He curled his lips up in a mocking smile and touched a pretend hat brim.

Even with the stretch of distance between them, he caught the slight wrinkling of her pert nose. She lingered there on the pavement. Here in the rookeries, where innocents were robbed of all and left bearing the scars of that onetime naivete.

Malcom balled his hands. She was not his problem. She'd come here of her own volition, risked her own foolish life and limb. One such as her, one who took on the care and responsibility of others, only found oneself on the losing end of life. That'd be her fate and not his.

No one was his problem—as he preferred it.

You have properties. Ones that you keep empty. Not caring that you sacked servants who needed work . . .

Aye, as she'd stated, he had properties, but empty ones without servants. A piercing pain shot to Malcom's temples. An agonized hiss escaped through tightly clenched teeth, and Malcom caught his head in his hands, applying pressure in a bid to dull that stabbing sensation.

But it was no use. Agony continued washing over him in waves.

A face flashed behind his eyes. A voice. A pair, conversing. A towering, liveried servant, glancing down at a small boy with his palms upstretched . . . *An extra biscuit is yours. Now be on your way, Master P—*

Gasping, Malcom jerked erect as the rest of that memory vanished. Sweat spilled from his brow and burnt his eyes, and he blinked back the sting of discomfort. He forced them open and searched again for the one responsible for the resurrection of demons that may as well have belonged to another.

Gone.

Upon the horizon, there wasn't so much as a trace of Verity Lovelace.

Malcom scrubbed the sweat from his face. How dare she? How dare she come here and call him out? She knew nothing of it.

For that matter, *he* knew nothing of it. Not truly. Not his past. All the memories were murky at best, blank at worst.

Until now . . . Until that distant echo of another place and another time with figures he couldn't place, yet innately knew. *I was that boy with that servant.*

"Enough," he croaked, needing to hear his own voice, to hear anything other than the loud buzzing in his ears in order to ground himself firmly in reality and focus on a safer outlet for his rage. The insolent virago who'd dared to enter his residence and call him out.

Not caring that you sacked servants who needed work . . .

He didn't care. He didn't.

And yet . . .

If he didn't care, then why not allow those people to remain as they'd been, tending an empty household and toiling away at their miserable existences, just as Malcom himself was?

"Bram," he thundered.

The bulky former tosher limped in several moments later. "Aye?"

Malcom frowned. As long as he'd known the other man, he had been lame. "It's gotten worse."

Scratching at his bald brow, Bram eyed him strangely.

And mayhap he *was* strange. The minx with all her accusations and questions had messed with him. "Your leg," he clarified, clipping those two syllables out.

"Ah." Bram brightened, and a wide grin split his heavily scarred face. "But moi eyes are better." Aye, they were indeed. "The little miss helped. Said she has something that would 'elp with my leg."

As the half-besotted tosher prattled on about the virtuous Verity Lovelace, Malcom's eyelid twitched.

Bram seemed to register that involuntary tic, for he abruptly stopped midpraise for the minx. "Is there somethin' ya wanted?" the old tosher put forward hesitantly.

"No," he gritted out. "Yes." What in hell was wrong with him? What madness had the witch inflicted?

As eager to please as he'd been since Malcom had hired him on, Bram stared expectantly back.

"Sanders . . . the . . ." Malcom grimaced. "My man-of-affairs." Because regardless of whether or not he wished it, the man answered to him. "Tell him to hire back the damned servants he'd previously sacked."

"And do what with them?"

"And . . . and . . . hire them back," he finished lamely, waving a hand. "Their former posts. Let them have them. If they want them."

"Anything else?"

He shook his head tightly, and Bram turned to go. Only . . . "Aye. Tell Sanders I'm done with his visits." Malcom had been patient enough, dealing with the transfer of the properties and the details surrounding the Maxwell title. There was nothing left for them to meet on.

"As you wish." Bram limped off.

"Bram." He stayed the old man at the door. "There is actually one other thing I'll require of you and Fowler."

Sometime later, after he'd gone, Malcom returned to the window and found the area on the pavement where he'd last spied Verity. A painted whore had since taken her place and was in the process of conducting a transaction with a garishly clad dandy. She caught the gentleman's hand and led him onward to whatever alley served as the place of her work.

And I'm not a fancy woman . . . I'm simply a woman attempting to do her work and care for her family. And you? You are so self-absorbed that you don't care at all about the plight of anyone . . .

I'll not think of it.

I'll not think of her on her own. Verity Lovelace without employment . . . She wasn't his concern, or his responsibility.

It was done.

He'd shut the door on the Maxwell title and the woman named Verity Lovelace.

Why did that not bring him the satisfaction he expected it should?

Chapter 15

THE LONDONER

Is Lord Maxwell a man . . . or a monster? Conflicting reports have been provided. The world, however, waits to decide for itself the answer to that question . . .

M. Fairpoint

"Well?"

Verity hadn't even closed the door behind her when that question greeted her.

Bertha stood in wait, wringing her hands.

Verity glanced off to the bedroom she shared with her sister.

"She tried staying awake but fell asleep about an hour past."

"Good," Verity muttered, rubbing at her sore right shoulder.

"Where've you been, gel?"

"Walking," Verity said quietly, and balancing herself on one foot, she tugged off first one slipper, and then the next. Letting the pair fall, she wiggled her toes in a bid to bring blood back to the digits, numb from the hours of walking she'd done.

"Walking?"

Think.

There had to be something . . .

Verity rested her forehead against the lead windowpane warmed from the sun.

"There has to be a way," she murmured. There always was.

"I have it," she whispered.

"I hope it doesn't involve that damned tosher," Bertha muttered, mopping the perspiration from her damp brow. "That one isn't about to help anyone but himself. Can't even share the damned sewers. As if he owns them," she mumbled under her breath.

And for the first time since she'd quit Malcom's residence and grappled with the uncertainty of her fate, Verity smiled. "Actually . . . it does have to do with Lord Maxwell."

"Mark my word, gel: he isn't one for you to rely on."

No truer words than those had ever been spoken. The help she'd have from Malcom North, the Earl of Maxwell, however, was one she'd herself take. "It involves his residence," Verity said quietly.

The other woman shook her head. "I don't follow you, Verity."

Racing over to the valise where her notes and notepads were tucked, she sifted through. *Where is it? Where is it?*

"I just organized all that for you," the other woman lamented.

Verity continued her search. "Here," she murmured, drawing forth the list. Rising in a whir of the same black skirts he'd gifted her, she held the page over to her nursemaid.

"What is this?" the other woman said, briefly scanning the perfunctory list.

"These are his properties." Three in total, uninhabited, vacant residences without so much as a servant seeing to their care. One in the heart of London. Her heart raced. Only, for the first time since she'd walked out of his apartments in the rookeries with her head up, it wasn't panic accounting for the erratic beat. "He has three of them."

"I see that. And you be thinking he's going to give any of them to you?" Bertha eyed her like she'd gone mad.

And mayhap Verity had because all this didn't seem like such a very bad idea, after all. "No." She smiled slowly. "I'm going to take it."

The other woman's eyes slowly widened into circles. "You're off your head." She made to hand the sheet over.

Verity ignored it. "I'm resourceful."

Bertha snorted. "Is that what you be calling it? You stealing from a lord?"

"Is it really stealing, Bertha—"

"Yes."

"If he has no intention of using it?"

The other woman paused; it was a discernible, pregnant one that indicated Verity's logic had forced her way past Bertha's reservations.

And then—

Bertha shook her head. "One such as him would happily see you hang."

On the heel of that warning came the ruthless words spoken by the gentleman in question . . .

Ah, yes, but then, I'm not the pitiable one humbling myself before a stranger, abandoning honor and good sense because of a sibling, am I?

Despite the sticky warmth of the early-summer day, Verity shivered. Nay, there could be no doubting that if he discovered she'd taken anything from him, again, he'd see her destroyed. She rubbed at her arms in a bid to rid them of the chill.

"You know I'm right about him, too, gel," Bertha murmured with a canniness that could only come from having bounced her on a knee when Verity had been just a babe. Sighing, her former nursemaid pressed the sheet into Verity's fingers, forcing her to take those notes about the earl.

The rub of it was, Verity did know it. However, until she managed to secure new employment, and then a residence, her life and those dependent upon her were in peril. "Our future is already forfeit, Bertha."

"You don't know the meaning of a forfeit life, Verity. You think this is the bottom." Bertha's eyes darkened. "But this is not it. This is not even close."

"Having no roof over one's head is as damned close to bottom as one could fall," she snapped, her voice carrying around the room. Verity looked to her sister's closed door, and this time when she spoke, she did so in hushed tones. "We'll be careful."

"You expect we're going to come and go as we please in some fancy end of London? Waltz through the front door without attracting any attention to the fact that we're commoners invading their fancy world?"

Verity chewed at an already-ragged nail. No, they could hardly venture through the front doors of some Grosvenor Square property. "We'll use the servants' entrance, and we'll do so when it's dark. Well after the respectable sorts take their beds."

Bertha snorted. "What do you know about their goings-on?"

Bastard born to an earl, it certainly wasn't her father and his connections to the peerage that had given her most of her understanding about that world. "You forget," she reminded the older woman. "My money over the years has been earned by understanding and writing about every detail around the lives of the nobility. I learned when they move about. When they retire for the evening. The hours they socialize. Just like I know the patterns of their servants." With every counterargument she put forward that silenced the old woman, her confidence in her plan grew. "Until I find work, we'll simply become shadows to the living."

Bertha pursed her mouth. "Ain't possible to become a shadow if you're going to have to leave the damned townhouse in search of work during the respectable hours."

"I'll be careful," she vowed. When the other woman went quiet, Verity moved closer. "What other choice do we have that you see? Where do you expect we'll go? Use the small amount of funds we do have on renting rooms for a night or two?"

They remained locked in a silent battle of wills.

Bertha sighed. "Very well," she said tersely. "But let it be clear that I find this idea a dangerous one."

Entering into the house of a man who'd warned her to never again cross him? Aye, there was nothing safe in that decision, and everything risky. She forced a smile she didn't feel. "He needn't ever find out."

Except she wasn't certain whether those assurances were for herself or the other woman.

⁓

Several hours later, when the streets had cleared and the cobblestones were quiet, Verity, Livvie, and Bertha descended from the hired hack in front of the unlikeliest of havens.

"The person who lives there is going to let us in?" Livvie whispered.

"Aye." Even if he didn't know it.

Quelling her own awe of the impressive stucco structure, Verity forced herself to close her mouth. She stole a glance about. The longer they remained out on these fancy sidewalks, the more they risked being caught about the streets of Grosvenor Square. There was no doubt that were someone to pass by or glance out their window at the trio with their mismatched luggage, they would summon a constable with rightful suspicions.

"Come," she said gruffly, taking one handle of the luggage while Bertha took the other.

Livvie hurriedly gathered the two valises and set out after them. "Is he a friend of Father's?"

"Shh," Verity and Bertha simultaneously whispered.

"Is he?" Livvie repeated in more measured tones.

"No," Verity said tersely. *A friend of Father's? Pfft.* If there'd been such a generous figure, he'd failed the Lovelaces magnificently these past years.

At last, her inquisitive sister ceased with her questions. When they reached the servants' door, Verity tried the handle.

Locked.

"What did you expect? That it would be left open?" Bertha muttered. "Here." Reaching past Verity, she slid a stickpin inside the lock.

Verity rounded her eyes. When in blazes had their nursemaid learned to pick locks?

"What are you doing?" Livvie asked the other woman. "What is she doing?" she demanded, putting that same question to Verity when the nursemaid remained fixed on the task of breaking them inside.

Verity touched a fingertip to her lips and gave a slight shake of her head.

A moment later, the lock gave with a satisfying click. "There." Bertha pushed the door panel open and grabbed one end of the trunk.

When Verity made no attempt to take the other side, she gave her a look.

Springing into movement, Verity took the opposite handle, and followed the older woman inside. Verity hurriedly closed the door behind them, erasing the miniscule hint of light that had peeked down from the night sky, and replacing it with a shroud of darkness.

"Can I talk now?" Livvie whispered.

Could she?

Could they?

Bertha glanced around uneasily. "You're certain he sacked the servants? Didn't keep on the butler and housekeeper, as is the way of the lords?"

"Who?" Livvie pressed.

Giving Bertha a warning look, Verity set down her end of the trunk and moved close to her sister. "Someone I know. A friend."

"The gentleman who saved you in the sewers?"

"Of a sort," she hedged.

Several lines of confusion creased Livvie's brow. "Either it is or isn't."

"Shh." Verity and Bertha spoke in unison.

Verity cleared her throat. "You were . . . correct earlier. In your supposition of Lord Maxwell and his kindness." She grimaced around that last word.

"Kind, indeed," Bertha muttered, and Verity shot her another warning look.

"But you said—"

"I was wrong. I heeded your advice. I called on him as you suggested."

Livvie's eyebrows touched her hairline.

And even in the pitch-dark kitchens, Verity caught the romantic glimmer in her sister's eye, followed by a sigh. There'd be time enough for alarm about that naivete. For now, it served its purpose.

Except . . . Livvie did a sweep of the rooms. "If he's allowed us to live here, why are we sneaking in?" Suspicion laced her question.

Why, indeed? Verity had drafted enough stories over the years that it should come as second nature as breathing to her. Only the work she'd done had never been fiction. She'd given facts and honesties the world had sought . . . to the point of offense in the opinion of many of those nobles who found themselves plastered upon the scandal pages.

"Well . . ." She felt Bertha's stare. The one Verity had faced many times as a girl trying to dance herself out of some mischief. Her sister, however, was deserving of the truth. When Verity had been her age, she'd been serving in the role of mother. "Livvie," she began, "you're correct. I've not been entirely forthcoming."

The door between the kitchens and the entrance of the corridors burst open, and two figures exploded through the doorway with seven-foot poles leveled at their trio. Gasping, Verity shoved Bertha and Livvie behind her. "Here, now," one of the voices boomed. "Wot's this—"

That familiar Cockney cut out as an even more familiar pair of men with white hair and thick brows stared back in dumbstruck silence.

Verity mustered her best smile. "Bram. Fowler. How very good it is to see you both again."

Chapter 16

THE LONDONER
INHABITED!

It has come to the attention of Polite Society that the servants previously dismissed by Lord Maxwell have been rehired, which remains nothing short of a curious development!

M. Fairpoint

Mayhap the world had accepted the truth: a tosher in the Dials would make no proper husband for any woman—lady or otherwise. Or mayhap it was that the gentlemen had witnessed the crude existence he'd lived, wholly apart from their fine, safe world, and had accepted, even with the title now affixed to his name, that he'd never be a gentleman.

Or mayhap it was just luck, which Malcom had possessed in spades through the years.

But the parade of debutantes and their desperate papas had at last ended.

His limbs straining from the exertion of holding himself aloft, Malcom focused his gaze on the front of the room, shutting out the pain that pulsated in his arms. His life had settled back into a familiar routine. His days were spent preparing physically for his search of the sewers. His nights were spent pillaging them.

His exchanges with those he called associates were no longer laced with ribbing and amusement at Malcom's changed circumstances.

There were no unwanted *guests*.

And there was no return of Miss Verity Lovelace.

That alone should have been cause for victory. The miserable termagant who'd shaken the foundations of his existence and signaled his identity—and whereabouts—to the world was one he would be fortunate to never again cross paths with. Single-minded in her attempt for nothing more than information about him, so that she could sell it to those rubbish pages that for all their meaningful contributions would be better served wiping arses than actually being read.

And yet . . . he had thought about her.

Every day since she'd proudly marched out, closing the door not with a bang, but with a damning and decisive soft click that had rung of its finality.

Of their finality.

"Good," he gritted out. Levering himself up another inch, and then carefully shifting his weight, he whipped his body around so that he remained perfectly balanced.

You don't know how lucky you are . . . You're content in this miserable end of London any one of us would sell our souls to climb out of. And all the while you sulk . . .

And Malcom didn't want to think of her as she'd been, vulnerable and pleading, desperate for the information only he could provide so that she might help her sister. "If there was even a sister," he muttered, sweat trickling down his cheek. Because it was no doubt another lie. Self-serving as the summer was insufferable in the Seven Dials, the woman wasn't capable of anything more.

Except even as he preferred thinking of Verity Lovelace as only a liar, in her words as she'd spoken them, there'd been such truth not even the greatest London stage actress could feign. That willingness to sell one's soul, because it was a sentiment he was all too familiar with. In the absolute absence of God, he'd bartered with Satan enough that not even his blackened soul was worth anything to that dark liege.

Raw in her honesty, her vulnerability reminded him too much of himself as he'd been long ago. So long that he'd forgotten what it had been like to be her: *afraid*.

Cursing, Malcom released himself. His feet landed on the floor. Whipping his arms back and forth, he brought blood rushing back to the limbs.

What was it about Verity that had left him haunted by the memory of her? That he remained unable to shake free of the thought of her? Or the feel of her in his arms?

And worse, the desire to feel her in his arms once more. To taste her. All the while exploring the voluptuous curves of her hips and buttocks. Desire surged through him.

KnockKnockKnock.

That rhythmic pounding at the door broke through his thoughts of her, and that usually unwanted intrusion proved a welcome diversion. Grabbing a towel, he wiped it over his face. "What is it?" he called, the white linen muffling his voice.

Giles entered, his sack looped over his arm. "North."

Treating those close to you as though they are somehow less . . . That is a sad way to go through life, Mr. North . . .

"It has nothing to do with that," he snapped.

Giles puzzled his brow. "What?"

"Nothing," Malcom grumbled. How dare she call out the method by which he dealt with his associates. "Giles." He issued that belated greeting. Malcom looked to the clock. Ten past nine o'clock. The other man's evening work should be beginning.

"A *greeting* and not a 'What the hell are you doing here'? I say, you're more cheerful than usual," Giles drawled. "Though I can certainly venture why . . ."

"I'd hardly say I'm cheerful," he muttered. The only cheer he'd allowed himself had been involuntary, and that amusement had been unwitting, a product of the mouthy minx who'd not hesitated to go toe-to-toe with him. In fact, he'd not even known he could enjoy himself in that way—or in any way.

"And you haven't tossed me out on my arse. I'd say that is as cheerful as I recall you in"—he perched himself on the arm of the carved, dark-walnut lounge chair—"*ever*." He let his bag fall with a thump. "I trust this has something to do with a certain . . . lady?"

By God, were his damned cheeks turning red? They *felt* hot. Only he didn't blush or give in to any other shows of emotion. "You'd be"—*right*—"wrong," he said, toweling the moisture from his arms, and then dropping the cloth. Giving his back to Giles, Malcom proceeded to the washbasin and pitcher and splashed his face. "If this is why you're interrupting me, you're in need of more work." He brushed the water from his eyes, and when he opened them, he caught the entirely too amused expression reflected back in the bevel mirror affixed to the stand.

"Oh, come, not even the dark-haired, smallish young woman?"

Malcom dunked his face once more in a bid to dull the heat. Damned Giles and his probing.

Giles sighed. "You suck the pleasure out of everything, including a good ribbing."

"Aye." The other man spoke an absolute truth. "Is there a problem with your assignment for the evening?"

Other toshers complained over the tunnel assignments; Giles had only ever accepted the weekly maps he'd been given and never questioned those orders. It was, in short, the reason Malcom had the relationship he did with him.

"I merely felt, given the news, that it required a visit to congratulate you."

The news? That gave Malcom pause, and carefully reaching for a dry cloth, he blotted his face. "Congratulate me on what?"

The other man blinked slowly. "Why . . . about your *news*."

Warning bells jingled in his mind. "What. News?" When the other man was too slow to answer, he growled, "I asked, *what news?*"

Giles jumped, and then muttering to himself, he leaned down, fished around in his bag, and drew out a stack of papers. Malcom was already crossing the room. "Here." He tossed the newspapers.

Malcom caught them to his chest.

"Front page. Of every newspaper."

He'd been on the damned front pages of every last gossip column for the first months of the discovery of his existence. When he'd eluded all their damned reporters, he'd been relegated to the safer middle and back pages.

Malcom's gaze collided with the headline across the front.

A UNION MADE IN . . . THE DIALS

All of London is abuzz with talk of the Earl of Maxwell's recent and unexpected marriage. The lady herself, as much a mystery as her husband, is known by Lady Verity, and was recently seen exiting the Grosvenor Square residence. Her past is as cloaked in secrets, with the exception of her romantic meeting and then whirlwind—

Courtship?

"Keep reading."

He glanced over the top of the paper.

Giles gave a nudge, urging him to finish, confirming Malcom had spoken aloud.

Returning to the article, Malcom resumed scanning the main story there.

It is a marriage that has taken the *ton* by storm.

For a long moment, Malcom didn't move. The page remained trapped in his fingers, his gaze riveted on the words before him. He'd read them, so he knew they were real. And yet . . . they couldn't be. For nothing captured in the article was in any way . . . accurate. The damned minx, determined to have a story, had provided another one. A different one . . . a fictitious one that involved a fake marriage between them. At last it made sense why the desperate fortune-hunting fathers and their daughters had stopped darkening his doorstep. And here he'd been feeling guilty about the young woman's state. He'd fought guilt—an unwanted emotion—at the thought of her alone. Hungry. Struggling to survive in the cold world they both had the misfortune of inhabiting. When all along, she'd been playing her usual games . . . all in the name of a damned story. God, there was no end to her ruthlessness.

"I trust you wished to keep it secret, then?"

"A secret?" What was the other man on about?

"Your . . . marriage?" Giles said, his words more a question than anything.

His fists curled into reflexive balls of rage, and he crushed the copy of *The Londoner*. Ignoring that question, he tossed aside the papers and grabbed for his lawn shirt. Pulling it over his head, he dragged on his boots and started for the door.

"Where are you going?" Giles called after him.

"I have a meeting," he gritted out. "With my *wife*."

God help her.

❧

"I shall love you forever. You have changed me in every way. There is no one and nothing like you." Verity's impassioned vow was met with a loud giggle from her sister.

"You're silly." Seated on the wide four-poster bed with her knees drawn up, her form was dwarfed by the mattress and bedding, making the young woman appear impossibly small and girlish.

"Oh, hush. You are not showing proper appreciation." Clutching the bar of shell-shaped soap, Verity held it to her chest and sighed.

"It's soap." Livvie giggled again. "We've had soap."

"Not like this and you know it."

Nay, the ones they'd had of the past were coarse against the skin. These were the comforts their father's other family had enjoyed through the years. Verity had never resented their existence, as they were no more responsible for their luck in life than she was for her ill fortune. But this? The smooth, fragrant bars, soothing against one's skin? She would have been hard-pressed to not find jealousy in them.

There was a light scratching, like the spare cat they'd taken in once to catch the rodents in their apartments. A moment later, the door was opened by a footman, and an army of servants came forward, bearing a porcelain tub and buckets of steaming water. Her cheeks heating with a blush, Verity hid the bar of soap behind her back.

Bertha came trailing in behind the small entourage with an all-too-familiar frown on her face.

"Thank you, Jemmy, Jeremy, Travis, and Miranda," Verity said after they'd set up the bath.

"My lady," they acknowledged with a series of matched sets of bows and curtsies before streaming from the room.

Miranda lingered in the doorway. "If there is anything else you req—"

Bertha closed the door in the young woman's face, drowning out the remainder of that offer.

"That was rude," Verity scolded.

"Schooling me on manners, are you? My, if you haven't fallen right into the role of household mistress and proper lady," Bertha drawled.

"If you were a proper lady, you'd know that lords and ladies don't thank the servants."

Frowning, Verity returned the creamy bar of soap to the floral porcelain dish at her vanity. "That is preposterous and rude."

"And it's the way of their world. Or should I say *your* world?"

At that slight emphasis, Verity felt another wave of heat bathe her cheeks in a blush. She stole a peek over at her sister; however, Livvie gave no outward indication that she'd detected those subtle nuances of sarcasm.

"Verity was just vowing her love to her soap," Livvie called over to Bertha.

"Was she?" Bertha asked, glancing to the younger Lovelace sister.

Livvie scooched herself to the end of the bed and swung her legs over the side of the mattress. "Oh, yes. Though I do say she's shown far more devotion and regard for her soap than she has the earl."

Oh, bloody hell. And with that, reality came ripping through yet another moment of pretend Verity had stolen for them. It wasn't *her* fault that society had taken her appearance in the formal residence as something more. Or that they'd believed her to be the countess.

Bertha folded her arms. "And why is that? Hmm?"

Drat her old nursemaid. She'd been opposed to Verity's plan since the start, and hadn't let up on her steely resolve to see them flee the only luxuries they'd truly known in more years than she could remember.

"And when am I going to meet him?" Livvie asked, glancing between Verity and Bertha. "I expected he should have come to live with us by now. Given that it is a love match." Her brow dipped, and she troubled her lower lip in a way so very similar to Verity's telltale gesture of unease. "It is a love match, is it not?"

That was an assumption Livvie had formed on her own. One that had been lent credence by the damned gossip pages. One that Verity had known, at the first utterance of it, would one day have to be explained for the lie it was. Later. Eventually. When they were gone. And yet . . .

Feeling Bertha's eyes on her, Verity joined her sister at the mahogany bed. Drawing herself up, she sat beside Livvie. "I . . . My arrangement with Malcom is more a matter of convenience." There, that much was true. It was a matter of convenience . . . for Livvie anyway.

Her sister's eyes were stricken. "You don't love him, then?"

"I . . . We are"—*mortal enemies*—"friends." Verity nearly strangled on that admission. *Liar. He'd happily cut you down if you came around when he discovered the truth of your deception.* Need he discover it, though? When he was so very determined to live a life of separate existence in the seediest streets in England?

Disappointment brimmed in Livvie's bright eyes. "I still expected that I'd have met him by now."

"Aye, me too," Bertha drawled.

Verity shot her a sharp look before shifting her focus to her sister. "He . . . Malcom"—because even fictional husbands required a name—"is merely finalizing matters in East London, and when they are complete, he'll join us." At which point, she'd have to craft some also-fictional accident that left her widowed, and hope that her sister never again asked about the missing Lord Maxwell.

Her sister yawned.

"You should go rest, Livvie. I have to speak with Bertha, and tomorrow we can talk more about Malcom." They wouldn't. Come the morn, she'd have altogether different reasons and distractions that precluded Verity from answering anything about her make-believe husband.

The moment Livvie had gone, Bertha faced her.

Her silence proved more damning than any words she might utter.

"What?" Verity groused.

"Oh, you tell me, gel. You're the one who has us living here with you as a pretend countess."

"I didn't make up that lie," she said defensively. "Society did that all on their own."

"I'm sure when His Lordship learns what you've been up to, he'll see it that way, too."

Aye, Verity had been besieged by those worries as well. That, however, had been before the comfortable beds. And the full bellies. And the untattered garments. And the soap and the lack of mice.

And by the fourth day, when servants had begun to flit around the household, removing the coverings from portraits and windows, and none had still yet called Verity and her family out for the lies they perpetuated, it had become increasingly harder to pack up, slip out, and simply move on to . . . Lord knew where. "He stated he had no intention to move to Grosvenor Square, and his . . . friends thought it was just fine that we remained."

"Aye, and by your own words and that fine research, he'd no intention of keeping on staff, but here we are."

"*Shh,*" Verity warned, stealing a frantic look at the front of the room. There'd been eager maids and footmen about, grateful for their posts and determined to please.

"This is madness, gel."

"I know," she muttered, struggling with the row of buttons along her borrowed dress. Another borrowed dress from the armoires of the former ladies who'd inhabited this household. This one was of fine silk, the hem several inches too long so that it dragged, and even so, the crystal beadwork along the hemline and neckline and the lace overlay skirt were finer than anything she'd worn now . . . or when her father had been living. "Will you help me?"

"No," Bertha said bluntly.

Verity glanced over her shoulder.

"Fine," the other woman muttered, and set to work on the row of buttons. "You're playing with fire, gel. And because you're playing with fire, I am, too. And if that doesn't mean anything to you, then Livvie's life and future should."

Verity frowned. "Is that what you believe?" Was her opinion of Verity truly so low? That she somehow thought that this was a game and Verity merely sought to play at blue blood? "All of this is because of you and Livvie."

Bertha grunted. "Is it, though?"

Wasn't it? Even as Verity spent her days searching for work at other scandal sheets and newspapers, she returned in the early-afternoon hours with a greater relief than she'd ever known to have a safe, comfortable roof over her head. One that did not leak. "This is for all of us," she finally said.

"We have to leave, Verity," Bertha warned, helping slide the dress off; the fine French satin rippled over her skin, gloriously soft and smooth.

And the rub of it was . . . Verity knew as much. Even as Fowler and Bram had been gracious enough to give her and her family shelter, now that the papers had run free with the erroneous story about Verity's actual place in this household, she was on borrowed time. She knew that she merely played make-believe and had stolen these moments of security, but they could only ever be temporary. Malcom wasn't one who'd remain ignorant to the sham she'd perpetuated here in West London, and he was not one who'd turn a cheek to that affront.

Particularly not when the guilty party is you . . .

"Here, step into the water, gel," her old nursemaid said gruffly, misinterpreting the reason for Verity's shivering.

Verity tugged off her undergarments and dunked one foot into the steaming bath.

She sighed and sank under the scented depths until the bubbled water concealed her shoulders. "No one was supposed to be here," she reminded Bertha.

"Aye, but they are. And we've worn out our welcome with the one who matters. It's only a matter of time before he comes for you . . ." That ominous warning echoed in the air.

"We'll leave." All her stomach muscles contracted, and Verity closed her eyes. They'd perish. A sheltered Livvie, an older woman, and Verity, with her experience working at a newspaper, didn't have the skills or references to do anything other than the career she'd come to love.

Bertha grunted. "That's the wise choice. We've coin enough to find smaller apartments."

Yes, but for how long? A week?

"Verity, if we stay here, we hang," Bertha said quietly.

Oh, and Miss Lovelace? If you cross me again, I'll ruin you . . .

Verity bit the inside of her cheek, scrabbling that flesh, welcoming the sting of discomfort over the fear that the mere echo of his warning instilled. She rested her head along the back of the porcelain tub and stared at the cheerful mural overhead. The recessed ceiling was intricately lined in gold with an oval carved at the center. Set within was a pale-blue, cloud-filled sky, that pretend window out to the world, as make-believe as the life Verity had stolen these past days as her own.

Except the faintest sheen of dust dulled the green inlay border, a taunting reminder that all this was a sham. All of it.

"Soon," she allowed before her courage deserted her.

"It's the right decision, gel." And as if she worried Verity might change her mind and debate her on the point if she lingered, Bertha quit the rooms.

As soon as she'd gone, Verity slipped under the water, submerging her ears and tunneling out all sounds but for the muted beat of her heart. She hated that Bertha was right, just as she hated that there were no options for them now. But then, there'd never truly been options. Not for women born outside the peerage. For that was what Verity had been the moment her mother had given her heart and body to an earl unwilling to marry outside his station. And for it, the pair that had been Verity's parents had doomed her and Livvie to their untenable fate.

Verity exploded from the water, gasping for a proper breath.

Damn them both.

She reached around for the cloth that had been draped somewhere along the side of the tub . . . when someone slipped that cloth into her hands.

Bertha. Verity set her teeth. She'd already secured Verity's agreement. "I've already agreed with you. Tomorrow is the day. You needn't worry that I've changed my mind."

"And tell me, Verity, what might you have changed your mind *about?*" At that steely whisper, Verity went absolutely motionless. Blood whooshed in her ears, smothering that voice. Slowly, she wiped the cloth over her eyes, brushing away the moisture. And then she held that fabric there.

Because as long as she didn't look at the owner of that low baritone, she needn't confront him and his fury. A palpable, thrumming one that vibrated in that coolly asked question.

Except . . . she'd made many mistakes in her life, but there was one certainty: she was no coward.

Reluctantly, Verity lowered the cloth.

Malcom sat with a hip perched on the opposite end of the bath; his gaze trained on her face. "Hello, Verity." That all-too-familiar, menacing grin that she'd come to recognize as patently false. "Or should I say . . . *wife?*"

Chapter 17

THE LONDON GAZETTE
THE HEART OF A GENTLEMAN . . .

So many have whispered with fear of the earl who will one day reclaim his rightful place amongst Polite Society. Now, however, with Lord Maxwell's having saved a young woman from certain peril, there is no doubting that he is not the monster the *ton* initially expected he would be . . .

E. Daubin

Fury had driven Malcom to his Grosvenor Square properties. Just as that emotion had compelled him abovestairs to the fancy chambers in search of the bloody thief of his secrets and now his material possessions.

And yet, all that safer fury had left him the moment he'd slipped inside the room and found the interloper, Verity Lovelace, naked and soaking in a bath with a light dusting of bubbles her only covering.

And damn him for his weakness as primal lust burnt more palpable than any of the anger he carried for this woman.

Seated on the edge of the bath, Malcom shifted in a bid to hide the telltale evidence of his desire. A mere physical reaction, and yet he'd be damned if he revealed any weakness to her.

"You've gone quiet, Verity," he said silkily. "How unlike you."

With a squeak, she slammed the small slip of fabric protectively against her breasts; that careless movement merely parted the water like a filmy curtain being drawn back to reveal the tantalizing display below. Unbidden, he devoured her with his eyes.

She squeaked again and sank lower so the sudsy bubbles touched her earlobes. "*Stop* looking at me."

"Do you know, I rather think I won't, Miss Lovelace." Pushing to his feet, Malcom glided around the curved porcelain bath until he reached her shoulder. "Or do I have that incorrect? Perhaps I should call you *Lady Maxwell*? Or is it *Countess*?"

"Perhaps we can continue our discussion after." She gave him a pointed look. "When I'm properly dressed."

Any other sane woman would have been blubbering with fear at having been caught in the deception that this one now carried out.

He grinned. "Oh, no. I rather prefer you precisely as you are, *dear wife.*"

The minx drew her knees close, fanning those bubbles once more, the suds parting to reveal the thatch of dark curls between her legs. Aye, if he were an honorable man, he'd look away. Alas, none of either East or West London would dare confuse Malcom North with anything other than he was.

Gasping, she buried a palm over that erotic sight. "You, sir, are *no* gentleman."

"Aye, at last you've come 'round to the way of it." Only that taunting barb came out guttural, from a place of maddening hunger for the slip of a woman before him.

Verity lifted her chin, defiance in that slight uptilt. Gloriously breathtaking in her arrogance . . . and pride. And then, the young woman lowered her legs and returned to the casual repose she'd been in before he'd stormed her rooms.

His rooms.

It was all his.

She'd merely taken it from him.

Just as she'd taken his secrets and the privacy he'd so craved and turned it over to the world as if any of it had been hers to give. And what was more, that theft was the one that grated worst of all. The one that felt like a betrayal from the one person he'd let in—in any way.

Those reminders proved sobering, restoring the rage that had sent him here. "Well?" he whispered.

Her mouth parted just slightly enough to emit nothing more than a slight exhalation. A slice of pink flesh darted out, and she trailed that tip of her tongue along the seam of that full lower and narrow upper lip. "I trust you're not happy about this."

She couched her words even still, carefully measuring the extent of his knowledge, no doubt to help in forming the next lie she'd feed him. "Oh?" Malcom folded his arms. "And which part might that be?"

"Any of it?" she ventured, offering a sheepish smile. One that dimpled both her cheeks, flushed red from the still-steaming bath.

Malcom narrowed his eyes and then slowly angled his face toward hers, so that only a handful of inches separated them. So that he could hear the audible intake of her breath. And see the ripple of her throat as it moved. From fear, or desire? No doubt the former. The chit was insolent in her gall, but she wasn't gormless. "You think this is a game."

"No." She was shaking her head. "I don't believe that at all. About any of this. Mine was a desperate attempt at survival." The young woman grimaced as though that price of her pride had physically hurt.

Pride.

It was a rare commodity in the streets of London. It was a gift most couldn't afford, and one that was traded early on, all in the name of survival.

And even with all that she'd taken, and the pleas she'd put to him, she clung to hers still.

It was a bond he didn't want to share with her.

"What am I to do with you, Verity?" he murmured, speaking that question aloud as much for her as it was for him. Of their own volition, Malcom's fingers caught her soaking plait from the water and squeezed the residual drops from those dark strands. "You're clever enough to know the fate of one who lies and gains entry into an earl's household. The resulting end for a thief"—her lower lip shook, and she caught it between pearl-white teeth. She knew, but he finished the reminder, anyway—"Newgate. A hanging."

"And is that what you intend? To turn me over to the constables?"

Sliding to his knees, he positioned himself directly behind her. "What should I do with you, Verity?"

Verity angled her head back so she might meet his gaze.

This closeness to her in all her naked splendor had been a mistake. Placing himself so very near her, her body flushed with the heat of her bath. And a porcelain tub the only divide between them.

Aye, it had been a mistake. He was weak. *She* was his weakness.

He lowered his mouth to hers.

The door exploded open. The moment was shattered, and he was already on his feet with a pistol drawn.

"He is here," a young girl exclaimed. "The earl . . ." And then her eyes rounded as she took in the gun pointed at her chest. "Oh," she whispered.

"Livvie," Verity said sharply. The water splashed and rocked as droplets sprayed Malcom, indicating the young woman had stood. There was a faint snap of fabric, and then Verity rushed over to the silent, still, wide-eyed girl hovering at the open doorway.

"I . . . was going to tell you he had arrived," the girl—Livvie—whispered. She peeked out past Verity's shoulder.

"I know," Verity said tightly.

"I . . . Do you intend to introduce us?"

So temerity ran between them, then.

Verity opened her mouth to speak.

Turning his gun, with the barrel toward the floor, Malcom returned it to the waistband of his trousers and dropped a bow. "Miss Lovelace, I gather?" he murmured, and two sets of near-identical eyes went to him. "Or rather, my sister-in-law?" He cast a jeering glance over the top of the girl's head to her furiously blushing sister.

The girl was either too innocent or too oblivious to note the mocking edge in his tone. She offered a hesitant curtsy.

"I've heard so very much about you, Miss Lovelace."

The younger Miss Lovelace widened her eyes. "You've spoken about me with Verity?"

Said sister closed the remaining distance between her and the girl. Verity's frantic movements sent the towel she wore about her slender frame gaping. "Livvie," Verity began warningly.

"Oh, indeed," Malcom continued on over her. "She spoke of the great sacrifice you made, giving over your slippers." If looks could slay, he'd have been split in half from the one being cast by his *wife*.

Darting out from behind her sister, Livvie Lovelace skipped over to Malcom. "My sister has spoken of you often, too."

His intrigue doubled. "Indeed?" he drawled, shooting another look over at the thorn in his side. "All wonderful, loving things, I take it, *wife*?"

Verity gnashed her teeth hard enough that the grinding punctuated the quiet.

"She spoke about how you rescued her." Saved the foolish chit who'd taken her life into her hands, navigating an underground hell that only devils like Malcom managed to survive in. A wistful, far-off glimmer lit the girl's eyes. "I told Verity she should come to you and try once more to sway you."

That struck somewhere in his chest, an uncomfortable pain that proved him . . . human. Her sister had put her up to it.

Then, contrary to his own inner tumult, a wide smile wreathed the younger Miss Lovelace's plump cheeks. "And look! Because of my guidance, you and Verity are now happily married."

"Happily married," he echoed. This time, he favored his fictional wife with a mocking look. "The happiest, are we not, love?"

If Verity's cheeks went any redder, she was going to catch fire. "Livvie, we'll continue introductions later," Verity snapped.

Hurt instantly flooded the young woman's face, revealing eyes that displayed a child's innocence that had no place in the streets where Malcom had grown up.

And it left him more rattled than the many times he'd had a blade turned on him in the London sewers and streets.

"Very well." Livvie gave a toss of her head. "I trust you both have much to say after your time apart."

Oh, he had much to say to the chit, indeed. Even so, he wasn't so much a monster that he'd deliberately scare a child. He dropped a short bow. "A pleasure, Miss Lovelace."

Verity's sister started. Surprise rounded her eyes. "Did you see that, Verity?" She giggled. "He bowed to me like I'm a lady."

"I saw, Livvie."

At his back, Verity's gaze bored into him.

Aye, the chit was wary enough, however, to expect he was that beast. But not sufficiently fearful that she'd not cross him. Again and again.

"My lord," her sister murmured, dropping her head.

When the girl had gone, Verity held her towel in place with one hand and turned the lock with the other. The makeshift covering draped over her frame placed her shapely legs on display. And yet, where there'd been a rash explosion of unwanted desire whenever he was near Miss Verity Lovelace, staring at the young woman with her back to him and shoulders slightly hunched painted her in a vulnerable light. And it killed any previous stirrings of lust.

She cleared her throat. "That is my sister," she said, directing that admission at the bronze hardware of the doorway. "As you obviously gathered."

"Aye." The sister with the slippers and in possession of blonde curls and fulsome cheeks, she couldn't be more than sixteen or seventeen. A mere girl. One who he'd previously taken as a fictional sibling created by Verity in order to rouse sympathies. However, that sister had proven real, lending credence to Verity's claims that she'd braved his presence and wrath for her. And he didn't want that to matter. It was, simply put, easier to accept that everything had been a lie, and Verity's motives ruthless.

Turning to face him, Verity fiddled with the towel.

"I expect you thought I made her up?" she ventured, accurately and eerily following his unspoken musings.

"Aye." She'd given him little reason to trust her and every reason to doubt.

"Thank you for not being rude to her."

He stiffened. That expression of gratitude struck like an insult she hadn't intended. It found its mark, unerringly. "I'm only a monster to those deserving of my wrath," he said coolly.

Her bare toes curled into the floor. "Fair enough."

"I see you've filled her head with the same romantic drivel you've written in the papers."

"I haven't filled her head with anything. She's simply artless." In other words, her sister's grasp on innocence was fleeting. Verity knew that. Accepted it, and still was hell-bent on preserving it anyway.

Had there ever been anyone like that in Malcom's own life? Had there ever been anyone who'd cared about him above everyone and everything . . . ?

You're going to get well, my boy. We are nothing without y—

That distant voice faded into a cough so real he could hear it in this very room. Malcom didn't move for several seconds. Or did minutes pass? When he opened his eyes, he found Verity's wary gaze still upon him. She was safer. This, his deserved outrage, and not some obscure memories that might be nothing more than conjurings in his own head. He took a step toward Verity to better search her for shades of truth and lies. He'd fallen prey to this woman before. The candles flickered, casting her face in shadow. "And I take it you've shielded Miss Lovelace from the harsh realities of the world?"

Verity's jaw tensed. "As best as I've been able."

With that grudging admission, she proved yet again that she'd acted not for ruthless gains—at least, not solely. Unnerved, Malcom gave her his back and wandered around the fine chambers. The fine rooms she'd commandeered. It'd been far easier to storm here with the threat of Newgate and retribution when she'd been a ruthless schemer. It was altogether different, knowing she'd acted on behalf of another—the sister whose identity she'd spoken of since their first meeting in the sewers.

How she lived her life, for another person, was as foreign to him as circling another planet. "You're not unlike her, though, are you?" he murmured. Completing his turn about the rooms, he positioned himself at the center. "Romanticizing my actions in the streets that night."

"I didn't romanticize them, Malcom. I wrote one article," she said tersely. "One piece that conveyed the truth of how you treated me that night." She smiled sadly. "You might take offense to my having written about you, but the facts remain: You did save me. You did provide me new slippers and a dress, and you did see me safely home."

He stiffened.

"Yes, I knew that," she said quietly, holding his gaze with her own.

She'd known that he'd followed her to see no harm befell her on her return journey through St. Giles, and yet she'd not printed that in her damned gossip column. *Why?*

"Everything I wrote about our first meeting was all true. The fanciful musings my sister has of what we . . . are . . . or shared . . . are ones that she created in her own mind."

Just as Polite Society had. For the world saw that which it wished, because they all wished to read a story of make-believe rather than see the rot that truly clung to a person's soul.

"I . . . suppose you wonder how I've come to be here," she murmured, bringing him back to the moment. Verity stared down at her endearing pink toes. "In your household," she added as if any clarification were needed.

"No," he said flatly. He didn't want to know those details, the ones that undoubtedly bespoke desperation and threatened his resolve. Nor did he want any further stories about her sister. He also knew that Bram and Fowler were responsible for allowing her entry. The damned traitors. "I don't wonder anything about you."

She elucidated anyway. "I happened to see your address and knew that you'd sacked your servants, and trusted the residence was empty. What harm would there be in staying, then?"

And as she spoke, it didn't escape his notice that she never mentioned Fowler or Bram. And resentment for the woman aside, he admired that loyalty. She didn't explicitly or implicitly state that the old codgers had let her in and given her shelter. A fact he'd confirmed the moment he arrived . . . to a pair of toshers who'd been wholly unapologetic and put out with Malcom. *With Malcom.*

"Except you didn't sack them, though." Her eyes softened, and she drifted closer. "You care about them, after all."

Oh, good God. He resisted the urge to yank at his collar. "No, Verity," he repeated. "I don't care why you've come to be here. I don't care about the servants, or anyone."

"I . . . see."

How was it possible for her two words to make a liar of him?

"There is, however, one question I do have . . ." Malcom caught his chin in his hand. "What to do with you?" He resumed another circle . . . only this one about the minx who'd single-handedly slayed his previously safe existence. "What to do with you?" he repeated.

Verity stiffened and notched her chin up a defiant fraction.

Did she believe he taunted her?

Ironically, eyeing the young woman, this proved a time when Malcom hadn't a bloody clue what he intended to do with her.

The immediate and obvious answer should be to turn her over to the constables. Let the law deal with her and be done with the termagant who continually popped up in search of his secrets.

Only he couldn't. To admit as much, though, would mark him continually weak where Verity Lovelace and all her antics were concerned. For some unexplainable reason, even if it would mean he was done with her and her interfering, he could not have that freedom attained with her at the end of a hangman's noose. And those reasons extended far beyond the doe-eyed sister who'd be left to fend on her own in these savage streets.

Malcom abruptly stopped and faced Verity.

Bloody hell. He hadn't a damned clue.

Verity lifted her right hand and waggled her fingers slowly, like an eager student currying favor with the instructor. "If I may?" she ventured. "You could provide me with the story I seek?"

A sharp bark of laughter burst from him. "God, you're mad."

"Then I'd be gone." She snapped her fingers. "On my way." When he remained motionless, she frowned and let her arm fall to her side. "It was an idea."

Aye, it was one at that. A bloody rotted one. "Tell me, what would I get out of that deal, *hmm?*" Nothing, was the immediate and *correct* answer. No good could come from revealing any part of how he'd lived these years. All that information would invariably trickle down from the *ton* to the dregs of East London, who'd in turn use that knowledge against him. Or they would try to anyway. "You'd have your story." He caught her damp plait between his fingers, and rubbed those silken strands. "And I . . ." His was a bid to taunt her, and yet once again, he only proved tempted by the siren. Her hair contained the richest shades of auburn and chestnut and chocolate. "And I . . ." Once again he became entranced by those silken strands, tresses that were kissed by every blend of brown.

"Th-there can be some good in that," she murmured, her usual singsong voice husky . . . *Good in what?* What was she saying? It was all mixed up in his mind. "Sometimes," she went on, "there is good in confronting one's past, Malcom."

And then it hit him, exactly what she was saying. What she even now suggested. By God, did she take him for a fool? That pull was shattered. He released her. "And how do you figure that, Verity?" At best all he possessed were distant memories so murky they may as well have belonged to another.

"Because it might prove healing."

"Do not make this about me, Miss Lovelace." He hissed out her name.

She recoiled but did not back down.

"Do not pretend that you in any way care about my past or any part of me beyond how it serves you. If I let you write your column, the *ton* would continue to eat up the shite drivel that makes them feel better about a man who's inherited a title in their ranks. I'll end up with another stream of desperate ladies and their equally desperate fathers, who'd sell me their offspring as easily as a whore sells herself in St. Giles." In that there was no disparity between the elite and the people under them. The parade of visitors he'd received since Verity had outed his whereabouts was proof enough of that. That reminder lit the wick of his fury once more. "No, there is nothing you can do for—"

Except . . .

"What is it?" she asked quietly.

220

Ignoring her, Malcom turned his back and let the idea fully flesh itself out in his mind.

She sought her position with *The Londoner*.

He wanted nothing more than to be left alone by the peers seeking him out as a potential match to their bankrupt families.

It was madness, and yet . . . Verity Lovelace, the woman who'd made him a mark amongst the peerage, ironically represented his path to freedom. Malcom turned back to face her. "I'll agree to your story."

Her eyes glowed, radiating a hope and brightness so mesmerizing he briefly looked away, steeling himself against its power. As soon as he returned his gaze to hers, a prudent degree of wariness had replaced that earlier light. "You wouldn't simply do this from the goodness of your heart."

"Nay." Darkness or goodness was neither here nor there. He'd no heart. He never had. "I wouldn't, Verity," he murmured, stalking a circle around her nearly naked frame.

More than a foot shorter than Malcom, the minx comported herself as though she were an equal in height and strength. And mayhap she was the latter. "Just what would you expect in return, Lord Maxwell?"

She expected an indecent offer. It was the correct supposition any woman born outside the ranks of the nobility would make. And it spurred those earliest questions he'd carried about Verity Lovelace and her past. "Marriage."

A lone early-summer wind whistling outside was the only sound.

"Marriage?" she echoed dumbly.

"A union between us, Verity. Husband and wife. Earl and countess."

She backed away from him, and continued retreating until she had the porcelain bath between them. "*You're* the one who is mad."

"Ah, but then, I'm not the one who risked life and limb by passing myself off as nobility, and invaded a Grosvenor Square townhouse," he gleefully reminded her.

The color leached from her cheeks. And then she bolted. He tensed, prepared for her to bolt past him, making a beeline for the door. Except her flight didn't take her to the door. Of course it didn't. Clutching her towel close, she swiped a night wrapper from the vanity and raced across the plush Aubusson carpet. She disappeared behind a French screen. There was a soft flutter of the towel falling, and a rustle of fabric. A moment later, she emerged in a modest white cotton wrapper.

"Good God, what is that?"

She followed his horrified stare. "It is a nightgown and wrapper."

He snorted. "It's nothing of the sort." With a high neckline, heavily adorned with ornate lace and flounced sleeves, the young woman couldn't be any more covered up than had she been wearing a gown and cloak, and yet, with her toes peeking out, there was something entrancing in the ruffled display of innocence. He'd sooner cut his tongue out than admit as much.

Verity drew the belt at her waist tighter. "Given the circumstances, I trust what I'm wearing doesn't truly matter."

"Aside from the fact that you stole it," he drolly reminded her.

"Er . . . uh . . . yes. Aside from that."

"You've robbed much from me, Verity, and I'd have something in return. It seems a fair price, does it not?"

She wetted her lips. And he waited with bated breath for her to throw Bram and Fowler under the proverbial carriage. Yet she continued to remain steadfast, claiming ownership of her decision. "Marriage," she repeated as if tasting the sound and feel of that word on her tongue.

And by the paroxysm of revulsion, the minx felt the same way he did about the state. Malcom drew the moment on, taking a savage delight in her horror.

Verity drew a deep breath, and swiftly exhaled her words. "You'll gift me the story in exchange for marriage."

"Of a sort." Malcom wandered over to the vanity the young woman had made her own. "All these comforts you've enjoyed. The bedding."

As he spoke, he gestured to the respective items in question. "The bath." He picked up an enameled looking glass. "The—" His gaze locked on the gold rose at the top of the soft-green, painted piece. A buzzing swarmed in his ears. A tinkling song played, tinny in his head. Malcom twisted the loose rose until it could not be tightened any further. The clever mechanical opened, springing forth a songbird.

Hmm-mmm—hm-mm—Dadadadadad—

You look like a princess.

If I am a princess, you shall be my prince. Now shall we dance, Percy?

Laughter echoed in the halls of his memory, rusty from the cobwebs of time. A child's high-pitched squeals and the brighter, fulsome, joyous expression belonging to a woman.

The mirror slipped from his grip; the ornate piece fell with a loud clatter and crack as the glass shattered. That tinny, discordant tune continued playing.

Gentle fingers touched his sleeve.

Rasping, Malcom shot a hand out, capturing that wrist, squeezing. "Malcom." Verity's pained whisper shattered the disjointed memory.

Verity.

A woman in the here and now.

Safe, and yet, dangerous for what she'd visited upon him, and what she continued to force upon him. But still far safer than the demons that lurked in his mind.

"Are you all right?" she whispered with such gentleness, he cringed.

Malcom abruptly released her, and his fingers clenched and unclenched into reflexive balls. Her astute gaze that missed nothing went to those shaking digits. He swiftly clasped them behind his back to hide that mark of his vulnerability. "Forgive me," he said sharply, exhaustion having made a muddle of whatever they'd been discussing. He searched his dulled mind, struggling to bring clarity of thought through the pounding at his temples.

Think. Think.

What was she doing here? What was *he* doing here?

And then it all came rushing back in a whir, crashing through the noise of jumbled memories. "Because of you, I'm being hunted."

Her high, noble brow creased. "Hunted by—"

"The peerage. Wastrels who've lost all at gaming tables and are in need of a fortune. They're thrusting their daughters at me." He lifted his chin in her direction. "All a credit to you, Verity."

"Oh." That single syllable emerged sheepish. "And so you wish to marry me so you needn't deal with a proper wife."

"It's all really quite simple, you see. I've no wish for"—he tossed his arms wide—"any of this."

Her eyes took in the expanse of the room.

"I want to live my life unfettered in East London." Where it was safe and comfortable and a world which he knew. Or the way it had been before his identity had been discovered and his existence thrown off-kilter. "I don't want to be bothered with title-seeking ladies and their fathers who would whore them out. I don't want the servants and the fine things." Malcom let his arms fall to his sides. "I don't want any of it."

Verity tugged her already impossibly tightly closed wrapper all the closer. "I'm afraid I do not follow, my—Malcom . . ."

"I wish for a marriage as real as the one you've created for us," he said flatly. "Temporarily. We present ourselves as the Earl and Countess of Maxwell."

"What?" she squawked, loosing that grip she'd had on her night wrapper, and the fabric gaped slightly.

It took a forcible effort to tear his gaze from that hint of generous flesh exposed. He took a step toward her. "In this arrangement I'm prepared to give you everything you desire . . . and more: your story." As he was able to tell it. Which was largely not at all.

She gasped. "You'd do that?" Then suspicion immediately darkened her eyes.

"During the course of our arrangement, you'll have the opportunity to live here with a roof over you and your sister's head. Full bellies. Fine garments. Security." He let that last word hang on the air as the gift it was.

He'd presented her with a mutually beneficial relationship that any struggling woman of their ranks would have leapt at.

She hugged her arms to her waist. "And then what happens afterward?" That question revealed Verity Lovelace to be a woman all too familiar with the precariousness of life.

His chest squeezed. Damn her for making him care.

"Why, we go our own ways as any proper lord and lady would. Society would expect nothing less of an earl and countess. My story, when sold, will bring you coin enough to keep you comfortable until you find yourself some other work, somewhere far away from"—*me*— "London." Then he wouldn't have to again think of all the ways in which he'd been played the fool by Verity Lovelace.

Her face fell. "I can't leave London. All the major newspapers are here."

Malcom dropped his hip on the back of the sofa. "Then it seems we are at an impasse, because the moment it was discovered the Countess of Maxwell was employed by some ragtag gossip column, questions would swirl. And then research would be conducted into our marriage. Whereas if it is understood you prefer the country, no one will give you"—and more importantly—"or me another thought."

"You've thought of everything."

He tried—and failed—to make something out of that quiet utterance.

Verity glanced past his shoulder, not meeting his eyes. "Why would you go through all of this?" Her voice faintly quivered.

"I get, simply put, the only thing I desire—my freedom. The ability to return to St. Giles and live there without intrusion."

Verity didn't say anything for several moments as she hugged herself in another lonely little embrace. "Can I ask you a question?"

"I suspect regardless of my answer you'd ask it anyway."

"Why would you want to return to the rookeries? Why would you want to face the threats that go with living there and doing what you do?"

It wasn't her business. She didn't deserve any more from him than she'd already taken, and yet for some reason, it was important that she understood. "Why do you write?"

She cocked her head.

Malcom motioned to that worn satchel that she'd stormed his home with weeks earlier. "There are other things you might do in the name of survival. Why choose writing for some newspaper?"

Verity thought for a moment. "It is what I know."

"Is it what you love or what you know?"

"Both," she said automatically. "I didn't always write for *The Londoner*, but I always wanted to. There is something freeing in the work I do. It's honest. It challenges me in ways that other, equally honest work wouldn't."

"And that is why I'm a tosher. That is why I've no interest in a fortune I didn't build from a family I don't even remember. I've built my existence with my bare hands." He turned his palms up. "Wading through muck and waste is eternally less glamorous than holding a fancy title, and yet there, I've been the master of my destiny." When there'd been none to save him, he'd saved himself.

Her eyes softened. "I see."

And he resisted the urge to shift because he saw that truth in her eyes.

Verity brought them back to the proposal at hand. "And my being banished from London. This would be—"

"Forever." He brought his lips up in a coldly mocking smile. "Given that you'd be trading a prison sentence in Newgate for an assignment in Grosvenor Square, I don't see there's much for you to consider."

She held his gaze. "What of my work?"

"What of it?"

"If I agree to your terms, I'd want to continue writing for *The Londoner* or any paper that would have my articles."

Articles that would be about him.

"They wouldn't all be about you. I would, however, exchange that story for employment, which I'd keep as long as we're together."

Regardless of the nightmare she'd made of his life, he admired the young woman's spunk. Verity Lovelace had to be the only woman in the realm who was looking her future, fortune, and title—albeit a false one—square between the eyes, and only asked after her job. Malcom shrugged. "As long as we're together, I don't care what work you do."

Wordlessly, she wandered over to the spot he'd quit at the vanity. Falling to a knee, she studied the remnants of that enamel mirror. Ever so carefully, she picked up shard after shard, dropping them into a neat little pile. Performing the work of a servant as though she'd been born to the role. And yet her language, the way she carried herself, everything about her, screamed of one who'd been born to an elevated rank.

Who was she . . . Miss Verity Lovelace? Who was she really?

And why do I have the hungering to have those questions about the young woman answered?

She abruptly stopped that distracted cleaning. "How long would our partnership be in effect?"

What in hell would be sufficient to satisfy the *ton*? "This is your world. What would you advise?"

"It is not my world," she said automatically. "I merely write of it."

"A year, then."

"A year," she cried out. "But . . ."

"The end of the Season is approaching, and then, come the next Season, there'll be too many questions if my new wife has suddenly gone missing."

She chewed at her lower lip. "If I do this, time will be carved out each day when I interview you." And now she would set terms of her own. "I get my story, Malcom."

"You get your story." And he would get back his freedom.

Verity took several jerky steps toward the door. As if to flee. As if to escape. And then she shifted course and headed for the window. Drawing the gold velvet curtain back, she peered out at the street below. That glass panel reflected every troubled plane of her expressive face. Unaware as she was of the vulnerable display that window made of her, she proved, for all his suspicions of her, just how lacking in artifice she, in fact, was. "And . . . will there be other requirements for me?" she murmured, her voice threadbare. "Carnal ones?"

Carnal ones? He repressed the grin pulling at his lips. "No, Verity. I'll not make love to you"—he layered a deliberate pause into his words—"unless you ask me to." In which case, he'd happily make love to her. He'd set out to tease, and yet a tantalizing image presented itself: Verity at the center of the enormous bed that was even now turned down. Verity, with her arms outstretched, reaching for him as she parted her legs and moaned his name.

He struggled to maintain an even breath.

"I wouldn't . . . ask you, that is. To . . . to . . ." Her toes curled into the carpet, scrunching the fabric and leaving little indentations upon it. "To do that," she finished weakly. "What else would be required of me while we are together?"

"To maintain a proper facade of husband and wife."

"Presenting ourselves before Polite Society."

Did she seek clarification or to talk herself into that task? Malcom himself would rather face a firing squad, and by the greyish-white pallor of her skin, this proved one area where they were remarkably the same. "Aye." This, however, would spare him from any more interested, potential fathers-in-law. "Those details you would be responsible for working out." He knew few of the secrets Verity Lovelace carried, but he'd wager his own life that she'd gleaned how the *ton* lived.

Verity dropped her gaze out the window once more.

And as he stood there, he had the niggling feeling that she'd say no. And he didn't know what in hell he'd do if she did. Because he couldn't turn her over to the law, even if the termagant had betrayed him and stolen from him. Her spirit didn't deserve to be crushed in Newgate. "What will it be, Verity?" he asked impatiently.

The young woman faced him. Fear and fury mixed in her eyes in an exquisite blending. Had he really found her ordinary at their first meeting? She was an entrancing specimen of courage and strength. "Very well," she said quietly. "I'll agree to your terms, Malcom."

He schooled his features to keep from revealing his shock. Sweeping his arms wide, he made her a mocking bow. "Then I shall leave you to your own. Until tomorrow morning, *wife*."

With that, he took his leave, unable to shake the feeling that the Devil was, in fact, female, and Malcom had unwittingly shaken hands in an agreement that could never end well for him.

Chapter 18

THE LONDON GAZETTE
RECENTLY MARRIED!

With the Lost Earl having wed, Polite Society is left now
with questions not only about the gentleman himself
but also about the woman he's taken as his wife . . .

E. Daubin

"You are cracked in the head."

Aye, sometime between the moment Malcom had left Verity's
rooms and a long, sleepless night, Verity had come to the *same* conclusion as her childhood nursemaid. Either way, it still couldn't be spoken
aloud. Any of this. "Hush."

"I won't," Bertha said. Roughly turning Verity by the shoulders,
she set to work slipping the pearl buttons into their respective hooks.
"What have you gone and agreed to?"

"A plan that will save us," Verity said tightly. Just as she'd been
responsible since she was a girl of twelve for the welfare of not only
a baby sister but also the older nursemaid who'd cared for that sister.
And yet, how easy it was for Bertha to call Verity out for the salvation
she'd grasped at.

"All you know of the man is that he's ruthless."

"I said hush," Verity whispered, looking pointedly at the doorway. Servants were always underfoot. Such knowledge came from the servants who'd been sources while she'd worked at *The Londoner*, as well as the short time she'd lived in Malcom's household. "And he's not . . . ruthless." She felt compelled to defend him. Because . . . it was true. He'd saved her before, and offered her security. And he'd vowed not to touch her . . . unless she wished it. *And you want him to touch you as he once did before . . .* "Not entirely ruthless," she muttered when Bertha forced her back around to meet her gaze.

"You'd romanticize what he's done?" Verity may as well have sprouted a second head for the way her former nursemaid eyed her. And using the same charges that Malcom had leveled at her. "He's threatened you at every turn, and now of a sudden you trust his word. Turn," she muttered, guiding Verity about once more. She slid the last button into place.

Fully dressed, Verity faced her protective nursemaid. "What other choice do we have?" she demanded, and displeasure tensed the older woman's mouth. "I'll tell you the answer to that: none. The answer is none. We've no home, no employment, barely any funds. Now we do."

"For how long?"

"It is for a year." Verity took Bertha by the arms and lightly squeezed. "A year of us not worrying about where we'll go or what we'll eat or wear. Think of it, Bertha." She spoke in cajoling tones.

"You made a deal with the Devil, gel," Bertha said, unmoved.

Aye, that was *also* true. "At least we'll not perish on the streets or end up in Newgate." With that reminder, she let her arms fall.

"We wouldn't have ended up in Newgate if you hadn't concocted a plan to pass yourself off as some nobleman's wife."

Blast Bertha for always being correct. "Regardless of the decisions I should or should not have made, it's done. He made the offer; I agreed." Stalking over to the pine double-door armoire, she clasped the heart-shaped handle and whipped it open. The row of bows and bon-nets hanging from hooks along the front panel shook. Verity grabbed the first bonnet her fingers touched, an intricately woven article with a distinct brim and a wreath of pale-pink primroses circling the crown.

"And what happens when you want to get out from under this life, Verity?" Bertha asked quietly, and Verity froze with the pronounced brim clenched in her fingers, the bonnet hovering just above her head.

Get out from under this life . . .

The other woman spoke of Verity one day tiring of the arrange-ment, as though it was a certainty. "It is just a year." And yet Verity had toiled for eighteen. She'd worked until her fingers had bled, and risen before the roosters. Now she'd be permitted to seek out employment as a reporter without the pressure of each story she penned being all that put food on her table and a roof over their heads. "This is the best I have to hope for," she finally said, jamming her bonnet on.

"Here," Bertha muttered, and coming over, she took the long pep-permint-striped ribbons and set to tying them. When she'd finished, she adjusted the neat bow under Verity's chin. "I don't want to see you hurt."

Like your mother.

It whispered in the air, not even needing to be spoken aloud.

"I'm not my mother." In love at seventeen with a roguish earl, she'd given up all hope of respectability and a secure life. "I'm thirty years old."

Bertha smiled sadly at her. "Age doesn't make a woman immune from heartbreak, gel."

Heartbreak? "Heartbreak. Heartbreak?" she repeated incredulously. "That is your worry, Bertha?" Verity had learned at her mother's knee the folly in trusting one's heart to the worst possible person. And there could be no doubting that as merciless, unbending, and dangerous as he was, the Earl of Maxwell was nothing if not the worst possible man a woman might entrust her heart to. "I assure you, I've no intention of having my heart broken over or by Malcom North." Malcom North, who looked at her as if she were the grime in the sewers he traveled nightly. Even as he set her heart racing whenever he was near. Even as she still found herself dreaming of the two moments he'd taken her in his arms and kissed her senseless.

"Aye, and that is the look that tells me I'd be mad to not be afeard for you, Verity."

At the old woman's ominous warning, shivers traipsed along her spine. "I'm going to be fine. Better than fine." She made her lips curve into a smile as she patted her former nursemaid's hand. "More than a year with nothing to worry after? It is a gift, Bertha. *Enjoy it.*"

Only, as she gathered up her satchel and started from the room, she could not shake the feeling that those false assurances had been as much for her as for Bertha.

With the nursemaid's warnings ringing in her head, Verity set out in search of her husband. Since she'd first met Malcom in the sewers, she'd faced his deserved suspicion and anger. Was such a man even capable of the pretense of a doting, madly-in-love spouse? Was she even capable of it?

A pair of maids were hurrying down the hall, and then stopped in their tracks the moment they spied her to dip matching curtsies. "My lady," they said as one.

Verity glanced about for the "my lady" in question before registering that they spoke to her. It was a foreign state she'd never become accustomed to. And one, for the deal she'd struck with Malcom, she'd be required to. At that reminder of her husband, she cleared her throat. "Do either of you happen to know where I might find Ma . . . my husband?" she amended. Nay, it would never feel right, referring to him in that light.

"'e's in his office, my lady." The youngest girl, Billy, tacked a curtsy on to her pronouncement. Girls younger than Livvie, who now had employment once more because Malcom had reflected on his decision to sack them. And one who spoke in street-roughened tones. Malcom had not only rehired back the staff he'd sacked but also given opportunities to a girl who'd been without.

"My lady?" Deborah ventured hesitantly. "Is there anything else you require?"

Verity started. "No. No. Nothing else." With a word of thanks, Verity wound her way through the halls, down the intricately woven Axminster carpets, the grandeur of the mosaic design so glorious in its detail and beauty, Verity found herself tiptoeing over the pale-pink and yellow floral pattern.

She reached the hall leading to Malcom's office . . . and then stopped.

How was she going to go through with this? Unlike her mother, who'd managed to smile in front of the earl when her heart had been breaking at the life she'd never have, Verity hadn't been one to dissemble. She'd been one to speak her mind and reveal precisely how she was feeling.

And then, to have to put on a show with Malcom.

Malcom, who now hated her.

If he'd ever even liked her.

Her heart pulled.

For there had been moments where he'd seemed to like her enough: when he'd scooped her up and dashed through London to keep them both safe. When he'd swindled her in a game of chess.

Except those moments didn't mean that he cared about her. They'd merely been a window into the fact that he, for all his gruff and hard edges and contrary nature, was, deep down, genuinely an honorable man.

"Something wrong with yar legs now?"

Verity jumped, and spun to face Bram. She found her first smile that day. "Bram," she greeted. The old tosher limped over, and she hurried the remainder of the way to save him walking the length of the long hall.

"Oi take it ya're meeting with North?" he asked when she reached his side.

"Aye." She slid a glance down the wide hall. "That is the plan." This time, Verity couldn't even manage a pretend smile. Aye, she was going to be rubbish at this arrangement, after all. "He's angry with me. With, of course, good reason," she said quickly. She was well deserving of his rage.

Bram lifted one large shoulder in a shrug. "'e lashes out to keep people out. Ya're no different from the rest of us. But 'e cares."

He cares.

Her heart did a funny jump in her chest. "Cares?"

Bram snorted. "About ya."

That organ in her chest did several more wild somersaults, and then promptly deflated. "He doesn't *care* about me. He hates me," she said softly. When their deal was up, he'd banish her from London just so he didn't have to share the same streets as her.

"He doesn't 'ate you. 'e's angry with ya. He's angry at all of us."

And guilt swarmed her. She'd come between Malcom and the small collection of people who mattered to him. "I'm so sorry if you've received his anger because of my actions."

He waved a bearlike palm. "Oi'm the one who gave you shelter. Fowler, too. Would do it again, too."

"Why?" she asked, unable to hold back the question she'd wanted to ask as to why he'd gone against his loyalty to Malcom and opened the townhouse to Verity and her family.

"Because Malcom brought you to his rooms that night, when he's never brought any person there before." It was the first time she'd ever heard anyone in Malcom's circle use his given name. A teasing glimmer lit his eyes. "And mayhap a little because you cured my eyes, and I'd hoped you could do the same for my leg." He winked. "Which ya did."

Laughing softly, Verity nudged him lightly with her shoulder.

And a ruddy blush splotched the old tosher's cheeks. "And mayhap also because ya didn't treat me as though Oi or Fowler were monsters just because of how we looked and where we lived. Now 'old yar 'ead up." Then the levity faded, and he was once more all seriousness. "Ya aren't right in mostly 'e's angry at himself because of all this." He gestured around the opulent corridor with satin wallpaper and gilt frames worth more than every most wonderful item she'd possessed in even her most prosperous days.

Going up on tiptoe, she kissed the old tosher on the cheek. "Thank you."

He swatted his palm about. "Get on with ya," he muttered and, not waiting about to see if she heeded his directives, took off quickly down the opposite hall.

Verity watched after him until he'd gone. Perhaps Bram and Fowler were correct. She and Malcom needn't be enemies. And more, mayhap they could even become . . . friends.

Friends, when he wouldn't so much as acknowledge that was precisely what the toshers who lived with him, in fact, were. What if she could make him see . . . ?

Hope filled her chest, and she resumed the same march she had earlier, before Bram's appearance.

When she reached Malcom's offices, all her courage deserted her.

"You can do this," she silently mouthed. Or . . . could she? This role she'd taken on, this agreement, was nothing but work. Of course, it was a different form of work than she'd been accustomed to over the years. Hers had been literary in nature; crafting words and shaping them into something people wished to read was what she knew. What she understood. Putting on a display of a besotted wife was a task better suited to a London stage actress.

Alas, she'd better perform this latest role. If she wished to stay living, and to see those she loved secure.

It was that reminder which gave her the courage to reach for the door handle.

Verity let herself inside. The well-oiled hinges of the door gave silently, and Verity remained unmoving at the entranceway of Malcom's Grosvenor Square offices. Malcom was there . . . but Malcom as she'd never seen him.

Unlike the past, where he'd been so attuned to her every movement that so much as lifting her slipper had earned his sharpened gaze, now he remained so wholly engrossed in the task before him that he displayed not so much as a hint of awareness that she'd entered.

Four neat piles of ledgers had been stacked high, forming a formidable barrier of those books. Malcom's head was bent over an opened one as his gaze scoured the pages, the speed with which he ran his eyes over the pages near superhuman in ability.

This side of him, with his guard down, was so unfamiliar. His unfashionably long hair had been drawn back in its familiar queue, and yet a lone strand fell over his brow. Periodically, he swatted at the piece, but remained riveted by whatever information was contained within that ledger. He'd the look of a child with a coveted book in hand, breathless with anticipation of what he'd find on the next pages.

Soft.

It was a word that could never be used to describe or define Malcom North. Or that is what she would have believed . . . before now. Those harsh features, typically set in an unforgiving mask, were devoid of their usual tension. When he worked, he creased his brow; four little lines furrowed there, in a way that made him . . . approachable and *real*.

And she found herself preferring this side of him. This real, unguarded version of Malcom North.

He stiffened, and it was the moment she knew he'd felt her presence there.

Malcom looked up, and then hurriedly slammed his book closed. "Verity," he greeted crisply.

Entering, she drew the door closed behind her, and joined him at the desk. She set her satchel down. "Malcom," she returned, loosening the strings of her bonnet. Suddenly not so very much in a rush to leave this place and seek out their first jaunt as a happily married couple.

"You didn't knock."

"Devoted husbands and wives don't have barriers between them."

"And you know so much about devoted husbands and wives?" he jeered.

He hated her. Her chest squeezed tight at the palpable loathing that rolled off him. Though in fairness, he hadn't even really liked her. It didn't matter what Bram wanted or thought was there. This was real. They'd merely been a pair united by danger in the streets that he'd provided Verity a safe haven from. *And you betrayed that by exposing his private life . . .*

"I don't," she acknowledged, removing her bonnet by its broad brim. She set the woven article down upon her lap. "Not firsthand, that is," she corrected. "I've written of . . . happy"—and unhappy—"spouses."

"Your gossip column." Derision continued to drip from his words.

Ignoring that bait, Verity caught the underside of her chair and dragged it closer to his desk. She studied the stacks of leather books lined up. What was he doing? Much like the ledgers that had filled his East London residence, here, too, there were neat stacks. Without thinking, Verity reached for one of them.

"What are you doing?"

Her hand hovered over the stack. "I'm sorry. I was . . ." Her lips pulled, and she shook her head.

Malcom rested his elbows on the edge of his desk and leaned forward. "Let us be clear, madam, as long as you are here—"

"Until the end of next Season."

"Until the end of next Season." He clipped out that echo. "You are not to avail yourself of anything unless I allow it. And you're certainly not to go through my belongings. While we are living together, as long as we are alone, we aren't going to put up some damned charade of a devoted, loving couple. We act the part when there are people about, but that is it."

Aye, he hated her, all right. With her newspaper article she had, without any input from the gentleman himself, opened Malcom in ways he hadn't wished to be before the world. As such, he was entitled to that rage, and she was deserving of that sentiment. Even knowing all that, she still had this urge to cry. Verity drew in a slow breath. "I know you don't like me."

He snorted.

"Hate me, even," she allowed, her heart pulling. How ironic that she'd made the decision she had as a matter of survival, and in the end, she'd earned his antipathy and hadn't even retained a job for that betrayal. "But servants are the eyes of a household, and if we're going to live together, with you *hating* me, no one will ever dare believe that charade. If the world is to believe our marriage was a love match, we have to play the part."

Malcom steepled long fingers, resting the bridge they formed upon his book, and smiled coldly. "And just what makes you think that ours need be passed off as a *love match*?"

Verity opened her mouth. No words came out. She tried again. "I . . . just assumed that would be easiest, to explain our hasty union."

"It doesn't matter what they believe or don't believe. Mayhap I wanted an heir. Mayhap I wanted a wife to oversee my properties when I go live my life. Perhaps we've had a falling-out."

Verity was already shaking her head. "The papers have already written of your rescue. They're going to be looking for signs of fissures. Of deception. They'll expect it of us." Certainly with Verity's origins . . .

"Us?"

Even as she'd built her life off words, the ease with which he wrapped a whole host of hatred and mockery around that one syllable still managed to stun her.

"You were . . . raised on the streets," she said needlessly. "I . . ." *I'm a bastard.* Her tongue grew thick in her mouth. It was only a matter of time before her own identity came to light. She'd long ago come to terms with who she was . . . what she was. But that had been different. That had been when she lived on the fringe of Polite Society, dipping her toes into their existence, solely for the purpose of earning a living. This? This would be different.

She was . . . what? This woman who'd deceived him, whom he'd entered into an agreement with, clung to her secrets with a greater tenacity than even Malcom himself.

She didn't want to share her history. And mayhap that was why he wished to know.

Liar. He'd been as eager for Verity Lovelace's secrets as she'd been for his. Only his motives had never been driven by anything but a need to know about her.

Which is what grates so much . . . , that voice jeered.

"And what of *you*, Verity?" Either way, turnabout was fair play.

"Me?" Her shoulders came up in a little shrug that another, less astute person might have taken for nonchalant. "What of me?" She was hedging. Searching for time, and her mind, for answers that would satisfy his curiosity.

Curiosity? He balked. It was more a need to know what there was about the woman he'd entered into a pretend lifelong arrangement with. Malcom brought his arms up and clasped them behind his head. "You expect me to lay myself out for you, then I should know *something* of the woman I'm married to."

She plucked at her skirts. Several moments passed before it became clear—she had no intention of saying anything else on the matter. In fact . . . saying *nothing* on the matter.

Malcom stood and circled the desk.

There was a mystery to the woman before him. And he yearned to draw forth the hidden details that made Verity Lovelace the woman she was. Malcom stopped behind her chair, and Verity stiffened. Lowering his head, he positioned his mouth close to the shell of her ear. She did not pull away. Her body only curved closer. "How . . . very interesting," he murmured. "Surely the woman determined to have me spill every part of my life that I've no wish to share would at the very least be equally forthright?"

An entrancing blush spilled over her décolletage and climbed to the long, graceful column of her neck. That damnable desire pulsed all the stronger. "It is . . . not at all the same."

Reaching around the back of her chair, Malcom rested his palms along its arms, and framed her. "Oh?" he whispered, so close that as he spoke, his lips brushed the curve of her ear in a fleeting kiss. One made all the more arousing for its evanescence. "And how is it different, Verity?"

Her breath caught. Or was that his? In this moment, it was all jumbled. "You never expressed a desire to know anything about me, Malcom. For you, my purpose being here, the role I serve . . . is singular. To fool. To deceive."

It was a fair rebuttal. And not even a day ago, she would have been correct. Some seismic shift, however, had occurred. One born of madness. One that required he know this woman he'd tied himself to in a devil's deal. He straightened. "Indulge me, then."

Standing, Verity grabbed her bag and strode around the chair with a strength the fiercest street warrior wouldn't have as effectively mustered. She stopped so abruptly her satchel was set to swinging at her side. "No."

That was . . . it? "No?"

"Aye." There was that natural, sultry husk to her reply. Slightly guttural in her acknowledgment. "That wasn't part of our arrangement."

Malcom ignored her latter words. "Aye," he repeated, a clue, and yet a mystery of Verity Lovelace's identity. "You've Scottish roots to you, Verity. Or Irish." There was no brogue, otherwise subtle or distinct.

She went close-lipped, and then: "My mum was Scottish. Her family owned a tavern in Fife, just between the Firth of Tay and the Firth of Forth, and my mum worked there." There was a finality to that admission, one that indicated that she intended to volunteer nothing more about herself.

"Scottish?" he repeated dumbly.

Verity's narrow shoulders drew back. "Aye. Is there a problem with that, my lord?"

Her question came as from a long tunnel, her clear English tones fading in and out of clarity, melding with another voice. A brogue that lilted, and a song that whispered forward.

GOOD lord of the land, will you stay thane
About my faither's house,
And walk into these gardines green,
In my arms I'll the embraice.

Ten thousand times I'll kiss thy face;
Make sport, and let's be mery:
I thank you, lady, fore your kindness;
Trust me, I may not stay with the.

For I have kil'd the laird Johnston . . .

A tentative palm touched his sleeve. "Malcom?"

It was, however, Verity's insistent question that brought him jolting back to the moment.

Malcom swiped the edge of his sleeve over the damning moisture that had beaded at his brow.

Those clever eyes took in all. "Are you all right?" she asked quietly.

Nay. "Fine." He was losing his damned mind, and he'd be damned if he did so before her.

"What of your father?" he urged, impatient to move them back to talk of her, and to draw himself out of the mire of his memory.

Verity drew her satchel close, the gesture a protective one. Her bag revealed watermarks upon the faded leather, and bits of the fabric having long peeled off. "My father was a man my mother was better off without," she finally settled for.

Malcom's stomach muscles tensed. She'd been hurt. Her pain didn't matter to him. Except if that was true, why did a bloodlust pump through his veins, along with a hungering to rip the entrails from the bastard's mouth? "He was cruel?"

Surprise lit her expressive features. "On the contrary. He was kind and loving. He was, however, not one meant for my mother." She briefly dipped her gaze to her bag. "He was an earl."

She'd been born the daughter of a nobleman. Even being illegitimate, with her regal bearing and grace, she was more of this world than Malcom had ever been.

Misunderstanding the reason for his silence, Verity's cheeks flushed. "I'm a bastard." Verity lifted her bold, unapologetic eyes to his in that show of spirit he so admired her for. "Therefore, if knowing that, you'd rather extricate yourself from our contract?"

He puzzled his brow. Extricate himself from their contract? *What . . . ?* And then it hit him. "You expect me to condemn you for your birthright," he murmured. It was there in the challenge that blazed in her eyes.

She shrugged. "You would not be the first. However, you will be expected to have a wife who is above reproach and—"

"I don't give a damn that you're a bastard, or what Polite Society expects or doesn't expect me to have."

Her lips parted. Her eyes softened. "Thank you," she said softly. So much adoration spilled from those expressive eyes, Malcom shifted on his feet. He didn't want her admiration or those damned doe eyes. Because, in short, he didn't know what in hell to do with all that emotion.

There was no place or room to let his guard down around the woman who'd pilfered his secrets and fed him to the members of both impolite and Polite Society as if his past and future were nothing more than a tasty morsel to be devoured.

That safe, burning anger stirred once more, kicking ash on any weakness about Verity Lovelace.

He was the one to break that connection. "Let us get on with it. What have you planned for us, madam?" he asked, returning them to the task at hand.

Verity reached inside the ridiculously ancient bag she carried about. "I've brainstormed a number of ideas," she explained, handing him a sheet.

"What is this?" He made no move to take it.

She waved it at him. "It is a list."

"And what do you have first at the top of it, madam?"

"Gunter's," she said, not missing a beat. Verity tucked her—their— plans back inside the satchel.

"Gunter's?" he repeated dumbly. That incessant throbbing in his head returned, and he fought the urge to jam his fingertips into his temples in a bid to rid himself of the sensation.

Verity looked up. "They sell ices. Lords and ladies sit in curricles outside. This way, we'll be on full disp—"

"I know what Gunter's is," he bit out.

"Unless you have another suggestion, *my lord*?" she asked in even tones that didn't fool him one damn.

He narrowed his eyes. The minx was "my lord-ing" him. She knew precisely what to do to get under his skin. "Very well. Let's get on with this." The sooner they deceived, the sooner he might continue on with his life, and she, hers.

"Of course," she murmured, and together in silence, they started from the rooms.

So they were doing this . . .

Chapter 19

THE LONDONER
SPOTTED!

The elusive Earl and Countess of Maxwell have been spied amongst Polite Society. Witnesses say there were many stretches of silence between them. All the *ton* is then left to wonder at the circumstances surrounding Lord Maxwell's marriage to the mystery woman. Extortion? Bribery? *Worse?*

M. Fairpoint

As a girl, Verity had heard tales of Gunter's. The stories had fallen from her father's lips as he'd regaled her with talk of London and all the places to see and all the things to do there. Peppered within each of those tales, there'd been the promise to one day take her there himself and allow her to try every flavor of ice.

Of course, as a small child, Verity had believed those promises. It hadn't been until the years dropped away that she'd learned her father would never bring her to Gunter's and all those wonderful places. That he'd never intended to, and all of it had been no different from the story he'd read to her from the fairy-tale book when he had come around.

As such, Verity had eventually come to accept that she'd never go to that illustrious place on Berkeley Square. Or taste those ices he'd spoken so excitedly of.

And yet, she was here now. Seated atop a curricle with a crystal glass of jasmine-rose ice, and she couldn't so much as muster a smile. All the muscles of her belly remained knotted and twisted. Survival had earned her immediate capitulation to Malcom's proposal. Now, the ramifications of living here, amongst her father's people . . . and his legitimate family? Verity clasped her hands tightly around her crystal cup.

I have every right to be here . . .

She may not wish to be here in this capacity, but she needn't be hidden away like a dirty secret. Why did it feel like she only sought to convince herself? Nor did it help matters that she was seated beside a man who despised her, and who hadn't uttered a single word to her since he'd all but tossed her atop the curricle.

"I'll have you know this is never going to work," Verity said from the side of her mouth.

For a long while she expected Malcom wouldn't even respond to that utterance. He scoured the streets, openly glaring at both onlookers and passersby. No one was spared his wrath. Not even her. *Especially* not her.

"What?"

"This." Careful to keep her palm low and out of visibility in the carriage, with her spare hand, Verity motioned between them. "*Us.* This ruse. None of it will ever work as long as you carry on as you are." The ease of their banter over chess was a distant memory made by two very different people, ones not divided over betrayal. A pang struck at that fleeting time she'd had with him. When they'd been two people hiding from a shared danger.

Suddenly, Malcom dropped an arm around her shoulders, wringing a gasp from her. "And tell me, dear heart, just how should I present myself?" he whispered against her ear. "Devoted? In love?"

Her body, traitor that it was, tingled where he held her. It knew nothing of pride, or of the mockery Malcom sought to make of her. "I'd settle for 'human,'" she muttered, and when faced with the option of her ice melting over the rim of her glass or taking a bite, Verity dipped her spoon and tasted the flowery-sweet confection. "You might at least smile."

"I don't smile," he said tersely. As if to accentuate that very point, Malcom glowered at a puce-clad dandy who stepped too close to the curricle.

The young man bolted off in the opposite direction with such alacrity his crimson silk Empire top hat tumbled to the ground. And the gentleman continued running, without so much as glancing back for the costly article.

Verity sighed. This was going to be a good deal harder than she'd anticipated.

"What *now*?" he demanded, that harsh question so hushed it barely reached her ears. At her side, Malcom tensed, his sinewy thighs tightening. The muslin fabric of her day dress did little to conceal the heat of him pressed against her. Or the weight of that heavily muscled limb.

Her breath quickened, and words escaped her. What had he said? It had been a question? Hadn't it? She took several frantic bites of her ice, shoveling the treat into her mouth. To keep from openly gazing at his splendid physique, impressively displayed within his tight-fitting black trousers and double-breasted coat.

"I suggest you say whatever it is you intend to say." His was a command that would never be confused for a question, and it also proved sobering, cutting across her pathetic musings of him.

"Actually, I do have something to say." *You're a damned fool . . . going weak-kneed over a man who despises you.* Who if he hadn't a need for her, would sooner turn her over to Newgate than talk to her . . . "You're not making any of this easy."

"And do you expect I should make it easy for you, Verity?"

She thought about that for a moment. "Well, no," she conceded. "But I'm not so much speaking of myself as you." Verity opened her mouth to explain when she caught a trio walking in neat precision, locked in step, with a bevy of maids following several paces behind.

Oh, blast and damn.

Sliding closer to Malcom, Verity slipped her arm through his, and favored him with her best I-adore-you-and-cannot-live-without-you expression.

"What in hell is *that?*"

Or her best *attempt* at an adoring smile.

"I'm besotted."

"You look foxed," he said bluntly.

Verity trilled a laugh and angled herself even closer to her make-believe husband. "Do you know who they are?" she whispered out the side of her mouth.

Had she not been studying him so closely, she'd have missed the slight shifting of his eyes over the top of her head to that trio who now lingered. "Should I?"

"The lovely one with dark hair is known as Queen Sarah. Also known as Lady Jersey," she murmured. "She is one of the patronesses of Almack's Assembly Rooms." Verity carefully positioned her spoon close to her mouth so her lips could not be read as she spoke. "One time, she denied entry to the Duke of Wellington himself because he arrived just seven minutes late."

"Horrific," he drawled.

"Hush." Except her heart thumped slowly in her chest. She preferred this version of Malcom. As he'd been in his East London residence, slightly droll, teasing. And not dripping with malice and loathing. "Well, the one to the left of her is another hostess of Almack's, Mrs. Drummond-Burrell. She is by far the greatest stickler." Verity stole a peek over at the trio, who gave no indication that they intended to leave. "And the other, that is Lady Cowper. Captain Gronow has called her the most popular of the hostesses."

"Should I be impressed?" His cool tones indicated anything but.

"Well, given that he landed himself in debtors' prison, many are of the opinion that his word is not . . ." Malcom gave her a look. "Oh," she blurted. "You were being sarcastic."

"Aye. I was being sarcastic."

Her cheeks warmed, and just then, the matrons unabashedly watching on erupted into a flurry of murmurs.

Undoubtedly they'd taken that blush for something more than the embarrassment it was.

"Be dismissive all you want, Malcom," she warned. "They are, however, the ones who will carry stories back to other members of the *ton*. Therefore, anything you . . . we . . . say or do is being observed and mentally recorded by them so they might in turn report to Polite Society." Scraping some of her ice onto the spoon, she held it to Malcom's lips.

"What are you—"

She shoved the small silver utensil inside, silencing the remainder of that question. Aye, he was terrible at this. "I'm being devoted."

"By f-feeding me?" he sputtered around the mouthful. "Give me that," he snapped, yanking the spoon from her fingers. "That's the act of a bloody nursemaid. Not a blasted spouse."

❧

Malcom had known at an early juncture in his life that he was going to hell.

No older than eight years, he'd followed an emaciated street urchin down an alley that had served as the boy's home. Malcom had nicked the smaller, younger child's sack of goods, the refuse from a bakery. He'd made off with it and ate heartily—a rarity in those darkest of days.

The next night, Malcom had come across that same lad, in that same alley, dead, his eyes sightless, pointed up toward the starless St. Giles sky. And not a wound upon him. Dead of hunger, and in the name of self-survival, Malcom had been the one to send the small stranger on to the hereafter.

Aye, as such, Malcom had known hell was the eternal fate one day awaiting him. He'd accepted it. At times, when the weight of life's struggles became insurmountable, he'd even welcomed it.

This, however? This was a special hell.

Attired in fine garments, out before Polite Society.

The Devil had a rich sense of humor, indeed.

He'd rather be wading through shite with an army of hungry rats bearing down on him than be where he was.

At least those discomforts and dangers were familiar. Ones he'd faced countless times, and survived to thrive from.

This? Being on display before fancily clad gents in ridiculously high hats and the ladies on their arms was a special kind of hell.

"It could always be worse," Verity whispered, unerringly following his thoughts. It was an uncanny ability she possessed, and proved continually unsettling.

"Oh, and just how do you figure that, *dear heart*?"

"Well, they could be seeking an audience with us," she rightly pointed out.

Malcom shuddered. "You are correct on that score."

She beamed, that luminescent smile wreathing her face, radiating her joy. His heart caught oddly in his chest. It was an all-too-foreign expression of unguarded emotion, and even as he should find himself only horrified by that candidness, he found himself . . . captivated against all his best judgment.

Her smile slipped. "What is it?"

"You smile like you mean it," he said flatly. And he didn't know what to do with or make of it . . .

Setting down her nearly empty cup of frozen ice, Verity dabbed at the corners of her lips. "And why shouldn't I?" With that, she closed her eyes and tipped her face up to the sun. Those rays bathed her cheeks in a soft glow, illuminating the details he'd not noted until now: a dusting of freckles along the sides of her nose. A cream-white quality of skin so soft to the touch that his fingers twitched with the desire to explore it once more . . . as he'd done a fortnight ago.

Resisting her quixotic pull, Malcom nudged her foot with his. Her already-wide violet eyes went all the rounder. "You find nothing disconcerting in this." He gave a discreet wave of his hand, gesturing out to the opposite end of the lake, where morning visitors to the park guided their curricles about.

"Oh, on the contrary." Verity gathered up her parasol from the bench. "I find *everything* disconcerting in it." Snapping open the frilly article, she angled it, putting up that slight barrier as though they were two lovers who sought to steal a moment of privacy from society's prying eyes. "I no more wish to be here than you. And yet . . . for the first time in more years than I can remember, I have no worries about where I'll live or whether there's enough food. Even this . . ." She tipped her parasol back so the sun's rays bathed their faces, and her eyes slid closed. "I've not had the freedom to so much as feel the sun on my face in the middle of a spring day."

Neither had Malcom, and yet, his had been a decision bred of preference. Verity's had been a product of the work she'd had to do. The same need for work that found her in a deal with his own devilish self. He forced his gaze away from her face, looking out, unwilling . . . and unable to meet her eyes. Because he didn't want to think of how Verity Lovelace's ruthless pursuit of him had been an act born of desperation. How there had been . . . was still, in fact, a younger sister with innocent eyes, a smaller, younger version of the woman who now sat before him. Because Malcom didn't want it to matter.

He didn't want *her* to matter, in any way. Unnerved, he settled his gaze on the crowded Berkeley Square streets.

"You should eat it."

He blinked slowly.

Verity motioned to the crystal glass of untouched ice. "If for no other reasons than because: one, you won't have to talk to me, and two, our terseness might be passed off as your enjoyment of the sweet treat." Her eyes twinkled. "And because you're very close to ending up with sticky fingers."

On perfect cue, a drop slipped down the rim of the clear glass, and landed on his knuckle.

Malcom cursed.

Leaning forward, she spoke in a conspiratorial whisper. "I told you." She winked, and then tugging free the monogrammed kerchief from his jacket pocket, she proceeded to wipe off the melted ice.

With her head bent to that task, Malcom stared on, unable to look away from her . . . or the task she completed. When was the last time anyone had ever undertaken such a small but tender gesture where he was concerned? For that matter, when was the first time? *Had* there been a first time? People knew better than to approach him, let alone touch him. There'd been whores he'd bedded, but their every action had been purposeful, driven by sex and devoid of tenderness.

"There," Verity said, and with a pleased little nod, she turned over his kerchief.

Reflexively, Malcom accepted back that scrap of cloth, and his gaze went to the gold letters embroidered upon the fabric. He ran the callused pad of his thumb over the TP EARL OF M emblazoned there.

Initials that belonged to another. The man who'd served in the role of earl for these past years. A man he'd never met, but who'd profited from Malcom's absence these past years. And according to Steele, the loss of parents that Malcom had no recollection of. Unbidden, his gaze drifted over the heads of those nosy biddies to the front facade of 7–8 Berkeley Square.

"You remembered Gunter's."

"Hmm?" It took a moment for that question to penetrate that all-too-familiar haze.

Only it hadn't been a question. Verity stared back with a solemnness to her eyes that revealed too much of her thoughts.

"Aye," he said gruffly.

"Did you . . . come as a child?"

Several drops of orange ice splashed the top of his hand, the moisture cool. He stared blankly down at them, more coward than he'd ever credited before this, because he couldn't meet Verity's eyes. "I don't know."

There it was . . . the truth. At best what had come before his time as an orphaned child on the streets of East London were murky shadows, buried in darkness. At worst, there was an emptiness.

Had she pressed him, he would have kept silent. He would have cursed her for asking, and mayhap the young woman knew that. Mayhap the same lady who'd demonstrated an eerie intuitiveness to what he was thinking and feeling had gathered as much. "My recollections are few." That allowance came grudgingly to his own ears.

Verity didn't say anything for a long moment, and then slowly, she brought her parasol closed. "Whenever my father visited, he always came with ribbons and these little flat chocolate discs, covered in nonpareils." She held her thumb and index finger in a tiny circle, demonstrating the size of that small treat. "After my mum died, he was forced to move us to a small apartment in London. He still visited. I never saw him smile much again after she died, but he'd visit," she tacked on as if it were important that Malcom know that much about the shameful man who'd sired her. As if she sought to defend him.

He struggled to follow through her unexpected shift in discourse and telling him about her family.

"The good thing about being in London was we were close enough that he could frequently visit, but far enough to keep us out of the eyes of Polite Society. I always wondered, how did he travel with chocolates without them melting? But they didn't." A wistful smile danced on her lips. "I digress . . . just before Papa came to visit, he'd send a note alerting us, because he knew one of my favorite things in all the world was to wait at the bottom step and then race to greet his carriage. It was my favorite part of the day." Her smile dimmed, and with it stole all the light. "Even when I was determined to hate him for having a legitimate family whom he needn't keep secret, rushing to meet him was one of my most beloved times, because when he was with us, I could pretend we were his real family." Her gaze grew as distant as her hushed, lyrical voice. It was the moment Malcom knew she'd lost herself in her telling and forgotten his presence.

Against all better judgment, against all control, he hung on, riveted to this, the widest window she'd let open on the questions he had of her own existence. That world she described, of a solitary girl, awaiting a beloved papa. Isolated even as it had been, it was far more than Malcom had ever known, and because of that, as fictional as the books he'd filched as a child from unsuspecting patrons outside Hatchards.

"One day," Verity carried on, her voice murmurous, "I received the missive, and I went out to meet him." Her expression darkened. "Only he didn't come. He wasn't there . . ." The long column of her throat moved up and down several times. "There was another. A man." Verity shook her head and returned to the moment—and to Malcom. "Apparently, he was my father's man-of-affairs. He'd come to inform us of my father's passing." She rested her callused, ink-stained fingers on his knee, and lifted her gaze up to meet his. "The thing of it is, Malcom . . . from that moment on, for so long I couldn't remember anything of that day: not the weather, not what I was wearing. Not what he said. And all the memories I carried of my father were lost. Occasionally, I would hear echoes of my own sobs. Or . . ." She creased her brow. "I *thought* they were my tears. It was as if they belonged to another. I couldn't make anything clear of the happiest memories that had come before it. I couldn't bring them into focus. Because it was just too h-hard." Her voice broke, and she immediately made a clearing sound with her throat. His chest constricted with an all-too-foreign pain . . . pain for another. For her. "Perhaps, Malcom, it is easier *not* remembering than fully owning the pain of that moment." There was a heartbeat's pause. "For me," she added softly. The meaning of her telling was unmistakable: he didn't remember because the memories were too dark. Too painful.

"And yet you speak of them now," he noted quietly, without recrimination and rather with a desperate need to know—to know about her and her past. To understand why his mind failed him. "How?"

"One day, when I was returning from my work, the skies opened and it began to rain . . . and a memory slipped in of my father and mother and I twirling in circles in a storm." Her gaze grew distant, and he knew the moment she lived within that memory. "And we were laughing and just so happy, and I realized I *wanted* to remember, Malcom. I wanted all the other happy remembrances I could have and every other in between." She held his gaze. "Even the ones that brought with them great sadness, too."

Malcom sat there with her words.

And then the truth slammed into him. He had fought to suppress those earliest parts of his life, and he'd done so because if he owned his past, fully, in every dark, evil context, then what would he be left with? What, other than lowered defenses that left him weak to all . . . this woman included?

That's what she would have of him. That is what she would have him do. He directed his stare at the front of Gunter's. Honest enough to admit that he was a coward and couldn't face her square on.

She rested her fingertips on his sleeve. His muscles jumped under that tender, unexpected touch.

He forced his gaze away from that palm that, even with the swath of fabric as a barrier between them, burnt.

"I understand you resent me." Nay, he didn't resent her. Not truly. He resented all this. Being thrust into a life he didn't want. He regretted that was what had brought them—and kept them—together. "But our agreement will have us together for . . . some time. And as such, I'd like to broker a truce."

Verity held out a gloveless palm.

He stared at it for a moment. "What is that?" he asked flatly.

"Well," she said slowly in those governess tones, as he'd come to think of them. "It is a handshake."

"A handshake?"

"During the medieval times, men would conceal weapons in their hands, and so shaking another person's hand conveyed that no harm was intended, and that is what I would convey to . . ."

Her voice faded out of focus, as something vague stirred in the chambers of his mind. Another echo, this one in a gentleman's voice.

"I know that story," he said hoarsely, cutting into Verity's telling.

And that is how the handshake has come to be, my boy . . .

Verity lowered her palm to her side.

Dark pinpricks flecked his vision.

She didn't ask how. And he needed to hear her voice. He needed her to anchor him to this moment, and pull him back from the memories that wouldn't come.

And then it came tumbling from her lips, her quietly spoken question, the mooring he needed. "Who?"

"My father. *It was my father . . .*" Only, that admission didn't suck him into the abyss, trapping him with thoughts of who he'd been . . . before. Rather, there came with that acknowledgment an unexpected buoyancy as the blackness tugging at his vision receded. Malcom drew a breath in slowly through his teeth, filling his lungs with it.

In that moment . . . he felt . . . free . . .

Chapter 20

THE LONDON GAZETTE

The Earl and Countess of Maxwell were recently seen
at Hyde Park. Despite the whispers and rumors of mari-
tal strife, witnesses maintain that the recently married
couple appeared very much in love . . .

E. Daubin

For nearly twenty years, Verity's life had been her work at *The Londoner*.
For three of them, she had been a reporter. Her nights had been spent
outlining stories, and then drafting interview questions for the subjects
of her article.

She began with a mock title. An outline. And then came the questions she'd piece together that would fill in the details of the story that
would ultimately be printed.

As such, she should be considering questions to ask and record for
her upcoming meeting with Malcom.

Instead, her notebook lay open before her, blank.

Since their quiet but not tense return to Grosvenor Square, she'd
been unable to think of anything but him and the last utterances to
leave his lips.

My father. It was my father . . .

It had represented a deeply personal admission that, once coaxed into further details, would likely have been sufficient enough to garner her work with any newspaper office. But in the immediacy of that moment, and even now, it wasn't her story or future employment she thought of.

She thought of him. Who Malcom had fleetingly been before he'd been forced to become someone else. The darkness he'd endured. And just as importantly, the point she'd never contemplated before now: What happiness had he known? The only son of an earl, he'd have been cherished for his role as heir.

And yet, he'd memories of Gunter's ices. And tales of handshakes. Information that had been imparted to him, that echoed in his mind still, all these years later.

And you'd ask him to expose those most intimate parts of himself to slake the hunger of gossips who don't truly care about the man Malcom North.

What alternative do you have, however?

Is his quest for privacy more precious than Livvie's and Bertha's survival?

Verity bit down hard on the end of her pencil, her teeth depressing the soft wood, leaving indentations upon it.

Footsteps sounded in the hall.

The pencil slipped from her mouth, and heart hammering, Verity jumped up. He was h—

Her sister slipped inside.

"Oh." Of course it wasn't Malcom. He'd mastered silence with a skill not even the dead of night could manage.

Livvie hovered at the entrance. "Is it all right if I join you?"

Forcing the cheerful smile she'd always donned for her only sister, even when Verity's heart had been breaking and the world weighing down on her shoulders, Verity stooped to gather her pencil. "You can always join me."

Leaving the door hanging ajar, with her hands tucked behind her back, Livvie walked hesitantly over. "What are you doing?" she asked as she climbed onto the leather button sofa alongside Verity.

Mindful of those recorded words about Malcom, Verity hurriedly closed her journal. "They're notes." She settled for vagueness.

"You're . . . working?" Her sister had the tones of one puzzling through a complex riddle.

"And why shouldn't I?" she countered.

"Because . . . you're a countess. And married . . ."

Leaning over, Verity gave a tug of her sister's plait. "And who says that a woman who is married should not be able to work?"

Livvie's brow pulled. "I . . . suppose I've never considered it, either way. I just expected that ladies didn't have to work."

"Aye, but I'm *choosing* to work. That is altogether different."

Her sister drew her knees to her chest, and eyed Verity's makeshift workstation. "Are you happy?"

Both that abrupt shift and the unexpectedness of that query from her innocent sister tied Verity's tongue. "What?" Yes. The answer she'd been expected to deliver was yes.

"Happy," Livvie repeated. "With the earl. With . . . your marriage."

No. "Yes," she lied. It had always been easy to lie to her sister. In doing so, she'd protected Livvie from numerous hurts and pain she didn't deserve. *Only . . . in lying to her, have you truly helped Livvie?*

In her bid to care for her family, Verity had made herself beholden to so many. Just as her mother had been beholden to the earl. *And what good has come from that?* a voice needled at the back of her mind. Setting aside her notepad, Verity drew her knees up and faced her sister. "Why do you ask?" she gently urged.

Without hesitation, Livvie brought her hands out from behind her back, and Verity's gaze went to the cover of that newspaper. "Oh," she said dumbly.

"It's written in here. Horrible things. Ones that suggest you've somehow trapped Lord Maxwell into marriage, and that he's desperately miserable, and"—Livvie lowered her voice into a hushed whisper—"if I'm to be honest, Verity? The earl does not seem at all happy when he is with you. At all. He seems angry and . . . not loving."

Well, given Malcom was angry, Livvie's observation couldn't have been more astute.

Sighing, Verity slipped the heavily creased newspaper from her sister's fingers, and unfolded it. She paused. "*The Londoner*?"

"I know, I know," her sister mumbled. "I simply wanted to see how they fared without your articles, and they're not. In fact, the only reason they're still surviving is because of the stories they're writing about you."

"They're just that, Livvie. Stories meant to sell newspapers," she said with a finality meant to end the discussion. And not long ago, that would have been sufficient to stymie the flow of questions and have Livvie continue on to bed. Livvie, however, was no longer the accepting child she'd been.

"But if it is untrue, then how come you and His Lordship are never together?"

Proud as Verity was of her sister's tenacity and insight, how much easier it would have been had she still been the small babe she'd raised like her own child. "We are, Livvie. Why, we were just at Gunter's this morn."

Again, that mention of the sweet shop was intended as a child's distraction, which her sister didn't take. "You've not taken any meals together. You're always in one room, working, and he's in another, doing whatever he does."

Verity's mind raced with some response that would satisfy Livvie's fervent questioning. In the end, she was saved from formulating a response by the unlikeliest of saviors.

She felt him before she heard him, his presence a palpable, thrumming energy in the quiet of the library.

Livvie forgotten, she glanced to the doorway, and every thought faded into nothingness.

Malcom.

Attired in black as he was wont to do, with his long blond strands drawn into a neat queue, he was a breathtaking blend of sophisticated lord and strikingly masculine self-made man who answered to none. He was breathtakingly beautiful in a way no person had a right to be.

When no greeting was forthcoming, he stepped forward. "Good evening. Forgive me for interrupting." One would never know he was a man who'd spent nearly the whole of his life on the streets, or that he despised one of the occupants of the room.

In the end, Livvie proved the greater hostess of their pair. She hopped up, and sank into an impressively competent curtsy. "My lord. We were just discussing you."

Oh, bloody hell.

Unleashing a string of black curses in her head, Verity shot a foot out, catching the back of her sister's knee.

Livvie jumped. "Ow." She shot a glare over her shoulder. "You *kicked* me."

Oh, double bloody hell. Verity gave her head the tiniest of shakes, praying her sister noted that unspoken plea for silence, and that she also honored it. Alas, God continued to prove himself an elusive figure in her life.

"We *were* talking about him."

Oh, Lord. Heat blazed across Verity's cheeks. "We weren't," she said tightly in her best, no-nonsense, bigger-sister tones.

"Uh, yes, we were. I was mentioning that you and Lord Maxwell are rarely together, and you said—*oomph*. Now, that is really quite enough," Livvie huffed and, drawing her leg back, hopped up and down as she awkwardly reached behind to rub the offended area.

His face set in its usual somber mask, Malcom glanced back and forth between Verity and her sister. Just like that, Livvie managed what

Verity had taken to be the impossible: she earned an honest, even smile from Malcom. One that crinkled the corners of his eyes and dimpled his left cheek. Verity's breath quickened.

And she didn't know whether to be wholly bewitched or mortified.

Malcom's smile deepened, doing even stranger things to her heart. He knew very well the traitorous thoughts running in her head.

The blighter.

Of course he should choose this as the time he would be smiling, delighting in Verity's misery.

No further invitation was required. Malcom came forward, his attention squarely on Livvie. "And just what did your sister have to say?" he asked as he stopped before them, shameless in his questioning.

So this is what it felt like for him and every last person she had put questions to over the years. Shame overwhelmed all her earlier embarrassment.

Albeit temporarily . . . Livvie hitched herself onto the curved arm of the leather sofa. "Well." She pumped her legs as she spoke. "Verity assured me you're both quite happy together . . ."

Malcom crossed his arms at his broad chest. "Oh?"

"Are you not?" Livvie latched on with a remarkable astuteness for one her age.

"How could I not be hopelessly enthralled by a woman who'd climb into the sewers of London?" A twinkle glinted in his eyes.

Hopelessly enthralled, indeed. "Enough," she mouthed.

He shook his head slightly. "I don't think I shall." He clearly enunciated each syllable.

Oh, this had really gone on long enough. Dismissing Malcom outright, Verity turned to her sister. "Livvie, His Lordship and I have more pressing matters to—"

"Verity pointed out that you'd gone to Gunter's."

"We did," he confirmed with such smug glee it was all Verity could do to keep from delivering a kick to the back of *his* legs.

This was to be her penance, then, for the years she'd spent prying information from others. "His Lordship and I have pressing matters to attend." Which wasn't untrue. She needed to be gathering information for her article, and those funds would be all that saved them after Malcom saw her banished to the English countryside.

He scoffed. "Not at all. I cannot imagine anything more pressing at this moment."

The pair continued on as though Verity's interruption had never happened. Folding her arms, she stuck a foot out and tapped it in an impatient staccato rhythm.

"I pointed out to Verity that you're otherwise rarely together."

Verity and Malcom spoke at once.

"We are not rarely—"

"You are not incorrect," his words continued over Verity's.

He would opt for blunt honesty, even with her innocent sister.

Livvie beamed, positively glowing in ways Verity was certain she herself never had been.

And there was surely a wicked deficit in Verity's character at the stab of envy at the attention . . . and warmth . . . trained on her blushing sibling. And the ease with which the pair of them got on.

Livvie ceased swinging her legs. "Are you? Happy, that is?"

I never smile . . . . What do you have to smile about? Her stomach tightened. Her sister wasn't one who could understand—

"Oh, undoubtedly."

Undoubtedly?

And with that, he shot a glance over the top of Livvie's head and favored Verity with a wink.

That brief but deliberate flicker of his lashes that alluded to a teasing game they two shared. Which, with the way he felt about Verity, was as preposterous as it was impossible, and yet in that very moment, she believed whatever game of pretend he put on for Livvie's benefit.

"Then where do you go during the day?" Livvie peered up at him through thick, golden lashes. Their mother's lashes, as Verity had thought of them through the years. The ones Bertha had claimed snagged an earl's improper attention and would be the crux of many problems for her—and them—in the future. It appeared the future was now. "Why aren't you ever about for mealtime?"

Verity ceased her distracted foot tapping. "Livvie," she said sharply. "His Lordship doesn't want to take questions . . ."

Malcom merely peered back. And then he crooked his four fingers, urging the girl closer.

Livvie hesitated, and then springing to her feet, she drifted over.

"I search the sewers of London," he said in a loud whisper.

"Stillll?" Livvie's mouth pulled. "I've heard as much. Crawling in tunnels for coins? I cannot see how you'd prefer spending your days in the sewers to living"—she threw her arms wide—"*here.*"

He scoffed. "Where's the excitement in that?"

"Security. There's security in it," Verity said before she could call the quiet words back.

Malcom briefly sharpened his gaze on her face. "There's long been greatness buried underground and in water, there for the taking. Have you ever heard of Decebalus?"

Who?

"Who?" Livvie gave voice to Verity's own question.

"He was king of a small kingdom in the Danube. He ordered the slaves to bury gold and silver in the riverbed Sargetia. Afterward, to keep concealed the treasures that dwelled below, he ordered the men executed."

If Verity were a proper lady and caregiver to her sister, there would have been horror at the story Malcom even now told. And Verity was filled with something unexpected . . . shame. She'd been so fixed on providing for Livvie she'd not thought of the education her sister was deserving of.

"Why would he do that?" Livvie piped up.

With a flair, he tossed his arms wide. "Why, to ensure that no one knew what was buried below."

This was another side of Malcom North. A new side of him. Kind and patient with an artless young woman, and God help Verity, that tenderness sent her heart into somersaults.

"And did anyone discover it?" The question tumbled out, and her cheeks instantly warmed as Malcom swung his attention back to her.

"Years later, one of his nobles revealed its location to the Romans, and it was uncovered."

And then it hit her . . . "They were pirates," she blurted.

Malcom pointed a finger in her direction, confirming her supposition.

"And that is how you see yourself," Livvie ventured slowly, as one puzzling through a riddle. "As a pirate of the sewers?"

"I see myself as one who came about a fortune by fair means. When people are forced to steal and . . . worse, there are those who dig deeper and find greater wealth than had by many noblemen."

And one more piece fell into the puzzle that was Malcom North. This gentleman who looked after crippled toshers and street urchins was the same man who'd refused to filch pockets, and instead had made his fortune as honestly as the fates had enabled him to.

And Verity was sure a corner of her heart would forever belong to him for it.

"Livvie, run along now," she said quietly. "There'll be time aplenty to speak with Lord Maxwell."

This time, her sister must have heard something in her tone that marked the end of the games she'd played. With a beleaguered sigh, Livvie hopped up. "Very well." She dropped another curtsy, this one smoother and more relaxed than the previous one. "My lord."

"No need for fancy titles." He bowed his head. "Malcom will suffice." His melodious voice came in crisp, refined tones that raised no question as to the gentleman's identity. He was noble born, in every way. And in every way that Verity wasn't.

It was a reminder that she'd not truly considered . . . all the ways in which they were . . . different. Why should that cause this peculiar tightening in her chest? After all, it didn't matter whether she was wholly unsuitable for the role of his actual bride; their arrangement was one forged of mutual necessity, insisted upon by a man who, if he didn't hate her, carried an immense dislike for her.

Chapter 21

THE LONDON GAZETTE

All Polite Society is aware that the more servants gossip, the less regard they have for their employers. Given the absolute silence from Lord and Lady Maxwell's staff, it is apparent that the earl and countess are very much respected by a staff determined to protect the family's secrets . . .

E. Daubin

Malcom didn't want to be here.

In fact, he wanted to be here even less than he'd wanted to be on display before the *ton*. Nor did his apprehension have anything to do with the woman standing across from him, and everything to do with what she sought.

Buying time for himself, steeling himself against the slew of questions she'd ask, Malcom closed the door behind her sister, shutting him and Verity away. Alone.

I don't want to do this . . .

Moisture slicked his palms and dampened the bronze handle.

Stop. You've faced head-on the threat of death and danger since you were a boy on your own . . . How difficult can an interview with Verity Lovelace be?

Why did it merely feel as if he sought to reassure himself?

To give his fingers something to do, he loosened the buttons of his jacket, and turned to face Verity. The slightly mocking words he intended were interrupted, but not with a question.

"Thank you," she said quietly.

Thank you? He furrowed his brow.

"For being patient with Livvie," she clarified.

"Did you think I should be a monster to a young woman?" he asked without malice. It wasn't the first time she'd insinuated as much.

Then again, neither of them had the greatest opinion of the other.

Verity colored. "I . . . no. I . . . I simply know that you don't like being asked questions about yourself, and Livvie's quite garrulous."

Aye, the girl was a talker. Like Verity. There'd been something oddly heartening in the banter between the sisters. Bickering, and teasing; there was a closeness to that bond that should have made him uncomfortable, but had only intrigued him.

Or mayhap it was Verity's magic once more. Everything about her fascinated him.

Verity sank into the folds of the leather button sofa overflowing with papers and notepads. Hurriedly, she went about tidying that makeshift workspace. "Would you care to sit?"

Waving off that invitation, Malcom shrugged out of his jacket and tossed it over the back of a mahogany library chair. As she organized her things, Malcom picked up a creased newspaper lying on the walnut rolling table.

He scanned the front page.

> The elusive Earl and Countess of Maxwell have been
> spied amongst Polite Society. Witnesses say there were
> many stretches of silence between them. All the *ton*
> is then left to wonder at the circumstances surround-
> ing Lord Maxwell's marriage to the mystery woman.
> Extortion? Bribery? *Worse?*

"Perhaps there was something to your suggestion of an amiable match," he muttered.

"Well, there's nothing Polite Society despises more than happy marriages," she explained, not lifting her head from her task. "There's some irony in it, however." Verity briefly paused. "Over the years, with the exception of my work, they've dabbled in half-truths and peddled nearly entirely in complete fabrications. How ironic that the closest they've ever danced to real truth should have been in the story they've written about us," she said dryly.

The irony rested in the fact that he was the only one in their party guilty of extorting her, coercing her into cooperation. In exchange for the story she'd write about him. Guilt stabbed at a conscience he hadn't even realized existed until this moment. He tossed the paper back down, and it landed with a loud *thwack*. "Why do you wish to work for a paper that doesn't have integrity?"

"Because I believe in what newspapers represent, and what they do," she said, looking up from the stack of notepads in her hands. "Because I believe with the right opportunity, I can make it better." She patted the empty space she'd cleared beside her.

Malcom hesitated, and then sat beside her. "Have you even tried?"

Her mouth pursed, that plump lower lip jutting out with her annoyance. "I've written pieces aside from gossip columns, if that is what you're asking. Of course, neither of them have been published."

"Of course?"

Verity set her notepads down. "As you pointed out, I write for a gossip column. There've been times I've written alternative pieces. More fact-based or moral-centered ones." She drew her knees up and wrapped her arms about them.

"And they were quashed?" he ventured.

"They were." Verity pressed her thumb and forefinger together. "Both of them."

Both of them? Which implied . . . two. "That's it?" he asked bluntly. She frowned. "I don't . . ."

"As I see it"—he stretched his legs out and crossed them at the ankles—"you've hunted me in the sewers, and invaded my private residence in East London not once, not twice, but three times."

"It was two," she defended. "You brought me back the first time."

"Aye." Against all better judgment that had screamed to be wary and to keep his guard up. She'd slipped past, and upended his life since. "I'll allow that. Two times, then, you've come to me. And invaded my townhouse. Yet you've only made a handful of attempts to push for a story other than the rot they required of you?"

Verity frowned. "I don't have the luxury to write anything else, Malcom." She delivered those words not with any self-pity, but with pure pragmatism. "The only luxury permitted me is survival, and as such I wrote the stories *expected* of me."

"Gossip."

Where in the past she'd bristled at his description of her work, now she sighed. "Aye. Gossip."

He lightly dusted his fingers over her chin, bringing her gaze to his. "And that is what I am to"—*you*—"the world? Gossip?"

Her gaze held his, so piercing, so intent as if she sought to crawl inside him and pull forth those secrets he was so determined to keep. "I don't believe that," she said quietly. "Society might initially see that for what it is. But once written, it is my hope that they find there is true substance to it, Malcom. It is a story of injustice and wrongs and . . . strife."

. And with that, it made sense.

He made to release her; as he unfurled his fingers and loosed his hold, that was his intention. Only, of their own volition, Malcom's knuckles did a slow, gradual upsweep of her jawline. A back-and-forth caress and re-exploration of skin soft as satin. Her thick, sooty lashes fluttered down, as if she herself was as entranced by that lightest of touches. "You felt the story was something more than it is," he murmured. "That's why you've been so determined to conduct your interview." It wasn't a question, and yet, as she forcibly opened her eyes and met his, she answered him anyway. "You see this as the ability to make the changes you wanted in the papers."

She nodded. "In part. There are those who believe 'the world doesn't want information. They want . . .'"—she pitched her voice to a high, nasally whine—"'the *right* information.'"

"Your employer?"

"My previous employer," Verity clarified. "He's since ceded the business over to his son. He'll allow any lie to be printed and any story to be stolen." Her gaze darkened. "Fairpoint," she muttered to herself.

She doesn't matter. Her plight doesn't matter. The work she did, and the people she was employed by . . . "Who is this Fairpoint?" Would Malcom have to break the cur's neck?

"A reporter who stole"—her cheeks pinkened—"my earliest story about you." She cast a sheepish look in his direction. "Either way, newspapers are struggling. The taxes are crippling, and reporters are turning on one another, all to maintain their work. And the most recent head of *The Londoner* . . ."

And in the dog-eat-dog world, they'd devoured Verity. Aye, he'd happily off the pair of those fellows. "He's proven more unbending than his father?"

"In the sense that he gave me an impossible task—" Her words immediately cut off. The color on Verity's cheeks deepened.

He sent a single brow arching up. "Me?"

Abandoning her curled-up position on the sofa, Verity shifted so that her feet touched the floor. His ears tried to make out the grumblings she made under her breath. Something that sounded very much like *"You are impossible."*

The right corner of his mouth pulled up in a half smile, one that didn't stretch quite so uncomfortably as the grins before it.

She scooched over so their legs brushed. "It wasn't simply that he assigned me the story of your whereabouts and past. It was that he did so anticipating that I'd fail so he would have sufficient reason to sack me without having to explain my severance to his father. He was always intending to sack me. One of those who doesn't believe a woman has any place in reporting." Impassioned, her eyes glittered with the depths of her outrage.

"He was a fool, thinking any man more competent than you in any task."

Her eyes immediately softened, her lips parted, and a little sigh whispered out.

Where women were concerned, there'd been any number of reactions they'd greeted Malcom with over the years: Desire. Fury. Suspicion.

Never had a woman looked at Malcom as Verity did now. He didn't know what to do with all that emotion. Any of it. He cleared his throat. "I'll have you know . . . my . . . anger in the park. It wasn't reserved for you. It was the discomfort of being there." Her brows dipped. "Not with you," he said on a rush. She was all that had kept him sane at that outing. Nay, she'd done more than that; she'd managed to make him smile, even. "It is my own"—*insecurity*—"dislike of Polite Society," he settled for.

Her eyes softened. "Thank you."

That was it: *thank you.*

He cleared his throat. "We should get on with it."

"Get on with—"

"The interview." The only reason they were together, and the reason they'd stay together until the end of the next Season.

The light went out of her pretty eyes. She blinked slowly, and then grimaced. "Forgive me. Of course you didn't need to hear all that."

Nay, he hadn't needed to. But he'd wanted to. And it was that wanting that scared the hell out of him.

He got to the heart of it. "I don't remember most." He grimaced. "I don't remember anything. The information you seek about my past?" About his parents and childhood before it had all been taken from him . . . "I've nothing to contribute." All he could offer was how he'd lived in the years after. Which was largely the whole of his life.

Silence fell, thick and uncomfortable, that tension a product of the fact that he'd never be able to give her what she fully sought, and yet, he intended to hold her to the agreement they'd reached anyway.

"Malcom, you were kidnapped," Verity said in somber tones. "You lost your parents, and when you were sick, found yourself stolen away by a faithless servant. The fiends who ripped off your title and your existence lived in comfort—opulent lifestyles of wealth and security and ease. While you struggled. While you, an earl's son, and at his passing, an earl by your birthright, learned firsthand the strife that exists for those born outside the peerage. You might not remember what happened to you"—she covered his hand with hers—"but never, ever doubt that you don't have something very powerful, something very meaningful to contribute."

The air effervesced from the force of emotion that passed between them, volatile and real and terrifying for the unfamiliarity of it.

"What do you want to know?" he asked gruffly, eyeing her notepads uneasily.

Except Verity drew her knees up once more and rubbed her chin back and forth over those pale-yellow skirts. "How did you become a tosher?"

That was the easiest question she could have put to him. He suspected she knew as much. Knew that was why she had asked it.

"A gent tried to bugger me. I escaped and scurried into a sewer. Down there, I found me a purse filled with guineas . . . and Fowler. I never looked back."

All the color left her cheeks.

Malcom tensed. He didn't want her pity. He didn't want any of her damned sadness and wide eyes. And he certainly didn't want useless apologies for what his life had been. "Don't expect that can be printed in the papers," he said with forced amusement.

She didn't take the bait of his teasing. "How old were you?"

He shrugged. "Twelve or thirteen." Twelve. He'd been twelve.

Her eyes slid briefly closed.

"I was small for my age," he went on. "Without a bit of meat to me. I was also quicker than bigger men and boys, which is what allowed me to get away and sneak into a grate that hadn't been properly shut."

"And Fowler . . . ?"

Malcom's mind wandered back to that long-ago night. The frantic beat of his heart as it pounded in his ears, muffling even his own ragged breathing. "I heard someone crying and thought it was myself."

"Fowler?" she breathed.

"Floods come sudden and unexpected in the sewers. One caught Fowler, and it carried him down more tunnels than he could remember. The force of it when it emptied into the chamber where I found him sent him slamming into a brick wall. Shattered his leg, and he couldn't get out." And somehow, more than a foot and a half shorter and fifteen stones lighter, he'd managed to get the tosher up and moving. "We've been together since."

Her eyes were riveted on him, her pencil frozen in her fingers.

"Are you going to write that down?"

She blinked several times. "What?" she blurted.

He nodded at the notepad.

Verity looked down, and then gave her head a shake. "No. No. I . . . I simply wondered how you two had come to be together."

That was all.

She'd not asked for her story. She'd simply asked because she wished to know . . . about him?

Never had he felt more splayed open and on display for another. Malcom shifted, the leather button sofa groaning under him. "And what of you, Verity?" he asked, the need for a reprieve from sharing of himself prompting that question. Except, even as he thought as much, he knew he lied to himself. He wanted to know about her, too. He'd wanted to since he found her in the sewers, fishing around for lost slippers. "How long have you been caring for yourself and your sister?"

She didn't even hesitate, freely answering. "I was twelve. My mother died in childbirth. My father died soon after. Before he did, he set me up with work at *The Londoner*."

She could have lived solely for herself without worrying about mouths to feed. And yet, she hadn't. She'd lost her mother and father, and then, only a child herself, she'd taken on the role of parent to a babe. It wasn't every day that Malcom could feel properly shamed, but in this instance, when presented with the selfless existence she'd lived compared with his own, he found himself . . . humbled. "Your father didn't see that you were looked after?"

She chuckled, the sound devoid of any mirth or happiness in an unexpected display of cynicism. "My father loved my mother, but he was a wastrel. He drank. My mum said his misery was because he could never be with us as he wished. My nursemaid always insisted it was because he was endlessly weak."

He was of a like opinion as the nursemaid. Malcom had killed many times in the name of survival. Even as every one of those devils had deserved it, he'd regretted that blood on his hands. And yet if her father weren't already dead, Malcom would have gladly done the deed all over for the state he'd left his daughters in. "You became a sibling and parent to Livvie."

Verity shrugged. "What else would I do?"

"You'd protect yourself," he said automatically.

"Protect myself, by . . . remaining alone?"

He went silent.

Verity, however, was tenacious. She scooted around so that she faced him. "And is that what you've done, Malcom?"

His body went whipcord straight. "Yes. Of course it is." Everyone in the rookeries knew as much about him.

"No."

He cocked his head.

"No," she repeated. "That is what you *think* you've done. You refer to Bram and Fowler as 'your people.' You call Giles an 'associate.' All of these defenses that you put up, these choices of words that strip away closeness from your connections, they cannot truly conceal the truth."

A sweat broke out on the back of his nape. Moisture trickled down his collar and streaked his back. "You don't know what you're talking about." Or was it that he didn't know what he was talking about? Everything was twisted. Illogical and confused.

"I do, though. I know that you're protecting yourself by pretending that they don't matter. But, Malcom." She rested a hand lightly on his sleeve.

He stared at those ink-stained fingers to keep from looking into her eyes and owning all the truths that spilled from her too-insightful lips. "What?"

"A man who doesn't care about others doesn't rescue men from the sewers. He doesn't stay with them, looking after them when they are old men who can barely walk from the injuries they've sustained." His hands formed balls at his sides. He wanted her to stop. He needed her to. But she was relentless. Verity moved closer so that barely a hand-breadth separated them. "A man who doesn't care doesn't send those old toshers to the finest residence in London so that they might live in comfort and never have to pillage a sewer again."

He glanced away, unable to meet her piercing gaze. That gaze that saw too much and knew even more. A million vises twisted his insides into knots. How had she known . . . ?

Verity proved unfaltering, wreaking further havoc upon him. "You wouldn't have made your right-hand man, one who is surviving on the streets with just one hand to defend and protect himself with, your associate." *Giles.* Verity laid her palms against his chest, and his heart thumped hard under that tender touch. "And do you know what I also know?"

He managed to shake his head.

"A man who'll do all that, who'll take in the woman who'd wronged him, along with her family, giving them security, is an honorable one."

Just like the romantic article she'd written about him in *The Londoner*, Verity simply saw that which she wished. "I'm not." A man who'd done the things he had could never be considered anything of the sort.

Verity smiled tremulously. She stroked her palms down the front of his chest, her touch soothing. "You continue to believe if you say one thing, that the words will, in fact, mean another."

Chapter 22

THE LONDON GAZETTE
A MATCH MADE . . . OF LOVE?

For all the original speculation about a nefarious union
between the Earl of Maxwell and his mysterious wife,
the couple is seen frequently about Polite Society, and
the *ton* is left with but one question: Is it love?

E. Daubin

In the following weeks, Malcom and Verity settled into their world of
pretend.

His days were spent courting his wife.

Their nights were spent conversing. Interviews that never truly felt
like interviews.

And somewhere along the way, make-believe had come to feel . . .
all too real.

Lying upon a blanket in Hyde Park with Verity's palms over his
eyes, Malcom knew there'd be time later for proper horror at the vulnerable place he'd let himself fall into.

"You're not paying attention," Verity accused.

"Very well."

She cleared her throat. "My first: the Serpentine doth wind.

"On to my second: which can only be a mistake.

"The third: abandoning of Eden."

His mouth moved silently as he repeated back those three clues. "You know, you really can remove your—"

"You're stalling for time, Malcom."

His lips curved up in a grin. Not even three weeks ago, he'd have sooner split his tosher pole in half than take part in any game. Since he'd been a boy, Malcom craved the dark and dank, and despised the light for the perils it posed. For in the day, there were no shadows in which to hide. As such, he'd not known what it was to have the sun on his face. Or a soft breeze upon his skin. At this end of London, he'd come to find just how very different this world was, and that its allure was even greater.

"Malcom," she said warningly.

"I assure you, I remain completely focused on the task at hand," he said drolly. "Ouch." He winced as she freed one of her hands and pinched his cheek. "What was *that* for?"

"You're not even—"

"A flower," he said over her. "It is a flower."

"Impossible!" Verity dragged her hands from his eyes. He blinked as the early-summer sun blinded him.

"Impossible that it's a flower? Or impossible that I've bested you . . . again?"

She swatted at him. "You are a poor winner."

"That seems quite contradictory, love."

"Oh, yes, I assure you it's not. You're very gloaty."

He flipped onto his side and braced himself on an elbow. "Is that a word?"

"It's not." She paused. "But if it were, it would be applied to you."

He grinned. A lightness suffused him, touching every corner of a place inside him that had once been dark, until he was buoyant.

Christi Caldwell

Malcom waggled his eyebrows. "In case you couldn't tell, I'm quite good at charades."

"And chess." Verity delivered another well-placed pinch.

"What was that for?" he mumbled, rubbing at the offended area.

"That one was just because," she said with a toss of her head.

"You are a ruthless competitor, you know."

"If you think I'm ruthless with charades, you should see me with"— air wafted over his cheeks, and the scent of mint flooded his senses— "lawn bowling," she whispered against his ear.

His heart pounded faster at her nearness. "Indeed?" he asked, as he was surely supposed to issue some reply, and a more meaningful one eluded him.

"Hardly," Verity clarified. "I've never played. I've always wanted to, though. My father would speak of bringing a set and teaching me."

And with her soft musings, an image danced forward of a sprawling country estate. A high-walled garden with steps that led out to rolling hills.

"I wanted to play lawn bowling, Papa." Malcom tugged at the hand in his. *"You told Mama we would, but we're not."*

His father stopped, and fell to a knee beside him. "Ah, yes, because I had to keep it a surprise."

Malcom stared, unblinking. "A surprise?" he whispered.

"We are picking flowers to make your mama a crown so she might be queen."

Lawn bowling forgotten, Malcom brightened. "Can I have a crown and be her prince . . . ?"

Malcom slowly opened his eyes, squinting at the bright flood of sunshine. He braced for the headache that accompanied such realizations—which this time did not come. The memory had been so vivid. So real. And letting it in this time hadn't crippled him with weakness.

280

He felt Verity's stare before he caught it, and glanced over. She'd dragged her knees against her chest, rested her chin atop them, and studied Malcom.

"You remembered something, didn't you?" she asked quietly, and where that query would have once set him off in a fury at her probing into his life, now he nodded.

"Aye." Scooping up a handful of debris at the edge of the blanket, he sifted through it. Settling for a small, smooth, flat stone, he sent it expertly skipping across the smooth surface of the Serpentine. The projectile bounced five times and then sank under the surface. "Sometimes that will happen. I'll see something or hear a word, and it . . . triggers a remembrance. But it's almost as if they aren't real to me. As if they happened to someone else. As if they are a dream."

Verity covered his hand. "But they aren't a dream, Malcom," she said gently.

Nay, they weren't a dream. She was correct on that score. His throat moved painfully around an uncomfortable ball that had lodged there. They were his life.

"Every morning, my mother would rise early."

He blinked at the sudden shift.

"Our cottage was small and I'd hear her, but I knew she loved her mornings. The quiet time before the world awoke. And I would lie there. I'd listen as she went through her morning routine. As she prepared water to make her tea. And every morn, she'd sing. It was an old Scottish folk song." Verity's gaze grew distant, and a smile played about her lips as she softly sang.

I've seen the smiling
Of fortune beguiling,
I've tasted her pleasures
And felt her decay;

Riveted, Malcom stared on. Unable to tear his gaze from her fulsome lips as she sang. This was how those sailors on their galleons were dragged out to sea. Lured by the soft, slightly off-key medley, made all the more mesmerizing for the discordancy.

Sweet is her blessing,
And kind her caressing,
But now they are fled
And fled far away.

"It is lovely," he said hoarsely when she'd finished and her low contralto had drifted into nothing.

"Aye." Verity flipped onto her side so that they faced one another. "When my mum died, I'd wake up nearly the same time every morn that I had when she was living. I'd drag my pillow over my head and hold it tight. So I couldn't hear anything. Because if I couldn't hear the silence, then it wasn't real. What had happened to my mum, and the truth that I'd never, ever see her again, wasn't real. In those moments before I removed that pillow, I was in control."

He froze, her meaning clear.

He'd been a master at keeping all the memories at bay. At forgetting the parents he'd known too briefly. Of the happiness they'd had together. But keeping thoughts of them buried didn't erase those moments in time. It hadn't. Nor would it ever.

"I've been here, too," he said quietly, staring past her. Through her. Off to the foreign gaggle of white pelicans. Several of the enormous white fowl basked on the rocks in the sun.

Just then, a lone bird sauntered too close to their blanket. It had a peculiar protuberance from its long, narrow beak.

"I was here. In this place. With these birds."

A sheen of moisture popped up on his brow, and he briefly closed his eyes. Willing that creature gone. Willing the buzzing at the back of his head gone. But it didn't leave. It remained, and grew increasingly incessant. The all-too-familiar pain knocked around at his temples. And this time, he fought it off and welcomed in the memory.

"Mama, Mama! That duck has a horn! I want to touch him . . . They are magnif—"

"They are magnificent, aren't they?" Verity asked, startling him from that memory.

Blankly, he looked over at the woman beside him whose echoed praise of some other boy, in some other lifetime ago, wrenched him back to the moment.

"The pelicans," Verity clarified.

"They're peculiar."

That was the only invitation to discussion Verity required. Gathering the forgotten parasol from the bench, she pointed the top of it toward the creatures in question. "Do you know how they came to be here?"

Malcom shook his head slowly.

Verity tossed aside the satin umbrella and scrambled closer. "Sometime in the early 1600s, James the First had this area drained and landscaped so that it might become a place for people to visit. He was responsible for the creation of a flower garden and a menagerie of wild animals." She stared back with a brightness in her eyes, one that expected he should be as impressed by that revelation as she herself was to give it.

And by damn, if he wasn't . . . but because of the woman in charge of the telling. Her enthusiasm was infectious. "Wild animals, you say?"

Verity nodded so enthusiastically her bonnet fell over her brow, concealing those bright eyes, and he mourned that small loss. "He had camels brought in. Crocodiles. Even an elephant, and the exotic waterfowl, of course."

His lips twitched, that natural movement so foreign to him it strained the muscles, and yet, with it came a . . . peculiar lightness in his chest. "Of course," he said, his expression deadpan.

Whether or not she heard the note of teasing infused in his words, she did not let it alter the rest of her telling.

"Charles the First continued to expand the pleasures at the park . . . until he was executed. Made his way there." Taking him by the hand, she forced him to either join her as she turned or pull her down. In the end, he could no sooner stop himself from doing as she bid than he could happily end his tenure as a tosher. "Do you see there?" Squinting, she pointed over a slight rise. "That is where Charles was marched in the dead of winter, all bundled up lest onlookers see him shake and mistake that response for fear. He and his dog, Rogue, were marched over that rise, and . . ." Her expression became grim, and she shook her head. "I trust you know the rest."

"Yes," he said automatically. Something slipped in and then tumbled from his lips before he could call it back. "'Sweetheart, now they will cut off thy father's head. Mark, child, what I say: they will cut off my head, and perhaps make thee a king. But mark what I say: you must not be a king, so long as your brothers Charles and James do live,'" he murmured.

Sensing Verity's eyes on him, he felt his cheeks flush with heat and color. "Or . . . I believe I recall he uttered something of that effect."

"That is precisely what he was quoted as saying to his son," Verity marveled, inching closer. "You've . . . heard that, then, at some point. And remembered it."

Sitting up, Malcom tugged at the loose cravat he'd donned. He did know the history of Charles's execution . . . but when . . . and where that knowledge had come from, he'd no recollection. Boys in the street weren't schooled in fine studies, and yet at some point, his education had come . . . from somewhere. Whether it had been from his father or a tutor . . . "I . . . don't recall anything more than that," he conceded gruffly.

"After Charles's execution"—*Cromwell*—"Cromwell took over. He sought to quash all hint of joy and outlawed anything that might bring pleasure." Verity settled back onto her seat, eyeing the pelicans nosing around their blanket.

With her silence, she made clear . . . she'd said all she intended to say, and if he wished to know more, then she expected him to give some indication.

Mama . . . where do the pelicans come from?

That child's voice he knew inherently was his own rang around the walls of his mind. Taunting him with echoes and shadows he couldn't make sense of. Just as he knew he'd asked that question, he also intrinsically knew the woman he'd called "Mama" hadn't had an answer.

Malcom's tongue felt heavy in his mouth. And yet . . . *this* . . . engaging with another on matters that had nothing to do with plundering the sewers of London, was as foreign as the languages one picked up in passing at the London wharves. "Why pelicans?" he made himself ask, his voice emerging harsh.

It was all Verity required. "Well, Charles the Second had an inordinate fascination with fowl himself." Her bonnet slipped once again, and she pushed the frilly article back. "Knowing that about the monarch, an ambassador to Russia presented the king with two grey pelicans." As she spoke, bright color suffused her cheeks, and she gestured animatedly. Malcom stared on, riveted. It was an impossibility to not be further entranced by the young woman . . . and her telling. "The original pelicans, however, were never successfully bred, and still today, they periodically replenish the population." She stared at him expectantly.

Another smile twitched at his lips. "That is an impressive breadth of information on the pelicans in Hyde Park, my lady."

"I conducted a story on it," she explained. The pelicans, having long tired of the lack of food and attention paid them, waddled off and set up in a new place upon an empty boulder. And she waited.

She never compelled him to speak.

She shared stories of herself so that he might see the reasons he denied his past. She let him understand just why he clung to the darkness.

And mayhap, after all these years, that was what gave him the strength to talk—to her.

"My parents brought me here. My father would ride." Cupping a hand over his eyes, he scanned the grounds, ignoring the lords and ladies strolling past. A tall, bespectacled gentleman at some point had stopped and stared blatantly upon Malcom and Verity. This time, none of those gossips mattered. "There," he murmured, pointing to a graveled path. "It was narrower. There was more brush and growth. My mother and I would sit on a blanket, feeding the pelicans." The remembrances slipped forth. "And chasing them." Just then, one of those enormous fowl waddled past, and then launched himself into the water. "I'd chase them about. My mother would pretend to scold me and come running after me, but then we were both chasing them together." It was so real, so vivid in his mind.

Her face.

Their laughing faces together.

A small hand slipped into Malcom's. Verity wound her fingers through his.

He didn't move for a moment, and then slowly Malcom curved his hand around hers.

Chapter 23

THE LONDONER
REVENGE

All society is well aware of the Rightful Heir's attempt to make a beggar of the previous Lord Maxwell, who'd stolen that respected title. All society is also left with one shared question: When will he have his final revenge on the man responsible for his miseries . . . ?

M. Fairpoint

Everything had changed.

Some seismic shift had occurred at Hyde Park, and nothing for Verity could ever be the same again.

But then—Verity studied her reflection in her vanity mirror—perhaps the shift hadn't been so quick, after all. Perhaps it had been with each and every exchange, a gradual breakdown that had occurred of those impressive barriers Malcom had put up.

And she should be thinking of her story and the interview she sought.

But could only think of him. Of being with him . . .

The following morning, Verity didn't know how to be with Malcom.

"Get that silly look off your face, gel."

She tensed.

Bertha stomped out of the dressing room.

"I don't have a silly look." Except . . . she stole a peek at herself in the cheval mirror, and blushed. Aye, there was a definite faraway wistfulness to her gaze, and glowing skin and—

"I knew ya were going to make a mistake with that one," Bertha snapped.

She bristled. "I haven't made a mistake."

"Do you think I don't see how you're moonstruck over the earl? All that sighing and long gazes."

She frowned. "I'm not some naive girl, Bertha. I'm a grown woman capable of protecting myself." Except, was she? Was she truly safe from the power of Malcom's charm?

"Your mother thought the same." There was a malice in that retort, the like of which Verity had never before heard from the other woman.

"Either way, it's not your place," she said crisply.

"Isn't it? I was taking care of you when you were a babe. And then when Livvie was born all those years later, I cared for her while you—"

"While I saw that we all survived," she interrupted.

"You're becoming your mother."

Indignation swelled in her breast. "I am nothing like my mother," she bit out. "My mother never put anyone before her love of my father. And—"

"And you're incapable of thinking about anything except your earl."

Her protestations faded away on the wings of fear and horror. Verity's skin went clammy. Nay. It wasn't possible. Her nursemaid was simply worried about the possibility of the past repeating itself. But Verity couldn't. She wouldn't . . . love a man who'd never belong to her. Want a future that would never be. Her heart hammered away. "You're wrong." She had to be.

"Am I?" Bertha asked with a sad smile. "And this one a ruthless sewer dweller too selfish to share those tunnels with other toshers."

"He is nothing like that," Verity snapped. "And you don't know him at all."

Tension blanketed the room.

Bertha dropped a small, mocking curtsy. "You should get on, my lady. I trust you have another meeting with the earl."

Refusing to allow the cynical nursemaid to ruin her outing for the morning, Verity grabbed her bonnet and quit the rooms.

When she reached Malcom's offices, she hovered outside.

Surely Bertha was wrong.

Verity appreciated Malcom. Admired him for looking after Fowler and Bram. She was grateful for the kindness he'd shown her and Livvie. It was nothing more than that . . .

Why did it feel like she was the worst sort of liar to herself?

"Are you going to lurk out there, or are you going to enter?"

His deep voice carried through the panel, his booming tones muffled by the heavy oak. Verity jumped. She tried to make anything of them warm or teasing or soft. Anything that harkened back to the gentleness and intimacy they'd shared at Hyde Park. And found . . . none of it.

Grabbing the handle, she pressed it and let herself inside. Moisture dampened her palms, and she resisted the urge to wipe them along the sides of her skirts. *Be breezy. You're a thirty-year-old woman.* "How did you know I was there?"

"Heightened senses are a product of life on the streets," he explained almost disinterestedly, his gaze focused on his cluttered desk.

Bonnet in hand, Verity joined him across the room and, not waiting for permission, seated herself. "What are you doing?" she asked, her curiosity getting the better of her and her nerves.

"Inventorying."

"Inventorying?"

"It is something that toshers do." He inked several notes upon a meticulous column of words and numbers. "You can mention that in your article."

Her article? It took a moment for that word, and then suggestion, to compute.

Malcom briefly lifted his head, and grinned at her. "Or rather, the good toshers do."

His smile proved contagious. Her lips turned up at the corners. Verity set aside the straw bonnet she'd grabbed from those left by the previous young lady who'd lived here. "May I?"

He hesitated.

He wanted to reject her request.

She'd come to know him enough, however, that not relinquishing the books suggested he cared more than he did. A vulnerability he'd not allow himself.

"Forgive me," she murmured. "It's not my place to pry into your important matters."

There was a wickedness in her that, in a bid to share his world, she'd turn that weakness against him. He grunted. "They aren't important matters." Malcom nudged his chin at her.

More than half fearing he'd gather the ploy she'd used and take back that offer, Verity plucked the tome from a pile, opened it, and began to read. She paused. This is what he'd meant by inventorying. Column after column filled the pages, containing an enumeration of items and a value alongside it. Nay, not just any items . . . but rather, articles that belonged to him. She flipped through the accounting. When she reached the end, she looked over at Malcom. These weren't items found in a sewer. "They are records of your estates and all your belongings."

"Aye." Malcom shifted in his seat. "Some of them, at least."

Returning the ledger to his desk, Verity measured her words for several moments. "There is nothing . . . wrong in taking interest in that which you've a right to, Malcom," she said gently.

An endearing blush splotched his cheeks. "It is a force of habit. I collect items, record their value, and sell or save them."

He offered a rare unsolicited glimpse into how he'd lived his life these past years. Only it wasn't her story that she thought of just then but instead him. She flipped through the pages, scanning as she went.

Everything from gold timepieces to embroidered kerchiefs to . . . horses.

"And is that what you intend? To . . . sell them?"

"Yes."

Verity paused in her searching and briefly looked up. "To what end?" Verity pressed. "When you receive the monies from selling everything, what do you do?"

"What do I *do*?"

"Malcom." Verity set the book down on her lap. "On this page alone there must be . . ." She glanced down and silently tabulated in her head, mouthing her count aloud. "One thousand pounds in material items." She sharply turned the next page, and silently added the numbers there. "And . . . and . . ." Her eyes bulged. "This is another two thousand pounds." Her voice climbed. "And that is just two pages." *My God, he must be worth* . . . She frantically flipped through the book, and sat back, stunned. "You're richer than Croesus." And just off the funds he'd inherited. The riches before her had nothing to do with what he'd amassed as a tosher.

"I should expect you'd understand the value in an accumulated fortune," he said without malice. Then he reached dismissively for his pen, dipped it into the crystal inkwell, and resumed writing.

That was it? That was all he'd say? "But—" He looked up suddenly, his unwavering stare commanding to silence her, and mayhap if she were a different woman with a greater modicum of fear and a desire for self-preservation, she'd have let the matter go . . . But she'd come to know that gruff as he may be, neither was Malcom North one who'd hurt her or anyone. She tried to reason with him. "Malcom," she said gently, turning the ledger around, "this is *so* much money." My God, she could provide for her and Livvie and Bertha for the remainder of their lives, and comfortably, on but one and a half of the items recorded here.

"And you'd have me give it away?"

"What is the point in keeping *all* of it?" she rebutted.

"I'm not keeping it."

"Fine, then selling it," she said, not missing a beat. Goodness, he was obstinate. "Why—"

"Let it be," he said sharply, a vein bulging at the corner of his temple. With that, he resumed his frantic writing, the staccato tap of the pen flying across the pages punctuating the quiet.

As he worked on, Verity studied his bent head. The lone blond tress that had escaped his queue lent an almost . . . vulnerability . . . to the stoic figure he presented to the world.

Malcom might not recall the specifics of what had happened to him in the earliest part of his life, but there was an inherent remembrance of having, and then . . . *not*. Her heart squeezed. If, however, he simply gave away these items, then he'd lose those pieces that linked him to the parents who'd died. The parents who'd undoubtedly loved him. With the losses of those items, so, too, went items that might jog any memory.

And mayhap that is what he wishes for, too. Whether deliberate or inadvertent, perhaps he was doing all he could to shut out everything except for the hardships.

As she exchanged the leather tome in one hand for another, he continued working, but she felt him tense. Saw his gaze creep briefly over to her hand as she gripped that book and pulled it to her.

He'd not acknowledge her actions, but he was aware of her and what she did.

More leisurely, Verity paged through the catalog. Unlike the previous volume of masculine possessions, these ones were—

She slammed her finger down in the middle of the page.

- Ladies' boots
- Gowns
- Day dresses
- Bonnets
- Aprons
- Pearl brooches
- Ruby tiaras
- Sevres box
- Ribbons
- Slippers
- Queen Ann wooden peg doll

Verity didn't move. Her heart pulled, and then splintered. "These belonged to a young woman," she murmured. She recalled the story of Lord Bolingbroke and his siblings. "Three of them."

When he said nothing, she looked up.

At some point, he'd ceased his writing and openly studied her.

"These belong to them, do they not?" The earl . . . Except that wasn't quite right. "Lord Bolingbroke's three sisters?" She needed him to say it.

"I suspect," he said with a casual shrug.

"What need have you of"—she glanced down at the three items which had ultimately given her pause—"worn slippers, ribbons, and a . . . wooden peg doll?"

"I don't."

"You don't."

That was all he'd say? "But they *did*, Malcom." Just as Verity had desperately needed the dresses and slippers and boots she'd been forced to sell at her father's passing. But this time, for these women, it had been Malcom who had been the one to see all that taken.

"Why don't you say what it is you're thinking?" he snapped.

It was a challenge. If he expected her to back down, however, he was to be disappointed. "Very well," she said slowly, resting the book on her lap. "They are no more responsible for the decisions of their parents than you are responsible for what happened to you that night." The night he didn't speak of . . . or remember. The one shrouded in mystery.

"You care so much for people you've never met?"

Verity angrily flipped through the book and stopped at the back. "And you should hate—" She froze. Her gaze landed at the center of the page. Her mind slowed as she struggled through those annotations.

"I did it because I hate them," he said quickly. Too quickly. "Don't make more of it than there is."

And yet . . . how could she not? Her eyes scoured the pages, making sense of the numbers and details written there. "You didn't intend to simply take their belongings," she said softly, stroking a finger over the words. Understanding at last dawned.

"Don't, Verity," he snapped.

"You were giving it all away."

A stiff silence met that revelation.

Verity fell back in her seat. Here she'd been berating him. Believing the worst. Accusing him of wrongly directing his anger at the wrong people. When all along, he'd been diverting those resources to others. Ones who were deserving in an altogether different light. "Malcom," she said softly.

He wiped a hand down his face. "As I said, do not make more of it than there is."

Only, what else *was* there to make of it?

- Salvation Foundling Hospital
- Ladies of Hope
- London Hospital

The list went on. He was so very determined that the world see him in the darkest possible light. He was content to be seen as ruthless, and yet at every moment, with every decision he made and every person he saved, he revealed himself to be one of great honor.

Verity lifted her eyes from that evidence before her.

He met her with nothing but a mutinous silence. Of course. Because he was determined that the world would despise him. He, in fact, made it easy for them to do so. "But you didn't just take it, though, did you, Malcom?" She needed him to acknowledge that truth. Not for her. But for him. "You gave it to others." Verity clicked the ledger shut, and set it down. "Just as you gave this townhouse to Fowler and Bram to retire. Because you knew." She shifted to the edge of her seat. "You *knew* they were too proud to not contribute, but were also too old to continue on in their current role as toshers."

Malcom looked away, confirming everything that had just slid into place.

It all made sense now.

He made sense now.

"I did it because I hated them." Fury rolled off Malcom in palpable waves, and there could be no doubting he spoke of Lord Bolingbroke and his family. He seethed as he spoke. "I took it all because why should they have known any comfort when they'd stripped me of mine?"

She weighed her words a moment. "No one will ever believe you aren't deserving of your hatred and every other emotion you're feeling for what was taken from you . . . and what was lost. And yet"—Verity tapped the ledger—"you didn't let your hatred destroy you." Hadn't that been her earliest opinion of him? "You used your resentment to give to others whom you saw as more deserving than that family who'd wronged you. You gave away belongings that were rightfully yours, the ones linking you to your past and your family, Malcom, and gave them new beginnings to help others."

A muscle rippled along his jaw in the only outward reaction that he'd been affected by her words. "I don't have a family."

And then it hit her like a blow to the chest all over again. They were the reason he kept the world at bay. Even if he himself didn't realize the intent behind his guardedness. His insistence that friends were associates and his desire for complete isolation. "You did. And now, you have a new family. In Fowler, Bram, and Giles."

The grip he had upon the arms of his chair drained all the blood from his knuckles, leaving that scarred flesh white.

"I thought we'd agreed your interviews would be conducted in the evening."

She was unable to stifle the hurt at his response. "That isn't the reason for my questions or words, Malcom. Not everything is about . . . that."

"Isn't it?" he asked curiously. He leaned forward in his chair, dropping his elbows on the desk, and proceeded to study her the way she'd observed the tiniest bugs crawling in the soil of her and her mother's Surrey cottage property.

"Not for me."

He continued to search her face. "Then why did you seek me out?"

Her heart broke for the wary way in which he moved through life. How very exhausting . . . How very lonely it must be for him. "Livvie and I intended to journey to Hatchards. I thought you might join us." There was a beat of silence.

"Hatchards."

"It is a bookshop."

His gaze grew distant over her shoulder. "I know what Hatchards is."

Just as he'd been familiar with Gunter's and Hyde Park. Whether he knew it or not, those small revelations offered a window into who his parents had been. Only . . . mayhap he *did* know it. Mayhap that was what made him so very determined to keep out the memories of what had been. And of what he'd lost.

"For appearances' sake, of course," she said when he still didn't speak. *Not because I yearn for your company and enjoy being about with you. Liar.* "Simply, it would be beneficial if we were seen about." *Stop talking.* Verity bunched her skirts, noisily wrinkling the light silk cloak. She made herself stop, and smoothed her palms along the top of one of his many ledgers. "If we were seen out *together*."

Setting down his pen, he cracked his knuckles. "I've an appointment."

Did she simply hear regret in his voice because she wished it? "Oh," she said dumbly, unable to explain the flood of disappointment that swept her.

What did you expect him to say? That he wanted to join you?

As if on cue, there was a knock at the door.

"Enter," Malcom's voice boomed.

A moment later, the aging butler pushed the door open and admitted a tall, heavily scarred man. A very familiar one.

"A . . . Mr. Giles," the servant announced, his wizened features pulled as if pained by that introduction.

Verity sat upright.

With a wool cap and coarse garments, none would ever dare confuse the man for one of the Grosvenor Square world. Having feared him at their first meeting, Verity now found there was a comfort in being in the company of someone who didn't fit with Polite Society. People who were like her. In ways that even Malcom wasn't.

The ancient butler shifted on his feet. "Do you require anything else, my lord?" he asked when no directives were coming.

A bark of laughter burst from Mr. Giles, earning a dark glare from Malcom. A look that would have quelled most men. Except this one.

"That'll be all," Malcom excused the servant, and with a speed suited to one thirty years his junior, Coleman bolted from the room.

The moment the butler had closed the door, Malcom's associate exploded into another round of laughter. "Why, hello, *my lord*." He sketched a bow so deep as to be mocking. "And here I thought you were going to invite me for a spot of tea," he jested in an impressive rendition of the crispest English accent.

"Go to hell," Malcom muttered as he snapped his books closed, and set to organizing them.

Verity hovered in her seat, forgotten, taking in the exchange between Malcom and the other tosher. At their first meeting, she'd been riddled with unease at his presence. And yet, unlike her make-believe husband, who kept a careful mask in place, his smile creeping out with the same reluctance as the English sun, Mr. Giles freely teased and laughed. Mayhap that was why Malcom had taken him on as the friend he referred to as an associate. Mayhap he unknowingly welcomed that levity in his otherwise stark world.

When it became apparent that no introductions were forthcoming, Verity stood, and setting down Malcom's ledger, she crossed over to his friend. "Mr. Giles. As Malcom will not do the honors and no formal introduction was made at our last exchange, welcome." She held her hand out. "I am"—not truly a countess, and neither of them had been born to the nobility as Malcom had been—"Verity," she settled for. "Please, call me Verity."

As Mr. Giles placed his sole palm in hers, she caught the glare Malcom leveled her way. Or mayhap it was reserved for Mr. Giles.

More likely, it was reserved for the both of them.

Giles looked at her for a moment and then doffed his hat. "These are altogether different circumstances than our first meeting."

A smile pulled at her lips. "Indeed."

He leaned down. "If anyone had told me the day you arrived to speak with North that he'd go and marry you, I'd have directed that blighter on to Bedlam." He winked.

"And I would have clarified the directions for that blighter," she said, her smile deepening.

Tossing his head back, Mr. Giles erupted into another booming chuckle.

"If you're quite done," Malcom snapped, "we've business to see to."

Verity's smile instantly withered. Malcom's words were a reminder that all this was pretend: Their relationship. Even the introductions between her and his associate. She wasn't part of his world. Even the exchanges in which they'd shared parts of themselves—all of it had been driven by their arrangement. And she'd be wise to remember as much. "Forgive me; I'll leave you both to your meeting."

And as she let herself out, foolish as it was, she found herself wishing that Malcom had *wanted* to join her at Hatchards.

Chapter 24

THE LONDONER

Despite appearances amongst Polite Society, it is re-
ported that at various points of the day, the Earl of
Maxwell . . . disappears. And the *ton* is left with one more
question about the gentleman: *Where* does he go?

M. Fairpoint

Having ridden from Grosvenor Square to the wharves of London,
Malcom had thought he'd managed to escape the questioning.

Alas, knowing Giles as he had through the years, he'd merely been
deluding himself.

"How is married life?" Giles asked as they walked the less traveled
shore of the Thames.

"Go to hell," he muttered.

"So as well as one would expect," the other man said dryly with his
nub adjusting his tosher pole against his shoulder. "And yet, also well
enough that you've not gone out nightly."

There was a question there. "I've had other work I've had to see
to." It was why he'd put Giles in charge in his absence. "Unless it's been
too difficult—"

The other man snorted. "Now *you* can go to hell."

Malcom kept his gaze forward. Giles was entitled to his skepticism. Since Malcom had started scavenging sewers as a boy, there'd not been a single day of rest. His had been a purpose-driven existence.

It hadn't been eating ices at Gunter's and skipping stones at Hyde Park. It hadn't been her . . . Verity Lovelace . . . with her endearing tendency to prattle on about Epsom salts and English history with like skill.

And yet, now that it was . . . now . . . those moments held on.

Beckoned.

And suddenly, this wasn't quite what it once had been.

It wasn't what it had been at all.

"Are you ready?"

There was a hesitancy in Giles's voice.

And Malcom glanced around.

They'd arrived.

"Of course I'm ready," he said tightly, and not allowing another question, he made his way into the tunnel first. Giles followed close behind, dragging the grate back into place, shutting out the light and plunging them into darkness.

There'd always been a thrill in stealing under London's cobblestones and uncovering the treasures buried below.

Except as they ventured along, slogging through the murky water, why was the thrill missing this time? Why, as he waded through muck and refuse, was Malcom even now thinking about Verity walking the aisles of Hatchards? Or wondering about the books she read? He'd venture material related to the work she did. Or mayhap she didn't? Mayhap she sought a diversion—

Something slammed into him.

Grunting, Malcom went flying forward. He managed to bring his tosher pole up, catching himself in time before he hit the water.

Behind him there was a sharp rumble and a crash.

Heart pounding, he stared at the small pile of bricks that rested where he'd been standing. Good God. It was the height of carelessness. Underground, a man had to be even more alert than one was on the streets. Here, even the ceiling and walls represented danger. And Malcom hadn't made a misstep, hadn't allowed himself to be distracted from the work at hand . . . since he'd started out at this life.

"I don't . . . Thank—"

Giles waved him off. "That's what friends do."

Friends.

You refer to Bram and Fowler as "your people." You call Giles an "associate." All of these defenses that you put up, these choices of words that strip away closeness from your connections, they cannot truly conceal the truth . . . I know that you're protecting yourself by pretending that they don't matter . . .

They were friends. He and Giles. And they had been since the moment he'd rescued the other man from certain death, and had been all the times Giles had been there for him. And owning that connection to another person didn't leave him weak. Verity had shown him that.

Everything was changing.

And he'd been so damned certain he didn't want any of it to change.

He'd been content with his life as it was and hadn't desired anything more.

At least, that was what he'd told himself. He'd told himself as much so many times, he'd actually believed it.

He scrubbed a hand over his face.

She'd been right about so much.

"You're out of practice," Giles said without inflection. And at any time before this moment, Malcom would have lashed out like a wounded beast at the insinuation. He'd have driven the other man into the pavement and asserted his place in these parts.

"Aye," he said quietly, his voice softly echoing off the bricks.

"And . . . it's all right if you are," the other man—his friend—went on. "If you don't want to spend your nights scrounging sewers, you could stop now." Giles chuckled. "You could have stopped almost ten years ago, by my estimation."

Malcom stared at the tosher pole in his fingers, the one Fowler had given him and commanded him to never let go of. And he hadn't. "It's all I've known." *It is all I want to know.*

Isn't that what he'd meant? Why hadn't he said that?

"Aye." They resumed their trek through the ankle-deep water, skimming their poles over the stone flooring as they went, dragging a small current in their wake, when Giles paused. "But do you know something?" The other man didn't wait for an answer. "This." He gestured with the place his left hand should be. "This is all I've known, too. But, North?" Giles held his gaze. "If someone came to me tomorrow and told me I was a damned baron, duke, or any other fancy lord, I wouldn't spit in the face of the universe. I'd grab that chance to get out of these parts and never look back." He jammed his tosher pole toward Malcom. "And none of us, not Bram, not Fowler, not me, nor anyone, would begrudge you leaving this shitehole."

How easy Giles made it all sound. Only this wasn't simply about living in the lap of luxury; it was where that lap was located. And all that went with it. And in Malcom's case . . . all that had once gone with it, too.

"And don't be a smug, all-knowing bastard."

"I didn't say anything," he muttered.

"I know you well enough. You didn't need to. You're thinking you don't belong there. Well, I've news for you, Lord Maxwell: you don't belong here, either."

That barb struck.

"Oh, go to hell, North. I didn't say what I said to get under your skin."

The other man's words, however he'd intended them, had grated because of their unswerving accuracy.

For what Giles proposed . . . it wasn't just about Malcom leaving this world . . . It was about entering a new one. One that he'd been born to, but didn't truly belong to. Not because of what he'd done. But rather, because of who he'd been. The darkest parts of him were indelibly tied to who he would always be. "Like I said, I've got no place there," he said with an underscore of finality. Even as he acknowledged as much aloud, memories slipped in: Verity with her palms over his eyes as they played word riddles. Verity stuffing a spoon of ice in his mouth.

Could he live that life away from this place . . . and could he do it with her?

Sweat slicked his palms, and he adjusted his hold on his tosher pole.

"You've got someone who can help you figure out how to navigate there, too."

It took a moment for both the statement and the meaning behind Giles's suggestion to sink in.

Verity.

His neck heated. "You're mad." *Except . . . why is it such a mad idea?* a voice whispered at the back of his brain.

"Because you don't like the gel?"

Nay, Malcom liked her well enough. He winced. Nay, he liked her a good deal more than that. A good deal more than he'd liked anyone.

"Or is it the whole matter of her being with the newspaper and whatever deal you forced her to agree to?"

"That's decidedly closer," he mumbled, and started on. "We're business partners, and nothing more."

Giles snorted. "Aye, business partners. Though in fairness, we're business partners, and I've never seen you eyeing me the way you eye that—" The remainder of that thought dissolved in laughter as Malcom splashed him.

"Can we get on with our work?" he groused, resuming his forward march through the tunnels. The bottom of his pole snagged something hard on the stone floor, and he shoved at it. He felt around the perimeter of the object, and then spearing it in the middle, he dragged the finding up along the wall. Wading through the water, Malcom removed the artifact from the end of his pole and studied it, turning the item over in his hands. An ornate gold-and-silver cuff bracelet.

It'd fetch a small fortune, and once would have elicited some greater sense of satisfaction.

These belong to them, do they not? Lord Bolingbroke's three sisters? . . . They are no more responsible for the decisions of their parents than you are responsible for what happened to you that night . . .

A bitter-to-his-own-ears-sounding chuckle shook his frame as he eyed the piece.

Oh, the bloody humor of it all. Here was he, the most merciless tosher of the rookeries, fishing out treasure and feeling badly about three women whom he'd never met and would never meet . . . women whose family had stolen all that had been slated in life for Malcom.

Good God, what madness had Verity Lovelace wrought upon both his sanity and his existence?

He tossed the bracelet back.

Whistling, Giles leapt forward with his arm outstretched, and caught the jewel before it struck the water, ringing it around his tosher pole. "I'll take that." Removing the bangle, he stuffed it into one of his many jacket pockets.

And as they continued their hunt, thankfully, the remainder in silence, Malcom couldn't shake the thought his friend had put forward . . . about a future with he and Verity in it, together.

Chapter 25

THE LONDONER
TROUBLE IN PARADISE?

Lady Maxwell has been spotted at Hatchards . . . sans the Earl of Maxwell. Polite Society can only speculate as to whether there's been a falling-out between the couple . . .

M. Fairpoint

Forty-two.

That was officially the count of questions her sister had put to Verity since the carriage ride and now short walk along the pavement to 89–90 Piccadilly, London.

"How come Malcom didn't join us?" Because he continued to push her away. Nay, because he wanted to keep her out. Alas, neither were suitable responses for her young sister. "Or is it you that he didn't wish to be with?" Verity opened her mouth. "Or mayhap it makes more sense that it is because I was coming that he didn't wish to join?"

Did those quickly strung-together questions count as three additional ones asked? Either way, Verity's head throbbed from the incessant chatter, all about her marriage. Ultimately it was far easier to focus on her sister's insecurity. "I assure you, his not accompanying us had nothing to do with you."

It proved the wrong thing to say.

"So it was because of you," Livvie said with her usual frankness.

Oh, blast and damn. "Hush," she warned, glancing about at the lords and ladies streaming all around them. "It was not because of me." *Are you altogether certain?* She ignored that jeering question.

"Are you certain?"

"I'm"—*not*—"certain. Malcom had business to attend."

She caught Bertha's snort and shot the old nursemaid a warning look.

"In his sewers?" Livvie speculated.

"In . . . in . . ." Whatever had been so pressing that he'd opted to not join her. "In matters that are none of our business."

They reached the front of Hatchards, and stopped. "But he's your husband. It's absolutely your business. Furthermore"—Livvie stayed Verity as she reached for the door handle—"it would seem that someone as progressive as you, who believes a countess can and should retain employment if she so wishes it, should also expect to be privy to her husband's business affairs."

And blast if her sister wasn't wholly correct. However, Verity's was a marriage of pretend. As such, she couldn't go saying as much to Livvie.

Silence proving safer, Verity drew the door open and motioned her sister in ahead of her.

Bertha followed close.

"Do you truly think you can go on for a year with that one not gathering that something is amiss?" Bertha asked in hushed tones as she shook out her skirts. "She's too clever by half, and not the small girl you used to bounce on your knee."

"This isn't the time or place." Verity spoke out of the corner of her mouth. She took in the crowded shop, the satin-clad ladies and top hat–wearing gentlemen who moved amongst the floor-to-ceiling rows of books.

"It never is, though, is it, Verity?"

"Bertha!" Livvie's exuberant cry saved Verity from answering, and also earned a sea of stares from disapproving patrons.

"Go look after her," Verity urged.

As Bertha made her way over to Livvie brandishing a small leather volume and waving it about, Verity took in the looks her sister and, by default, she herself continued to receive. Her neck heated, and it took a concerted effort to bring her shoulders back and her chin up.

Her gaze collided with that of a young gentleman, yet another patron boldly staring.

She made to take a step but lingered. Something in his warm eyes compelled her to remain. There was something vaguely memorable about him. With the spectacles perched on the edge of an aquiline nose, he had the look of many men she'd worked alongside at *The Londoner*. His finely cut wool suit, however, set him apart from those other commoners like herself.

Giving her head a shake, she ventured deeper into the shop. She may have written stories on the nobility over the years, but every last one of them was a stranger to her.

Still, some air of familiarity tugged at her, and she tossed another glance to where he stood.

At some point, he'd gone.

Verity resumed her stroll through the bookshop. And as she wandered the rows, she studied titles. Periodically, she'd pluck one from the shelf and tuck it into the fold of her arm. Purposeful in her selection, she'd six titles in hand when she turned to go.

Gooseflesh popped up on her arms.

A different stranger stood at the opposite end of the aisle. Though also well dressed like the other man who'd been studying her a short while ago, that was where all similarities ended. His skin was faintly pockmarked. But it was his eyes. There was a coldness in them. They were eyes that emanated a threat.

Her heart racing, Verity bolted in the opposite direction.

A stockier man blocked that exit, bringing her up short. *Trapped.*

She spun sideways so she could keep an eye on both foes.

Verity hugged her books tightly, the spine of one of her volumes biting painfully into the soft flesh of her upper arm. "Step out of my way," she commanded, proud that her voice didn't shake. "I'll scream." Her heart hammered out of control. She whipped her head back and forth between the two men.

"Now why would you go and do that?" The taller of that menacing pair started forward. Stalking her. "If you did, Miss Lovelace, then we'd not have the opportunity to speak on what it is we want."

Miss Lovelace? It took a moment for that correct usage of her name to register.

A hard, empty smile curled his lips. "Or is it Countess Maxwell? It's all very confusing, isn't it?"

Her pulse picked up its beat. He knew. This man knew she wasn't married. Or mayhap it was merely speculative . . . ?

"Step out of my way," she repeated.

"I will," he offered.

At her back, she registered a sharp snap as the shorter stranger cracked his knuckles.

"Once we make something clear to you, Miss Lovelace."

He stopped before her.

Verity's mouth went dry. Reflexively she hugged the books in her arms all the tighter.

"Your story? About the earl? Kill it."

It took a moment for that warning to penetrate her fear.

"What?" she blurted.

"There's those who don't want that story out, miss. People who'd rather you be . . . silent."

Silent. Or *silenced?*

Verity shivered. *Bolingbroke.* Who else would these henchmen be here on behalf of? And yet she'd be damned if they quieted her. And she'd certainly not silence Malcom's story, not when it would open the world's eyes to the abuses those who lived beyond the lap of luxury suffered. For all the times she'd been silenced before this one, and all the stories she'd been prevented from telling, and the directives she'd taken, they had brought her to this moment. "No."

He tipped his head. "What did you say?" The brute exchanged a look with his partner.

"I said no. You can go back to whomever has sent you here to try and intimidate me and let them know I'll not be cowed. Whatever Lord Maxwell, *the rightful Lord Maxwell*, wishes to share with the world will be shared." Her chest rose and fell quickly from the force of her emotions. Or fear? Or mayhap a blend of both. "Nor do I truly believe you're going to kill me in public at an establishment filled with patrons." Adjusting her hold on her books, Verity gathered her skirts in her other palm, and took a step forward. "Now get out of my way."

Neither man budged.

"We aren't going to kill you," he scoffed. "We only came to warn you."

He swiftly caught her by the nape of her neck, wringing a gasp from her . . . which he promptly buried under a meaty palm.

The books toppled from Verity's arms, the sound as they clattered about her feet muted by the pounding of her heart. She scrabbled at those unforgiving hands. Dimly aware of the bespectacled figure charging forward, the unlikeliest of saviors.

"You there!" That shout came from somewhere in Hatchards. That voice vaguely familiar. But everything swirled in her mind; it was twisted and jumbled by fear and panic.

The gentleman with the glasses was quickly brought down by the stocky fellow at her back.

Verity's eyes bulged, and she scrabbled all the more with her assailant.

"Consider yourself warned," he whispered against her ear. And then he slammed her headfirst into the wood shelving.

Verity didn't blink. Surely, she was supposed to cry out. To make some sound. The vicious crack of her skull. The agonizing thud surely merited even just a sigh or whisper of breath. Except she couldn't make a noise. Her ears buzzed. Her vision swam.

And then, collapsing against the bookcase, Verity crumpled onto the floor—and remembered nothing more.

Chapter 26

THE LONDONER
ATTACKED!

The Countess of Maxwell was assaulted in the middle of Hatchards. Her attack serves as a reminder of the Countess of Maxwell's and the Earl of Maxwell's dark pasts. As long as he moves amongst Polite Society, there will be a threat . . .

M. Fairpoint

She hadn't come.

Or rather, she was late.

Standing at the empty hearth, his arms clasped behind his back, Malcom stole a glance at the porcelain ormolu clock. He squinted in a bid to bring the small circular dial into focus in the dimmer lighting of the room. Grabbing the gilded cherub by the head, Malcom picked it up and consulted the piece once more.

Ten minutes late, to be precise. When she'd never been late before. He set the clock down.

Mayhap because she'd found her books or even now saw to her work.

Or mayhap it was because she was fine enough without him.

He began to pace.

And furthermore, he should be just fine with her tardiness. Hell, he should be even more thrilled if she didn't come. Because then there wouldn't be questions and probing into his past, and yet—

He stopped midstride, the tails of his jacket slapping wildly at the abrupt cessation of movement.

Somewhere along the way, he'd ceased minding the questions. At some point, sharing those parts he'd buried or fought to repress had ceased to be a battle. Instead, with every remembrance she'd coaxed forward, there'd come an ease in accepting his past and those memories as ones that had belonged to him.

Footsteps echoed from out in the corridor.

Even as he turned to face the entrance of the library, he knew it wasn't Verity.

The steps were more minced than Verity's deliberate, confident ones.

And yet, as he faced the interloper, there was also a striking similarity, an unrepentantly direct Lovelace gaze.

"Malcom," Livvie greeted with a flawless curtsy.

He yanked at his collar. Girls and curtsying. Aye, this was a realm of foreignness of which he'd no finesse. He cast a glance over her shoulder, searching hopefully for the elder Miss Lovelace. "Miss Lovelace, would you care to . . ." Livvie was already shutting the door behind her.

". . . join me," he finished wryly.

"I'll not waste either of our time, Mr. North." She stalked over with long, purposeful strides. Grabbing one of the leather wing chairs, she used her hip to shove it into her desired place. When it was almost perfectly aligned with the button sofa, she jabbed a finger at it. "If you will?"

And under siege, and wholly outmaneuvered by a slip of a girl, Malcom did the only thing that made sense.

He sat.

Livvie Lovelace plopped herself into the opposite seat so they faced one another . . . and drumming her fingertips on the leather arms of her chair, she waited. Silently assessing him. Her impressively unflinching stare remained unwavering.

Over the years, Malcom had faced any number of opponents, people of all ages and sizes. In thinking of that impressive catalog of adversaries, he'd venture the one before him might prove to be the most formidable. For in that moment, Malcom acknowledged the gross underestimation he'd made—there was nothing mincing about this one. In fact, he'd wager her entrance a deliberate show to set him off-kilter. And he tipped his proverbial hat to the young woman, and notched his appreciation for her tenfold.

Tap-Tap-Tap-Tap-Tap-Tap-Tap-Tap. As she drummed along to that rhythm, Livvie slowly brought her eyebrows into a single line. "My sister thinks I'm an idiot, North."

Well, of all that he anticipated she *might* have said . . . that had not been in it. He'd brokered peace in the rookery, but never had it been between quarreling sisters. As such, he was completely useless of words.

Fortunately, Livvie had enough for the both of them. "I'm not an idiot. I'm quite observant, you know."

"Indeed."

There, that was certainly a suitable reply.

By the further narrowing of her eyes, however, the young woman remained *suitably* unimpressed.

Malcom shifted on the bench, and stole a hopeful look at the door. Alas, rescue would not be coming from Verity.

"And do you know why my sister believes I'm an idiot?"

"I couldn't even begin to imagine." There, that much was true.

"Because Verity believes that I believe that you're really married."

The ticking of the clock was inordinately loud.

"And as you seem to think that I believe that, as well, Lord Maxwell"—Livvie ceased tapping her fingers—"then on the matter of my intelligence, that would mean you are of a like opinion as Verity."

He'd danced through knife battles in the street less precarious than this exchange. "I would never presume to question your intelligence; however, I feel this might be a discussion—"

"Better reserved for my sister?" She shot a brow up. "Never tell me you think you can be free of this discussion that easily? If that's the case . . ." She muttered the remaining something under her breath that sounded a good deal like *You're, in fact, the lackwit.* "And do you know why I have no intention of leaving?"

"Because you're stubborn?"

"Because of my sister."

"I . . . see . . ." And he saw not at all.

"No, you don't. Don't simply say you do so that you've some reply. You're better off saying nothing."

Aye, Verity's sister was clever, after all. Even more clever than he'd credited at the start of their dialogue.

"Either way, I've not the time to lecture you on how to have a proper conversation. I was the one who insisted Verity go to you, and do you know why I did that?"

"Because you are a romantic?"

Unlike Verity, who'd bristled at having that descriptor applied to her, Livvie Lovelace preened. She sat up all the straighter in her chair. "Precisely. As such, when she recounted what happened that night you met, I heard what she didn't hear. And I was the one who believed if you could be heroic, then you'd be the one to help us."

Us.

That was what had set Verity apart from him and how he'd lived his existence. It had marked him different from her or her sister. They saw themselves as a family; they never divorced themselves from that connection.

While Malcom had taken more than fifteen years to own up to such a bond with his own . . . kin.

And with her faith in him, he'd failed to meet those expectations she'd had. Instead, Verity had come to him, and he'd turned her away. Shame pitted his belly.

"Well, do you have anything to say? Speak up."

Aye, terrifying now, she was going to rule England should she so wish it, come ten years from now.

"What I am trying to sort through, Mr. North, is whether you are actually a good man or not . . . so which is it?"

Decidedly not was the immediate and accurate answer that sprang to his mouth. Mayhap he was getting weak through the years, that he could not bring himself to snarl or even utter that response at the young woman. While they sat, tensely studying one another, Malcom considered his response. In the end, he settled for raw truth. "I've not been a good person," he said quietly. "I'm trying to be better."

"Hmm," she said noncommittally. With that she hopped up, and he was saved from any further questioning. Or, he almost was. Livvie lingered at the doorway. "Do you care about Verity?"

That blunt, unexpected question hit him square between the eyes. "I . . ."

"It is just that I never knew my mother. Verity has been the only one I've known. As long as I've been alive, she's worked to support me. And she's always soothed my hurts and allowed me my dreams. She's protected me." A warning glint sparked in Livvie's eyes. "And I'll not see her hurt by anyone. And certainly not by you. So if you think you can't care about her, or that you don't love her, then we're done here." She paused. "All of us."

"I . . ." His mind swam, and he tried to dredge up a reply. Only, Livvie Lovelace had confounded him. What she spoke of . . . loving Verity . . . was foreign to the world he'd built. One that the elder Miss Lovelace had single-handedly dismantled. And yet to open himself so wholly, so completely . . . "Thank you for the talk," he replied. For whatever he had to sort through couldn't be done with this slip of a woman, or any observer, about.

"North," she murmured. She made to go, and then paused once more. "Oh, and I should mention, in the event that you *do* care, you should be aware that my sister was attacked earlier today."

With that, Verity's sister let herself out. Her words echoed in her wake.

Malcom didn't move. He didn't so much as blink.

Surely he'd heard Livvie wrong. Surely with the casualness of that deliverance, his mind had simply twisted whatever she'd said.

And then blood went roaring through his ears.

Malcom exploded to his feet and bolted from the library, cursing the endless, winding corridors. Slightly out of breath from fear and his exertions, he reached the stairs and took them two at a time. The moment his feet hit the landing, he took off running once more, skidding to a halt outside Verity's room.

Breathing hard, he pressed the handle, and let himself in. And then he found her.

Or more specifically . . .

Them. Malcom found them.

Based on the ominous pronouncement Livvie had dropped, during his endless streak to this very moment, Malcom had conjured all the worst imaginings.

Verity: Unconscious. Bleeding. Broken.

Of all the sights he'd expected after his talk with Livvie, this had not been it. Verity perched at the left side of the mattress with her back to him; she had Bram and Fowler before her. The old toshers sat in two delicate, scrolled armchairs like dutiful pups, albeit enormous pups that tested the constraints of that seating. "I told you, it's an absolute cureall," Verity was saying, wholly engrossed in whatever latest apothecary sat next to her bed. Their hands outstretched and dunked in bowls of water, the trio remained focused on whatever it was they were doing. "You'll want to do this several times a day. It will soften them."

"Ain't nothing wrong with a callus." Fowler grunted.

"There is when they break and then you get dirt in them, and well, it's no different from getting dirt in an open wound."

Malcom lingered at the entrance.

Mayhap it was relief so strong that managed to stir an even more unfamiliar sentiment—mirth.

And he didn't know whether to be relieved or irate with the young woman who'd sent him—

Verity glanced over her shoulder. "Oh, hullo," she greeted.

And the floor fell out from under him.

Since he'd taken his leave of her that morn, a round knot had formed at the right side of her forehead. A vicious knob, a product of a blow.

The air hissed between his teeth.

"Get out."

Stiffening, Verity shoved to her feet. "I'll not."

"Not you, madam," he ground out.

Those enormous eyes blinked. "Oh, uh . . . well, because I was going to say I'll not be ordered about."

Fowler and Bram exchanged a look, and then simultaneously jumped up. The pair of toshers shuffled guiltily over to the door and made their exit.

Good. They should feel guilty, the blighters.

Malcom fixed on that outrage to keep from descending into panic. She was all right. She was . . . sporting an enormous bruise, which according to her sister, was the product of an attack.

And where was I? Diving into sewers, fishing out treasure I don't need. Wealth that other people in the dire circumstances he'd once found himself in desperately needed.

Malcom slammed the door shut, hard.

"You needn't do that," she chided, tidying up the little workstation she'd arranged for herself between the chairs previously occupied by her patients.

Her patients.

When *she* was the one who should be lying down with a—

"Doctor—" He already had the door opened and was thundering for a servant.

Billy popped out of the shadows. "Ya called, sir," she piped in.

"The butler . . ." What in blazes was the man's name? Why hadn't he bothered to learn it? He'd be the one with those connections Malcom—and Verity—needed in this moment.

"Coleman, my lord."

"Have Coleman fetch a doctor."

"Malcom, I don't need a doctor."

The girl was already darting down the hall.

"One has already come," Verity called, sailing over to the door.

"Then you'll see a different one." To be certain she wasn't truly hurt. "You should be in bed," he squeezed between clenched teeth as she took the panel in her fingers and ducked her head—her injured head—out.

"I don't need a doctor, Billy."

The little girl stopped.

"Fetch the doctor."

Billy took a step forward. She wavered back and forth, her arms outstretched and a hopeless look etched in her small features.

"You're confusing the girl," Verity chided. "Stop it." Stepping out into the hall, she spoke in a gentle but insistent voice. "I don't require another doctor at this time, Billy, but if I do, I'll be certain to let you know."

And in an absolute display of which one of them held actual power in this household and over people, Billy dropped a curtsy. "As ya wish, moi lady."

It wasn't enough.

"You need to be checked again, Verity," he said tightly as she closed the door.

"I've been—*eep*." Malcom swept her up, an arm under her knees, and cradling her against his chest, he carried her over to the bed. "I can walk, Malcom."

Had she been able to walk in the immediacy of the attack? Was she even now putting on a brave show through the pain? His chest tightened.

"It doesn't matter that you can. You're not doing it." He lay her down gently in the middle of the mattress. And hovered there, uncertain, when he'd always had answers. When he'd never feared anything. He feared for this woman. It was an enervating, crippling panic that chipped away at all coherent thought. Somewhere along the way, she'd come to mean more to him than anyone. "Do you have nothing to say to me?" he managed when he trusted himself to speak.

"You heard about the attack."

"I heard about the attack," he confirmed.

"Oh." She twisted her fingertips in the lace coverlet.

How was she so calm? How, when a raw rage set every nerve to vibrating? When he wanted to hunt down and end the one who'd dared put his hands upon her?

"Livvie?" she ventured.

"Livvie."

"Livvie," she muttered under her breath.

God love the girl. Had it not been for her, Malcom would still be waxing on in his mind about everything he felt—and feared feeling—for the woman before him.

Verity abruptly stopped that distracted toying with her bedding. "I thought you'd be grateful for a reprieve?"

His blond brows came together in a fierce line. By God, was she . . . ?

"I take it you're not amused?"

"I'm not amused," he whispered.

Chapter 27

THE LONDONER
THE HUNTED BECOMES THE HUNTER...

Our sources report upon learning of the assault on his wife, the Earl of Maxwell went half-mad... and he's revealed the ruthlessness which he's kept carefully concealed from Polite Society... until now.

M. Fairpoint

Over their course of knowing one another, Verity had encountered many shades of Malcom's anger, and at any number of times.

But never had she seen him like this. His sharp features tensed in lines of fury, veins bulging at his temple, his eye twitching. His self-control was thin, and she'd only ever seen him in command of it . . . and himself.

And he should be upset . . . about her?

Something in that evidence of his caring sent a warmth unfurling in her breast.

On the heel of that was the call to reality. "I assure you, I'm quite well to continue on with our arrangement, Malcom."

He narrowed his eyes, and then dropping a knee on her bed, he climbed onto the mattress. "Is that what you believe?" he whispered. "That I'm concerned about the deal we've struck?"

Something in his tone suggested she weigh her answer and provide the correct one. In the end, she offered him what he deserved—the truth. "I don't know, Malcom." She well knew how she felt about him. She knew that her heart was lighter whenever he was near. That he'd made her open her eyes to the stories she should have been fighting these years to tell. But she didn't know what he felt or how he felt about her.

He stopped his advance, kneeling beside her.

With an infinite tenderness that sent warmth spiraling all the more, he brought his palm close to her cheek. It hovered there. This man, uncertain in ways that he'd only ever been fully in command of. Then ever so slightly, he touched his callused fingertips to the corner of her injury.

She bit her lip.

"Oh, V-Verity," he said hoarsely. His voice cracking as he misunderstood her response for one of pain. And aye, her head throbbed still from the bashing it had taken, but the feel of him so close, and caring as he did, threatened to shatter her.

"I'm fine," she whispered, placing her palm over his.

"What happened?"

"Someone slammed my forehead into a bookcase."

His eyes slid closed. "I should have been there."

She'd wanted him to be there . . . but not out of any sense of obligation.

"I fainted. When I came to, I was already in the carriage. A gentleman had helped carry me from the shop and sent us on our way."

The muscles of his throat moved rapidly.

"A doctor was here most of the day. He insists it is a superficial wound."

Malcom gently framed her face between his long fingers; the tenderness of that caress brought her eyes closed.

"Verity, are you attempting to reassure me?"

She sat up. "Is it working?"

"Not at all. Who?"

It had been inevitable. That particular question that could never end well . . . not for Malcom. It would lead to scandal and controversy and conflict he didn't need. Not with what his life had been. "They were strangers," she hedged. "Two of them."

"What did they want?"

He'd never be content in believing it was a random attack at a London bookshop.

He sat back; his keen gaze worked her face. "You're not telling me for a reason."

Blast him for being so astute. "Someone who wants me to keep your story silent."

Malcom fell back on his haunches. "Bolingbroke."

"I don't know that," she said quickly, even as he confirmed her initial supposition at Hatchards. "And you don't know that, either." No good could come from Malcom entering into a battle with a peer of the realm, one whose family had already proven ruthless.

Frost glazed his eyes. "I'll kill him."

And despite knowing Malcom as she did, Verity found herself shivering at the dark threat blazing from those golden depths.

Verity came up on her knees before him and took his face between her palms. "You won't, because you're not one to simply charge after someone without knowing facts."

"You don't know—"

"I do know that about you."

The muscles under her palms jumped and moved. He was a volatile ball of thrumming nerves and energy. Verity worked her eyes over him. "Malcom, I don't want you to run off and fight battles for me. I've been alone for eighteen years, and when I leave this place at the end of next year's Season, I'll be fighting them on my own. While you, you'll be living with and amongst these people."

"I don't care about any of them. Any of this." Emotion hoarsened his voice. "I care about you."

Her heart jumped several beats.

"And I want to fight this battle for you."

She stroked the back of her knuckles along his jaw. "Oh, Malcom. You don't get to decide that. I do."

"You are maddening, Verity Lovelace," he whispered.

"Aye." Verity smiled softly. And yet, when had anyone truly looked after her? Oh, there'd been Bertha and her mother and, periodically, her father about. But even in those earliest days when life had been easiest, Verity's well-being and happiness had fallen second to her emotional, brokenhearted mother. Too often Verity had been focused on seeing that her mother smiled, as had Bertha, but no one had been there for Verity. Not truly. Going up on her knees, she leaned forward and pressed her lips to his.

He froze, and then kissed her back with a desperation that matched hers.

Malcom broke the embrace as quick as it started. "Why . . . ?"

"Because I want to," she said simply. "Because I want to be in your arms." *Because I love you.* And when they parted ways, she'd live on as a spinster, and when she did, she'd have this moment, with this man, there as part of her memories. This time when she kissed him, there was a desperation to their embrace.

She came alive all at once.

They came alive together.

He groaned and caught her around the waist, drawing her closer as if he needed to feel her against him. And she luxuriated in that evidence of his desire. She herself needing to feel *him* in every way. "You've thrown my existence off-center, Verity."

Aye, as he'd done to hers. And she'd never recover. "Then we're even, Malcom North," she panted out between each lash of his lips on hers. God help her, she didn't want to recover from this upside-down world.

And there would be time enough to panic about her need for this man. But for now, there was only them. For now, she wanted it to be only them.

Verity parted her lips, and he slipped his tongue inside to taste her as he'd done twice before. "I've dreamed of doing this every moment since our last kiss."

"Then our dreams are aligned, *tooooo*." The remainder of that broke down into a moan as he nipped and teased the corner of her mouth.

"You taste of chocolate and mint and honey."

They dueled with their tongues.

"Is that a g-good thing?" she asked when he moved his lips down the curve of her neck.

The depth of desire in his eyes touched her to the quick, hot, like a physical caress. "Aye. It's an all-intoxicating sweetness I've never known in any way, Verity Lovelace."

Verity Lovelace.

I want to be joined with him. In every way.

Thrusting aside those regretful musings, not allowing this moment to descend into what she truly longed for and what would never be, she kissed him again. Their tongues lashed against one another, an erotic dance with no predefined rules or movements.

And then he broke away from her.

Verity cried out. "What? Why . . . ? Why did you stop?"

❦

He wanted her. He wanted her as he'd never hungered for another. And yet he could not simply take the gift she held out. Even as he yearned to. Even as he resented this belated discovery that she'd, in fact, been correct; there was a shred of honor that lived within his worthless soul, after all. Panting, Malcom pulled away, a concerted effort that took every bit of self-control he'd fought to master through the years.

Her lashes, thick and heavy, fluttered up, revealing the question in her eyes a moment before it spilled from her lips in a single hoarse utterance: "Why?"

"I don't want this as payment." He managed to force that admission between sharp gasps for breath.

Some of the desire receded from her eyes, and she leaned up, straightening from her haunches. "Is that why you believe I'm doing this? To pay you for the gifts you've given me?"

He winced. "No. Aye." Malcom dragged a hand through his hair, unloosening his queue. Everything was upside down. "I don't know," he confessed. He knew only that he wanted her. That he wanted her to want him. But that never would he have her in any way but one that was of her own choosing, one that came from a place of only desire—for him.

"Oh, Malcom," she whispered, and then leaning up once more, she touched her lips to the corner of his—first one and then the other. A butterfly-soft caress that weighted his eyes shut. "This is me making love with you because I want to, Malcom." The lilting timbre of her voice emerged like a seductive song, and it sent a fresh wave of desire thrumming through his veins. "I'm a woman and I know what I want." Desire darkened her eyes. "I want you."

And with that, he was lost.

Or mayhap, he'd been found.

Mayhap he'd truly been found the day he'd discovered her in the sewers of London . . . and his life would never be the same.

Groaning, Malcom worked his lips down her neck. He flicked his tongue out, teasing the flesh, until breathless moans spilled from her; his shaft went impossibly hard at the unrestrained evidence of her desire. "You are so beautiful, Verity," he said between each kiss on her satiny-soft skin.

"You. Are. Too." She gasped those three words out, wringing a smile from him. He brought his hands up between them, cupping her supple breasts. "Y-you are." She panted, her head falling back, allowing him better access. "I th-thought it the first . . . *mmm*"—her speech dissolved into an incoherent, keening cry as he lowered her neckline and swooped down to worship the creamy swells of her breasts—"time I saw you," she said, her words running together on a rush. As if she'd never draw proper breath to speak a proper sentence, but needed him to know those truths.

He was on fire, set ablaze by her yearning. Sweat beaded along his brow; it trickled down his cheek, and Verity lifted fingers that shook to brush that perspiration away.

Their gazes held; in her violet depths was reflected back all the desire singing through him. Not breaking contact with her gaze, Malcom undid the handful of buttons on his jacket, and shrugged out of it. He reached for his shirttails the same moment Verity did. Together, they divested him of the lawn article.

Her lips, swollen and damp from his ministrations, parted as she eyed him.

He stiffened, seeing the same scarred canvas littered with the marks left by daggers and injuries he'd sustained dwelling underground in London.

Verity stroked her fingertips over the jagged scar alongside his navel. He tensed, but then she bent down and touched her lips to him.

"*So* beautiful," she whispered between each caress of her mouth on him.

Malcom released a hiss through tightly clenched teeth, fisting his hands at his sides.

It had never been like this with a woman. Tender and slow, and yet also burning and frantic. Sex had been nothing more than a physical act, a satiation of his lust that brought an all-too-brief, mindless release from the hell that was life.

With Verity, it was . . . more.

Because she was more than he'd ever dared believe himself worthy of.

She drifted her trail of kisses lower, grazing the top of the waistline of his trousers, where a scar started.

It was too much.

He groaned, low, deep, and guttural, the sound lodging in his throat.

Drawing her up, Malcom took her mouth under his once more, and set to work on the tiny buttons down the length of her dress. In between each frantic meeting of their lips, he spoke. "Why are there so many damned buttons?"

"I like them," she said breathlessly, her voice ragged like the night of their first meeting, when she'd run, frantic, through London at his side. "Th-they're v-very delicate."

He wrenched at the buttons down the front of her dress, and the fastenings gave with a pop. And then pinged and hopped along the floor, bouncing on the table, all around them. The gaping fabric revealed her chemise underneath. Malcom and Verity ceased moving; their chests rose and fell hard and fast in a matched rhythm. "I'll buy you more."

"You needn't—"

He swallowed those protestations with another kiss and then guided her back down.

Verity stretched her arms up, reaching for him, and lowering himself, he braced his weight on his elbows.

Then, bending his head, he drew the tip of her right breast into his mouth, and suckled that pebbled, pale-brown nipple.

Verity groaned, long and low, and let her legs splay wide.

His shaft jumped, all the blood rushing to that throbbing flesh.

Malcom pulled back once more, and Verity cried out, scrabbling for him.

But he was merely shucking off his boots, and then his trousers. And as he bared himself before her in all his scarred imperfection, Verity reclined on her elbows and simply watched him.

In her eyes, there was no pity or revulsion. Or even the sick fascination he'd encountered in the past liaisons he'd had in his life.

"So beautiful," she said, her breath coming in rapid little bursts.

Malcom resumed his previous ministrations. Worshipping the previously neglected breast, he palmed the bounteous mounds that were overflowing in his callused palms. Her skin was like pure silk upon his flawed flesh, and he laved and teased the engorged peak until Verity was crying out. Keening his name. Lifting her hips in a frantic up-and-down, primitive thrusting.

Unable to look away from her tightly clenched eyes and the contortions of her face as she surrendered to the magic of their embrace, Malcom cupped the thatch of dark curls shielding her womanhood.

Verity went motionless, her eyes flying open, sharp surprise emanating from them, matched by the little circle of shock her lips formed.

And then Malcom slid a finger inside the tight, sodden sheath.

Verity cried out as he stroked her slowly at first, and then at a quickened pace. He slipped another finger inside, and Verity bucked her hips wildly. Thrust and retreat. Over and over. They set up a perfect rhythm, moving conjointly.

Her movements grew more frantic, her breath hissing.

Or was that his own?

The blood rushing in his ears made it near impossible to make any sense of any sound through the pulsing of his own heartbeat.

"Malcom." She moaned his name, an entreaty that sent another wave of lust pumping through him.

Her movements grew more frenetic.

She was so close, the scent of her impending climax hanging in the air, an aphrodisiac that pushed him near the edge of madness.

Malcom shifted, replacing his fingers with his erection. Wet, her body slicked the way for the glide of him.

Everything within him screamed for him to plunge deep and complete their union.

And it took everything else within him to summon the restraint.

"I-is this going to h-hurt?" Her breath came in quickened respirations.

"Aye, love." He brushed a palm along her cheek. His hand shook. All his body did, trembling from something more than physical desire. From this closeness. He'd never been this close to anyone before. And he never wanted to be close with anyone but her.

"Y-you are n-nothing if not d-direct, Malcom N-North." Verity laughed, her body shaking slightly, and he clenched his teeth as the walls of her sheath constricted around him, testing his self-control and restraint.

He reached between them and resumed stroking her, gliding inside her, as he pushed deeper and deeper.

And all mirth faded as Verity was reduced to a sound that was both a groan and a whimper. "Malcom." His name emerged a plea, and he was lost.

"I'm so sorry." He rasped out that penitence, and thrust home.

Verity cried out, her entire body bucking, and yet the pain of that did not drive her back. Instead, she clasped her arms about him, holding on tightly.

He dropped his sweaty brow atop hers, and concentrated on breathing.

There had never been a feeling like this, him buried deep inside such constricted heat and wetness. Malcom fought the primal need to keep thrusting and complete the act his body begged of him in the name of surcease. And yet with the pain he'd inflicted, and the desire to reawaken her body to the pleasure she'd previously known, his raw need mattered not at all. Malcom touched his lips to her forehead. "Forgive me, Verity."

"It w-wasn't all bad," she murmured, her thick lashes sweeping up. She flashed him a tremulous smile. "Everything before it was rather quite nice."

He grinned. There was the courage she'd shown at their first meeting. The one that had ensnared him, and had since held him bewitched. Lowering his mouth to her right breast, he resumed his previous teasing of that nipple.

Her breath caught.

"Is that quite nice?" He paused to murmur against her heated flesh.

In response, she tangled her fingers in his hair and anchored him there, preventing him from doing anything other than attending the sensitized tip.

Bringing her breasts together, he flicked his tongue back and forth, until Verity's hips began to move and desperate cries pulled from her lips.

And he moved with her. Slowly. Accustoming her body to the feel of him.

Then they were moving. Their bodies in perfect concert as he thrust, and she lifted up into each glide of him inside her.

"Malcom-Malcom. *Malllcooom.*" She wept. Just one word. His name. Over and over, a mantra that lent a desperation to every thrust of his hips. He was close.

"Come for me," he begged, when he'd never pleaded with a soul in the whole of his life. But Verity Lovelace was also unlike anyone he'd ever known in the whole of his existence. She was light and mirth and all clever wit and courage.

Her body stiffened, and then she screamed her release. Cursing and pleading, until she went limp. And her surrender threw him over that edge where pleasure and pain melded in an exquisite torture.

He withdrew and emptied himself in an arc on her belly, groaning and shuddering until his body ceased to shake, and then collapsed atop her. Catching himself at the elbows to keep from crushing her. Their bodies continued to tremble until a calm crept in.

And as he lay there, Malcom had the terrifying sense that the arrangement with Verity would never be enough.

When Verity was a girl in Epsom, the villagers had been less than discreet in their whispered slurs: she was a whore's daughter, and a whore's fate awaited her.

Verity, however, had never been one to self-flagellate for the sins of another. Or as the case had been, the decisions of another. Her mother had taken a lover, and thrown away any possibility of an honorable, respectable match with a man who'd been willing to make her his wife. That decision, however, had belonged to Lydia Lovelace. It hadn't been Verity's. As such, even as the insults had stung, she'd still held her head high because she wasn't her mother. She'd prided herself on the fact that she would never give herself to any man, in any way, outside of marriage.

Of course, having worked since twelve, there'd been even less thought of marriage than of surrendering her virtue.

Until she'd at last understood.

Lying precisely as she'd been since Malcom had gently cleaned the remnants of his seed from her person, atop his chest, with her legs twined through his, it all made sense to her.

This moment had been the one to bring it all 'round to clarity: She understood her mother. She understood what it was to want and need a man so desperately that in a moment of passion, there'd not been a fraction of a thought spared for principles such as honor or respectability or virtue.

She'd known only that she needed to know Malcom in this way. That were she to part from him, and never have lain in his arms, it would be a regret far greater than any she'd ever carry over words like "respectability" and "honor."

Smoothing her palms over the curls matting his chest, she threaded her fingers through that light tuft.

She loved him.

And mayhap she was her mother's daughter after all, because there was none of the deserved panic that realization should elicit. There was just a contented peace. An absolute sense of rightness in them. For however long that was.

And this time, a pang of regret did strike . . . for that reason alone.

Thrusting back those bleak musings, refusing to relinquish the time she did have to regret, Verity propped her chin up on his chest. "Are you sleeping?" she whispered.

"Am I even alive?" he asked, his voice still hoarse and weak, and she found herself smiling.

She pinched his side, and his eyes flew open. "Bloody hell. What in blazes—"

"Alive." She beamed. "I was just confirming for you."

Muttering, he rolled her lightly under him. "Minx," he breathed against her lips, and then mindful of her bruise, he drew back and lightly probed the tender area around her lump.

She anticipated the question that had formed on his lips. "I'm fine."

"I shouldn't have made love to you." Where there had been desire before, and then sleepiness after, now there was remorse. And she'd have none of that.

Verity jammed a finger into his chest, earning a grunt. "First, I made love to you, Malcom. Second, I assure you, I'm fine. Just a little ache," she promised.

He smoothed a palm over one of her thighs in soft circles that elicited a moan.

"Now that, however, feels delicious."

Malcom shifted so she was once more atop him, and proceeded to glide his hands lower to the curve of her back, and she sighed. "And that feels even more wonderful." He palmed her buttocks, pressing her lightly against his erect shaft.

She giggled. "Behave."

"Am I to take it that doesn't feel wonderful?" he murmured teasingly, thrusting lightly against her, and a sharp ache settled at her core.

She bit her lip. "Oh, no." She was faintly breathless. "It does. You do." He rotated his hips, and even as he moved, Verity's eyes closed and words failed.

"What was that, love?" Malcom took her mouth in a slow, deliberate kiss. A teasing one that he broke too soon, dragging a regretful moan from her.

Through the haze of desire, she caught the self-satisfaction in his gaze, and she pinched him again.

"Ouch."

"Don't be smug," she chided. "That isn't why I've awakened you, though we can certainly do more of that after."

He barked with laughter, his frame shaking under her, and she joined in. This side of Malcom, that clear, honest expression of his amusement, absent of the rage that had been such a part of him, proved contagious. After their mirth had abated, Verity slid off his chest and scooted to the nightstand at the side of her bed.

Leaning over, she pulled the drawer open, and fished out the notebook resting there. Head lowered, she stared at it for a moment, and then pushed the drawer back into place and joined Malcom.

"Here."

"What is this?" he asked, already taking it from her fingers.

"It's the story."

He went still, his gaze locked on the first page, the title there.

"You're trying to get out of the arrangement," he said flatly.

"No." She scrambled onto her knees. "It has nothing to do with that. I'll stay as promised." Because she'd sooner sever her arm than give up any time she could steal with him. "But that is the story. The only one I'd tell, Malcom."

Sitting up, he edged to the side of the mattress, and for a moment, she thought he'd reject the piece. That he'd set it down and lash out as he'd done so many times when the past came up between them.

Only this time, he sat and read. Motionless except for the occasional glide of his fingers as he turned the pages.

Until he reached the end.

Her heart hammered.

She'd often wondered how readers had felt about her work. Even as she'd written the pieces as a requirement from her employer, there'd been the hope that there was someone out there who'd appreciated the words she put to the page.

But those stories, they'd all been empty. Gossip, as Malcom had rightly claimed. And the opinions of those strangers had not mattered at all. Not compared with him. This man before her.

When he sat in silence, Verity wetted her lips. "Well?"

"It is . . . perfect," he said quietly. "It is perfect."

And as he took her in his arms a moment later and made love to her all over again, Verity found perfection once more.

"You are going to be the death of me, Verity Lovelace." He groaned, an arm flung over his eyes.

"If one must die, this would be a preferable way to go," she teased, giggling when he lightly swatted her buttocks.

"Minx." He ran a hand in slow, wide circles over her back. That caress so gentle. So soothing.

Sliding her fingers into his, Verity rested her head against his chest, the light mat of curls soft against her face. How . . . right this was. Being in his arms. All her life, she'd only seen acts of intimacy between a man and a woman as folly and weakness. Now, having made love with

Malcom, she saw how wrong she'd been. There was beauty in lying in the arms of a person one cared for.

Her sleepy gaze on their interlocked fingers, Verity lightly squeezed Malcom's in a slow, deliberately rhythmic pulsing.

When she registered Malcom's absolute stillness.

She abruptly stopped. Propping her chin on his chest, she swept her eyes over his stricken face. Gone was all hint of the earlier desire or teasing; in its place was raw, unbridled emotion. "What is it?"

His mouth moved, but no words were immediately forthcoming. Verity followed his tumultuous stare. His eyes remained locked on their joined palms.

Verity made to release him, but he clung tight, as if her hand were a lifeline, and she gripped him all the harder. "Malcom?"

"I just . . . I . . ."

She waited, allowing him his time.

"My mother . . ." His whisper emerged hoarse and gravelly. Malcom drew in a shuddery breath and began again. "As a boy, I was always running off, seeking and finding mischief, and before I would go, she'd take my hand and . . . squeeze it as you did as she said:

'I love thee, I love but thee
With a love that shall not die
Till the sun grows cold
And the stars grow old.'"

His eyes slid closed. "She'd say it whenever we parted, and when she tucked me into bed." Then his words came quickly. As if he feared in not speaking them, he might lose them and the memory he held dear. "She would press my hand in time to the rhythm of that sonnet. B-because . . ." His voice wavered, and Verity closed her other palm over their joined hands. "'Because my h-heart beats for you. It always has and it always will, and even after it ceases to beat, my love will live on in you.'" A ragged sob tore from him, and he clung to her fingers, clenching tight.

Tears clogged her throat and blurred her eyes, and Verity just held Malcom. Lying against his chest, she allowed him to weep with the pain of all he'd lost and the memory that had at last come to him. His body shook and trembled from the force of his emotion. Verity held him all the while, with time meaning nothing, and then his crying stopped.

She pressed a kiss to the corner of his temple, and squeezed his hand several more times in that rhythmic beat, and willed him to feel the love she carried for him.

Chapter 28

THE LONDONER
THE MEETING!

Lord Maxwell was seen breaking down the front door of the Baron Bolingbroke. Society was agog, and now salivating for details on the fight that undoubtedly erupted between the Lost Heir and his nemesis, Lord B.

M. Fairpoint

Over the course of his life, Malcom had sought—and attained—revenge on more enemies than he could remember or count.

Never, however, going into battle had he felt this. Bloodlust pumped through him, primal and raw. It heated his veins and coursed through him, spreading a venomous poison where only one word took shape: *destroy*. This upcoming meeting didn't have to do with territory or right of ownership or the simple primitive need to exert control and display dominance.

This was about her—Verity, and what had almost befallen her.

Not bothering with a knocker like any civilized guest would, Malcom pounded hard at the modest panel. The heavy oak rattled, and he pounded all the harder.

But he wasn't going anywhere. This meeting had been ordained following the attack on Verity at Hatchards. Nay, if he were being honest with himself, it had been ordained long before that. Back when he'd been a boy smuggled from his family's Kent estate in a burlap sack, taken for dead, and passed off like trash.

And now he was back, reclaiming his past life.

That brought him up short with his knock, and he froze, his fist halfway to the oak panel.

Could he?

Forget moving amongst the world in daylight. Could Malcom move amongst the *peerage*? Polite Society, which he still wanted no part of. He was a man trapped in an "in-between" in which he'd never truly belong. Neither the sewers nor the fanciest end of London.

But the possibility of a future he saw, it wasn't a place.

It was with her . . .

It was with Verity.

He wanted to be wherever she was. It's why for the first time ever, he'd wanted not to be scouring for treasure but instead at Hatchards with her.

Home was wherever Verity was.

I love her . . .

Malcom shot a hand out, catching the stair rail, managing to keep himself upright. *Christ.* It was a prayer from him, a man who'd never been religious, and yet that was all he was capable of. He loved her. He'd loved her since he'd stumbled upon her in his sewers, a tart-mouthed spitfire challenging him at every turn as if she'd forever dwelled in those tunnels and set herself up as queen.

With their every exchange, he'd lost more and more scraps of a heart he'd not known he possessed: Verity, as she'd doled out chess lessons. Verity, as she'd gone toe-to-toe with him to defend two old toshers. Just Verity. It would only ever be Verity.

And she was the reason he was here even now.

Steadied once more, Malcom let his fist fly with a thunderous boom that rose above the din of the early-morn Mayfair traffic.

And then the door was opened. Suddenly, by an ancient butler with white hair. "May I help you?"

But for his flawless English, the man might as well have been Fowler or Bram. A servant who, by his advanced years, should have retired some time ago but remained. For what reasons? A lack of pension? Loyalty? Surely it was not the latter. Not given Bolingbroke's family history. That brought Malcom back to the task at hand, the whole reason for his visit. "Bolingbroke."

The servant hesitated. "I'm afraid His Lordship is—"

Malcom shot an elbow up before the door could be closed in his face. "He'll see me." Or Malcom would tear down the bloody door with his damned hands, and then hunt the other man for the fiend he was.

"I said, he's not receiving," the butler said with an impressive resolve, and this time the old servant slid the door forward.

By God, he wouldn't. He shot a hand up—

"Florence, is there a problem?"

In the end, it wasn't a stone-cold Baron Bolingbroke who cut through the butler's resolve but a slender young lady with a mass of black curls and an even greater amount of curiosity brimming in her eyes.

"Just someone who's arrived without a meeting, my lady. And His Lordship is not taking visitors."

The young lady stayed the butler with a hand, and then crooked her fingers, motioning Malcom to enter. "I am the Baroness Bolingbroke," she said softly, confirming her identity. "My husband is otherwise engaged at this hour. Might I be of any assistance in the interim?"

As he'd been visited by Sanders, and given the permission and then directives to make Bolingbroke pay and then pay even more in interest, Malcom hadn't thought of the wife. Or the sisters.

And yet even as there was a shred of humanity within him still that regretted in this moment that this woman found herself an unwitting player upon a chessboard designed long ago by different players, there was another woman who mattered far more than her. Another woman who mattered more than anyone else. And Malcom would sell his soul ten times over to protect her from harm. "My name is . . ." She stared patiently back. "I am the Earl of Maxwell." And he didn't break with that admission of his rightful title.

She went absolutely still . . . and then that earlier veneer of warmth was doused by a blanket of ice. "I see, my lord. My husband isn't accepting—"

"I'm not leaving until I see him."

The young woman hesitated, and he felt the desperate look the butler shot her way. And the battle she fought with herself.

"Very well," she said stiffly. "If you'll follow me?" And whipping about, she started down the hall.

As Malcom fell into step alongside her, the butler followed their strides. And then the moment they disappeared around the next corridor, loyal footmen followed in the shadows. Malcom felt them there, too. Lurking in loyal wait.

Aye, but wasn't that the way . . .

No one saw themselves or their people as the monsters. It's always the other who's in the wrong.

"I've oft wondered if you'd call, my lord." The lady kept her eyes trained forward as she walked at a brisk clip his longer legs easily kept stride with. "Or whether you were content to lurk in the wings, waiting like a bogeyman, delighting in the power you wielded."

How ironic that she should speak of his influence. "How unfortunate . . ."

The young woman fought a futile battle with herself. "What is?" she snapped.

Malcom flashed a cool smile. "That *six months* of your husband's past twenty years has proven so unpleasant. For him." When the reverse had held true for Malcom's own existence. When Malcom had been beaten and robbed, and stabbed and spit on.

The young lady missed a step, her gaze stricken.

Aye, so the young lady was clever enough to hear that unspoken gibe.

She didn't say another word the remainder of their long march through the sparse townhouse. Where Malcom's inherited properties dripped wealth and extravagance, Bolingbroke's new homes reflected the sorry state of his affairs.

Lady Bolingbroke slowed her step, and planting her hands on her hips, she lifted her gaze to his. "You don't know my husband. You only know"—*what I endured*—"what was done to you." She entreated him with her eyes. "But those actions, they were never Tristan's. He was a boy at the time those wrongs were committed. And you were both victims." She grimaced. "Albeit in . . . very different ways," she finished lamely, at least sounding properly sheepish with that ludicrous charge that Malcom and Bolingbroke had ever been alike in their sufferings. The baroness ventured forward.

"Hullo, love, I thought you were never going to join me."

Malcom followed that booming greeting across the ballroom . . . and found him.

His foe.

Or . . . his cousin. Odd, he'd never thought of the other man in that light. The distant relative whose parents had sought to off Malcom and had succeeded in erasing him from the world.

Malcom had to remind himself the proper pattern to breathe: In and out. Easy. Measured cadence.

"Tristan," the young lady greeted, hurrying across marble flooring haphazardly covered in paint-covered sheets. Worktables littered the room with sculptures and clumps of stones set out.

What in God's name . . .

Malcom took it all in.

Either the man was mad or . . . Nay, there was nothing for it. The man was mad. He hurled blue and green paints at a wall already sloppy with color.

"You're late, love."

"Tristan!"

This time, that insistence penetrated the baron's levity. He turned . . . and stopped.

"You've company," his wife said as she reached his side. "Lord Maxwell."

Missing a jacket as he was, the baron's lawn shirt did little to conceal the other man's muscles as they coiled. He, too, was a man braced for battle.

Aye, mayhap there was blood shared between them, after all.

"I want a word, Bolingbroke," he called from the middle of the room, content with the distance between them and the booming of his voice off the soaring walls. "Alone."

Except . . . the baroness slid her hand into her husband's, her meaning clear. And then Malcom noted with some shock the baron weaving his fingers through the young lady's. "Whatever you can say, you can say in front of my wife," he said with a calm Malcom no longer felt.

He remained locked on those joined hands.

And had he not been fixed as he was, so closely attending that silent gesture of support, he'd have failed to note the slight rhythmic pulse as the lady squeezed Bolingbroke's palm. Just as Verity had done not even eight hours earlier.

And for the first time since he'd stepped foot inside Bolingbroke's residence, Malcom found himself the one knocked off-balance. He struggled to regain his footing. "Are you intending to hide behind your wife?" Because there'd be no secrets this day. There'd been secrets enough for two decades.

"I have nothing to hide," the other man replied, his voice quieter, and yet, it still carried. And contained within was a conviction from a man who believed the words he spoke.

"You threatened my wife." How easily that descriptor slipped out. How right it felt. Because Verity, she was so much more to him. *I want her to be so much more . . .* Staggered by that realization as it hit him square in the chest in the presence of his greatest enemy, it took a moment to heed the long beats of silence.

"I beg your pardon," the baron sputtered.

Releasing his hand, his wife took a step forward. "How dare you? My husband is a man of honor. He would never dare threaten or harm anyone, let alone a woman."

"And yet, he's the son of a couple who'd steal a child and everything that child owned."

The baroness blazed to life with a stunning, if incoherent, defense of her husband.

"Poppy," the other man said quietly, lightly tugging her arm. He repeated it again more forcefully, and penetrated her outrage.

A look passed between them, an intimate glance belonging to two people who required no words in one another's presence.

I've felt that with Verity . . . I know that with her . . . I want that with her . . .

Lady Bolingbroke shook her head.

Her husband nodded.

She gave another shake.

And after she gave him a prolonged look, her shoulders sagged. Brushing a hand through those curls that hung loose down the lady's back, the baron leaned down and whispered something. And then placing a kiss against her temple, Bolingbroke stepped away.

"You're not wrong, Maxwell," the baron said solemnly as he abandoned the previously staked-out corner of the ballroom. This most unlikeliest of places for a showdown. But then, this paint-splattering, endearment-calling gentleman was also the unlikeliest of opponents. "My family wronged you. My parents . . ." The baron averted his face. But not before Malcom caught the fury, shame, and rage that crumpled the other man's features. When he looked back, he was a man once more in control. "I will not diminish in any way what was done. My parents committed the greatest of evils upon you. And no apology will suffice. Anything would be inadequate." He stopped several feet from Malcom.

The two men sized one another up.

Enemies who'd come together at last in a long-overdue battle.

"Still, all I can do is convey how sorry I am. If I could undo it, all of it, I would. Not because I give a damn about the scandal or the loss of funds." Bolingbroke spoke with an ease that could come only from a place of forthrightness. "But because of what was done to you. I do not profess to be a good man. I'm not." The baron ignored his wife's protestations at his back. "I've gone to battle and killed men. I lived a meaningless existence upon my return from war . . . when you"—he took a step closer toward Malcom—"you were the one who should have known those luxuries."

And yet, would Malcom have ever met Verity? Would their paths have ever crossed?

Mayhap that was what fate had intended all along . . . Mayhap fate had known that Malcom North, as Percival Northrop, the Earl of Maxwell, would have never crossed paths with the courageous newspaper reporter who'd captured his heart . . .

"I've hurt many. But I've never hurt a woman, and never would. And I'd never let myself, for any reason, visit suffering upon you for what you've known."

It is an act . . . It is a show . . .

It had to be.

Because what was the alternative? That the man he'd spent these past months secretly resenting and gleefully knocking down, was, in fact, a man who'd himself been dragged into this mire, much as Malcom himself had?

Just as Verity had said.

Husband and wife exchanged a look.

Aye, because something was expected of Malcom here.

During the medieval times, men would conceal weapons in their hands, and so shaking another person's hand conveyed that no harm was intended, and that is what I would convey to . . .

That was why she'd handed out that lesson, and in doing so invoked that reminder . . . She'd known Malcom would need that gesture.

As Malcom stretched a hand out and placed his palm in the baron's, he was not besieged by shame or any sense of weakness, but rather an inherent right.

It was done.

And it was because of her . . . Verity.

Verity Lovelace . . . a woman who'd come to mean more to him than anyone. A woman he wanted in his life . . . forever.

He stiffened. A woman who'd come to harm at the hands of someone . . . someone who'd not been Bolingbroke. Ice tripped along his spine. For if the baron was not responsible for the attack on Verity, that meant there was some unknown foe who sought to hurt her.

❦

At six o'clock in the morning, Verity came awake to find Malcom leaving the townhouse. Even as she'd hurried through her ablutions in a bid to catch him, knowing what he intended, she'd proven too late.

And thirty minutes later . . . her life fell apart.

Although, in fairness, it wasn't really her life. This was all pretend. A game of make-believe.

So why, if it was pretend, was she coming apart inside? Why couldn't she breathe?

Once more, it had all fallen apart because of a newspaper.

When Fairpoint had stolen her words, Verity had imagined there could be no greater affront she could suffer. The rage and indignation had been so staggering that surely nothing could have surpassed it.

How wrong she'd been . . .

"Ahem. Is there anything else you need . . . my lady?" The young maid who'd delivered the newspaper didn't meet Verity's eyes. Though in fairness, motionless in the middle of the gold parlor, Verity hadn't managed to wrench her eyes away from the words inked across the center page in bold, damning letters.

THE LONDONER
SCANDAL . . . AGAIN . . . !

A great ruse has been perpetuated, and Polite Society made to look the fool. Should anyone expect anything else from one raised in the sewers, even if he was born an earl? The Earl of Maxwell, who would live life in the rookeries, would also lie so easily about having a wife . . .

His pretend wife is none other than Verity Lovelace, the bastard-born daughter of the late Earl of Wakefield.

Verity tried to breathe. She desperately tried to suck air into her lungs.

In the end, she failed.

Verity's legs gave out from under her, and she sank onto her knees in the middle of the parlor.

"Verity!" Livvie's voice came muffled from the doorway.

Livvie, who, capable of words and sound, proved braver than Verity, who couldn't sort through the chaos in her mind.

And then there was a stampede of unwanted interlopers.

Bertha hovered at the front of the room, uncertain, while people swarmed around Verity, Malcom's servants circling, and she was like that fish she and her father had pulled from the lake and she'd kept in a bowl in his absence, to remember him by. She and Bertha and Mama would peer down, and he'd look up, and God help her. Verity shook. It was too much.

"Get out!" Livvie shouted, and as quick as the cluster of maids had come, they left, filing from the room. The moment they'd gone, Livvie fell to the floor beside her and rescued the newspaper. "Who would do this?" she whispered. "Who could have done this?" As she frantically shook those damning pages, she looked hopelessly between Verity and Bertha.

Dimly, Verity noted Bertha lingering at the doorway. Her cheeks splotched red. The old woman stood on the fringe when she'd only ever been in the heart of the family.

Verity froze.

And just like that, she *knew*.

Oh, God. No.

Vomit churned in her belly.

She didn't know. Because it would mean that the woman she'd known, the woman she'd trusted and seen as family, all along had been just another person capable of great treachery and deceit. Which was impossible.

And yet . . . not.

Verity managed to push herself to standing. "Livvie, will you leave me and Bertha alone a moment," she said quietly. How was she so calm? How, when she was breaking apart inside? Nay, when she'd already broken apart? She held a quaking hand out, and Livvie looked at it a long moment before relinquishing *The Londoner*.

The minute she'd gone, Verity spoke. "How could you do this?"

"I'll make no apologies for what I've done. I'd do it again."

Verity jerked. The other woman didn't even deny it. "You've hated him from the start." Not once had the closed-minded nursemaid taken the chance to see who and what Malcom truly was: One who gave of himself. One who lifted up those who most needed support.

"Aye, I have. He's a selfish, greedy devil." Bertha's voice crept up a fraction. "He didn't need those tunnels. He'd a damned earldom waiting for him. A bloody fortune. But was it enough?" She jumped in, not allowing Verity a word edgewise. "No, it wasn't."

Something tickled the back of her memory. A conversation traipsed in, in drips and drabs.

Hush. You think it so shocking that I might have found myself a suitor? . . . He's a tosher. He's a sewer hunter. Scavenges. Pans and retrieves tosh . . .

Verity's eyes flew open. "Your sweetheart . . . ," she whispered. "That was how you knew Malcom's identity." And all along, Verity hadn't truly given thought to how the older woman had attained the information she had. Even the idea of a "sweetheart" had been secondary. All she'd been focused on was locating her "story."

"You want to know the manner of man you've gone and fallen in love with?" Bertha asked, startling her out of her musings.

"I already know precisely the manner of man he is," she said quietly. And this spiteful, bitter woman before her was the last who'd ever truly know Malcom North.

"Staked his claim on the entire sewers and threatened my Alders. Your earl had him blubbering himself."

A sound of disgust escaped her, and Bertha slammed a fist against her open palm. "We were going to have it all: You would get that damned story you were so determined to tell. Alders would replace that bastard in the tunnels." The glint in her eyes lent her a half-mad look. "And in the end, neither of us got what we deserved. Because of him."

Verity's stomach continued to churn, and she forcibly swallowed back the bile elicited by the other woman's poison. She clutched the curved back of the nearest sofa, keeping herself steady, keeping upright. "You ruined his name. You ruined my name," she cried. The woman who'd held her and cradled her and been a mentor to her through the years had thought nothing of humiliating her and Malcom before the world.

Bertha shrugged her bony shoulders. "Neither of you truly had a name to ruin," she said without inflection, stating as fact her opinion on Verity's and Malcom's worth.

"He's a greater man than, with your twisted soul, you can ever know or appreciate."

Bertha scoffed, "He's a bounder just like your father."

Verity snapped. "He is nothing like my father," she spat, flying across the room, a finger outstretched. "My father left us nothing. He left me, and Livvie, selling our things and me working as a child. And Malcom?" Her heart flipped over in love and sorrow at a dream which had ended too soon. Even as that dream would have never been enough, she'd have greedily stolen all those moments as she could have. "Malcom has cared for those he called family. He's given a home to them. Provided security—"

"Bah," Bertha spat, spittle forming at the corners of her tense mouth. "You'd hold him up on a pedestal for what he's done for others. Tell me this, Verity: What has he done for you? He's trapped you, that's what. He's used you." Her voice pitched around the room. "He's bedded you. And in the end, he'd turn you out."

"They were my decisions," she cried out, shaking. "All of them. Everything I did was because I wanted to."

"You're just like your mother."

Once that would have struck like the insult it was surely intended as. Verity lifted her chin a notch. "At least she was capable of love. Your heart is only full of hate."

The old woman jerked like she'd been slapped. "I did this for you."

"You didn't do this for me. You did it for you. Get out," she said tiredly, and for the first time in her life, she turned and presented the former nursemaid with her back.

"After all the years we've been together, you should doubt me?" Bertha whispered.

Verity stiffened as her nursemaid came around and faced her, with a hand outstretched.

Wordlessly, Verity took the page, and read it.

Two hundred pounds paid out by Mr. Fairpoint.

I'm going to be ill . . . "You *worked* with him?" Verity cried.

"He gave me coin here and there to tell him little things. Things that didn't matter."

Verity felt the blood leave her face.

"What?" Bertha said defensively. "I used that coin to help pay our rent and put food upon our table."

"What things did you tell him?" she asked, her voice pitched.

Bertha frowned. "Where you were going to conduct your research. When you'd be working on cases. And for that he gave us a sizable coin for a story you wouldn't have made half for, had your name been put to it. He was always going to see you sacked, Verity." The old woman shrugged. "I just managed to secure us funds before he did."

Verity's knees weakened. "Oh, my God," she breathed.

The threat at Hatchards. Her stomach revolved. Why, even the night she'd been followed. Fairpoint had been attempting to scare her out of doing her work in order to secure his own position. And Verity's loyal nursemaid had gone and thrown all her support to one such as him. Verity made to tear up the note, but crying out, Bertha surged forward.

Verity froze. For all that had come to pass, Bertha had still spent the whole of her life with Verity and Livvie. Wrinkling the note into a ball, she tossed it at the other woman. "Get out. I never want to see you again."

"Verity." The old woman shook her head, disbelief stamped on her features. "This is me. You don't mean that."

"I've never meant anything more, Bertha."

Tears glassed the nursemaid's eyes. A moment later, she turned . . . and was gone.

Verity didn't move for several moments, and then all the life drained from her legs and she sank onto the edge of the nearest seat.

The rapid clip of determined steps carried from the corridor.

Her heart squeezed. She wasn't ready to face him. Not yet. Feeling like one facing her executioner, Verity climbed to her feet.

Only, two figures filled the doorway. Neither of whom was Malcom. The butler and a stranger who was . . . not a stranger. Bespectacled, tall, the gentleman was since sporting a bruise from their last encounter. "You," she blurted. The man she'd come across at various outings. But who yesterday at Hatchards had attempted to come to her rescue.

The butler cleared his throat. "The Earl of Wakefield to see you."

The Earl . . .

She whipped shocked eyes up to his.

The young man doffed his hat and dropped it awkwardly to his side. "Hello," he said quietly. "Please, if you'd call me Benedict."

And Verity found herself struck dumb for a second time that day.

He was her half brother.

Chapter 29

THE LONDONER
TREACHERY!

Is it any wonder with her bastardy, Miss Verity Lovelace
committed the ultimate deception against Polite
Society? It is a wonder, however, that her half brother,
the Earl of Wakefield, paid her a call. What was dis-
cussed at that *reunion . . . ?*

M. Fairpoint

"Where in hell have you been?" was the snarled curse Malcom found
himself greeted with upon his return six hours later.

With one hand, Malcom tugged off his hat while loosening the
clasp of his cloak with the other. "I had business to see to," he said,
tossing those articles to a waiting footman.

"All this time later?" Fowler snapped. "There was trouble while you
were gone."

Malcom came up short. "Verity," he rasped, reaching for Bram.

"Aye. Slow there, lad," Bram barked, catching Malcom by the back
of his jacket. "The girl is fine. Sad. But fine." The old tosher yanked

a folded newspaper from inside his jacket front and slammed it into Malcom's chest.

"What is this?" he asked, alternating between the silent pair.

"Ya haven't heard about that yet?"

Heard about . . . ? Following his meeting with Bolingbroke, Malcom had taken care of two important matters, the most pressing of which was seeking out Steele's services and putting him on the task of determining . . . His gaze scanned the front page of the gossip column. He cursed. "Where is she?"

"In her rooms . . ." The words hadn't even left Fowler's mouth before Malcom was off and running, and once more, as he reached her rooms and let himself in, he hadn't been sure what he'd expected . . . but this was certainly not it.

"Hullo, Malcom." She spoke quietly, standing alongside a tattered trunk and valise.

Malcom entered slowly. "Verity." He clicked the door shut behind them. All the while, his pulse knocked away, skittering out of control. She intended to leave. *Or does she think you intend to send her away?*

Her gaze took in the scandal sheets clutched tight in his fist. "I trust you've seen the newspaper," she murmured. It wasn't a question, and yet, as he didn't have any coherent reply in this instance, he nodded and answered anyway.

"Aye." He relaxed his grip, and then dropped the hated pages on a nearby table.

"It was Bertha, you know."

He froze.

Verity's throat moved quickly, and she looked past his shoulders at the door panel behind him. "She resented you. She had a sweetheart. A tosher. A man named Alders."

Christ. Malcom dragged an unsteady hand through his hair. "He robbed Fowler. Beat him . . ."

Verity waved a hand, dismissing that defense for what he'd done. "She believed I was repeating the sins of my mother, and that you were the one responsible for taking me down that path, and she wanted us out of here." Her voice broke. "Away from you and the arrangement we'd struck." At last, she looked at him squarely. "She sold the story to Fairpoint, the man whom I was competing with for work. He's been the one attempting to silence me, and Bertha helped him." Her voice dissolved on an agonized whisper as she hugged herself.

Malcom took another step closer, wanting to take her in his arms, but she retreated, and that slight distance hit like a physical kick to the gut. Another time, rage would have clouded all reason. Now what radiated strongly first was the need to comfort. To take her close . . . even as she didn't want that offering in this instance.

All along, the woman Verity had seen as family, one whom she'd protected and cared for. And in the end, Bertha had delivered the ultimate betrayal . . . Knowing Verity as he did, she'd be ravaged inside. "She wasn't entirely wrong."

That brought Verity's gaze whipping over. "What?"

He took a slow, careful step closer. Wanting to be near her. Wanting to keep her close and never let her go. "I'm the one who forced you to come here. I dangled a threat over your head."

She scoffed, and it was the first hint of her in-command self. "Malcom, I came here of my own volition, just as I searched you out each time. You didn't make me live with you and take part in your plan. I did that all on my own."

Aye, not even the Good Lord himself could bend Verity 'round to his thinking if Verity were of a different opinion. That conviction was just one of the reasons he'd fallen so hopelessly for her. God, how he loved her . . . and if she left, he'd never recover from the loss of her. He wanted her in his life forever. If she would have him in all his imperfection. His hands went damp. And never before had he wished he was one of those urbane gentlemen with all the right words so that this moment would be the one she deserved. "Verity, there is something I would—"

"My brother came."

He cocked his head at that interruption.

She turned her palms up. "My half brother. The Earl of Wakefield. He . . . learned about Livvie and me, and he's been searching me out. I saw him at the bookstore that morn. I didn't know who he was. He tried to stop it . . ." She ceased her ramblings.

"And . . . what did he want?" he asked slowly, trying to slog through anything that made sense. Anything past the black dress she now wore. The one he'd given her at their first meeting. Not the pieces she'd adopted since she'd come here. His heart slipped another fraction at the implications of that, and of the articles at her feet.

Verity drew in an uneven breath and ran her hands over her skirts. "My father was useless when it came to finances. My half brother, he's been working to repair the family fortunes. He's offered a little cottage to Livvie and me. A place to live, with a small stipend on which to survive."

The earth swayed under him. "That was a generous offer," he said, his voice muffled in his ears. The earl had also offered that which Malcom should have unconditionally put forward for Verity. "And what did you say?"

"I thanked him. I appreciated that he cared and sought to make our lives better, but said that I'd different hopes for my future."

The Londoner.

His throat bobbed.

Verity drifted ever closer. "I told him that I'd fallen in love." His heart jumped. "That I'd fallen in love with you." She slowed to a stop before him. "That I wanted to marry you." Laying her palms on his chest, she leaned back so she could hold his gaze. "If you—"

Malcom swallowed the remainder of that question with a kiss. His body shook from the force of the laughter and light moving through him. "Good God, Verity Lovelace," he strangled out through the joy. Cupping her face, he rested his forehead against hers. "You're the only woman who would beat me to a proposal."

Her eyes formed perfect circles. "Were you—" She gasped as he fell to a knee.

"I'd come here intending to ask you to marry me. To spend your life letting me work to be the man you deserve. Loving you."

A sob burst from Verity's lips. "Yes," she cried out, her arms coming up—

But he stopped her. "And then I'd also intended to offer you . . . your freedom, if you so choose." He withdrew the notes from inside his jacket.

Her lips parted, Verity took them and quickly worked through them. Another gasp escaped her.

"I was otherwise delayed today because I paid a visit to the owner of *The Londoner*. I purchased the papers, because what they do is rubbish and what you would do with them would transform the world."

Tears glazed her eyes. "Malcom," she whispered, those crystalline drops winding down her cheeks.

He brushed them back.

"And as I wanted to beat your Fairpoint to a pulp, I thought it only appropriate to leave you the honors when you stepped into the office as the proprietress."

She threw her arms around his neck, toppling the both of them.

Malcom came down hard on his back, grunting as she fell atop him. "By your response I trust you've accepted option two?"

"I love you, you silly man," she rasped. "I want a life with you at my side." Verity claimed his mouth, and he angled his head to receive her kiss. And infused within was all the joy and love he felt for her, and he tasted it on her lips and in the whisper of her breath. And it made him whole in ways that he'd only ever been empty. Verity broke the kiss. "I accept both options, Malcom North," she teased. "A future with you and one with *The Londoner*." Her smile wavered. "Would you accept that? An unconventional wife who conducts actual work?"

He brushed the strands that had come free from her chignon, tucking them behind her ear. "I wouldn't have you any other way, Verity," he said hoarsely. "I'd only ever have you as you are."

"And I you, Malcom North," she whispered.

And as Verity leaned down and kissed him once more, Malcom smiled.

At last, he'd been found.

Epilogue

Two months later
St. Giles

Everyone was there.

From the most revered members of the *ton* to the poorest of the toshers to the wealthiest of the merchant class, all had come out that morn.

The eclectic gathering of people now sat in a crowded auditorium.

As they spoke, their voices rolled together; coarsened Cockneys, blended with the crispest of the King's English, echoed from the twenty-foot ceilings.

People born of different stations, who rarely acknowledged the others' existence, had been joined in an unexpected commonality: rabid curiosity. After all, it was the story everyone wanted. Or rather, the *latest* story everyone wished to hear. Someday there would be a fresher piece of gossip, or a newer story, that men and women would crave the details of.

But for now, this was the one that consumed people.

Once, Malcom would have only been riddled with rage at those interlopers scrounging for details about his life the way the poor begged for scraps in the streets. That anger had since left him.

Because of her . . .

As if she'd heard those unspoken thoughts, Verity slipped her fingers into his. She gave a light squeeze, and raised them to her lips for a gentle kiss. "You are going to be brilliant, Malcom," she said softly.

"Yes, but will I still be brilliant alone?" When the other key player was missing.

Verity held his gaze. "You're never alone, Malcom."

His throat worked. "No. No, you are right on that score, love." His gaze traveled out, bypassing the strangers in the crowd and homing in on the first row . . . the front row of the auditorium occupied by Bram, Fowler, Giles, and Billy. The four of them sat, shoulder to shoulder, pride beaming in their eyes. Malcom wasn't alone. In those he'd spent a lifetime with on the streets, he'd found family. And in Verity.

And behind that family, there sat another.

A row of ladies and gentlemen who were strangers, and yet connected to him by another.

Together, they stood there, side by side, surveying the room as one.

"Are you nervous?" Verity asked.

He hesitated. "Yes," he allowed, giving her that truth. For the first time in the whole of his life, there was no shame in that acknowledgment. Before Verity, he'd have seen the admission as a weakness he couldn't dare own. Nor was it worry about appearing before that crowd. Rather, his unease came in appearing before them alone. Malcom reached inside his jacket and grabbed the folded paper there. "None of this makes sense if he doesn't arrive." As guests began claiming their seats, true panic began to set in. "I'll have to rewrite it. Only . . ." He grimaced. "There's not time to rewrite anything. I'll have to reorder my thoughts." Malcom cursed. "I should have prepared an alternate speech—"

Verity pressed her fingertips lightly against his lips. "He will be here," she said simply.

"You're so certain."

"He'll be here," she repeated.

The "he" in question being none other than Baron Bolingbroke. Bolingbroke, who'd been due nearly ten minutes ago. Except, what if the other man had simply gotten what he needed from Malcom . . .

"And his coming, Malcom, will not be because you've forgiven the debt that once hung over him and Poppy," Verity murmured with her usual uncanny ability to sort through the thoughts roiling in his head long before he was able to himself identify the source of his unease. "He'll be here because he promised he would," she said simply.

"And if he isn't?" he insisted, forcing a casualness he didn't feel.

"Then you will be fine without him."

"What faith you have in me, lady wife."

She bristled. "And how could I not? A man who's accomplished all you have? The most successful tosher to ever—"

Malcom claimed her lips in a sweet, tender, too-brief kiss.

He drew back, and Verity blinked slowly.

"Thank you," he said quietly.

"For what?"

For attempting to distract him from the words he'd soon deliver to the crowd beyond the corridor. "I wouldn't have been here had it not been for you." He'd not be moments away from entering that room before a sea of strangers and saying any words, let alone the ones he intended to speak: about his life and the lives of so many here in London.

Giving his hands another squeeze, Verity drew them close to her chest and held them against the place her heart beat. "Yes, you would have, Malcom," she said softly. "You would have found your way to this place whether or not I'd been part of your life." Her eyes twinkled. "It would have just taken you far longer."

"Minx," he growled, and took her in his arms, guiding her against the wall and making love to her mouth. In her arms, all was right. There were no fears. There was no anger. There was just an absolute rightness.

An exaggerated cough brought them quickly apart, and they faced a tardy Baron and Baroness Bolingbroke. The young woman looked between Malcom and Verity. "Hello!" she greeted them with a smile.

Her husband, on the other hand, with his red-splotched cheeks, made a show of studying the ceiling.

"Hello, Lady Poppy," Verity returned, dipping a flawless curtsy.

"None of that, now," the baroness chided. "We agreed to dispense with formalities. It is so very lovely to see you both again. Isn't that right, Tristan?"

The baron kept his gaze skyward. "Indeed. It—*oomph*." That at last managed to bring the other man's head down.

The baroness flashed a blindingly bright smile. "If you'll excuse us a moment?" Without awaiting permission, she took her husband and steered him onward several paces.

"What was *that* for?" Bolingbroke demanded in tones that would have been hushed and entirely lost to any person who'd not been raised in the streets. Alas, heightened senses and hearing would never afford the lords and ladies of London privacy.

"You were a rogue, Tristan. You shouldn't be discomfited by displays of affection."

The couple spoke on a flurry of whispers, and Verity shifted closer. "They are . . . something. Are they not?"

Malcom stole another glance at that wildly gesticulating pair: One, a man he'd secretly hated, who also happened to share his blood. A cousin. And the gentleman's spitfire wife. "They are not what I expected," he conceded. They were . . . real. Real and flawed and human in ways he'd erroneously believed a nobleman and noblewoman couldn't be.

How narrow his view had been of the world. How much Verity had opened his eyes to it.

The Baron and Baroness of Bolingbroke, their arms linked, rejoined Malcom and Verity. "Forgive us for arriving late. I'd not been . . . feeling well." The baroness slid a palm over her slightly rounded belly, and her husband's throat moved, the emotion in his gaze raw. "And my husband was insisting that I rest—" She peeled her lips up in a grimace as if she'd uttered a heinous epithet. "That he'd come without me."

"And my wife insisted on being here with us."

Us.

The word paired them: Malcom and Bolingbroke. They and their wives.

"I'm so glad you are here," Verity said softly, moving to take the baroness's palm. "Both of you."

"As am I. We should be seated and leave our husbands to their business." The baroness held out her arm.

Verity's gaze drifted to the back of the hall, where the reporters swarmed for the best view of the front of the auditorium. Her frame tensed. "If you'll excuse me for but a moment? There is just something I'd see to before our husbands begin."

"Of course." The baroness rushed off to rejoin her husband.

Malcom, however, reserved his focus on just one. *Mitchell Fairpoint.* Rage coursed through his veins. Bully as he'd been to Verity, the man now towered over a young woman, berating her.

"The cur," Malcom clipped out.

Verity looked to Malcom. "Would you be opposed to waiting several moments more while I see to him?"

He smiled. "Of course not. Would you have me join you?"

"No." She narrowed her eyes in a way that almost made him pity Fairpoint. Almost. "I have it."

"Go then, love." This was a moment long overdue. One he'd allow Verity to own in every way.

Her eyes softened, and leaning up, she took his lips in a brief kiss. "I love you."

"And I love you, wife."

And as she slipped out of the corridor and marched through the throng of observers who'd come that morn, Malcom followed her with his gaze; she moved like a warrior in battle, purposeful and single-minded in her intent. If possible, as she wove through the onlookers, making for those other reporters, Malcom fell more and more in love with her.

Four figures appeared at the hall, blocking Malcom's line of vision. He quietly cursed. "What are you—"

"Ya surely aren't going to ask wot we're doing?" Bram cut him off.

"Actually, I had—"

"Because the only person deserving of that question is *ya*," the old tosher went on. "Wot in blazes are ya *doing*?"

"Wot's the girl doing?" Fowler demanded.

"Righting wrongs," Malcom murmured, not taking his gaze from his wife.

An elbow collided with his side. Grunting, he glanced over at the old toshers.

Bram and Fowler wore matching frowns.

"What in hell was that for?" Malcom muttered, rubbing at the wounded flesh.

Fowler gave him another hard nudge. "Ya should be there when the Mrs. speaks to that bastard."

"They are worried again," Livvie said by way of explanation. As if there could be a doubt to the "they" in question, the girl motioned to Bram and Fowler.

"Bloody right, we are worried." Bram nodded. "Go to her now, boy."

This time, Malcom evaded the next blow the old toshers sent flying.

"Mrs. North ain't need anyone's help," Billy piped in, her worshipping gaze centered on Verity. The girl's adoration had been there from the moment Verity had entered Malcom's household, and since Billy had been relieved of her work as a servant and made another member of the family, those sentiments had only intensified.

Now, as one, they watched Verity move with the grace of a queen. "Billy is correct," Livvie announced with a toss of her curls. "My sister doesn't require assistance."

"Aye, listen to the ladies, you old toshers." Warmth spiraled in Malcom's chest as he fell in love with Verity all over again. "Verity is capable of handling her own battles."

"Don't ya want to beat the blighter within an inch of his goddamned life?" Fowler demanded.

"Lord knows Oi do." Bram slammed a fist against his open palm and glowered at the source of his hatred. Several young fops and ladies turned white and immediately scurried off in the opposite direction.

"Aye, I want to beat him senseless." In fact, it had taken every last shred of restraint he'd honed on the streets of East London not to. Just then, Verity reached Fairpoint's side.

***

He'd no right to be here.

And more, Mitchell Fairpoint had no right to this story. Not because of any sense of ownership on Verity's part, but because of the significance of this day and how it should be preserved in papers.

Verity reached the back of the hall.

Fairpoint, with his back to her, towered over a small woman with elfin features and enormous spectacles. "You've no right to this seat," he was saying. He thumped his notepad. "Do you know who I am? Do you know what newspaper I'm with?"

The young woman shook her head wildly. But still, she hesitated, not immediately relinquishing her spot. It was a detail another person might have missed or underestimated. Verity, however, had been this woman. She'd journeyed to the point of finding her voice in a world dominated by males so very determined to keep the respectable work to themselves.

"Mr. Fairpoint." Verity finally spoke to him, relishing the way Fairpoint stiffened, and the slowness to his movements as he turned and faced her.

"Miss—"

She lifted a brow.

"My lady . . ." And she reveled in the pained way he delivered that proper form of address and taut bow.

Dismissing him and his greeting, she looked to the young woman. "Is there a problem here, Miss—"

"Daubin," she said quickly, adding a curtsy. "Miss Daubin."

"And you are with . . . ?"

"*The London Gazette.*"

With that information, Verity turned back to Mitchell Fairpoint. "As I see it, Miss Daubin of *The London Gazette* has every right to be here." She paused. "In fact, I'd argue, given her work with that respected newspaper, she has even more right to be here, Mr. Fairpoint, than you do."

He sputtered, "That is preposterous! *The Londoner* has a longer history, one that affords me a greater respect than some inkwell filler sent here by her employers."

"Ah, but that is where you are wrong."

He tipped his head.

Verity took a step closer. "You see, that seat"—she pointed to the source of the earlier contention—"is not your seat. And the paper you reference?" She paused. "It is not your paper."

"What are you on about?"

With glee, Verity leaned in. "I mean, my husband and I purchased *The Londoner* from Lowery."

Fairpoint stared at her a moment, and then exploded laughing. "Lowery wouldn't ever sell to you. He knows women don't belong in this business."

Verity waited until his amusement abated. "Lowery never truly cared about this business, Fairpoint. He only cared about the coin to be made in it." As she spoke, she took relish in the way the color slowly seeped from his cheeks. "And so even his archaic views on a woman's role fell second to his greed."

"What are you saying?"

Reaching inside the pocket sewn along the front of her dress, Verity extracted the page that was never far from her person and handed it over. "I suggest you have a read, Fairpoint."

He grabbed the sheet from her fingers, and as he read, color flooded his cheeks and the page shook in his hand. "What is this?" he demanded, turning the document over, back and forth, several times, as if doing so would somehow miraculously alter the words written there.

Verity folded her arms at her waist. "My husband paid a sizable sum with the stipulation that the transaction remain secret until I was ready to claim ownership." She smiled coldly. "And I've never been more ready. Therefore, Miss Daubin's seat"—Verity gestured to the wide-eyed young woman—"belongs to her. And *The Londoner? The Londoner* is mine, and you've no place here."

Mitchell Fairpoint's cheeks drained of all color. "This is . . . I don't . . . You can't . . . He wouldn't . . ."

"Ah, words fail you again," she taunted. "Only, now there's no one to rob for a proper response, is there?"

His reed-thin frame shook violently.

All these weeks, since she'd learned of the gift Malcom had given her and bided her time for the right moment, she'd wondered what it would be like. Nothing could have prepared her for the thrill of triumph. This revenge taken on behalf of every woman he'd robbed of a place at *The Londoner*. For the story he'd stolen from her. For the misery he'd made her existence. "Now, my husband is set to speak, and you are neither wanted nor allowed to be here. I suggest you go of your own volition, Fairpoint, or I'll have you thrown out on your thieving arse."

And with the row of reporters staring in wide-eyed wonderment, Fairpoint scrabbled with his collar, and then turning jerkily on his heel, he scurried off.

"That was well done, my lady," Miss Daubin said softly.

"That was long overdue." Fishing inside her pocket once more, Verity withdrew a card. "Your refusing to relinquish your place was impressive as well, Miss Daubin. If you are ever in need of work, please seek me out."

Scrambling to take the card, the young woman strung together a series of incoherent thank-yous.

Her shoulders back, Verity started to the front of the auditorium. She made the long march past the rows of lords and ladies present: most strangers . . . some not. Her gaze found her half siblings. The twin sisters sat beside their husbands, and at the end sat the bespectacled Benedict. He caught her stare, and tipped his head in acknowledgment. A watery smile formed on her lips as she returned that silent greeting.

She reached the front row, and Bram and Fowler immediately jumped up.

"Do we need to kill 'im?" Bram asked without preamble.

"Because we'll do it," Fowler jumped in.

Still seated, Livvie rolled her eyes.

"Behave," Verity warned her sister before looking once more to the old men. Going up on tiptoe, she kissed each tosher on the cheek. "I've handled it."

"Told ya she would," Billy chimed in with a victorious grin as they resettled into their seats . . . and waited.

From her spot at the end of the row, Verity glanced to the corridor where Malcom stood speaking with his cousin, Bolingbroke. The pair of them conversed as easily as ones who'd known one another their entire lives. And though their reunion had been recent, most days since had involved visits between the men: Planning and discussions. Dinners.

And with every exchange had come a greater and more visible peace in her husband.

As if he felt her stare, Malcom looked to Verity.

She pressed her fingertips to her heart, and then motioned to her husband.

"I love you," he mouthed.

"I love you, too," she said softly, her voice lost to the buzz still echoing around the hall.

And a moment later, Malcom stepped out, ushering in a blanket of silence so thick and pronounced that the gentleman's footfalls could be heard as he took his place at the dais.

"'e 'ates this," Bram bemoaned, wringing his hands together.

Verity, Livvie, and Billy spoke simultaneously.

"'e's foine."

"He's going to be fine."

"He is fine."

As Malcom walked, he glanced throughout the room. The muscles of his jaw rippled in the faintest hint of his unease.

Verity curled her palms into tight fists. She hated this moment, not because of any fear that he'd make a misstep but because she knew how he despised this. Knew how desperately he sought privacy in his life and of his past, and yet he'd open himself to the world. Was it possible to love him any more than she did? She willed his eyes to hers.

And then he found her.

Again, Verity pressed a palm to her heart. "I love you," she mouthed once more.

His throat moved, and he gave a slight nod, and then spoke. "Many of you know me as Percival Northrop, the Earl of Maxwell. And some twenty years ago, that is who I was. I was kidnapped. I lost the home I once knew. I lost the family I had still remaining." His deep baritone carried throughout the hall; his words, coupled with the somberness of his tone, commanded silence and brought people to the edge of their chairs. "And I lived in the darkest side of England. I was an orphan on the streets." A little sob filtered into his speech—some lady in the audience who stifled that response. "But this day," Malcom went on, "is not one of sadness. I was one of the lucky ones. I survived. I found a family." He looked to the front row.

Tears filled Verity's eyes, blurring his beloved visage.

"And I've reconnected with the family I did have," Malcom said quietly.

And gasps went up as Lord Bolingbroke stepped from the corridor and made the short walk, joining Malcom atop the dais.

"You see," Malcom went on, his voice growing increasingly powerful as he spoke, "it is so very easy to give in to hatred. To carry resentment for wrongs committed. And yet those sentiments, they will only destroy a person. Which is why Lord Bolingbroke and I have come together to lay to rest the painfulness of the past, and to anoint a new beginning."

The baron stepped forward. "We are here today to announce the construction of three foundling hospitals. These, however, will be more than the orphanages that the most unfortunate children of society call home." He turned to Malcom.

"Together, we've committed funds to building places throughout England, where boys and girls might learn and laugh and have greater hopes for their future, and where they might also know"—Malcom's gaze locked with Verity's—"family."

And as Malcom continued on with his appeal to society's most powerful and influential members, tears slipped down her cheeks. She glanced down the row at Bram and Fowler, both wiping furiously at their eyes. And Billy burying her own reddened ones behind her palms. All while Livvie smiled softly on.

And when Verity looked back once more, her and Malcom's gazes locked.

"Our family," she whispered.

This was their family.

Acknowledgments

If an author is fortunate, she has a person who believes in her characters and the world she's creating. I've been so very blessed to have an entire editorial team at Montlake who believe in my stories, and my vision, for the not so always *conventional* hero and heroine. (Malcom, my dear, beloved sewer scavenger, being just one of many!) To those at Amazon Publishing who support my creative process, I'm so very grateful.

About the Author

Christi Caldwell is the *USA TODAY* bestselling author of the Sinful Brides series and the Wicked Wallflowers series. She blames novelist Judith McNaught for luring her into the world of historical romance. When Christi was at the University of Connecticut, she began writing her own tales of love—ones where even the most perfect heroes and heroines had imperfections. She learned to enjoy torturing her couples before they earned their well-deserved happily ever after.

Christi lives in southern Connecticut, where she spends her time writing, chasing after her son, and taking care of her twin princesses in training. Fans who want to keep up with the latest news and information can sign up for Christi's newsletter at www.ChristiCaldwell.com.